EXQUISITE TORMENT

"Take your hands off me," Lorelei cried, pushing frantically at Reeve's broad chest. His response was to pull her even closer, until her breasts were pressing against the shiny brass buttons of his coat.

"No, Miss Montgomery," he ground out, his face mere inches from hers. "Not until you've learned the consequences of playing with fire."

His lips crushed down upon hers in a kiss that was at once merciless and captivating. She moaned low in her throat, determined to resist him.

But no matter how desperately she tried to prevent it, she found herself swaying against Reeve as the kiss deepened. Her traitorous hands crept up his arms, and she grasped weakly at his shoulders.

Just like it had the night before, passion flared hotly and rapidly between them. Had her brain not been clouded by desire, Lorelei would have been aghast at her own boldness, for soon she returned his kisses in full measure and did not tremble with the least bit of proper maidenly outrage. The madness gripping her was wild and sweet, and so forceful that nothing mattered save Reeve Cameron and the exquisite torment he was only too happy to inflict upon her . . .

CATHERINE CREEL

WILD TEXAS LOVING

ZEBRA BOOKS
KENSINGTON PUBLISHING CORP.

*To my sweet, spirited daughter Caitlin . . .
I love you, Miss Firecracker.*

ZEBRA BOOKS

are published by

Kensington Publishing Corp.
475 Park Avenue South
New York, NY 10016

First printing: April, 1992

Printed in the United States of America

One

Old-timers had predicted it was going to be another summer straight from the fiery depths of hell.

They were right, of course. But not a one of them was inclined to rejoice over being so capable a prophet, not when it was all they could do to get up in the morning and drag themselves down to their usual "congregatin' place" in front of the Longhorn Mercantile. Hot wouldn't even *begin* to describe what was going on. Hell, it made even their bones feel parched.

June wasn't half over yet, and already it looked like the county proper, not to mention all other parts around, was in for a record-breaking scorcher. The heat seemed to rise up and take on a life of its own as the sun baked the land with relentless fervor. Rain, its merciful blessing prayed for with great vigor every Sunday in church, was at an all-time premium. Creek beds were fast drying up, buzzards filled the sky like so many black clouds, and even the slightest stirring of the pungent, dust-choked wind threatened to send the good citizens of Fort Worth scrambling for cover.

If any relief *was* forthcoming, it was a carefully

5

guarded secret—kept by a Mother Nature gone haywire. One of the more popular sayings about the accursed predicament was "days are getting longer and tempers shorter."

Lorelei Montgomery's temper was no exception.

Musing irefully that the present situation was enough to make even a triple-haloed saint give more than a passing thought to murder, Lorelei released an audible sigh of exasperation and narrowed her splendid, fiery blue eyes at the line agent. She was hot and tired and in no mood to wait any longer. Her full-length skirts and tightly laced corset, combined with the near-torturous burdens of a chemise, petticoats, drawers, and stockings, brought to mind the hotel clerk's earlier observation that "Texas ain't a whole lot like Georgia."

That was an understatement if ever there was one, she thought with a frown, her sapphire gaze darkening. Great balls of fire, nothing had gone right so far! She could only hope that her luck improved by the time she reached Fort Concho.

She lifted an angry hand to tuck a strand of her thick, frequently wayward auburn hair back into place and tried not to think too much about what lay ahead. It took a great deal of self-control to swallow the blistering malediction that rose to her lips. This certainly wasn't the first time she had been tempted to forget she was a lady born and bred; nor would it be the last. But her fine Southern upbringing was about to undergo a trial by fire . . . *Texas-style*.

"In the highly unlikely event it has escaped your attention, Mr. Billings," she offered in tones of exaggerated patience, "our departure has already been delayed for the better part of an hour!"

The target of her remark, a bald and bespectacled man on the other side of the counter, gave no indication of having heard her. He continued with his work, making entries in one of the stage company's thick and surprisingly well-kept ledgers.

His rudeness made Lorelei see red, but nevertheless she decided to employ a more amiable tactic. Her grandmother had always said a person could catch more flies with honey than with vinegar.

"I'm so very sorry if I sound a bit out of sorts," she told the agent sweetly, as she forced a winning smile to her lips, "but surely you can understand my difficulty." She added a soft, dramatic little sigh for good measure. "Isn't there *any*thing you can do to—"

"Not a thing, ma'am." With the same maddening complacency he had displayed for the past fifty-two minutes, Homer Billings shook his head and reiterated, "Like I told you before, the stage won't be leavin' here 'til all passengers are present and accounted for." He spared her only a brief, perfunctory glance.

"You mean one particular passenger, don't you?" She flushed with renewed anger at the thought. Her fingers clenched around the fan she had been wielding in a hopeless attempt to cool the air about her face. "It is completely beyond belief that you would see fit to subject the rest of us to this . . . this sweltering inconvenience because of one man's complete lack of regard for schedules! Who is he, anyway?" she demanded sharply. "Some rich, puffed-up old banker? Or maybe one of those terrible carpetbagger politicians with more influence than brains? For Heaven's sake, I doubt if even President Grant himself would go so far as to keep everyone waiting this long!"

Her words apparently struck the man as funny. A sudden grin flashed across his heretofore impassive features, while a quiet chuckle rumbled up from his

throat. He reached up to adjust the elastic-banded vi-
sor which lent him—or so he hoped—the appearance
of an important member of the local business com-
munity. His eyes met Lorelei's at last.

"Somehow, ma'am," he drawled, "I doubt if any of
the Camerons, 'specially Reeve, would put a whole
lot of salt in havin' their manners held up to Ole Red-
Eye's."

His observation made her bristle all the more. Her
nerves were already worn to a frazzle—she had been
worried sick about Hadley ever since receiving the
news of his arrest. God help her, this delay was only
making things worse.

"You listen to me." Her voice, while low and show-
ing firm evidence of roots in the heart of a more genteel society, held a note of fury. "I don't know who in
the blue blazes Reeve Cameron is—nor do I care!
The stage was scheduled to leave at seven o'clock this
morning. Don't you understand? I must get to Fort
Concho right away!"

She spun about, her bright gaze holding a silent
plea for help as it crossed the faces of the other passengers, who were seated along one wall of the
cramped, stuffy office. There were only three of
them—an older man who looked back at her with
weary indifference, a woman of indeterminate age
whose true calling in life was announced to the world
by a tight, scandalously low-cut gown of green satin,
and a slender youth who could not be much above
seventeen years of age. He was the only one of the
three to offer Lorelei a response, which came in the
form of a quick, gallant tip of his battered hat. But
he said nothing.

"Don't schedules mean anything at all in this godforsaken place?" fumed Lorelei, rounding on the
damnably unruffled Homer Billings again. All she

got in reply was yet another of the man's hopelessly backhanded comments. There was no doubt that he took great pride in his own wittiness.

"You're in the wrong of things there, Miss Montgomery. Matter of fact, it's been said the good Lord favors Texas more'n any other place on earth."

"I fully intend to take this matter up with the proper authorities, Mr. Billings!" she vowed, unamused.

"Won't do you no good."

"And why is that?"

"On account of I'm the only *au-thor-i-ty* in town," he enunciated smugly.

"Then I insist you provide me with the address of the company's owner!"

"You won't be needin' that." He actually smiled again. His eyes moved slightly to the left of her before snapping back. "You'll be meetin' one of the owners any second now."

"Will I?" Her brows knitted into a frown of disbelief and she sighed again. "What are you talking about?"

"Unless I miss my guess, he's talking about me."

Lorelei whirled at the sound of the low, deep-timbred voice behind her. Her breath caught in her throat, while her blue eyes grew very round.

There in the doorway, his tall, muscular frame silhouetted against the harsh morning light, stood the most striking man she had ever seen. He was handsome, but it was more than that. A whole lot more. There was an air about him, an air that was so completely self-assured, so thoroughly masculine, that she felt her pulse quicken.

She watched as he reached up and unhurriedly drew the hat from his head, revealing thick, sunstreaked brown hair. His features were rugged perfec-

9

tion, tanned and chiseled and sure to please many a feminine heart, while his deep green eyes were so steady and piercing that her cheeks grew warm beneath his gaze. Although he was dressed in a simple, double-breasted cotton shirt and fitted denim jeans like many another cowboy on the streets of Fort Worth, she sensed he was different from all the rest.

She wanted to look away but found she couldn't. His gaze remained locked with hers, matching stare for stare. A sudden, heart-shaking current of feeling, raw and more potent than anything she'd ever known, burst through her.

Merciful Heavens, what was happening? She felt positively shaken. It was an unfamiliar sensation, one which served to confuse and intrigue—and alarm—her at the same time.

The tall stranger began moving toward her now, his boots almost soundless on the dusty wooden floor. He walked with an easy, virile grace. The merest hint of a smile tugged at his lips, and Lorelei could have sworn she glimpsed a twinkle of rakish amusement in his eyes.

Finding herself at a rare loss for words, she watched his approach with barely concealed apprehension. She swallowed hard when he drew to a halt just inches away. He towered above her, making her feel quite small, as well as uneasy at his proximity. She didn't like this feeling of anxious vulnerability one bit; she was accustomed to things being the other way around when it came to men.

His gaze narrowed and grew warm as it traveled swiftly, although quite thoroughly, over her well-formed curves. Stung by the uncomfortable sensation that he could see right through the pearl gray foulard of her traveling suit, and even through her "shimmy" beneath, she colored again and

10

lifted her chin in a proud gesture.

Her breasts, which swelled provocatively above the lace-trimmed, round neckline of her corseted bodice, received more than their fair share of the bold cowboy's attention before his eyes finally returned to her face. She would have been shocked if she'd had any notion of the true extent of his appreciation for her charms. Shock would have given way to dismay if she had known about his wicked thoughts that resulted from the appreciation.

As it was, she took exception to his insolence. Outrage had always proven a great restorative for her composure.

"Am I to understand, then, that you, sir, are the owner of the stage line?" she questioned loftily, her eyes like blue ice now. She had always been good at putting men in their places with a single look, a look which more often than not made them feel chilled to their very souls. It was a skill honed by many years of practice.

This man, however, appeared as hot-blooded as ever. Not only that, but he managed to turn the tables on her with a dangerous look of his own. Sweet mercy, she had never felt so absolutely *branded* by a pair of eyes before.

"Well?" she demanded when he did not answer immediately. There was a telltale tremor in her voice. "Are you the owner or not?"

"I guess you could say that. In part, anyway." Again, that perplexing ghost of a smile.

"And which part is that?" she retorted on impulse. But she regretted the words as soon as they were out of her mouth.

"That depends." The light of humor in his gaze grew even more unholy.

"On what?"

11

"On which part it is you intend to single out for—" he paused, his eyes flickering significantly downward for an instant before he finished, "—attention."

Homer Billings chuckled out loud, and so did the brassy-haired floozy who was ogling the newcomer with undisguised interest. Lorelei crimsoned at his teasing, her chin lifting even higher.

"I don't know who the devil you think you are, but—"

"Why, this here's Reeve Cameron," Homer interjected. He looked back to Reeve and explained, "The lady's none too pleased with the delay. Name's Montgomery. Lorelei Montgomery. Came all the way from Georgia."

"The *lady* was under the impression—quite mistaken, I now see—that this was a reputable transportation company!" said Lorelei. She clutched the fan in her right hand and pointed it toward the line agent. "Mr. Billings is well aware of the fact that I have been waiting in this confounded hothouse you call an office for more than an hour!"

Snapping the fan open vengefully, she agitated the air about her face once more while returning her stormy gaze to the man responsible for the morning's tribulation. All traces of amusement quickly vanished from his countenance as he listened to her.

"I have neither the time nor the inclination to stand here making pleasant conversation with you, Mr. Cameron. You have already caused everyone enough trouble! Now, if you don't mind, may we *please* be on our way at last? I suppose it gives you some kind of perverse satisfaction to keep others waiting like this, but I for one don't appreciate watching the entire morning waste away when a matter of life or death awaits me at Fort Concho!"

Reeve said nothing. The only indication he gave of

12

having heard her was a slight, almost imperceptible narrowing of his eyes. But if she had known him at all, she would have noticed the sudden tensing of his hard-muscled body.

Another taut silence rose up between them. The line agent seized the opportunity to intervene again.

"Miss Montgomery claims she's got real pressin' business out at the fort. Yessir, seems—"

"You heard what the lady said." Reeve cut him off with quiet authority. He raised his hat to his head and turned away. "Let's get on with it."

Lorelei watched in surprise as he disappeared outside without another word. The other passengers obediently followed his lead, offering her no expressions of gratitude for having expedited their departure. All she received for her troubles was a fleeting, indulgent grin from the young cowhand.

She stared after the odd trio for several seconds, then mentally shook herself and retrieved her carpetbag from underneath the bench. If she was going to have to share the close quarters of a stagecoach with them for the next two days, she should at least be glad for the fact that her ears would not be bent.

Emerging from the office, she discovered that the slender youth had already seated himself next to the blonde woman inside the stagecoach, leaving her no choice but to take her place beside the older, dark-suited man, who cut her an unwelcoming glare. Reeve Cameron, she noted, was talking to the driver and paid her little mind.

The streets were still practically deserted, although there were beginning to be definite signs of life in front of the mercantile and the livery stable. Lorelei became aware of the scents of horses and woodsmoke, cattle and fresh lumber, breakfast and dried hay, all mingling together and borne aloft on the morning's still-awakening breeze. She had spent only one night in this burgeoning cowtown on the banks of the Trinity River, and she could not deny a certain fascination with its determined, rough-hewn atmosphere. It had the feel of new life about it.

New life. She repeated the phrase in her mind, offering up a silent prayer that the same could be said of what lay ahead for Hadley, and for herself. Whatever came, the two of them would face it together . . .

The sound of a horse's hoof pawing impatiently at the ground brought her back to the present. Shielding her eyes from the sunlight with one gloved hand, she lowered her bag to the dust-caked boardwalk and gathered up her skirts.

A strong pair of hands clasped her firmly about the waist from behind. Before she could protest, they lifted her effortlessly up into the coach. She ducked her head just in time, pivoting about to face her self-appointed caretaker as she lost her balance and sank heavily down upon the cushioned leather seat. Reeve's fingers lingered a moment longer than was necessary before he relinquished his grip.

"Thank you," she muttered stiffly, determined not to let him know how affected she was by his nearness. His touch still burned upon her flesh, even through the protection of several layers of clothing.

"The trip won't be an easy one, Miss Montgomery," he cautioned, watching while she settled her full skirts about her.

"Nothing worthwhile ever is, Mr. Cameron."

"It isn't too late to change your mind."

"Change my mind?" she echoed, frowning in puzzlement. "About what?"

"About going to Fort Concho." His handsome face

14

was forebodingly solemn. "It's no place for a woman."

Lorelei's frown deepened as she met his penetrating gaze squarely. Before she could ask him what he meant, the buxom blonde seated opposite suddenly gave a husky laugh.

"Why don't you try tellin' that to all them 'poor females' there now?" she challenged Reeve good-naturedly. "There's many a wife and sweetheart would give you an argument." She administered a quick, calculated pat to her bleached curls. "It so happens I'm bound for Fort Concho myself. Been there once, just last year. Not to the post, exactly, but to Santa Angela, 'cross the river. There's always plenty of work near them cavalry boys."

"The devil's work," the man beside Lorelei muttered with a scowl. He shifted uncomfortably on the seat, hugging a worn leather valise to his chest.

"Better that than what you do, sellin' some no-account snake oil all over kingdom come!" the cowhand blurted in her defense. He didn't have any real notion of what he was defending, but he felt honor bound to do it just the same. "You're the one hooked up with the devil, you old coot, spreadin' nothin' but high hopes and misery with that poison of yours!"

He was rewarded with a broad, coquettish smile from the woman, who linked her arm through his and cast the peddler a triumphant smirk.

"There now, honey," she purred to her young champion, settling even closer to him, "ain't no use in tryin' to make his kind see reason. You could talk yourself blue in the face, and he'd still see things the same way he does now. If you ask me, he looks to have a mean streak in him a mile wide."

"Jezebel," the man bit out under his breath. The cowhand narrowed his eyes in warning.

15

"Take my advice, Miss Montgomery," Reeve told Lorelei, ignoring the others. "Go back where you belong."

"And how would *you* know where I belong?" Her eyes flashed with annoyance at his presumption. "Until five minutes ago, you and I were complete strangers to one another. We are still little more than that. You don't know anything about me, Mr. Cameron. And what's more, it is most assuredly none of your business *where* I choose to go!"

"I know more than you think."

With that he stepped back and closed the door, snatching up her carpetbag but refusing to admit defeat just yet. His gaze seared across to hers through the open window. He told himself it was useless to try and dissuade her, but something he could not yet put a name to prompted him to make the effort.

"You don't know what you're letting yourself in for." He spoke in a voice that was whipcord-sharp. "The danger of an Indian attack increases tenfold once we leave Fort Worth behind. Even if we manage to avoid a run-in with the Comanches, there's still the matter of—"

"I'm afraid you are wasting everyone's time again," she interrupted stubbornly. "Nothing you say will change my mind. I am going to Fort Concho." To emphasize the point, she leaned back and folded her hands primly together in her lap. A cool smile touched her lips. "Goodbye, Mr. Cameron."

Reeve's mouth tightened into a thin line of displeasure. His eyes glinted as he tossed the carpetbag up to the driver at last.

"Not goodbye, Miss Montgomery." Curtly he tugged the front brim of his hat lower. "Not yet. Not by a long shot."

She leaned forward again. "I don't understand." It

occurred to her to wonder why he should sound so angry with her.

"I'm a passenger on this stage, too — remember?" He did not wait for an answer, but climbed up to take his place beside the driver, apparently meaning to ride shotgun for the duration of the trip.

Lorelei closed her eyes and groaned inwardly. How on earth could she have forgotten? After all, the past hour's maddening discomfort had been caused by this man's tardiness. The prospect of traveling all the way to Fort Concho with him was not an agreeable one. Not at all.

"Get up there!" the driver shouted in a voice loud enough to wake the dead. He snapped his long whip expertly above the horses' heads. "Hang on!" he yelled to the foursome inside the coach. His warning proved all too necessary.

A gasp broke from Lorelei's lips when the coach gave a violent lurch forward. She instinctively grabbed for support at the leather strap hanging above her head, then noticed that her fellow wayfarers had already done the same. The wheels beneath them rolled and bounced across the rutted dirt road, setting the coach swaying rhythmically side to side as it headed westward.

"You'll get used to it before too long, honey," the other woman consoled her with a not unkindly look. Upon closer inspection, Lorelei thought, she appeared to be only a few years older than the freckle-faced cowboy beside her. "Come nightfall, you'll think you was a babe bein' rocked in your cradle again."

Lorelei managed a rather half-hearted smile in response, then closed her eyes again. She had already come so far; she was weary in body as well as spirit. But anything was worth enduring if she could save Hadley—*anything.*

She was startled when the vision of Reeve Cameron's face came unbidden into her mind, forcing all other matters to retreat. Her eyes flew open, and her fingers curled even more tightly about the strap. She caught her lower lip between her teeth as a dull flush crept up her face.

It would do no good to pretend she wasn't aware of his presence next to the driver above her. The best she could hope for was to try and focus her attention on the passing countryside. It was to this purpose that she shifted on the dusty leather cushion and began vigorously fanning herself in time to the rocking of the coach. She felt a sharp twinge of guilt for finding it necessary to school her mind at all.

She couldn't allow anything—or anyone—to interfere with what she had traveled all the way from Georgia to do. Solving Hadley's plight would require her full energies and commitment. Hadn't that always been the case? She sighed, her blue eyes clouding with remembrance before drifting inexorably upward.

The cause of her disturbing reverie, meanwhile, was waging a losing battle to keep his own thoughts fixed on the stagecoach's progress beneath the sun's deep golden blaze.

Lorelei Montgomery. Reeve's gaze darkened anew, the expression on his rugged features becoming even more grim. He swore to himself, bracing his booted foot against the iron rail around the driver's box. The movement of the coach was second nature to him; he'd ridden atop this particular Concord, and many another like it, more times than he cared to remember.

It was no coincidence that the beautiful redhead who had set his blood afire shared her last name with

18

the accused, and he knew it. The possibility that she might be Hadley Montgomery's wife seemed more than a little farfetched, especially since the report he'd been given had listed the trooper's age as a mere nineteen. Besides, he now recalled having read something about a sister . . .

"Guess you're glad to be gettin' back out to the Concho," the bearded giant of a man beside him boomed out above the din of straining harness, rattling chain, and thundering hooves. "Been away a long time, ain't you?"

"Longer than I wanted to be," admitted Reeve. He had known the driver, Ollie Newcomb, for a good number of years. It was Ollie who had first taught him how to handle a team. "Washington will never pass for Texas, not for me," he shouted with a sardonic half-smile.

"How long you aimin' to stay this time?"

"I don't know." Lorelei's face swam before his eyes again. He frowned and tossed a glance into the cloudless, astonishingly blue sky. "As long as it takes."

"Headin' for trouble, are you?" asked Ollie. He had always been a perceptive friend.

"In more ways than one."

Reeve's brow cleared at the sound of his own prophetic words. His green eyes filled with an intense, almost savage light. It was a light which, had she seen it, would have struck fear in Lorelei's unsuspecting heart.

Two

The first day of the journey was one of the longest and most difficult Lorelei had ever endured.

By the time the stagecoach rolled to a halt in front of the station where they were to spend the night, she was feeling bone-weary, battered from head to toe, and was covered with more dust than she'd ever known to exist. She didn't offer a single protest when Reeve opened the door and lifted her bodily from the coach. He immediately set her on her feet again, but kept one steadying hand at her waist. His mouth curved into a soft, thoroughly disarming smile.

"A hot bath will help."

"There isn't enough hot water in all the world to help," she pronounced dispiritedly. Her gaze fell before the amused sympathy of his, and she pulled away as if the contact had suddenly burned her.

"Welcome to Cantrell's Station!" a stout, black-haired woman called to them from the doorway of the simple log structure. A handful of cottonwood trees surrounded the building, with a sturdy barn and split-rail corral situated nearby. "Come on inside! I've got a pot of coffee boilin' on the stove and a side of beef sizzlin' in the oven!"

20

None of the passengers needed any further encouragement. They were all much too tired and hungry to care if the coffee was hot or if the meat being served was the least bit recognizable. But Lorelei hesitated before going inside with the others. While she busied herself with the pretense of shaking some of the dust from her skirts, her eyes sought out Reeve as if with a will of their own.

She saw that he had gone to assist Ollie, and a man she correctly assumed to be Mr. Cantrell, with the horses. He certainly looked none the worse for wear. Indeed, she mused with a spark of resentment, he appeared as strong and vibrant and devilishly handsome as ever. She had seen him only twice during the day, when they had paused to rest and water the horses, and of course, he had scarcely spoken to her. It was almost as if he had been avoiding her. The thought provoked an inordinate amount of wholly feminine anger to spring to life within her.

"Ain't you comin', Miss Montgomery?" the slender cowhand called eagerly to her from where he waited, hat in hand, just outside the doorway. His name was Virgil Baker, and he had told her all about himself—in truth, a good deal more than she or any of his fellow travelers had wanted to know. Still, he was a pleasant enough young man, and he reminded her a little of Hadley.

"Yes, Mr. Baker, I'm coming."

She tore her eyes off Reeve and managed a wan smile as she continued toward the main house. Her graceful movements were not lost on Reeve. His eyes followed her every step of the way, burning across the twilight-cloaked grounds of the station.

"Pretty, ain't she?" Abraham Cantrell put forth,

21

his own gaze matching the direction of Reeve's. "A real lady, unless I miss my guess."

"You never do," grunted Ollie. He noticed the sudden tightening of Reeve's countenance, but he knew better than to comment on it.

"Nope," Abraham was only too happy to acknowledge. "That other one, though . . . well now, Martha's not too likely to take a shine to her."

"Doesn't have to," Ollie pointed out. He freed the lead horses and handed the reins to Reeve, who accepted them with a curt nod and led them away to the corral.

"Any sign of trouble today?" the station owner asked the driver. He already knew the answer, but it was good manners to ask. And it had become a sort of tradition between them over the years.

"None at all. Things are quiet," said Ollie, his thick, bushy brows drawing together like two caterpillars above his dark eyes. "Almost too quiet. Reeve seems to think something's brewin'."

"What do you think?"

"Hell, I think he's right."

Abraham nodded in silent agreement. He and Ollie knew that Reeve Cameron had always possessed a sixth sense when it came to Indian trouble. It might have something to do with the fact that his grandmother had been a full-blooded Cherokee, but then again it might have just as much to do with the fact that he had spent the first half of his thirty years living right in the middle of some of the most dangerous Indian country on the face of the earth. Either way, they had learned to trust his instincts.

Supper was already being served by the time Lorelei took her place at the long, roughly fash-

22

ioned table a short time later. She had washed up using the bowl and pitcher provided, then tidied her hair as best she could, but with no great success — she still felt woefully disheveled. Taking solace in the prospect of a bath generously promised by Martha Cantrell, she sank down upon the uncushioned bench beside Virgil. Reeve Cameron, she noted with displeasure, was directly opposite.

"Eat up, child!" Martha exhorted the new arrival, bustling maternally about the table. Her red calico skirts and freshly ironed white apron made a pleasant, sweeping sound as she went. She came round to Lorelei and popped a well-buttered biscuit onto her empty plate. "Here you go. This and some of them meat and potatoes down there will perk you up for sure."

"Martha cooks up the best food you're liable to get in the whole of Texas," Abraham Cantrell boasted of his wife. He was reed-thin and possessed of a full head of gray hair, the very antithesis of his plump, dark-haired spouse. Like any good host, he sat at the head of the table and kept a watchful eye on everyone else's progress throughout supper. "The best this side of Dallas, anyways," he saw fit to clarify.

"That ain't sayin' much." One corner of Ollie's mouth twitched up. He gave Martha a conspiratorial wink while she piled some of the mashed potatoes onto Lorelei's plate. "I had me a meal in Dallas once."

"My last job was over in Dallas." This came from the satin-clad blonde, who had earlier identified herself to Lorelei as Charity Pardee, and Lorelei was struck by the irony of the name. Charity filled her mouth with a forkful of potatoes before complaining, " 'Course, the pay wasn't worth a damn, but—"

"I don't allow that kind of talk in my place, Miss Pardee," Martha cut in with a stern frown of disapproval. She thrust the spoon back into the bowl of potatoes and took her seat on the other side of Lorelei. "You want to talk like that, you might as well get on back to Dallas to do it!"

It was obvious to everyone that Charity took offense at being called down like a child at the supper table. She colored angrily and opened her mouth to give the older woman a piece of her mind.

"How long have you and your husband operated the station, Mrs. Cantrell?" Lorelei intervened impulsively. Her appetite had fled, but she was making a valiant effort to eat. She happened to glance up and meet Reeve's eyes, only to look away hastily.

"Ten years now, ain't it, Abraham?" was Martha's answer.

"Ten years," her husband confirmed with a nod.

"I'd never have stayed on this long if it hadn't been for the children," added Martha, a sudden shadow crossing her face.

"The children?" Lorelei echoed in surprise. She had seen nothing to indicate the presence of any children about the place.

"Two. Both of 'em boys. They're buried out there on the other side of the corral."

"Oh . . . I—I'm sorry," murmured Lorelei, her heart twisting at the thought of the couple's grief. She had known so much loss in her own life, and now the memory of it, coupled with what she had just heard, caused her to fight back tears.

She could feel Reeve Cameron's gaze upon her again, could feel as well the other guests' eyes shifting uncomfortably back and forth between herself and Martha. An awkward silence fell about the table. One of the men cleared his throat unnecessarily.

"Most folks in this part of Texas have lost young 'uns to the fever. Or to the Indians," Ollie finally said in a low, gruff voice. There was unmistakable compassion in his dark gaze. He pushed away his plate and folded his arms slowly across his massive chest. "This here land is wild enough now, but it was a far sight worse back during the war. Back then, a man couldn't hardly step out the door without facin' off against one tribe or another. The war took just about anyone of fightin' age, some of 'em still wet behind the ears. There wasn't too many of us left behind."

"Those of us too old to fight Yankees, well, we stayed put and did what we could to keep them Indians from takin' back the whole blessed country," Abraham reminisced to the table in general. He gave a nod in Reeve's direction. "Reeve Cameron, now, he could tell you how bad things was when he came home that first time, after takin' a round in the leg at Gettys —"

"Oh, shame on you, Abraham Cantrell!" Martha scolded with mock wifely reproach. She had clearly set aside her momentary sadness and now smiled with fond indulgence at the man who had shared her life, good and bad, for the past twenty-odd years. "None of these young folks want to hear those worn-out stories about the old days." She leaned toward Lorelei and shook her head, remarking in an undertone, "Once you get my Abraham and that Ollie Newcomb wound up, there'll be no reinin' the two of them in for the rest of the night!"

25

"You fought in the war?" Virgil asked Reeve, his eyes wide with sudden interest and in his voice a discernible note of awe.

"I did," Reeve affirmed quietly. He had finished off his own plate of food and now settled back in his chair. While he gave the appearance of being completely at ease, his eyes glinted with a cold, unfathomable light. "But I make it a point not to talk about it."

"Well, that's the first time I've ever heard that!" Charity exclaimed in disbelief. "Any man I've ever known was plumb tickled to sit and bend my ear for hours, runnin' on and on about how brave he was while all them Yankee bullets were flyin' all around him."

She took a sip of coffee, then shifted her ample hips on the bench so that her bosom was displayed to its best advantage in the warm lamplight. The look she gave Reeve made it all too clear that she would dearly love to know him better.

Lorelei, aware of the silent, audacious invitation proffered by the well-endowed blonde, met Reeve's gaze once more.

She wished she had not. Whether he was receptive to Charity's appeal she could not tell, but there was an obvious spark of amusement in the gold-flecked depths of his eyes when they met hers. She was almost certain he was laughing at her, and *that* was something she would not tolerate, especially in her present turbulent state of mind.

"I think Miss Pardee has a point, Mr. Cameron," she announced coolly, her sapphire gaze issuing an unspoken challenge. "It has been my experience that a man who refuses to talk about himself has something to hide."

26

"We all have something to hide, Miss Montgomery." A faint, mocking smile played about his lips.

"I don't," Virgil was quick to disagree. He gave a sigh of youthful dissatisfaction. "Hell's bells, I —" He caught himself and looked guiltily to Martha. "Sorry, ma'am. I was meanin' to say that I ain't lived enough yet to have anything worth hidin'."

His rueful comment elicited chuckles from Abraham and Ollie, and a smile from the others. Even Lorelei could not help smiling, but she frowned in the next instant when the conversation took an unexpected turn.

"Why are you headed out to Fort Concho, child?" Martha asked her.

"I . . . I am going to visit my brother." It was partially true, she thought.

"He's stationed at the fort?"

"Yes."

"She's come all the way from Georgia to see him," Charity disclosed, proving that she had been listening back at the line office after all. "And she's in a hurry to get there, ain't you, Miss Montgomery?"

"Yes, Miss Pardee, I am."

Folding her napkin with more care than was necessary, she placed it beside her plate and sat with eyes downcast. She did not want to pursue this topic, did not want to answer any more questions about Hadley. The fewer people knew about the painful circumstances, the better.

She made the mistake of looking at Reeve again. His eyes seemed to bore right through her, as if he suspected the truth, as if he had somehow guessed that her journey had been prompted by something other than a simple desire to see her brother. She

27

told herself it was perfectly ridiculous to be concerned about what this man thought, but his steady, piercing gaze continued to trouble her all the same.

Rising abruptly to her feet, she turned to Martha with a forced, apologetic smile. The sound of wood scraping on wood filled the dining room, for the men had no choice but to stand, too.

"I'm sorry, Mrs. Cantrell, but I'm not very hungry this evening."

"That's all right," the older woman assured her. She stood up and placed a supportive arm about Lorelei's shoulders. "It's been a long day. I'll go ahead and put the water on to heat for your bath."

"A bath?" Virgil swiped at some of the dust coating his shirt. "Looks like I could do with one of those myself."

"Sorry." Martha shook her head. "Ladies only inside. You men'll have to make do down at the creek." She suppressed a smile at the crestfallen expression on the young cowhand's face. "Abraham, show him where to wash. And you could do with a good scrubbin' yourself, old man."

It was after midnight when Lorelei's eyes opened. She had fallen asleep almost immediately, too exhausted to do anything more than get in her side of the bed she was to share with Charity. Martha, apologizing for the close quarters, had explained that there was only the one room for female travelers. The men would bed down on the floor of the dining room.

Lorelei had been too tired to mind the lack of privacy. The bath had soothed her aching muscles considerably, so much so that she had been unable to muster the energy to give her hair its usual one

28

hundred brushstrokes. She had abandoned her efforts at forty, secured the gleaming auburn mass into a single long braid down her back, and crawled beneath the covers. She hadn't even been disturbed when Charity slipped into bed beside her.

Now, more than three hours after retiring, she found herself wide awake. She glanced toward the gingham-curtained window, only to discover that it was still quite dark outside. The room was lit by a soft, silvery glow spilling down from the quarter moon above. All was quiet.

She lay perfectly still and listened to the steady breathing of Charity for a few moments. Her thoughts wandered aimlessly over images of her brother, memories of home, and the disturbing, more recent memory of Reeve Cameron's eyes burning into hers. Great balls of fire, she mused irritably, *he* did not belong in her thoughts. He was just a stranger, a man she would never see again once she reached Fort Concho.

Charity stirred, murmured something unintelligible, and rolled over. Lorelei waited until the blonde had settled her bountiful form into the feather mattress again, then released a pent-up sigh. She knew she'd have little success if she tried to go back to sleep just yet. Her eyes moved back to the window.

Seized by a sudden restlessness, she eased herself from the bed and tossed a floral wrapper on over her cotton nightgown. She padded barefoot across to the door, opened it slowly, then peered up and down the narrow hallway that separated the back portion of the log cabin into two halves. Her searching gaze, growing accustomed to the darkness, fell upon the rear door of the building, and she hesitated only an instant before heading toward it.

The long, heat-soaked day had, miraculously, given way to a cool and pleasant summer night. Lorelei stepped outside, closed the door behind her, and wandered a short distance away from the cabin. She was glad of the wrapper about her shoulders, even though her high-necked, long-sleeved white nightgown covered her very nearly from head to toe. She tied the belt at her waist and turned her face up toward the sky.

A million stars twinkled in its magnificent blackness. Somewhere in the hills nearby, a lone coyote wailed plaintively for its mate. The night air smelled of sagebrush and wildflowers. Folding her arms across her breasts, Lorelei closed her eyes and inhaled deeply.

"Didn't anyone ever tell you to watch out for snakes?"

She started in alarm at the sound of that low, splendidly resonant voice. It had become all too familiar to her. She spun about, her eyes full of fire—and of a fear she would never acknowledge.

"What are you doing out here?" she demanded in a furious whisper. She caught her breath and took an instinctive step backward when he emerged from the shadows into the pale moonlight.

"The same as you," Reeve answered softly. "I couldn't sleep."

He was still fully dressed. She wondered if he had been to bed at all.

"You had no right to startle me like that!" she snapped. Her prim, haughty manner belied the wild pounding of her heart.

"It's dangerous to walk about at night." He

offered no apology as he drew closer.

"I wasn't walking about! I was just . . . I felt the need for some air. And some privacy!" she added pointedly.

She was surprised to hear his soft laugh. Sheer, stubborn pride prevented her from moving away when he came to stand close beside her. She would not give him the satisfaction of knowing how uneasy he made her. It certainly wasn't proper for them to be out there alone together at that hour of the night, but she'd be hanged if she'd turn coward and run.

He lifted a hand to the trunk of the cottonwood tree directly behind her, his arm nearly touching her head. She gazed up at him in breathless anticipation and impulsively crossed her arms over her breasts again.

She had no idea what an appealing vision she was, standing there with her braided hair hanging down her back like a schoolgirl's and her delectable curves hidden beneath nothing more than her nightclothes. It was all too easy to imagine what she would look like with her hair unbound and her body revealed in all its sweet glory; all too easy to imagine what she would feel and taste like . . .

Reeve Cameron groaned inwardly at the thought. His green eyes darkened, and a tiny muscle twitched in the clean-shaven ruggedness of his cheek. He took a step closer, cursing himself inwardly. His boots disturbed the flimsy gathers of Lorelei's nightgown.

"Whatever your reasons," he cautioned in a tone that sent a shiver down her spine, "you shouldn't be out here at all. I meant what I said about snakes. And there are other dangers as well."

"Are there indeed?" she retorted caustically. Try as she would, she could not force herself to ignore the way the moonlight set his dark hair aglow and gave his handsome face an even more rakish look than usual. She swallowed a sudden lump in her throat, tilting her chin up bravely. "I suppose you are referring to Indians, Mr. Cameron. Or wild animals, perhaps. Well, I am not easily frightened by tales of half-naked savages and prowling wolves!"

That was true enough. She had read a good deal about Texas and all its perils, of course, but she found it difficult to believe everything she had read. She was more inclined to believe that the "firsthand witnesses" had exaggerated in order to make their stories fascinating enough for publication.

"You're even more of an innocent than I thought, Lorelei Montgomery," murmured Reeve, making her feel that he was capable of reading her mind. A strange half-smile touched his lips, then suddenly he straightened and allowed his arm to fall back to his side. His dark brows drew together into a frown. "Get back inside."

"What? I—you have no right to order me about!" she sputtered indignantly, her beautiful eyes flashing anew. "I will go inside when I am good and ready, Mr. Cameron, and neither you nor anyone else—"

"Damn it, you little fool!" he snarled, startling her with his fierceness. His expression softened an instant later, and he gave her another brief smile. "I'm sorry, Miss Montgomery." His tone was calm and measured now, his manner all that was gentlemanly. "But I meant it when I said it isn't safe out here. Besides, we leave at first light in the morning, and it's getting late."

"But I am not sleepy."

She was quite accustomed to holding her own against overbearing males, and she saw no reason to make an exception with this one—no matter how affected she was by his nearness. If only he would stop looking at her like that!

"Goodnight, Mr. Cameron," she said by way of dismissal. Unfolding her arms, she turned and began walking away, only to stop and toss back over her shoulder, "I would appreciate it if you granted me some time alone with my thoughts."

"I can't do that."

"Can't—or *won't?*" She rounded angrily on him again.

"You're my responsibility. I'm not about to let you get yourself carried off."

"I am *not* your responsibility!" she snapped, bristling at the suggestion.

"Until we reach Fort Concho, you are." He narrowed the distance between them again and stared down into her angry upturned face. It required great strength of will for him to resist the sharp, powerful urge to touch her. "As long as you're a passenger on the Cameron line, you'll do as I say."

"I most certainly will not!"

"Go back to bed, Miss Montgomery," he commanded grimly. "Go back to bed before I do something we'll both regret."

Lorelei gasped. She eyed him with a combination of fury and apprehension, wondering if he had any intention of making good his threat. What exactly did he mean by it, anyway? She was suddenly tempted to slap his face, but settled instead for giving him a well-deserved piece of her mind.

"Why, you insolent, rattleheaded cowboy! Am I

33

supposed to be impressed by your threats? I am not some witless, weak-spirited little mouse like the other women of your acquaintance, Mr. Cameron! I will not be bullied, by you or anyone else, do you understand? If I were a man, I would improve your manners with a good—"

"If you were a man, I wouldn't be finding it so damned hard to keep my hands off you," he drawled lazily, despite the desire that her fury-heightened beauty sent shooting through him.

He had gone too far. Lorelei muttered an unlady-like oath and raised her hand. Before she could strike, however, Reeve caught her wrist in a viselike grip. She cried out as he twisted her arm behind her back and brought her up hard against his lean, powerfully muscled body.

"Aren't you afraid I'll hit back, Miss Montgomery?" he challenged in a mocking undertone.

"Let me go!" she hissed, struggling violently.

She balled her other hand into a fist, but as she swung he caught it as well. Another gasp broke from her lips as her thinly clad lower body came into contact with the undeniable evidence of his masculinity. Her eyes flew wide in alarm. She opened her mouth to scream.

Reeve silenced her in the most effective way known to man, his lips crushing down upon the parted softness of hers. She struggled again, but to no avail. She was locked within his hard, almost punishing embrace.

And then something happened. One moment she was fighting to escape—and the next she was pressing closer to the man who held her captive. She had been kissed before, more than once—*but never like this*.

Reeve's kiss demanded a response: not an innocent, tentative one, but the wholehearted response
of a real, flesh-and-blood woman. Lorelei gave a
sharp intake of breath when his tongue suddenly
plunged between her lips to ravish the startled
sweetness of her mouth. She was scarcely aware of
the moment when her wrists were released. Her
arms crept up about his neck with a will of their
own, and she kissed him back with all the passion
he was awakening deep within her. His sinewy arms
tightened about her, drawing her so close that her
every curve found a perfect, corresponding fit in
the hard planes of his body.

The kiss rapidly intensified, all flash and fire and
heat of the moment. Desire, pure and white-hot,
blazed between them. Everything was forgotten save
this wild yearning, this fierce hunger which, though
neither of them had wanted to admit it, had sprung
to life the first time they had set eyes on one another.

Lorelei felt her head spinning. She swayed weakly
against him, her emotions waging a fierce battle
with her conscience. And her conscience was taking
a beating . . .

But all was not yet lost. The coyote's howl rose
up again in the night air. Lorelei would later
wonder if the sound had been Heaven-sent.
Reality hit her like a dash of cold water in the
face. What on earth was she doing? She had never
let anyone hold her the way Reeve Cameron was
holding her. Color flamed in her cheeks at the
thought of how she must look, standing there in
the darkness in nothing but her nightclothes while
this man, an almost total stranger, kissed her as
though he had every right to. Shame joined with

righteous anger to give her strength.

"No!" she cried brokenly, tearing her lips from his. "Let me go!"

She pushed at his chest with all her might, but he refused to release her, his fingers digging into the soft flesh of her upper arms as he forced her to be still.

Reeve was unprepared for the way his heart wrenched at the sight of her stricken face. Tears glistened on her cheeks, and there was a wild look in her eyes, like some helpless, trapped animal. Though his body burned for her, he could not ignore more than a twinge of guilt for having lost his head. He hadn't meant to touch her, hadn't meant for things to go so far.

"Get inside," he muttered hoarsely, forcing his hands away.

Lorelei flung him one last reproachful glare, then snatched the disheveled wrapper closely about her trembling body and scurried back across the moonlit grounds. Her fingers shook upon the latch, but she managed somehow to get the door open. Seconds later, she lay in the sanctuary of the bed once more, her heart thundering in her ears and her hands dashing furiously at her tears.

"Damn you, Reeve Cameron!" she whispered, her fiery gaze slicing toward the window. "Damn you straight to hell!"

It wasn't at all like her to invoke such extreme condemnation on anyone's head, and she knew she didn't truly mean it. She remonstrated with herself for even thinking such a thoroughly uncharitable thing. But she very nearly hated him at that moment, and nearly hated herself as well. How *could* she have been such a fool? She had thought herself safe with him. She had mistakenly believed him to be a gentleman; a rough-edged gentleman, to be sure, but a gentleman all the same.

Oh, it was downright disgraceful, the way she had behaved. She had always believed herself to hold such high moral principles; now it seemed that she had misplaced them somehow. Great balls of fire, she had behaved every bit as wickedly as one of those scarlet women who give in happily to temptation!

Yes, she concluded with a ragged sigh, she was wicked all right. Wicked and stupid, and more wretchedly miserable than she had been in a long time.

Her lips compressed into a thin line of bitter displeasure as she became aware of the woman snoring softly beside her. Charity would have felt no shame, of that she was certain. The thought of Reeve Cameron kissing Charity the way he had kissed her made her blood boil all the more. He probably made it a habit, grabbing any woman he pleased. She could well imagine such a thing — just as she could well imagine that most women would be active participants in the grabbing.

Another long, unhappy sigh escaped her lips. Thank Heaven she would never see him again after tomorrow. She would forget all about him. She would make herself forget . . .

Outside, Reeve stared in the direction of Lorelei's room. He was dangerously close to getting in over his head, and he knew it. His plans didn't include getting tangled up with the sister of the man he had been sent to investigate. In fact, his plans didn't include getting tangled up with any woman at all. He had managed to avoid that particular distraction thus far, though there had been a few times when he had been tempted to let personal feelings interfere with duty.

He had never done it, though. God knew, he was certainly no saint, but the women he'd known, and there had been a number of them over the past dozen or so years, had been willing to accept a temporary involvement.

Lorelei Montgomery, however, was different. She was the kind of woman a man either married or forgot. If he was honest with himself, he'd admit that there was little hope of being able to achieve the latter. The flame-haired wildcat was unlike any woman he'd ever known before. The memory of what it had felt like to hold her in his arms provoked another blaze of desire so intense it almost hurt.

Still, he concluded, his green eyes narrowing, he would *have* to try and forget her. There was too much at stake not to.

Turning away, he headed back to the front of the cabin. The beauty of the summer night was lost to him now; he cursed the impulse that had brought him outside in the first place.

Just as he had done for more nights than he cared to remember, he sought the cold loneliness of his bedroll. He had little doubt that his sleep would be troubled. He could master his emotions, could call upon his iron will to follow through on life's unpleasant decisions — but even he could not control his dreams.

Three

They reached Fort Concho in the late afternoon of the following day. The stagecoach had rolled away from Cantrell's Station shortly after dawn; the hours had once again stretched into an interminable odyssey of heat and dust and motion. Lorelei had been grateful for small favors—neither Virgil nor Charity had talked as much as before—but it had certainly not been easy when she had come face to face with Reeve Cameron that morning, and then twice more during the long day.

Troubled was too mild a word for what she was feeling. Her traitorous mind refused to cast out thoughts of the bold Texan. Guilt and shame still burned within her, but no matter how diligently she tried, she could not vanquish the memory of last night's humiliating madness.

"Big, ain't it?" Virgil remarked beside her, craning his neck to get a better view.

"What?" she asked blankly. Comprehension followed immediately as she turned her head back toward the window. Her eyes, stung by the dust kicked up by the stagecoach's halt, blinked and then widened in surprise at what they beheld.

To their right lay a wide river, and on the other

39

side of it lay the army post, her destination. From this vantage point she had a clear view. Fort Concho was not at all what she had expected. If first impressions counted for anything, the sturdy brick barracks, officers' quarters, and various outbuildings rising so impressively out of the parched ground provided a true refuge in the midst of the vast, mesquite-dotted prairie frontier. Or a refuge for everyone save Hadley, she reminded herself bitterly.

"But why have we stopped here?" she wondered aloud. The coach had pulled up along the main street of a town, although *town* was really too generous a term for the collection of ramshackle wooden buildings sprawled on the banks of the North Concho River. "I thought we would —"

"This is Santa Angela, the end of the run," Charity explained matter-of-factly. Her eyes were gleaming with anticipation at the thought of her new employment. She gathered her skirts up quickly and was ready when Reeve opened the door to help her alight. "I expect I'll see you at Miss Hattie's tonight," she told him in what she hoped was her most enticing manner. She was pleased to see his eyes drop momentarily toward her half-exposed bosom as he swung her down. "You and me could get to be on speaking terms real fast," she said archly, swaying closer once her feet met the dirty, splintered boardwalk in front of the town's one and only hotel.

"I'm not much in the mood for conversation, Miss Pardee," he answered drily. He softened the rejection with a brief, crooked smile, but it required no great effort on his part to let her go.

He turned back to Lorelei, who had moved into the coach's doorway. When he went toward her, her reluctance to submit to his touch was obvious. "No, thank you, Mr. Cameron." It wasn't easy maintaining her composure around him, especially when every time she met his gaze she was certain he was remembering the way she had allowed him to kiss her with such hot-blooded passion. She'd gladly perform any penance Heaven demanded if the whole painful episode could be undone. "I do not require your assistance," she added stiffly.

"I don't recall offering it."

His ungallant words were contradicted by his actions, however, for he seized hold of her about the waist and lifted her bodily down from the coach. An inscrutable smile played about his lips while she glared vengefully up at him.

"Take your hands off me and *keep* them off!" She jerked free and took an unsteady step backward. "If I never see you again, Reeve Cameron, it will be too soon!"

"I warned you not to come," he reminded her, solemn now.

"Yes, but for entirely different reasons! And might I point out that we did not once face any of the dangers you predicted?"

She reached up, unpinned her white straw hat, and dragged it from her head. The sunlight turned her upswept auburn tresses to red-gold fire, a fact which was not lost on Reeve. His features tightened imperceptibly as his gaze traveled over her. Even though her traveling suit was creased and dusty and her hair a tangled, windblown tumble of curls, she was still beautiful. Damnably beauti-

41

ful. And every inch a lady.

"How long are you planning to stay?" he demanded, as if he had a perfect right to do so.

"I fail to see how that is any of your concern." It gave her some perverse satisfaction to note the way his green eyes darkened with displeasure. "Goodbye, Mr. Cameron."

Ollie had thrown down all the baggage by this time. He made a halfhearted effort not to eavesdrop, but he just couldn't leave off straining to catch every word passing between his longtime friend and the young woman with the face of an angel—and the devil's own temper.

Lorelei, spying her carpetbag on the boardwalk behind Reeve, attempted to brush past him. He caught her arm.

"If you won't listen to reason, at least get yourself a decent place to sleep." Forcing his hand back to his side, he offered her a conciliatory smile. "I know a woman over at the post. Her name's Merriwether."

"Well it's none of your business, but I intend to secure accommodations at the hotel." She glanced toward the whitewashed building to her left, doing her best to ignore the perplexing warmth that crept over her each time he set hands on her. It seemed so odd to be carrying on a conversation with the man who had virtually ravished her the night before.

"I don't think you'll like sharing close quarters with a dozen or more buffalo hunters."

"Buffalo hunters?" she echoed in surprise. Hastily scanning the area, she saw that sure enough, there were several bearded and roughly dressed men walking about, almost every one of them looking as if they hadn't bathed in months. And the few women to be seen in the waning afternoon light were decidedly not the sort to command respect.

"Santa Angela's no place for a lady," Reeve told her. He did not add that it was called *Hog Ranch* by the soldiers; the term was an appropriate one. "You'll find nothing but saloons and gaming halls here."

He turned away and picked up her carpetbag. Lorelei tried not to notice the way his denim pants stretched tightly across his lean, hard-muscled thighs and buttocks. She averted her gaze and cleared her throat gently.

"Is that a boarding house?" she queried, nodding to indicate a two-storied building a short distance away. She couldn't quite make out the weathered sign, although the second word appeared to be a woman's name. "The one with the lace curtains—"

"No. That's Miss Hattie's. I'd advise you to stay away from it."

"Why?"

"Because, Miss Montgomery, there aren't many men in this town who will bother to find out whether or not you're one of Hattie's girls. They'll carry you upstairs first and ask questions later."

Her mouth formed a silent *O,* and she was dismayed to feel a hot blush staining her cheeks. She watched in silence as Reeve, battling the impulse to smile at her naïveté, tugged the front brim of his hat lower.

"Let's go."

"Go where?"

"I'm taking you across the river."

"You most certainly are not!" She tried to snatch the carpetbag from him, but he would not let go, and her temper flared. "For Heaven's sake, will you please give me my bag? I am perfectly capable of making it to the fort on my own!"

"Maybe you are," he allowed quietly, "but—"

"Since we have arrived at our destination, I am no longer your responsibility," she protested firmly. Her eyes sparked with rapidly increasing anger. "I have no earthly idea why you have taken it upon yourself to . . . to *bedevil* me at every turn, but I refuse to put up with your high-handed interference any longer!"

It dismayed her to realize how easily he could send her emotions into utter chaos. She took a deep breath, mentally counted to ten, and raised her head proudly. There was nothing to be gained by arguing with him. And Hadley was waiting.

"I am going to the fort now, Mr. Cameron. My bag, please," she demanded, extending her hand for it. The calm, measured tone in which she spoke was in direct contrast to the annoyance and confusion—*and fire, blast it!*—still racing about within her.

"I'll be glad to walk over there with you, ma'am," Virgil Baker offered as he came forward. He had just that moment returned from escorting his new friend Charity down to the very place Reeve had warned Lorelei about. "I ain't got to be out at my uncle's ranch 'til tomorrow, anyhow."

"Thank you, Mr. Baker." Smiling gratefully at Virgil, she sent Reeve a triumphant look. "Well,

44

Mr. Cameron, it appears I won't be needing your assistance after all."

He hesitated only a moment longer before relinquishing the carpetbag into the young cowboy's care. His penetrating gaze held a mixture of amusement and determination when it met Lorelei's again.

"Appearances can be deceiving, Miss Montgomery."

"*Goodbye,* Mr. Cameron," she said, with finality. She turned and took Virgil's arm. They set off across the street, heading toward the wooden bridge that linked Fort Concho's homesick and lonely cavalrymen with the raucous pleasures of Santa Angela.

Lorelei could feel Reeve's eyes upon her, but she refused to look back. She and Virgil were forced to dodge a trio of horsemen, and seconds later they were nearly run down by a wagon rumbling hell-bent for leather down the middle of the street. Driving it was a man anxious to make the best deal for his precious cargo and then squander a goodly portion of his money on whiskey and women. The flatbed wagon was piled so high with buffalo hides that it was dangerously top-heavy.

"I thought all the buffalo had been killed off by the Indians," Lorelei remarked, shuddering at the awful sight of the bloodstained skins.

"There's still a pretty big herd or two if you head north," said Virgil. "But it ain't the Comanches who are doin' much of the killin' any more. It's these white fur traders."

They reached the bridge and started across. Lorelei glanced down, only to see that the river

45

was little more than a trickle in the midst of its high, tree-lined banks. She pressed a lace-edged handkerchief to her nose as protection against the cloud of dust when another wagon, this one laden with supplies destined for an outlying cattle ranch, came thundering across the wooden planks. The entire bridge shook, prompting her to grasp Virgil's arm more tightly.

The impressionable youth was delighted by her action and felt a surge of masculine protectiveness. Already more than a little infatuated with her, he couldn't help thinking that, while a woman like Charity Pardee was all well and good for an easy friendship, a true lady like Miss Montgomery was the kind of woman he'd want beside him when it came time to settle down.

It was his bad luck that she was too old for him. Already past twenty, if he had to guess.

"Does your brother know you're coming?" he asked, his heart giving a sudden flip-flop when he turned his head and met her sapphire gaze.

"Yes. I—I notified him of my plans before I left Georgia." She looked away hurriedly, then asked herself why she should feel either guilt at fibbing or shame about the truth. Hadley was innocent; of that she was certain.

"I hope I'll be seein' you again before too long. I'll only be twelve miles north of here. My uncle's ranch is called the Double Bar S. If you need any-thing—"

"Thank you, Mr. Baker." Preoccupied, she gave him a smile. "I'm sure everything will be fine."

Her eyes clouded as they swept across the fort just ahead. It was much larger than she had imagined it would be. The wide, rectangular parade ground was flanked on one side by a long row of enlisted men's barracks and mess halls, the powder magazine, corrals, and stables, and behind all that the washhouses and laundresses' quarters. On the opposite side were the officers' quarters—eight separate structures that were each two stories high and had the luxury of a columned front porch. The guardhouse, hospital, headquarters building and storehouses were situated at either end of the parade ground.

Lorelei recalled what her brother had written about Fort Concho. In the beginning, nothing could have dampened his excitement. His letters had been full of details about how it was founded nearly twenty years earlier, about its strategic location on the old Butterfield Trail along the river and the army's resultant power to control one of the few water sources in the area, and about its all-important responsibility to provide military protection for the ranches, stage lines, and cattle trails.

He had also mentioned how the buildings had been fashioned of locally quarried stone, their construction overseen by a group of skilled German artisans brought in from Fredericksburg. He had apparently been quite impressed by the amount of money the army had spent on this lonely frontier outpost that had, over time, become more and more a world unto itself.

Even the fort's name had been of interest to him—he had explained how, more than two hundred years earlier, Spanish padres had been prompted to christen the adjoining river *Concha*

47

because of the numerous mussel shells left along the banks by the Indians. With his usual good humor, Hadley had closed that letter with an observation designed to make her smile:

And so here I am, my dearest Lori, granted the perfect opportunity to replace the string of pearls you lost on your sixteenth birthday. Regretfully, they will not be of the same high quality, and it may require a year or two to locate enough productive shells, but I am confident that you will have your gift by the time I am mustered out . . .

"Where are we headed, ma'am?"

"Headed?" Drawn out of her reminiscence, Lorelei frowned thoughtfully at Virgil's question. Her gaze cleared as she returned to the present. "Oh, I . . . to headquarters, I suppose."

"Headquarters. Well, I'd say that'd be the building up ahead, the one where the flag's flying." He nodded toward it and shifted the carpetbag in his hand.

"Yes." She stopped, smiled wanly and reached for the bag. "Thank you for your assistance, Mr. Baker, but I would like to proceed alone now, if you don't mind."

"You sure about that, Miss Montgomery? It's no trouble at all to—"

"I'm quite sure," she asserted, her thoughts already elsewhere.

She had been dreading this moment for days; now that it had finally come, she was dismayed to feel her courage fleeing. *Be strong,* she exhorted herself silently. *Be strong for Hadley's sake.*

"All right then," Virgil capitulated with obvious reluctance. He handed her the bag and quickly

48

drew off his hat. "I'd like to call on you, if it'd be all right, ma'am. I'll be headin' back into town on Saturday." She might be a bit past her prime, but hell, it couldn't do any harm to enjoy her company while she was at the fort. And anyway, Charity would be too busy to pay him much mind. A man needed to be around a woman now and then. "We could go for a ride. I could even take you out to the ranch."

"That's very kind of you, Mr. Baker, but I am not in a position to make any plans at the moment. You see, I don't know how long I will be staying."

She softened the rejection by offering him her hand. He took it, but then appeared to be at a loss as to what to do with it. Lorelei, her eyes aglow with momentary amusement, curled her fingers warmly about his before drawing her hand away again. She turned without another word and began her purposeful march toward headquarters. Virgil didn't move for a long time, his eyes following the gentle, provocative sway of her skirts while his face reddened at the thoughts running through his mind.

Virgil wasn't the only one staring.

The soldiers had been going about their usual daily routine—grooming their horses, cleaning out the stables and barracks, chopping wood, and hauling water. A number of them stopped dead in their tracks as Lorelei approached, their mouths falling open and their eyes growing wide with amazement at the sight of the beautiful, auburn-haired woman who had suddenly appeared out of nowhere.

Half the regiment was away on yet another maneuver against the increasingly aggressive Indians of west Texas. Still, there were close to two hundred men at the post. They would soon be assembling for afternoon drill and target practice, an event that provided its participants with some much-needed relief from the monotony of their duties, while at the same time offering the women and children of Fort Concho the opportunity to gather and watch proudly.

Officers' wives and the laundresses were already beginning to line the edges of the parade ground. Though equally concerned with the men's activities, these women were at opposite ends of the fort's long-established social scale. An officer's wife lived in superior quarters, had servants to do the majority of the cooking and cleaning, and busied herself with tea parties, sewing bees, and the like.

Most laundresses, on the other hand, were married to enlisted men and lived in an area known derisively as "Suds Row." They earned meager wages for their hard work. In addition to washing a mountain of soiled clothing for their husbands' companies twice a week, they also served as midwives and nurses, and even teachers. They had respect, of course, but little else.

Occasionally, an unmarried woman was hired as a post laundress. Her "duties" might well include something of a more personal nature than laundry. There were two such women at Fort Concho, and they kept themselves apart from the wives. Their eyes burned with jealousy when they saw Lorelei, for they knew that any new female, particularly one as young and pretty as she, would be deluged with suitors.

It wasn't as if they hadn't received proposals of marriage over the past few months. They had— countless proposals—but none they had been tempted to accept. The truth of it was, enlisted men couldn't offer them a life any better than the one they had. And officers didn't make a habit of marrying women who had been on first-name terms with half the fort's male population.

As yet, Lorelei was blissfully unaware of the rigid class structure—and of the attention she was attracting. Reaching headquarters at last, she gathered up her skirts and swept inside. The two blue-coated guards flanking the doorway apparently saw nothing suspicious about her, for they let her pass without interrogation. They did, however, exchange looks of disbelief once she had disappeared into the single-story building.

"Think she's one of Hattie's new girls?" the younger of the two whispered to his comrade.

"You blind?" the other man retorted in disgust. "That there's a real lady, boy."

"Yeah? And what makes you so sure of that?"

"There ain't no mistakin' quality, Junior. You live a while longer and pay close attention, you might just be able to tell."

"Damn it, O'Shaughnessy, you call me *Junior* one more time and I'll beat the—" he broke off as an officer approached.

The low rumble of their voices had reached Lorelei's ears, but she hadn't quite been able to make out their words. She hesitated for a moment just inside the doorway while her eyes adjusted from the sun's brightness to the interior's more subdued lighting, which came from two uncurtained windows at the front and two at the rear. The room in which she stood was large and cluttered with various military odds and ends. The walls were lined with photographs of presidents, Texas heroes, and well-known Indian fighters. Unfortunately, it wasn't much cooler inside than out. She detected the faint, unpleasant odor of sweat and tobacco. She lowered her carpetbag to the dusty floor and pushed a windblown strand of hair back into place. She was tempted to take off her jacket, but decided she would look more mature and businesslike if she kept it on. Besides, she reflected, she could remove every stitch of clothing she was wearing and still not escape the awful heat.

Noticing a man seated at a desk near the window, she approached him straightaway.

"Would you please tell me where I may find Colonel Mackenzie?" she requested firmly.

The young corporal had been so absorbed in his paperwork that he was startled by the sound of her voice. His head jerked up, the irritation in his gaze turning to surprise and then pleasure. Coloring guiltily, he leapt to his feet.

"Sorry, ma'am, I . . . I didn't see you come in," he stammered.

"I wish to speak to Colonel Mackenzie. *At once.*"

Her no-nonsense tone belied the increasingly frantic racing of her pulse. She kept telling herself that there was nothing to be afraid of, that she had always managed to talk herself and

52

Hadley out of trouble in the past.

But her reason told her that this predicament was far worse than any the two of them had ever faced before. It would require a good deal more than talking to solve it.

"Colonel Mackenzie?" echoed the corporal. He frowned and shook his head, his pale gray eyes apologetic. "I'm afraid he's not here, ma'am."

"Not here?"

Her spirits plummeted. She knew it would do her no good to speak to anyone but the fort's commandant, for he was the only one with the authority to free Hadley. She wanted desperately to see her brother, to assure him of her support and make certain he was being treated well, but she had decided to present herself as his advocate the moment she arrived. She met the young officer's eyes again and demanded, "When do you expect Colonel Mackenzie to return?"

"Not any time soon. He's off chasing Comanches." He smiled and offered helpfully, "But Colonel Jameson's in command during his absence."

"Then may I please speak to Colonel Jameson?" Her eyes clouded as she fought back a sudden wave of lightheadedness. The effects of the long, difficult journey, combined with a lack of sleep, were beginning to make her regret her decision to charge ahead without resting first. "I—I have a matter of the utmost urgency to discuss with him," she added.

"Yes, ma'am. If you'll tell me your name, I'll see if he's agreeable to meeting with you now."

"My name is Lorelei Montgomery. Tell him I must see him right away."

"Montgomery?"

He seemed about to say something else, but changed his mind and nodded to her before disappearing through a doorway at the far end of the room. When he emerged again a minute later, it was with the welcome news that Colonel Jameson would see her.

Thanking the corporal as she passed him, Lorelei forced herself not to hurry toward the commandant's office. When she entered through the open door she saw a tall, somber-looking man, apparently in his forties. He rose to his feet behind a desk covered with half a dozen neat stacks of paper, and greeted her with a polite smile. If he was surprised by the fact that a beautiful, if travel-weary, young lady professed the need to see him with such urgency, he gave no indication of it.

"Miss Montgomery. Please come in." Gesturing toward a chair opposite his, he wasted little time in preamble. "Corporal Diller informed me you've something important to discuss with me. What is it?"

"It *is* important, Colonel," she confirmed, sinking gratefully down into the chair. She hadn't realized until that moment just how weak her knees had begun to feel. "It concerns my brother, Hadley Montgomery."

"I was unaware that Private Montgomery had any family," he remarked with little interest. "However, I have been in command for less than a week, so I haven't had the time to concern myself with the details of my men's private lives."

He sat down again, somehow managing to look cool in spite of the fact that his double-breasted

54

blue coat, impressively hung with medals and insignia, was buttoned up to his neck. His black hair was streaked with gray, his golden eyes devoid of warmth. Lorelei sensed that he was a thoroughly by-the-book officer, the sort Hadley had complained about in his letters.

"Still, you are aware of my brother's predicament, are you not?" she challenged, noting the disapproval in his gaze as it flickered over her.

"I am familiar with the charges brought against your brother."

"Well, then, surely you can understand why I am here."

"Not entirely."

"Hadley is incapable of committing the crimes of which he stands accused!" She spoke with great feeling, fire sparking in her blue eyes.

"If you'll pardon me for saying so, Miss Montgomery, I would hardly consider you an impartial judge." He gave her a faint, condescending smile and leaned farther back in his chair. "I would expect any man's sister to defend him."

"Have you met my brother, Colonel Jameson?" she demanded sharply.

"I have spoken to him briefly," the man admitted, then his brows knitted together into a frown of rising impatience. "But I fail to see—"

"What you must have *seen* is that he is little more than a boy! He is neither a cold-blooded murderer nor a traitor!"

She drew in a deep, unsteady breath and made a valiant attempt to remain calm. Nothing was going the way she had planned; she had intended to state her case rationally and with utmost composure. But now that she was here, she found herself a victim of her own emotions. She cared too deeply to be able to exercise restraint.

Her eyes full of helpless desperation, she placed a hand upon the edge of the desk and entreated the commandant to listen.

"Please, Colonel Jameson, you must believe me. Something is terribly wrong. Hadley couldn't have killed anyone. He couldn't have! And as for the charge of treason—why, there simply isn't a man alive who loves his country more than my brother does! Indeed, Colonel, that's one of the very reasons he joined the—"

"I'm sorry, Miss Montgomery," he cut her off brusquely. "I can, of course, sympathize with the pain you must be feeling as a result of your brother's arrest. But I'm afraid I can do nothing to alter the situation. Private Montgomery is facing a court-martial, wherein the truth of the allegations against him will be decided by a military tribunal. At this time, the only comfort I can offer you is the assurance that he will be tried fairly."

"And what will happen to him if he is found guilty?" she asked, her voice low and quavering slightly.

"A guilty verdict will bring with it the sentence of death."

He stood as a signal that the meeting was over. His eyes were uncompromising, and his lips were compressed into a thin line of displeasure.

Lorelei rose numbly to her feet. A terrible ache gripped her heart as a result of what she had just heard, but she refused to admit defeat.

"Will you . . . will you not at least explain how

these charges came to be leveled at Hadley?"

"I was under the impression that your brother had already confided in you regarding that matter."

"No." She shook her head and silently cursed the tears which sprang to her eyes. Blinking them back, she swallowed hard and revealed, "The only communication I received from him was a telegram informing me of his arrest. I immediately left my home in Georgia to come here."

"Well, then"—he frowned again and stepped from behind his desk—"your brother stands accused of murdering an officer and conspiring with the enemy."

"Enemy?" she repeated blankly. "What enemy?"

"The Indians, Miss Montgomery," he explained, his tone suggesting she possessed only half a mind.

"But that is impossible!" Her gaze widened in astonishment and confusion. "Why would Hadley—"

"I'm afraid that's all I can tell you for now. I am not at liberty to discuss the details surrounding this case any further," he insisted, though Lorelei suspected he was merely anxious to be rid of her. He moved closer and took her arm in a gentlemanly but nonetheless compelling grasp. "I will arrange for you to speak with your brother—now, if you like."

"Thank you," she murmured, her head still spinning. She did not protest when he led her toward the doorway, but she held back once they had reached it. Her beautiful face wore a look of fierce determination as she turned and met his

57

gaze. "You have not heard the last from me, Colonel Jameson," she promised. "I know my brother is innocent, and I will do everything in my power to prove it!"

"Take my advice, young woman, and leave his defense to those who are better qualified to provide it." For the first time, a glimmer of kindness appeared in his eyes, but he quickly resumed an air of dispassionate courtesy. "Good day, Miss Montgomery." He released her arm and stepped forward to nod curtly at the young, fair-haired officer in the outer room. "Corporal, please escort Miss Montgomery to the guardhouse."

"Yes, Colonel."

"You may have five minutes alone with your brother," the commandant told Lorelei.

"Five minutes?" she repeated, her voice tinged with disappointment. "But—"

"The afternoon drill will commence at four-thirty," he explained. He entrusted her into the corporal's eager care and disappeared back inside his office. The door closed firmly behind him.

"We'd better hurry, ma'am," said Corporal Diller. "No one's allowed in the guardhouse during drills."

Lorelei nodded in silent agreement and obediently went with him. She was both excited and apprehensive at the prospect of seeing her brother again after so long. Their parting had been very difficult. Angry words had passed between them before Hadley, with all the fervor of a nineteen-year-old male, had declared his independence once and for all. They had each apologized in those first letters to one another, of course, but still . . .

it would be so good to be with him again, to reassure him of her love and let him know she would find a way to help him.

But why did their reunion have to take place under such awful circumstances? she lamented inwardly. It all seemed like a nightmare. More than anything in the world, she wished Hadley had never left home. If only he had listened to reason! But then, he had always had a streak of willfulness. The thought prompted a rueful smile to tug at the corners of her mouth. She couldn't very well hold *that* against him, not when she was every bit as headstrong as he.

Everything Colonel Jameson had told her continued to burn in her mind as she hurried along with the corporal. *Murdering an officer and conspiring with the enemy.* How could anyone believe Hadley guilty of such treachery? *The sentence of death.* As God was her witness, she would never let that happen. Never!

Once again, she scarcely noticed the inquisitive stares directed her way. There was murmured speculation among the women concerning her reasons for being at the fort, but the soldiers were much more concerned about whether or not she would be a candidate for their feverish attentions. The most attentive of all these observers, however, was a man watching her from the center of the parade ground. His steel-gray eyes narrowed and gleamed intently beneath the braid-trimmed hat of an officer, while his aristocratic features expressed a good deal more than simple curiosity.

The guardhouse was located only a short walk away, just beyond the long row of barracks. Even in her present, troubled state of mind, Lorelei was struck by the orderliness of what she saw. She had expected the fort to be far more primitive. Hadley had complained at great length in one of his letters about the lack of bathing facilities, the constant invasion of such insects as centipedes and scorpions, and the never-ending dust, which found its way into everything, even the food.

Strangely enough, she realized, he had never complained about the heat, which she found quite oppressive. She raised her handkerchief and pressed it gently to her temple for a moment, longing for the time when she could finally grant herself the luxury of a cool bath. Of course, she realized with an inward sigh, she had to find a place to stay first. She frowned, remembering Reeve's disparaging remarks about the town's only hotel.

"Here we are, Miss Montgomery," Corporal Diller announced.

They had paused in front of yet another stone building, built in the same style as the barracks but with telltale iron bars on the windows. Preceding her escort inside, Lorelei found herself standing in a central room, where a single guard stood abruptly to attention. He appeared to be even younger than Hadley, his uniform hanging loosely on his slender frame and his hat tilted sideways above his freckled face. Her eyes moved past him to scan the guardhouse hastily.

As she would soon discover, the eastern third of the building consisted of one large room for general prisoners—those arrested for drunkenness or other minor infractions—while the third to the west of the room she stood in contained eight small cells. These were reserved for men accused of more serious crimes. Locked doors stood between the central room and the other sections.

"Private Montgomery has a visitor," Corporal Diller informed the guard.

"Yes sir." Trying his best to look manly, he noisily cleared his throat and instructed Lorelei, "Right this way, ma'am."

She followed him in preoccupied silence, her skirts gently rustling and her laced-up boots stirring up a cloud of dust from the floor. The guard unlocked the door, then stepped aside and allowed her to walk alone through the doorway and down an arched stone corridor. She glanced anxiously about her as she went, searching for her brother. All the cells she passed were empty, until finally, she reached the last one.

"Lori!"

Four

Hadley Montgomery's handsome young face lit with the most profound pleasure and relief he had ever known. He rushed forward to the heavy wooden door of his cell, his fingers curling tightly about the bars. The square opening was just large enough to allow his sister to see his head and shoulders.

"I've never been so glad to see anyone in my life!" he confessed with an uneven laugh.

"Oh, Hadley, thank God you're all right!" Lorelei fought back a wave of tears as she quickly closed the distance between them and raised her trembling hands to his. "You *are* all right, aren't you? Sweet mercy, I can't believe this is happening to you! How did you get into this—"

"I'm fine! If you'll give me half a chance, I'll explain everything!"

"Yes, but we've only got five minutes! Colonel Jameson—"

"You've seen the colonel?" he interrupted with a worried frown.

"Of course I have! How else could I be here?" Gazing across into a pair of eyes that were nearly as blue as her own, she forced a bolstering smile to her lips. "Everything's going to work out, Hadley, you'll see!"

"Damn it, Lori, don't meddle in this!" he warned, his frown deepening into a scowl. "You'll only make things worse!"

"How can things be any worse than they already are?" she retorted.

Her eyes were alight with both impatience and affection as they traveled over his well-defined features. He had changed while he had been gone, she noted with surprise. His face looked tanned and healthy above the unbuttoned collar of his white shirt, his slender frame had grown more muscular, and his eyes held a new maturity. He seemed taller; surely he couldn't have grown so much in a matter of months?

He was no longer a boy, but a man. The realization caused her heart to swell with pride. That pride, however, was tempered with sadness, for she knew she would never again be as important to him . . .

"Well?" she challenged, returning to their present argument.

"I don't suppose they can," admitted Hadley, releasing a heavy sigh. He pulled a hand away and raked it through his thick, reddish-brown hair. "I shouldn't have sent you that blasted telegram!"

"Don't be an idiot! You know very well I would never have forgiven you if—"

"Well, it's too late now. You're here. And I *am* glad you've come, dearest Lori!" He grasped her hands with both of his again and gave her an endearingly crooked smile. To look at him, one would never guess he was facing death. "How long are you planning to stay?"

"Why, until you're free, of course!" she proclaimed, her expression leaving little doubt what she thought of such a question. "I promise you, I'm going to do everything I can to get you out of here as soon as possible. I arrived only a short while ago, so I haven't yet had time to do anything more than speak with Colonel Jameson."

"It didn't go well, did it?" he asked, though he had already guessed the answer.

"No," she conceded reluctantly, then stiffened with determination once more. "But it doesn't matter! Great balls of fire, Hadley Montgomery, do you honestly think I'm going to stand by and do nothing while you're convicted of a crime you didn't commit?"

"Two crimes," he was obliging enough to point out, his eyes gleaming with indulgent humor at her spirited response. He told himself it was entirely useless to try and persuade her to let justice take its natural course. She had never allowed anything or anyone to stand in her way when it came to righting a wrong. God help the man who tried.

"Why do they believe you guilty of murder? And how could you possibly be suspected of treason? Colonel Jameson said it had something to do with the Indians, but —"

"I'm afraid it's all rather complicated." His amusement had vanished now, and in its place was a grim resignation. "I swear, Lori, I had nothing to do with Lieutenant Fitzhugh's murder," he declared somberly. "The simple truth is, I'm being framed."

"Framed?" she echoed in astonishment. "By whom?"

"There's more than one person involved. I can't give you any names right now. You'll just have to believe me."

"Of course I believe you!" she assured him with great feeling.

"Lieutenant Fitzhugh was killed because he knew too much," Hadley continued in an undertone. He glanced cautiously toward the outer doorway as he spoke. "There's a secret group here at the post. I don't know who all the members are, but I do know they include officers as well as enlisted men."

"And these men are responsible for your arrest?"

"Yes." He nodded and chose his words carefully. "They arranged for Fitzhugh to be killed. And they arranged for me to look like his murderer."

"But what does that have to do with the charge of treason?"

"The group takes an active 'interest' in the raids going on around here. Their involvement may be even more far-reaching than I originally believed."

"Are you telling me that our own *soldiers* are responsible for the Indian attacks?" She was incredulous at the thought.

"It's my belief that they are."

"But why? What possible motive could they have for doing such a thing?" It sounded incredibly far-fetched, this secret conspiracy among the cavalry's ranks, she told herself with a frown. But if Hadley believed it, then so would she. He had never lied to her.

"Profit, of course." His mouth curved into a faint, humorless smile. "Greed can be a powerful incentive."

"Why don't you tell Colonel Jameson about your

suspicions? Please, Hadley, you must tell him at once! He'll *have* to let you go when he hears this!"

"No, he won't. I haven't any proof. And all the talk in the world won't do me any good until I get it."

"Then *I'll* tell him!" she vowed.

"No!" His adamance startled her. His fingers tightened about hers until she winced, and the look in his eyes made her heart leap in alarm as he continued, his teeth clenched. "You can't say anything to anyone, Lori, do you understand? If the men involved find out that I've told you, they'll kill me — and you as well!" He relaxed his grip and sighed again. "I only told you because I wanted you to know the truth. For now, the best thing you can do is feign complete ignorance of the situation. We're both safe so long as you do that."

"Dear Lord, Hadley, surely you can't mean to keep quiet and let them find you guilty! Colonel Jameson said the punishment would be death, if—" She broke off abruptly, hot tears stinging her eyelids in spite of her efforts to quell them.

"Don't cry, Lori," her brother murmured soothingly. He managed another quick smile. "All's not lost yet. There's still reason to hope the truth will be discovered before my court-martial takes place."

"How?" she demanded, her voice edged with bitterness. "If this group you've told me about is so secret and powerful, who will have enough courage to stand against them? No, Hadley, I won't let them do this to you! There must be some way to get the proof we need, some way to—"

"We? Didn't you hear a word I said? You *can't* get mixed up in this!" he reiterated angrily.

"I can and I will!"

Hadley opened his mouth to offer yet another warning, this one in language she would be sure to understand, but he never got the chance. Corporal Diller stepped into the corridor and announced that their five minutes were up.

"I'm sorry, Miss Montgomery, but the men are beginning to assemble for drill. You'll have to leave now."

Lorelei nodded in acquiescence, then turned back to Hadley. There was so much she had meant to say to him, so many questions she still wanted answered.

"I'll visit you again tomorrow," she promised.

"The colonel might not allow it."

"The colonel can go to the devil for all I care! I *will* come again. And in the meantime, I'm going to see what I can find out."

"Lori," her brother warned in a low, threatening tone.

"Goodbye, dearest Hadley!" She flashed him a smile that was half defiance, half endearment before taking a step backward. "Please try not to worry. If there's anything you need, I will try and get it for you. I haven't much money left, but—"

"The only thing I need is for you to remember what I said!" he countered, then couldn't help returning her smile with a loving, exasperated one of his own. He sobered in the next instant and murmured, "I'm glad you're here, Lori."

"I love you, Hadley. I would do anything for you," she replied softly.

"Miss Montgomery?" Corporal Diller called again from the doorway.

"Yes, Corporal, I'm coming."

Reluctantly she retraced her steps back down the corridor and into the central room. The guard closed and locked the door behind her. Listening to the key turning in the lock, she closed her eyes and silently repeated her vow to see Hadley freed. Seconds later, the strident sound of a bugle echoed throughout the fort to signal the official start of the day's last drill.

Having lost her escort to his military duties, Lorelei returned alone to headquarters to retrieve her carpetbag. She paused for a moment when she re-emerged into the late afternoon sunlight, watching as the blue-coated men marched in unison across the wide parade ground. The officers shouted orders, the men obeyed instantly, and the whole maneuver was accompanied by a rolling cadence of drums. It was an impressive sight—or it would have been, had she felt the least bit inclined to be impressed with the United States Cavalry at that moment.

Hadley's story about a secret conspiracy at the fort still seemed incredible, and yet she knew he had spoken the truth. Her blood boiled at the injustice of it all. Her brother, an innocent man, was imprisoned in the guardhouse, while the guilty men were free to carry on with their lives. They were probably somewhere on the parade ground right now. The thought provoked a surge of vengeful fury deep within her. Hadley may have warned her about the dangers, but it was completely unthinkable for her *not* to interfere.

Of course, she realized unhappily, she had no idea where to start. Colonel Jameson would obviously be little help. Perhaps she could ask Corporal Diller a few questions. She'd have to be careful not to arouse his suspicions; what if he was one of the members of the secret group? No, she decided quickly, he wasn't the sort to be involved in such treachery. But she'd have to be careful just the same.

Her pensive gaze shifted to where the women stood, their children playing within a safe distance, observing the drill from their vantage point along the gravel walk. It was quite possible that she would learn the most from them.

"Back to town—or not?" she murmured aloud, suddenly recalling that she had still to find a place to spend the night.

Santa Angela's no place for a lady. She bristled with renewed irritation at the memory of Reeve Cameron's high-handedness, then found herself wondering if he would be staying at the hotel himself. Of what possible interest were his whereabouts to her? she mused angrily. After all, she would never see him again.

"Miss Montgomery?"

She was surprised to hear a feminine voice, and turning her head, she saw a tall, dark-haired woman of perhaps thirty approaching her with a friendly smile. The woman was very attractive, and she was wearing a well-tailored dress of embroidered white cotton. Lorelei's brow creased in puzzlement, for she had believed her identity would be known only to the men she had encountered thus far.

"Yes?"

"I was told you might be in need of accommodation. My name is Abigail Merriwether."

"Oh, I—I recall having heard your name," Lorelei

69

stammered in response. So, Reeve Cameron was still trying to interfere in her life! She should have known he would take it upon himself to arrange things. Hastily recovering her poise, she gave the other woman a polite smile and said, "How do you do, Miss Merriwether."

"It's 'Mrs.'—my husband is Captain John Merriwether." She extended a hand gracefully toward one of the nearby officers' quarters. "We have an extra room. It's not in the main building, I'm afraid, but in a smaller one out back. Still, I can assure you that it's very comfortable."

"Thank you, Mrs. Merriwether." Although tempted to accept, she did not immediately do so. The prospect of being in Reeve Cameron's debt, even in this small way, perturbed her greatly. "I certainly appreciate your kind and generous offer, but—"

"Please, call me Abigail. And I simply will not take no for an answer." Her green eyes sparkled with good-humored warmth as she stepped forward and linked her arm companionably through Lorelei's. "Come along, my dear. You must be positively exhausted after so long a trip. We'll get you settled right away. To tell the truth, it will be wonderful having someone new to talk to!"

"Well, I don't know how long I will be staying," Lorelei pointed out.

"That doesn't matter, you may stay as long as you like. The children will be glad of your company, and I give you my word that John is in perfect agreement with me about this. John is always in perfect agreement with me—except when it comes to military matters." She sighed dramatically and began

70

leading Lorelei toward the house. "It is my opinion that this post would run a good deal more smoothly if the men bothered to heed the advice of their wives!"

Lorelei made one last halfhearted attempt to decline the Merriwethers' hospitality, but she was overruled by the delightful, talkative Abigail and escorted to the small, whitewashed building that would serve as her home for the duration of her stay. The room proved to be every bit as comfortable as her hostess has promised. The furnishings included a carved oak rocker, a brass bed covered with a wedding ring quilt, and a washstand. A large chest of drawers sat opposite the bed, and ruffled gingham curtains hung at the windows. The floor had been recently scrubbed with lemon and beeswax. A pair of braided rugs added a welcome touch of color, while a pot-bellied stove rested in the far corner, waiting for the time when it would be useful again. During the relentless heat of summer, it was difficult for anyone to remember how harsh the winters at Fort Concho could be.

"I'm afraid the furniture has seen better days," Abigail remarked with a momentary frown, "but it's very sturdy." Her face brightened again after she had thrown open the two windows. "You'll be wanting a bath, of course. It will be another two hours before supper is served, so you'll have plenty of time to rest."

"Thank you, you've been very kind," Lorelei declared sincerely. She wondered what Reeve Cameron's relationship with the Merriwethers was, and wondered as well what he had told Abigail about her. But she did not ask. If first impressions

71

counted for anything, she knew Abigail would reveal everything in the near future. "If you hadn't come along, I would have had to find a room at the hotel in town," she confessed on sudden impulse.

"In Santa Angela?" Abigail looked shocked. "Oh, no, my dear, that's the one place you must avoid at all costs! There are times when necessity forces us to visit the general store, but we are always reluctant to do so." She wrinkled her nose in an expression of distaste. "It's been said that there are so many gamblers, murderers and horse thieves in town that it is unsafe to pass through after dark. A wretched assortment of saloons and . . . well, houses of ill fame, that's all you'll find there!"

"So I have been led to believe," Lorelei murmured dryly.

"And rightfully so." Abigail patted the younger woman's arm and swept back to the doorway. "You'll be taking your meals with us. I'll see about that bath now." With that, she was gone.

Lorelei felt as though she had been caught up in a whirlwind. She smiled to herself and sat down upon the bed. She peeled off her jacket at last, then removed her boots and stifled a groan at the sudden twinge of pain in her back, which reminded her all too clearly of the many hours she had spent in the stagecoach. She put her feet up and settled herself comfortably. The sounds from the parade ground drifted in on the warm breeze and brought her yet another unwelcome reminder—this one of the task before her.

It was still difficult to believe that Hadley's life, and her own, had taken such a calamitous turn. These past eight years had certainly been far from easy, but at least she and her brother had been able to comfort one another through the bad times.

There was little she could do to comfort Hadley now. He needed her more than ever before, and yet she feared she would fail him. And her failure might very well mean his death, she thought disconsolately. There had to be *some* way to prove his innocence, some way to convince Colonel Jameson that the wrong man had been arrested. But how?

Admitting to herself that she was much too tired to be able to think rationally, she surrendered to the temptation to lie back and close her eyes for a few moments.

She was sleeping soundly when Abigail returned with the first bucketful of water for her bath. The kindly woman did not have the heart to wake her, so she tiptoed out and closed the door softly.

It was two hours before Lorelei finally bathed and dressed for the evening meal. She might very well have slept the whole night through, but six-year-old Caroline Merriwether had taken it upon herself to go and inform the family's new guest that they were having the wondrous delicacy of sweet potato pancakes for supper. The deceptively angelic-looking child, a smaller replica of her mother, had sneaked away from the main house to the small building where "the redheaded lady" lay sleeping. Opening the door softly, she had said her piece and scampered away again with an unrepentant giggle after making certain she had been heard.

Lorelei had not minded in the least; in truth she had been grateful for the enthusiastic awakening. She discovered that the nap had left her feeling much improved, and the quick bath Abigail hur-

73

riedly provided served to lift her spirits even higher.

Abigail began the introductions as they gathered in the dining room shortly after seven o'clock that evening. "Miss Lorelei Montgomery, this is my husband, Captain John Merriwether." Her voice held a note of maternal pride when she presented her three children—the precocious Caroline, a three-year-old boy named Weston, and a happy, apple-cheeked baby of eight months who would immediately be known to anyone as his father's offspring. He and the captain possessed the same dark eyes and the same tumble of thick, wavy brown hair.

"Welcome to our home, Miss Montgomery," Captain Merriwether said amiably. He was quite tall and looked authoritative in his crisp blue uniform. His voice carried easily throughout the house, which was furnished with mismatched, albeit much treasured, items collected during ten years of cavalry life.

"Thank you, Captain," said Lorelei. She considered pressing him for details about Hadley's arrest, but she resisted the urge and bestowed a polite smile upon him instead. "It is exceedingly generous of you and Mrs. Merriwether to allow me to stay."

"Not at all." He waved her gratitude aside, then, waiting until all three children and both women had taken their places, he took his own traditional seat at the head of the linen-covered table. He intoned a quick, rather perfunctory blessing upon the meal before reaching for a platter laden with a meat Lorelei could not easily identify. "My wife tells me you hail from Georgia, Miss Montgomery."

"Yes." She accepted the platter from him, eyed its contents dubiously, and forced herself to transfer a portion of the meat to her own plate.

"And that you have come to visit your brother," added John, looking to her for confirmation.

It was precisely the opening she needed.

"Yes, Captain, I have," she answered in calm, measured tones. She glanced at Abigail, who appeared uncomfortable with the subject. Wondering with renewed annoyance what Reeve Cameron had told the woman, she returned her attention purposefully to the man beside her. "My brother is Hadley Montgomery. I suspect both his name and his plight are already familiar to you."

"They are." A hasty, conspiratorial look passed between him and his wife. "I have known Private Montgomery for some time now."

"Do you also know that he is innocent?" demanded Lorelei, her eyes holding an unmistakable challenge.

"His innocence or guilt is not for me to judge." Although his manner was all that was correct in an officer, his eyes reflected genuine compassion. "I'm sorry, Miss Montgomery, but it would be highly imprudent of me to discuss the case with you. Please believe me, however, when I say that a full investigation has been launched." His features relaxed a little as he cast a glance about the table. "Now, if there is any way we can make your stay here more comfortable, you've only to let us know."

"Can you not at least tell me when my brother's court-martial is scheduled to take place?" She tried, unsuccessfully, to keep the anger and bitterness from her voice. It wasn't right to blame him for what had happened, she told herself; and yet thus far she had met with nothing but maddening resistance in her efforts to aid Hadley.

"Have you spoken to Colonel Jameson regarding this matter?"

"I have." Her eyebrows pulled together in a frown of intense displeasure. "He was far from communicative."

"Please, John," Abigail interceded at this point, "what can be the harm in telling her?" She extricated her hand from the baby's potato-encrusted grip and smiled sympathetically at Lorelei. "You must understand, my dear, that such caution is a way of life in the cavalry. One can never know when the smallest detail might result in—"

"Abigail," her husband admonished quietly, but firmly.

"Private Hadley Montgomery is going to hang," Caroline suddenly piped up. It was put forth quite matter-of-factly.

A pained expression crossed Lorelei's face, and her hand trembled slightly as she lowered her fork to her plate. She was acutely conscious of five pairs of wide, examining eyes fixed upon her.

"*Caroline!*" Abigail finally scolded in shocked dismay. "How on earth could you say such a horrible thing?"

"It's true, Mama!" the little girl insisted defiantly, her dark curls bouncing as she gave an emphatic nod.

"Who told you that, Caroline?" Captain Merriwether asked in a quiet, stern tone.

"Nobody told me, Papa," Caroline hastened to disclose. In contrast to her previous nonchalance, she was now visibly upset. "I heard two men talking about it in front of the stables this morning.

76

They—" She broke off and swallowed hard. Her eyes fell to where she was pushing her food aimlessly around with her fork. "They said Private Hadley Montgomery is going to hang because he's an Indian lover and a murdering son of a—"

"That's enough!" her father snapped. Caroline promptly burst into tears.

"Oh, Lorelei, I'm so terribly sorry!" Abigail apologized in embarrassment. Her distressed gaze shifted to the wailing child and back again. "I'm certain she did not understand what she was saying!"

"It's all right," reassured Lorelei. Her eyes shone with compassion as she smiled across at the hapless Caroline, whose sobbing had subsided into a lingering case of sniffles. "Please don't cry, Caroline," she entreated soothingly. "It isn't your fault that you overheard those men. But they were wrong, you know. My brother isn't a murderer. He is a very good man."

"He is?" the little girl murmured, glancing uncertainly at her parents. She was relieved to see that neither of them appeared angry with her any longer.

"He most certainly is."

"Finish your supper, please, children," Abigail instructed softly. The smile she cast Lorelei held gratitude as well as affection. Even John's hitherto rigid features relaxed, and he offered a fresh sourdough biscuit to Lorelei.

"I will speak to my daughter later, Miss Montgomery," he promised in an undertone.

"There is no need, Captain." She meant it, for she didn't blame the child at all. But Caroline's words continued to haunt her. *Private Hadley*

As if reading Lorelei's mind, Abigail gave her husband an imploring look.

"Please, John, it seems cruel to keep her in suspense. Why, how would you feel if you discovered yourself in such a position? It will surely jeopardize nothing if we let her know—"

"No, Abigail." He cut her off with another cautionary frown. "You know very well that I am under orders not to speak of it." His gaze encountered the searching blue intensity of Lorelei's, and she could sense that he was torn between duty and sympathy. He made a none too subtle attempt to change the subject. "I was in Georgia during the war, Miss Montgomery. From what I recall, the countryside was—"

"Well, *I* am under no orders!" Abigail startled him by proclaiming in a rare burst of defiance. Her three children watched in silent, wide-eyed fascination as she turned purposefully to Lorelei and confided in a breathless tumble of words, "Washington is dispatching a special investigator to look into your brother's case. It is no real secret—the entire post is aware of his imminent arrival, even if Colonel Jameson chooses to think otherwise."

"By thunder, woman!" Captain Merriwether ground out, forgetting for a moment that they were not alone. A flush of anger crept over his face, and the look in his eyes promised a husbandly retribution on his errant wife. "You have no right to—"

"I have every right!" retorted Abigail bravely. Two bright spots of color rode high on her own cheeks, but she went on to tell Lorelei, "I cannot reveal his name, of course, but I thought you should know that something is being done to ensure your brother's fair treatment."

"Thank you," Lorelei offered in heartfelt gratitude. Her mind raced to think of a way to make the information useful. After a few seconds' indecision, she hastily rose to her feet. "Excuse me — I must speak to Colonel Jameson about this at once!"

Her announcement was greeted with an expression of somber disapproval from John, while Abigail began to look as if she regretted having said anything at all.

"No, Miss Montgomery, I must advise against such a course of action," said the captain as he rose from the table as well. "Colonel Jameson will not like having his privacy disturbed at this late hour. And," he added, torn between protectiveness and simmering displeasure when he glanced briefly toward Abigail, "I would not want it known that my wife was the one—"

"You needn't worry on that score, Captain," Lorelei assured him earnestly. "I will make quite certain he does not suspect the source of my enlightenment."

Murmuring an apology for her abrupt departure, she hurried from the room and out of the house. Caroline's melodious voice called out a goodbye behind her. She smiled at the sound of it; she would not have smiled at the conversation which took place in her absence.

The sun had dipped below the horizon, and the long summer day had nearly completed its surrender to twilight. Darkness would soon cloak the wild, windswept Texas prairie, but life at the post continued its routine. The enlisted men were enjoying a supper of warmed-over beef hash, bread, and coffee; the horses had been groomed and fed; and the parade ground was virtually deserted. The entire garrison would reassemble for retreat within the next half hour, at which time the buglers and drummers would accompany the formations and the flag would be lowered.

Across the river, the saloons were already starting to get crowded. Faint strains of music and laughter reached Lorelei's ears. A sudden image of Reeve Cameron crossed her mind, and she wondered if he was among those who would spend the night in drunken pursuit of gold and women. The thought brought an inexplicable spark of fury to her eyes.

Gathering up the long skirts of her rose silk gown, she quickened her steps toward the headquarters building. She realized that the commandant would in all likelihood be at home, but she had forgotten to ask Captain Merriwether where his quarters were located. Perhaps Corporal Diller would still be on duty. She was certain she could convince him to tell her where to find Colonel Jameson. If not, then she would search the entire post!

She had decided that it was imperative to ask him why Hadley's arrest should be of such interest in Washington. There was a good deal more to the situation than anyone was willing to let on, and she was determined to get to the bottom of things. At least there was a glimmer of hope now.

She was surprised to find that there were no guards on duty, but happily she discovered the door to the building to be unlocked. She swept inside, her eyes lighting with satisfaction when she saw the lamplight streaming from beneath the closed door to the commandant's office. Corporal Diller was no-where in sight, so she proceeded across the room. She knocked, then determinedly opened the door without waiting for a response.

"Colonel Jameson?"

"Miss Montgomery!" The colonel, standing at the window, spun about to face her. His initial startle-ment gave way to more than slight irritation as he hastened forward. "You should not be here," he scolded curtly. "Please leave at once!" His eyes glanced to the shadows in the far corner of the room, but Lorelei did not notice.

"No!" She lifted her head proudly, and her hand tightened resolutely about the doorknob. "I have heard that Washington is sending someone to inves-tigate the charges against my brother!"

"And where did you hear that, may I ask?" Once again, his behavior toward her was all that was mili-tarily correct, but his harsh gaze left little doubt about his true feelings regarding both her intrusion and the apparent lack of discretion at the post.

"I happened to overhear a conversation between two of your men," she lied, anxious to protect Abi-gail. "Well, Colonel? Is it true?" She waited several seconds for him to answer, all the while eyeing him closely to gauge his reaction.

"Yes," he admitted finally. He frowned across at her, then turned back to the window. "Come inside and close the door, Miss Montgomery."

Taken aback by his sudden unexpected coopera-tion, Lorelei did as he said and moved toward the desk. She was just about to take a seat when the colonel added a second surprise to the first.

"It so happens that the investigator appointed to

your brother's case has already arrived."

"Already—" echoed Lorelei, only to break off in confusion. "But why didn't you tell me this before?"

"Because, Miss Montgomery," he explained with what looked suspiciously like a smile, "I did not know it myself until a short time ago."

"Well, then, where is he?" she demanded.

Colonel Jameson did not answer. Instead, the man whose presence had so far gone unnoticed by Lorelei emerged from the shadows.

Five

"*You!*" gasped Lorelei. Her sapphire eyes widened in shocked amazement.

"Miss Montgomery, this is Major Reeve Cameron," announced Colonel Jameson. "Major Cameron, I'd like to present Miss Lorelei Montgomery. She is, as I have already informed you, Private Montgomery's sister."

Lorelei had wondered why the commandant had capitulated and allowed her to remain, but she was a good deal more concerned with what she had just heard.

"*Major?*" she echoed in disbelief at the revelation. Her eyes moved back to Colonel Jameson. The look on his face convinced her that he had spoken the truth.

Stunned to discover that Reeve Cameron was the special investigator Abigail had told her about, she grasped the back of the chair for support and tried valiantly to hide her agitation. Her heart pounded and her senses reeled. How was it possible that this man, the insolent cowboy who had ridden shotgun on the stagecoach from Fort Worth, was a high-ranking officer in the United States Cavalry?

Great balls of fire, this couldn't be happening!

And yet there he was, looking unbearably handsome, tall and commanding in his dark blue uniform. It was as though a different man stood before her. But no, she told herself, with more than a touch of indignation, he was the same—the same arrogant, overbearing man she had vowed to forget. And although she hated to admit it, the memory of his kiss haunted her still.

"Miss Montgomery and I have already met," Reeve confessed to the colonel. His gaze, steady and penetrating, locked with the deep blue fire of Lorelei's while he slowly advanced upon her. "I trust you are comfortable at the Merriwethers'?" he queried with seeming politeness as he stared down at her. There was a faint glimmer of amusement in his eyes that did not go unnoticed by Lorelei.

"Tell me, *Major*," she enjoined, her voice angry and accusing, "isn't there some sort of regulation forbidding you to deceive others by passing yourself off as a civilian?"

"Deception was never my intent."

"Then why were you out of uniform these past two days? And why did you conceal your identity from me?"

"Patience, Miss Montgomery. I'll explain everything to you later," he promised in a low, resonant tone that would brook no defiance. He transferred his attention to Colonel Jameson, who had watched the couple's brief, highly charged interchange with a frown of confusion. "I suggest we conclude our discussion now, Colonel. Shall I expect that report first thing in the morning?"

"Of course, Major."

In spite of the fact that he outranked the younger

man, the commandant's tone showed considerable respect. It wasn't every day the fort received such a distinguished visitor. From what he'd heard, the major was one of the best when it came to cracking difficult cases like young Montgomery's. On top of that, he was a highly decorated war hero—although it was too bad he'd fought on the wrong side. That was a mystery in itself: just how *had* a Johnny Reb come to be so popular with the high command up in Washington?

"Good night, Colonel," said Reeve. He moved to Lorelei's side and took hold of her arm. "Miss Montgomery, I'd like to have a word with you."

Although reluctant to cause a scene in front of the colonel, Lorelei resisted when Reeve tried to lead her from the room.

"One moment, if you please, Mr. Cameron!" she demanded sharply. She would have extricated her arm from his grasp, but he would not allow it.

"It's 'Major,' " he reminded her with provoking equanimity.

She battled the temptation to strike him. Shooting him a blazing look that spoke volumes, she turned to the colonel.

"Please, Colonel Jameson, I must speak to you at once. My conversation with my brother yielded some shocking and important information! If you will only listen to what he—"

"I will arrange for you to visit your brother again tomorrow." Colonel Jameson cut her off with pointed swiftness. He glanced toward Reeve and back again. "In accordance with Major Cameron's request, all matters pertaining to Private Montgomery's arrest will henceforth be referred to directly to him."

"But Hadley is being framed!"

"I'm sorry, Miss Montgomery. You'll have to rely upon Major Cameron's indulgence from now on." There was a note of finality in his voice, and his features had taken on the cold, unapproachable look she remembered all too well. "You are welcome to make use of my office, Major," he told Reeve. He strode past Lorelei and offered her a curt nod. "If you'll please excuse me, my wife is expecting me." And he left them alone together, closing the door on his way out.

Lorelei hesitated only a moment before jerking her arm free. She rounded on Reeve with fiery-eyed vengeance.

"Why the devil didn't you tell me you were coming here because of my brother?"

"I wanted to get a few answers myself first." That was at least partially true.

"Indeed, Major? And did you get those answers?" she demanded with biting sarcasm. Her anger was only fueled when she realized again how dashing he looked in his blue uniform. He had even more medals than Colonel Jameson, she noted, then told herself he probably won them by taking part in some outrageously devious maneuvers. "Well? Did you?" she prompted, her temper flaring almost beyond control.

"Some of them." His mouth curved into a sardonic half-smile. "I'll get the rest of them soon enough."

"Why did you let me believe you were nothing more than a . . . Texas *cowboy?* And how can you possibly serve in the cavalry and run a stagecoach line at the same time?"

"I *am* a Texas cowboy," he replied nonchalantly. "As far as the line is concerned, my father owns it. I just help out whenever I'm passing through." He did not add that he hadn't been home on leave for more than a year.

"Blast it all, none of this makes sense!" She frowned and spun away in a burst of exasperation, her silk skirts rustling about her white-stockinged legs as she stormed across to the widow. "I don't understand. I knew — Abigail told me a man had been dispatched from Washington," she blurted out, and then flushed guiltily when she realized she had broken her word. She turned hastily to face Reeve again. "Good Heavens, I promised Captain Merriwether that no one would know —"

"Don't worry. Your secret is safe with me," he assured her solemnly. He closed the distance between them once more and subjected her to a long, oddly disturbing scrutiny. He towered above her, and his piercing green eyes were full of a warmth she did not want to acknowledge. "Abigail told you the truth. I left Washington a week ago."

The urge to touch her was very powerful. His gaze dropped to where her breasts rose and fell rapidly beneath the square-cut neckline of her bodice. He cursed the sudden fire in his loins, and forced his eyes upward again. The rose silk she was wearing made her hair look even redder in the lamplight, he mused appreciatively. Damn, but she was beautiful. Beautiful and spirited, and more intriguing than any woman he'd ever known.

"But why?" Lorelei demanded. "What is it about

87

my brother's arrest that is of such interest to Washington? And why were *you* chosen to investigate?"

The ghost of a mocking smile touched his lips. Lorelei grew alarmed at the way her pulse raced.

"I hope that isn't an insult to my capabilities, Miss Montgomery," he drawled. Then, growing serious, he went on, "Your brother's arrest simply coincided with another matter that was worthy of a more in-depth exploration." Again, it was a partial truth.

"I don't believe you! I think you came here for the express purpose of investigating the events surrounding my brother's arrest!"

"Do you?" The challenge was offered with deceptive indifference. Only the wary light in his eyes betrayed the fact that her words had caught his interest.

"I most certainly do!"

Her gaze fell for a moment while she tried to decide whether or not to reveal what Hadley had told her. She was acutely conscious of Reeve's proximity—Heaven help her, she could literally feel the heat emanating from his virile, muscular body—but she tried not to think about that. Right now, the only thing that mattered was helping her brother. And if that meant she had to endure Reeve Cameron's damnably unsettling presence, then so be it.

"My brother *is* being framed," she insisted, raising her eyes to his again. They seemed to bore into her very soul. She suffered a sharp intake of breath and gently cleared her throat before continuing. "Hadley is innocent of all the charges. He . . . he did not kill Lieutenant Fitzhugh, nor did he enter into a conspiracy with the Indians."

88

"What makes you so certain?" Reeve asked quietly.

"My brother has never lied to me, Major Cameron. And—" She left the sentence unfinished and turned away again. Reeve's eyes narrowed almost imperceptibly while he watched her take up a stance behind Colonel Jameson's desk. It was as though she suddenly felt the need for a barrier between them.

"You're going to have to trust me, Lorelei."

She was startled at the sound of her name on his lips. Her eyes widened and an inexplicable warmth spread through her entire body. It was all she could do to maintain her composure.

"I don't recall having granted you permission to—" she started to protest.

"We'll get to that next," said Reeve. "For now, let's stick to the subject at hand." There was something in his low, deep-timbred voice that made her want to give him the trust he was demanding. "I'm here to find the truth. You claim your brother's innocent. All right, then, help me prove it. Tell me everything you know."

"I'll have to speak to Hadley first," she declared, still cautious in spite of the temptation to divulge the whole incredible story.

She remembered Hadley's words of warning, remembered the fear in his voice when he had mentioned the possibility of reprisal. But surely Reeve Cameron couldn't be part of the conspiracy. She didn't know why it was so important to her to believe that, and yet she sensed it had more to do with her own feelings than with her brother's predicament.

89

"I — I'm afraid I can't tell you anything until I've discussed it with him," she reiterated, her gaze falling beneath the burning intensity of Reeve's. "I'll ask him tomorrow."

"You do that." His handsome face appeared forebodingly grim. "But keep in mind that we don't have much time."

"What do you mean?"

"His court-martial is scheduled to take place at the end of next week."

"Next week?" She glanced up at him in dismay. Dear Lord, she wondered, how could she hope to discover the truth by then?

Reeve's heart wrenched at the pain and anguish he saw in her eyes, but he schooled his emotions quickly. He had never taken such a personal interest in a case before. He was treading on dangerous ground; disaster lay ahead for them both if he lost his head again.

"I'm sorry. I tried to get the proceedings postponed. But I don't intend to let an innocent man hang," he assured her. Somehow, she knew he meant it.

"That's precisely what will happen if my brother is found guilty."

Her voice broke at the end, and she was visibly fighting back tears as she gathered up her skirts and headed for the door. Reeve moved to block her path.

"Please allow me to leave, Major!" she choked out, attempting to push past him. His hands suddenly closed about her upper arms. She struggled, but with a weary resignation. Her spirits were perilously low at that moment, and the last thing in the world she either wanted or needed was to do battle with him again. The touch of his fingers scorched her through the thin layer of silk. "No! Let go of—"

"Listen to me, Lorelei," he commanded. His words achieved the desired effect, and she stilled within his firm, surprisingly gentle grasp. As she stared up at him, her beautiful eyes were wide and luminous.

"Why should I?" she countered. "You have done nothing but deceive me and . . . and humiliate me from the first. Don't you understand? My brother's very life is at stake!" Furiously she blinked back the tears and lashed out at him with a reproachfulness she could not suppress. "Would to God his fate had been entrusted to a man who had enough decency to keep his . . . his lustful inclinations under control!"

"I wondered when we'd get back to last night," he remarked with a faint, ironic smile. "I did nothing more than steal a kiss, Lorelei."

He had wanted to do a hell of a lot more than that, of course. Even now, her nearness sent liquid fire racing through his veins. Lorelei apparently read his thoughts, none of which were of a virtuous nature, for she blushed hotly and narrowed her eyes at him.

"I hardly think stealing a kiss from the sister of a man you have been assigned to investigate would be deemed acceptable behavior by your superiors!"

"Maybe not. But no matter what happened between us—no matter what happens from here on— I'll do the job I was sent to do." Forcing himself to release her, he shook his head slightly and pointed out, "You're wrong about one thing. I don't hold your brother's fate in my hands. That will be decided at the court-martial." In truth, though, he knew his influence would be considerable; he had been given full power to direct every aspect of the trial.

"Yes, but it's *your* evidence that will be used to reach a verdict!" There was no doubt that her strength was returning. When she next spoke, it was with her usual proud defiance. "Go ahead and conduct your investigation, Major Cameron. Find out everything you can about Hadley and the charges against him. But I offer you fair warning—make the mistake of turning the military tribunal against him, and I'll see you repaid!"

"Is that a threat, Lorelei?" he queried softly, trying in vain to remain impervious to the way her anger heightened her beauty.

"Make of it what you will!" was her enigmatic response. She marched to the door and flung it open, then paused to add haughtily, "And stop calling me 'Lorelei'! It so happens that I find your familiarity offensive in the extreme!"

"Liar."

She gasped at the insult, which actually sounded more like an endearment. Her eyes widened, first in disbelief, and then in outrage.

"Why—how *dare* you?"

"I'm as anxious as you are to keep our relationship on a strictly professional level," he asserted, then snatched back the reassurance with his next words. "But we both know that's impossible."

There, damn it. He'd said it. There was no use in denying it to himself any longer—he couldn't treat her with his usual cold detachment. She might be

Hadley Montgomery's sister, but she was also a captivating and thoroughly desirable young woman. He'd have to be made of stone to be immune to her charms. Still, he wasn't yet ready to throw all caution to the winds.

"We're going to be seeing a lot of each other in the next few days," he remarked in a conciliatory manner. "We might as well admit we've progressed past the first round of formality."

"Speak for yourself, Major!" retorted Lorelei. She drew herself rigidly erect. "I, for one, do not intend for us to spend any significant amount of time together. You have your work to do — and I have mine!"

"What are you talking about?"

"Merely that I am not going to sit back and rely upon your 'indulgence,' as Colonel Jameson so charmingly put it. It may surprise you to learn that you are not the only one capable of searching out the truth."

She felt a warning deep within her as she saw his rugged features tighten abruptly. His green eyes darkened and took on an unfathomable expression. There was no trace of amusement in his manner now.

"You're not going to get mixed up in this." It was a decree, not a request. Lorelei bristled at his presumption.

"And what makes you think you have the right to —"

"You'll do as I say," he interjected masterfully.

The thought of her being in jeopardy made his blood boil. He suspected that the situation at the fort was even more volatile than Colonel Macken-

93

zie's initial report had indicated, and he couldn't have this redheaded wildcat running around stirring up trouble while he tried to conduct his investigation. He had never before allowed a woman to distract him, and he'd be damned if he'd let it happen now.

"Stay out of it, Lorelei," he commanded, then added fuel to the fire with, "That's an order."

"I am not in the cavalry, *Major!*" she reminded him with considerable feeling. "You have no authority over me!"

"Ah, but I do. If I catch you interfering in any way, I'll have you placed under arrest." His voice was deadly calm.

"You wouldn't dare!" she scoffed indignantly.

"Wouldn't I?" Though spoken softly, his words were strong as steel. "You are at present enjoying the hospitality of the United States Cavalry. If you wish to continue doing so, you'll think twice before disobeying me."

She opened her mouth to offer him a fittingly scathing reply, but then thought better of it. She looked daggers at his handsome face. Inwardly, her reason warred with a fury that was both vengeful and intense. On the one hand, she could see the advantage of letting him believe his threats had worked; but on the other, she was still sorely tempted to defy him. Nothing would have given her greater pleasure than to inform him he could take his blasted military authority and go straight to the devil.

The solution to her dilemma arrived unexpectedly.

"It's getting late," pronounced Reeve. He was reluctant to end their meeting, no matter how strained things had become between them, but he had plans for the night. And though he certainly wished otherwise, his plans didn't include spending any more time in the company of the woman he considered so dangerously attractive. "Come on. I'll walk you back to the Merriwethers'."

At first Lorelei was too engrossed in considering her next course of action to offer any resistance when he crossed the room in two long strides to stand beside her. As his fingers closed about her arm, however, she came to life again—with a forcefulness that surprised them both.

"Let go of me, you arrogant bastard!" The epithet rolled easily enough off her tongue, in spite of the fact that she had never uttered it before. Then her anger took her one disastrous step further. She raised her hand and delivered a hard, stinging slap to Reeve's clean-shaven cheek. It was an impulsive action, one she immediately regretted; but the harm had been done.

Reeve's face became a mask of inscrutability. His gaze, steady and penetrating, burned down into the shocked roundness of Lorelei's. He did nothing at all for several long seconds, during which time she could only stare up at him in silent, breathless anticipation. She could literally feel the tenseness of his body, could feel as well the barely suppressed violence simmering just beneath the surface. A shiver ran down her spine.

Without warning, his hands suddenly shot out and seized her about the waist. A sharp gasp broke from her lips as he yanked her roughly against him. She had no time to struggle before his powerful arms enveloped her and forced her supple, alluring body into searing contact with his undeniably masculine one. His relentless hold on her made it difficult to breathe, and she was ashamed to realize just how afraid of him she felt at that moment.

"Take your hands off me!" she cried, her voice hoarse as panic welled up inside her. She pushed frantically at his broad chest. His response was to pull her even closer, until her breasts were pressing against the shiny brass buttons of his coat.

"No, Miss Montgomery," he ground out, his face mere inches from hers. "Not until you've learned the consequences of playing with fire!"

"I don't know what you're talk—" she started to deny furiously.

Reeve's lips crushed down upon hers, silencing her with a kiss that was at once merciless and captivating. She moaned low in her throat when his warm, insistent tongue thrust inside her mouth.

No! her mind screamed. She couldn't be a willing partner in her own humiliation once again. She couldn't!

But no matter how desperately she tried to prevent it, she found herself swaying against Reeve as the kiss deepened and grew even more compelling. Her traitorous hands crept up his arms, and she grasped weakly at his shoulders, conscious of the way her every curve fitted with sensuous perfection against his lithe, muscled hardness.

Just like it had the night before, passion flared hotly and rapidly between them. Before Lorelei knew quite what was happening, Reeve had kicked the door shut and pressed her back against it. His mouth ravished hers in a delectable assault on her senses, while one of his hands reached up to entangle itself in her thick, luxuriant mass of auburn tresses.

Had her brain not been clouded by an increasingly awakened desire, she would have been aghast at her own boldness, for she returned his kisses in full measure and did not tremble with the least bit of proper maidenly outrage. The madness gripping her was wild and sweet, and so forceful that, for the moment anyway, nothing else mattered save Reeve Cameron and the exquisite torment he was only too happy to inflict upon her.

She inhaled deeply when his hand roamed downward to where her bosom swelled above the lace-edged neckline of her corseted bodice. His fingers trailed across the décolletage, then closed possessively over one of her breasts. She squirmed against him, half in alarm and half in pleasure, while an unnamed yearning built to fever pitch deep within her.

"Damn you, you little witch!" he murmured huskily, tearing his lips from hers at last. She was given no respite, however, for his mouth immediately seared a fiery path downward along the silken column of her neck. Her eyes flew open at the first touch of his lips, hot and branding, upon her exposed flesh.

"Reeve!" she gasped. The protest lacked conviction, even to her own ears.

He pressed a series of tantalizing kisses upon the tops of her breasts, his hand pushing their ripe, creamy fullness even farther upward into his moist caress. Lorelei felt her knees weaken and her whole body tremble. Reeve's strong, sinewy arm tightened about her waist and her fingers clutched at his shoulders for support. Catching her lower lip between her teeth to stifle a cry of shocked pleasure, she closed her eyes and struggled to control her highly erratic breathing.

Her flame-colored tresses escaped their pins at last, cascading down about her face and shoulders in glorious disarray. Reeve's mouth returned to its wondrously skillful conquest of hers once more, his lips and tongue demanding a response she was only too willing to give. Her low moan of surrender delighted and inflamed him, as did the slow, innocently seductive motion of her body against his. God help him, his own desires were on a collision course with the very disaster he had been determined to avoid . . .

Lorelei's eyes flew open when he suddenly tangled his hand in her hair and yanked her head back. Though not painful, it was quite unexpected. She stared up at him in mingled startlement and confusion.

Reeve offered no explanation for several long, tense moments. His smoldering gaze raked over the woman in his arms, taking in the sight of her beautiful, flushed face, the riotous tumble of curls streaming all the way down to her hips, and the full breasts he could envision spilling out of her bodice with one good tug on the silk. He groaned inwardly and forced his eyes upward. She looked like a wild angel.

But what the hell was he doing? he asked himself. He had to be out of his mind, letting things go so far. It wasn't like him to let a woman get under his skin like this. And it wasn't like him to jeopardize an assignment, no matter how tempted he was to forget everything that stood between him and Lorelei Montgomery. Damn it, she wasn't his for the taking.

Not yet, anyway. He swore silently at the unbidden inner voice, but he couldn't deny how much the idea appealed to him.

Still battling emotions he knew he had no business feeling, he released Lorelei and set her firmly away from him. His features tightened with a surge of anger, but it was directed more at himself than at her.

"We've got to get you home," he said, his voice cold and clear. None too gently, he moved her aside and opened the door.

Stunned into speechlessness, Lorelei gasped at his arbitrary rudeness. Hot waves of embarrassment washed over her, and outrage soon followed as she realized he was dismissing her, just as he had the night before. She was also horrified at her own behavior: in spite of all her prior indignation and determination, she had actually allowed him to kiss her again.

Only, dear Heaven, she recalled as her face crimsoned, he hadn't settled for merely kissing her this time. Besides shame she felt a lingering pleasure she would not acknowledge at the memory of his hands and lips upon her breasts. She had never before permitted such an intimate caress from any man, so why, oh why had she allowed it from *this* one? And why in the blue blazes hadn't she been able to summon either the strength of character or the pride to resist him?

The answers eluded her, but it made no difference. She was much too incensed—and hurt, though she would never admit it—to care.

"I'll see myself home, if you don't mind!" she declared with biting sarcasm. Shooting her handsome tormentor one last withering glare, she flung open the door, gathered up her skirts, and stormed out of the room. Reeve caught up with her easily.

"You can't go out there like that." His hand closed about her arm, pulling her to a halt.

"Leave me alone!" She didn't ask him what he meant, but instead gave a hard kick on the shin. He bit out an oath and momentarily relaxed his grip. Jerking free, she continued her hurried flight toward the main doorway.

Reeve battled the temptation to go after her, for he was afraid of what he might do once he got his hands on her again.

"Lorelei!" he called out in a quiet but commanding tone of voice. She chose to ignore him, a fact which made his eyes darken and narrow. "Don't be a fool. If anyone sees you looking like that, they're bound to—"

"You, *Major*, can go to the devil!" It gave her great satisfaction to fling an insult at him, and it wasn't until she was safely outside that she realized what he had been trying to warn her about.

She gasped in dismay and stopped dead in her tracks when she saw the large group of soldiers assembled on the parade ground a short distance away. Night had fallen, but the torches lining the walk cast an all too revealing glow upon her. The men stared at her with even more interest than before, making her suddenly and quite painfully aware of the fact that her hair was cascading down about her face and shoulders. Her eyes fell instinctively to the creased and disheveled fabric of her bodice.

Although she blushed in dismay, she lifted her head proudly and headed toward the Merriwethers' house. She wondered if Reeve would emerge from the building and thereby send rumors flying, but she dared not look back. Let everyone think what they would, she told herself defiantly. She and Hadley would be gone soon enough!

Reeve, meanwhile, had chosen not to risk compromising either his military credentials or Lorelei's reputation. Returning to the colonel's office, he settled his hat on his head and turned out the lamp, then eased open the window. This means of exit was not unfamiliar to him. There had been more than one occasion when circumstances had made it necessary for him to seek an alternative exit—although he couldn't recall ever having done it with the added purpose of preserving a young lady's good name.

His feelings for Lorelei were more than a little contradictive, he mused, his green eyes darkening again. One minute he wanted to kiss her until she begged for mercy, and the next he wanted to protect her. Thinking of the former prompted him to smile faintly and wonder if maybe, just maybe, the battle had already been lost.

He frowned at the thought of the latter, however, for it reminded him of what he had told Lorelei about staying clear of his investigation. She was too headstrong to be trusted on that score, he knew. He'd have to work fast if he hoped to save both her brother's life *and* her beautiful hide.

It was to this end that he climbed out into the darkness behind the headquarters building and closed the window behind him. The buglers were already sounding the call to night retreat, but he had no intention of taking part in the assembly. His long, purposeful strides carried him swiftly away from the post and across the river, to where the music and laughter of Santa Angela held the promise of tongues loosened by drink — and the opportunity to keep himself so damned busy that Lorelei Montgomery wouldn't dominate his every thought.

Six

Being awakened by the sound of reveille before sunrise was an experience Lorelei would gladly have forfeited. Still, she was eager to see Hadley again, and to interrogate her gracious hostess on the subject of Major Reeve Cameron. She felt a twinge of resentment that Abigail hadn't bothered to mention the fact that their mutual "acquaintance" was not only an officer in the United States Cavalry, but was also the investigator sent from Washington. Of course, she reminded herself, his name had never even entered into their conversation thus far. Now, she told herself determinedly, it was high time it did.

She refused, absolutely *refused,* to let him prevent her doing whatever she could to help her brother. One thing was for certain—she would have to avoid him at all costs. There was little doubt in her mind that he would carry out his threat of imprisonment. Her eyes flashed at the memory of both his arrogant words and his supercilious behavior. If he dared to lay hands on her again, she could make him wish he had never been born. Major or no major, he would soon learn that a Montgomery never backed down from a fight.

A good night's sleep had left her ready to do battle. She chose to wear a gown of blue and white striped lawn, trimmed at the bottom with a gathered bias flounce and edged with a narrow pleated ruffle. It was one of her prettiest day dresses, one she had made herself with only minimal assistance from Aunt Matilda, and she was pleased with the way the fitted, heart-shaped bodice accentuated her slender waist. She did not pause to consider her reasons for the choice of such unabashedly feminine attire. If she had, she would merely have told herself that confidence in her appearance would lend support to her courage.

The aroma of freshly brewed coffee greeted her when she stepped into the Merriwethers' dining room shortly after seven o'clock. Apparently the first one to arrive for breakfast, she took a seat in the same chair as the night before and allowed her gaze to wander toward the open window. A slight breeze, warm and heavy and scented with woodsmoke, stirred the gingham curtains. The morning sun was hidden by thick, ominously churning clouds, which promised to release a veritable torrent upon the earth within the hour. Somewhere in the house, the cries of the baby mingled with the exuberant giggles of his brother and sister.

"Good morning!" Abigail said brightly as she appeared in the doorway to the kitchen. She quickly dried her hands on her starched white apron while hurrying across the room. "Please forgive me, Lorelei! I'll be right back to get your breakfast. The children are making a terrible racket, aren't they? They're very likely driving their poor father to distraction!" came her breathless apology before she disappeared into the hallway.

A soft smile of amusement tugged at Lorelei's lips. She wondered idly what it would be like to balance the care of three small children with the duties of a wife and the demands of running a household. She'd always had Hadley to care for, of course, and there had been plenty of work to keep her busy, but she knew it wasn't the same. On the other hand there had been no one, other than a brother young in years as well as in outlook, to hold her tight and reassure her when things seemed darkest. Aunt Matilda, bless her soul, had done her best under the circumstances, but the poor woman had been a good deal more concerned with appearances than with the day-to-day care of two orphaned siblings . . .

The memory sent a shadow of pain across her face. She heaved a long sigh of discontentment and stood abruptly to her feet.

She looked back to the doorway. Deciding that the very least she could do was help Abigail with breakfast, she wandered into the kitchen. Her eyes widened in astonishment when they beheld the topsy-turvy condition of the room where, incredibly, all the meals for the Merriwether family were prepared.

She had expected to find perfect order and cleanliness. Instead, pots and pans were strewn everywhere, unwashed plates were piled high beside a sink that looked as though it hadn't seen soap and water for a week, and the floor was dusted with a generous coating of flour. Footprints, both large and small, were clearly visible, and seemed to indicate a remarkable amount of activity within the confines of a room that was neither spacious nor uncluttered.

"Oh dear, it's truly awful, isn't it?" remarked Abigail, suddenly materializing behind her. "Please don't judge me too harshly, Lorelei! You see, I've been at my wit's end ever since Mrs. Denton—she is, or rather *was,* our cook—took it into her mind to visit her sister back East. I've been trying to find a replacement, truly I have. There are two women—'ladies' would be an entirely inappropriate term, I can assure you—who have expressed an interest in the position, but I shudder to think what the other wives here at the post would say if I dared to employ either of them!"

This was all said in her usual highly animated manner, prompting Lorelei to smile again. Her blue eyes sparkled with genuine warmth as she turned and made her way, carefully, to the sink.

"The two of us can put things right in no time," she said encouragingly. She spied another apron hanging on a peg beside the cast-iron stove, and did not wait for a reply before pulling it down.

"Oh, but you . . . that's very generous of you, my dear, but you are our guest, and—" stammered the brunette, torn between the desire to accept and a nagging sense of duty.

"I am no stranger to the kitchen, Abigail," Lorelei assured her. "And since you and Captain Merriwether have refused to accept any payment for my accommodations or food, I would feel much better if I were allowed to assist in some way."

"Oh, but of course we couldn't accept payment for our hospitality!" She looked aghast at the notion.

"Why not?"

106

"Because . . . why, because you and . . ." Her voice trailed away while a telltale blush stained her cheeks. Hastily she averted her gaze from Lorelei's and made a forced attempt to steer the conversation onto safer ground. "John and the children will be down any minute! Now where did I put that bowl?" she wondered aloud, starting an intensive search among the jumble on the worktable.

"It's because of Major Cameron, isn't it?" demanded Lorelei, her eyes narrowing in suspicion. Abigail's sheepish expression provided all the confirmation she needed. A horrible thought suddenly occurred to her. "Good Heavens, is *he* paying—?"

"No!" the other woman hastened to deny. Abandoning her search, she came forward to take Lorelei's arm in a gentle, consoling grasp. "No, my dear, it's not like that at all! Major Cameron and my husband are old friends, you see, and so we were more than happy to have you as our guest!"

"But I scarcely know the man!" That was true enough, she mused, then groaned inwardly when she felt her own face flaming with secret guilt.

"Perhaps so, but he was quite concerned for you and asked that we provide you with a room for the duration of your stay at the post. It was no trouble, really! We've had no visitors for so very long, and after Ree—Major Cameron explained the circumstances to me, I was insistent upon your coming here."

"Why didn't you tell me Major Cameron was the special investigator from Washington?" There was a rather accusing tone in her voice, but no real anger.

"Because John would have had my head! You don't know what it's like being a cavalry wife, Lorelei," she complained with a heavy sigh. "These men are a breed unto themselves. They always have their little secrets and mysteries. John confides in me only so much, and then it's as though a curtain suddenly falls between us. It has to be that way, I suppose, but it can be frustrating in the extreme!"

"I'm sure it can. But please, Abigail, you must tell me whatever you can about my brother's arrest, and about Major Cameron as well!" Her gaze held a desperate appeal for understanding as she clutched the apron tightly to her chest. "I swear to you, Hadley is innocent! There are others responsible for the crimes, others who must be exposed before it is too late! You must help me!"

"Oh Lorelei, I — I *cannot* become involved!" cried Abigail. Her eyes were full of mingled sympathy and remorse. "I know how you must feel, truly I do, but there is nothing I can do! The children and I were away when Lieutenant Fitzhugh was murdered, and although I have heard talk regarding the involvement of others, I can offer you no real facts."

"But don't you see? If there are rumors circulating, then what Hadley told me must be true!" Hope stirred anew within her breast. She fixed Abigail with a sharp, penetrating look. "What betrayal can there be in simply relating to me the talk you have heard?"

Abigail did not respond immediately. She stood with eyes downcast, waging a battle with her own conscience. The faint sound of a child's voice drifted down from the room above.

"None, I suppose," she conceded finally, with obvious reluctance. She shot a quick glance toward the doorway before adding in a cautious undertone,

"Mind you, I have heard no mention of specific names. What I *have* heard is that there are some officers here at Fort Concho who can lay claim to an unusually high level of obedience from their men. I don't know if their power stems from their military experience, or from some other means of persuasion. And several of the wives have voiced suspicions regarding Lieutenant Fitzhugh's death, although I doubt that their suspicions hold any merit."

"But what is the connection between those two facts?" Lorelei asked with a frown of confusion.

"These same officers have supposedly been heard to threaten severe punishment for any man who speaks of the matter." She sighed again and, turning away, began cracking eggs into the bowl, which had been in plain sight all along. "What I've told you is probably not at all significant. It really is best to let Major Cameron handle everything, Lorelei."

"And why is that?" she challenged, a discernible edge to her voice. "Why should I trust *him* to see that Hadley does not hang?"

"Because according to John and a good many others, Reeve Cameron is the best investigator the United States Cavalry has," Abigail told her solemnly. She tossed the eggshells to one side, took up an iron skillet, and set it on the stove. As she continued with her preparation of breakfast, there was little doubt her attention remained with the young woman, whom she had liked from the beginning. "I have known Reeve since the first year of my marriage to John. Our paths may not have crossed often, but I can say without hesitation that he is a man of honor."

"I have not found him in the least bit honorable!" Lorelei disputed, with telling vehemence. She slipped the apron on over her head and furiously tied the strings. "I'm sorry, Abigail, but I neither like your Major Cameron nor trust him! And that is why, no matter what you or he or anyone else says, I intend to search out the truth myself!"

"No, Lorelei, that is something you must not do!" the other woman cautioned, her eyes very serious. "He will not allow it, you know, and . . . well, you are an outsider here. If you try questioning anyone, you'll very likely find yourself ostracized completely!"

"Why the devil should I care about that?"

"You must believe me, it will only make things harder for your brother. Besides," she added, casting yet another wary look toward the doorway, "I think there is a more effective way to make use of your presence here." Her manner was decidedly conspiratorial, and Lorelei glimpsed a defiant light in her eyes.

"And which way is that?" she pressed, more calmly now.

"Major Cameron, of course! He is your only hope."

"I thought we had settled—"

"No, I mean . . . oh dear, how shall I put it?" Pouring the eggs into the hot skillet, she turned back around to face Lorelei. "John would be furious with me for telling you this, but my goose is already cooked, as Mrs. Denton used to say, so I may as well charge ahead!" She gave a perfunctory stirring to the eggs, then confided, "While it is true that Reeve is the investigator assigned to your brother's case, his influence is even more far-reaching than that."

"His influence?" echoed Lorelei, her brow creasing into another frown. Though grateful for Abigail's willingness to help, she found it difficult to follow her train of thought. "What are you talking about?"

"Only that, if I were you, Lorelei, I would not be so hasty in my unflattering assessment of him. His opinions are sought by men occupying the highest positions of command, and I have heard John remark on more than one occasion that if it were not for Reeve's unfortunate choice of loyalties during the war, he would be a full colonel or even a general by now. Of course, he *is* something of a renegade, but no doubt that is what makes him so very successful at what he does."

"I am vastly relieved to hear he has the confidence of his superiors," Lorelei remarked with a touch of sarcasm, "but I fail to see how that changes—"

"It is more than confidence," insisted Abigail. Smoke rising from the skillet warned of scorched eggs, but she merely beat at them a bit more with the spoon and said, "He is the only one who has a chance of ensuring that your brother's life is spared. No matter what the outcome of the court-martial is, if Major Reeve Cameron recommends leniency, then the tribunal will most assuredly follow his advice."

"Are you saying that I should swallow my pride and beg him for mercy?" The idea was thoroughly repugnant to her.

"Not 'beg,' exactly," Abigail clarified, with a strange little smile. "It should be more like a gentle persuasion. I think we both know how to use our talents to our best advantage when it comes to men."

Lorelei's blue eyes widened with incredulity. She watched, speechless, while Abigail turned back to rescue the eggs. At first stunned by the other woman's suggestion, she allowed her eyes to wander toward the ceiling and felt the idea slowly taking seed in her mind.

"Reeve is interested in you," Abigail went on with studied nonchalance. "I could sense it when he spoke to me about you yesterday afternoon. You are a beautiful and intelligent young woman, Lorelei. It would not require much encouragement on your part to—"

"This is absurd!" exclaimed Lorelei, trying to convince them both. She snatched up a pan of biscuits that was waiting to be baked, pulled open the oven door, and thrust the pan inside. "I cannot believe I am even tempted to embrace such an outrageous scheme!"

"What is so outrageous about it?" Abigail countered defensively. "For Heaven's sake, my dear, it isn't as though I am suggesting you sacrifice your entire future! There is certainly no disgrace in a simple flirtation. Why, anyone would tell you that you can always gain more by friendly and engaging behavior than by proud incivility."

"I'm quite sure Major Cameron has received more than his fair share of friendliness," she murmured caustically.

"Yes, I'm quite sure he has," the brunette agreed. "He is so very attractive, after all, and John once told me—" She broke off, colored guiltily once more, and busied herself with scooping the eggs

112

onto a plate. "I am truly sorry if I offended you with my advice, Lorelei, but I still think you should appeal to Reeve to intervene on your brother's behalf. In truth, what harm can it do?"

"More than you know."

Abigail started to ask her to explain that enigmatic remark, but Caroline chose that moment to come barreling into the kitchen with the news that Weston had taken a tumble down the stairs—his third in so many days. Lorelei was left alone with her troubled thoughts while Abigail hurried off to see to her shaken but otherwise uninjured son. A great racket ensued, as all five Merriwethers seemed to be talking or crying at once. The morning fatigue call mercifully put an end to the mayhem, sending the tardy captain off to his duties and the four others into the dining room.

Lorelei managed to consume a small portion of the eggs, a single biscuit, and a cup of coffee that reminded her of a peculiar, rather unwholesome Southern adage regarding the virtues of "strong coffee and weak women." Promising to return soon in order to help Abigail with the dishes, she left the table and approached the front door with the intention of visiting her brother.

The impish Caroline pushed an umbrella into her hand on her way out. She smiled gratefully at the child and said she would be delighted if the two of them could take a walk together later that day. Caroline's little face beamed with pleasure.

"We can walk to the stables! I'll show you my horse—he isn't mine exactly, but Papa says we can pretend that he is. Do you have a horse?"

"I used to," replied Lorelei. She gave a faint, wistful smile. "Her name was Delilah and she could gallop like the very wind."

"What happened to her?"

"She was taken away."

"Who took her?"

Having anticipated that question, and not at all certain how much of the truth to reveal, Lorelei opened the door and stepped out onto the front porch.

"Some men who said they needed her more than I did," she explained, choosing her words carefully. "It was during the war. A great many things were taken away during the war." She smiled again and tossed a glance overhead at the darkening sky. "I think it will rain before I can make it to the other side of the parade ground, don't you?"

"Yes. And your dress will get muddy," said Caroline. She grinned, waved goodbye, and sped back inside to finish her breakfast.

Although it had been light for less than an hour, the soldiers were already about their duties. Lorelei opened the umbrella and gathered up her skirts, nodding politely at the men who offered her a greeting as she directed her steps toward the guardhouse. As she had predicted, the first drops of life-giving moisture fell just after she had passed the headquarters building. She breathed deeply of the fresh, rain-scented air and gave silent thanks for the respite — however brief it turned out to be — from the oppressive heat that had plagued her ever since she had arrived in Texas.

The gentle shower had turned into a summer cloudburst by the time she entered the guardhouse. She closed the umbrella and left it beside the doorway, then approached the young man on duty. He immediately stood to attention.

"I am here to see my brother, Private Hadley Montgomery," she announced. She was pleasantly surprised to encounter none of the trouble she had anticipated.

"Mornin', ma'am," said the burly private, doffing his hat and trying hard not to let on how nervous he was about being in the presence of such a beautiful and well-spoken lady. It struck him that she was every bit as pretty as Montgomery liked to brag she was. "Colonel Jameson left orders you're to have as long as you want."

"He did?" she responded in bemusement. Silently wondering what had prompted such a generous turnabout, she followed the guard through the doorway and down the narrow corridor.

Hadley was already waiting at his cell door when she reached the end. He managed to smile at her through the barred opening, but she could sense that his spirits were perilously low that morning. She waited until the guard had left them alone before rushing forward and covering his hands with hers.

"What is it, Hadley? What has happened?" she demanded anxiously. Her gaze searched the similarly blue depths of his.

"Bad news, I'm afraid," he admitted. His face looked pale, and there were dark circles beneath his eyes. Lorelei's heart wrenched at the undercurrent of defeat in his voice.

"Dear God, Hadley, what is it?"

"Damn it, Lori, I might have had a chance if he hadn't turned tail and run!" he burst out, his fingers clutching the bars until his knuckles turned white.

"Who?" Her voice was sharp with worry.

"Taggart! Private Joseph Taggart. He's the only one who could have cleared me!" He sighed heavily and explained, "He knows what happened the night Fitzhugh was killed. He was there."

"He was there? Sweet mercy, Hadley, if that's true then you've got to tell—"

"It won't do any good," insisted Hadley. He shook his head and gave her a look full of such pain and resignation that she felt hot tears well up in her eyes. "He's gone. I just got word of it this morning. Someone said he'd been talking about deserting to New Mexico Territory, that he was afraid of what would happen to him if he didn't clear out."

"Well, he—he will have to be found! If he is a deserter, then surely the cavalry will attempt to bring him back to justice," she pointed out in desperation.

"It will be too late by then."

"No, it won't! I'll talk to Colonel Jameson right away! I'll demand that your court-martial be postponed until—"

"The colonel isn't in charge of things now, Lori. Major Cameron is." His mouth curved into the ghost of a smile. "I heard the two of you are already acquainted."

"You've spoken to him?" she asked in surprise.

"Yes," he confirmed with a nod. His youthful features fell again, and his eyes glinted dully. "He paid me a visit first thing this morning."

"What happened?"

"I think he expected me to cooperate. He said he wanted to hear my side of the story, and he gave me

116

his word that whatever I told him would remain confidential; but I wouldn't talk."

"Whyever not?" demanded Lorelei, frowning at him. "For Heaven's sake, he's come all the way from Washington to investigate your case!"

"I know that," he muttered with another sigh. Suddenly, he narrowed his eyes at her in suspicion. "What did you tell him, Lori?"

"Nothing!" she hastened to assure him, then was dismayed to feel her cheeks burning. Quickly averting her gaze, she regained her composure and faced him squarely once more. "I made it quite clear to him that I would not betray your confidence. But I do think you should tell him everything you know! There is so little time, and I . . ." She swallowed a sudden lump in her throat before remarking disconsolately, "Oh, Hadley, I honestly don't know if I will be able to uncover any useful information before next week. Nothing is as I thought it would be. Major Cameron has warned me against trying, and even Abigail Merriwether insists that I leave everything in his hands. It seems his abilities are highly regarded, and—"

"I can't tell him, Lori," Hadley interrupted in a low, unsteady tone that gave evidence of his own fears. "I want to, but I can't. As long as I keep my mouth shut, there's a chance I might get out of this alive. You know, it's odd," he commented with a look of wonderment, "but Major Cameron seemed to understand that."

"Please, Hadley, I beg of you—tell him what you know!" she entreated passionately. "You've got to trust *someone,* and I've been told he has a great deal of influence in such matters."

117

"It isn't a question of trust." For a moment, he looked like the frightened little boy he used to be. "I . . . I don't want to die. But I'm prepared for whatever comes."

"How can you just give up like that?" Lorelei demanded with a catch in her voice, as she angrily blinked back the tears. "The two of us have never given up on anything, Hadley Montgomery, and we never will!" She tried one last time to make him see reason. "Please, for my sake if not for your own, let Major Cameron help you!"

"I can't."

There was no sign of the boy now. Before her stood a man who was both proud and implacable, a man who had made up his mind to let fate have its way with him.

She knew then what she had to do.

"All right. But don't expect me to abide by your decision," she cautioned him quietly, her own voice full of steely determination.

"What are you planning to do? Confound it, Lori, I told you—"

"I have to leave now." She forced a smile to her lips. "But I will return later. It appears that Colonel Jameson has decided to grant me the privilege of visiting you whenever I like. Are you certain there is nothing you need?"

"Stay away from Major Cameron!" he ordered, ignoring her inquiry altogether. "If the two of you are seen talking together—"

"Everyone will assume it's because we enjoy one another's company," she finished for him. Her calm demeanor belied the storm of emotions raging within her. "I must go now."

118

"Where are you staying?"

"With Captain Merriwether and his family." She started to turn away, but was stopped when she saw the sudden tensing of his fingers about the iron bars again.

"Lori?"

"Yes, Hadley?" Her throat constricted at the expression on his face. She wanted nothing more than to be able to gather him close and promise that everything would turn out all right.

"Is it true what Major Cameron told me, that the two of you have become friends?"

"He told you that?" She gasped in disbelief, her eyes growing widening within the delicate oval of her face.

Hadley nodded wordlessly, and did not miss the rosy blush which stole over her face.

"The major has greatly overestimated his charm," she answered, with cool evasiveness.

"Be careful, Lori. He's not like any of the men you've known before."

Lorelei opened her mouth to ask him exactly what he meant by that, but decided she would rather not know. Finally she took her leave, remembering at the last moment to retrieve her umbrella on the way out.

It was still raining quite heavily. She glanced down at the path and frowned when she noted that it had been transformed into a river of mud. Lifting her skirts as high as she dared, she grasped the handle of the umbrella tightly and stepped down, her boots sinking into a reddish-brown puddle. She had traveled no more than a few feet before she collided with someone.

119

"Oh! Oh, I beg your pardon!" she apologized breathlessly, tilting the umbrella back so that she could see her unfortunate victim.

"It was my fault, Miss Montgomery."

She found herself staring up at a man who, though obviously aware of her identity, was a complete stranger to her. He was tall, with dark hair and gray eyes, his features both swarthy and aristocratic. Clad in an officer's uniform and a canvas slicker, he stood smiling down at her in the rain. She realized that his hand was grasping her arm.

"Please forgive me!" she said, and endeavored to move past him. He astonished her by taking hold of the borrowed umbrella to shelter them both, and drawing her arm through the crook of his.

"I'm Collin McNeil. Captain McNeil," he announced smoothly. "Were you on your way back to the Merriwethers'?"

"Yes, but—"

"Then allow me to escort you there." Without waiting for her consent, he began leading her along with him.

She had very little choice in the matter. Realizing that it would be ridiculous to stand about arguing with him while the rain soaked them to the skin, she couldn't help feeling a trifle irritated, nevertheless, at his assumption that she would welcome his company.

"How did you know my name, Captain McNeil?" she asked, trying in vain to keep her long skirts clear of the mud.

"It wasn't difficult to learn. Everyone at the post is talking about you."

"Are they indeed? And what are they saying?"

"Only that you are Private Montgomery's sister and that you are staying at the Merriwethers'." He turned and met her inquisitive gaze. She felt an inexplicable chill run through her.

"That is true enough," she murmured.

Acutely conscious of her body's contact with his, she attempted to put some distance between them. He merely pulled her close again under the pretext that they needed to stay huddled together beneath the umbrella.

"Abigail Merriwether will never forgive me if I deliver you in less than perfect condition," he remarked with a soft laugh. He was attractive and obviously meant to be charming, but Lorelei couldn't help feeling uneasy about him.

"Have you been at Fort Concho long, Captain?" she asked, pleased to see that they had nearly reached the officers' quarters by now.

"Less than a year. Your brother was once under my command, Miss Montgomery."

"He was?" She glanced up at him in surprise.

"Yes." He smiled again, but she noticed that the smile did not quite reach his eyes. "I suppose Hadley has mentioned me."

"No. No, I . . . we haven't had much opportunity to talk." She didn't know why she said that; perhaps it was because Hadley had cautioned her to trust no one.

"I'm sorry for your brother's trouble. If there's any way I can be of assistance, please let me know," he offered gallantly.

"Thank you, Captain."

She breathed an inward sigh of relief as they climbed the steps to the front porch of the Merriwethers' house. Lorelei gently disengaged her arm while Captain McNeil lowered the umbrella and took off his hat. He watched as she bent and shook out her skirts.

"Will you be staying at the post long?" he asked, his steely gaze almost predatory as it raked over her.

"I don't know." She straightened, gave him a polite little smile, and turned to open the door. "Thank you for your escort, Captain McNeil."

"Aren't you forgetting something, Miss Montgomery?"

She felt his hand closing about her arm again. Her eyes flashed with anger at the familiarity of his manner, but she battled the impulse to jerk free and instead faced him with a cool, quizzical look.

"Your umbrella," he supplied. He handed it to her and then made a slight bow. "Good day, Miss Montgomery. I hope to see you again soon."

"Good day, Captain." She could feel his eyes on her as she turned and went inside.

Making a mental note to ask Abigail about him, she placed the umbrella on the carved, mirrored hall tree in the entrance foyer. She caught sight of her reflection, smoothed her hair, and sighed as her troubled thoughts returned to Hadley.

Heartsick at his refusal to cooperate with the investigation, she realized that now, more than ever before, she had to take the initiative. She couldn't count on justice being served, not when the military's brand of justice might very well result in a guilty verdict.

The time had come for drastic measures.

Reeve is interested in you . . . a chance of ensuring that your brother's life is spared . . . it would not require much encouragement on your part. Abigail's words came back to her, burning themselves into her mind. She closed her eyes for a moment and conjured up the disturbing vision of Reeve Cameron's face.

"So be it," she whispered; then felt as though she had made a pact with the devil himself.

Seven

The opportunity to put her plan into action arrived sooner than she had expected.

A post dance had been planned for that same night, a dance to which not only officers and their wives but also a select number of enlisted men had been invited. Lorelei had not learned of it until after she had finished helping Abigail set both the kitchen and the parlor to rights.

"I am so very sorry I forgot to tell you sooner, my dear, but it completely slipped my mind!" her hostess apologized, her eyes full of contrition as she tugged the kerchief from her head. "I can't imagine how I forgot. I suppose it was because I'm not accustomed to having someone to talk to while John is on duty. The children are absolute darlings, of course, and I love them dearly, but it is such a delight to have another woman in the house."

The two of them had enjoyed a pleasant, rambling conversation. They had traded details of their childhoods, exchanged views on the latest fashions as well as a variety of other subjects, and had scrupulously avoided any mention of Reeve Cameron. Caroline had done her fair share of the talking, too, keeping Weston entertained with books and toys at the dining room table while the baby gurgled happily or drifted off to sleep in his wooden playpen. The remainder of the morning and the early afternoon had virtually flown by.

Lorelei had been glad for the work, for it had served to turn her thoughts away from her troubles. Of course, it was impossible to forget them altogether. The decision she had made earlier hung over her like a dark cloud.

"It doesn't matter," she now assured Abigail about the dance, her eyes making a broad, critical sweep of the transformed kitchen. "To tell the truth, I don't feel much like celebrating."

"Oh, but you *must* come! It will do you good to meet some of the other wives, and I fully expect Major—" She broke off with a sharp, guilty intake of breath. Then, lifting her chin defiantly, she opined, "I think it would be foolish of you not to take advantage of this evening!" Her meaning was perfectly understood.

Reluctantly, Lorelei agreed. She had to face him again sooner or later; there was no use in postponing the inevitable. Besides, she reminded herself, time was running out. She had to act quickly.

And so it was that, shortly after taps had sounded and the majority of the soldiers were drifting off to sleep in their narrow bunks, she accompanied the Merriwethers to the separate mess hall located at the far end of Barracks Row. The building was the frequent site of such gatherings, for it was large and spacious, and easily accommodated more than a hundred people at a time.

Caroline and her brothers had been bundled off into the care of another officer's wife, an older woman who had made no secret of the fact that she would much rather spend the evening in the company of three rambunctious children then thirty times that many adults. Lorelei smiled softly as she recalled Caroline's affectionate goodbye. She had managed to make good on her promise to walk to the stables with the little girl that afternoon, once the rain had finally stopped and the river of mud had dried a little.

She had also kept her word to Hadley. Her eyes clouded at the memory. Their brief visit just before sundown had yielded no more results than the previous one. But it had made her determination much stronger.

The sky was perfectly clear now, the moon adding its silvery radiance to the glow of a million twinkling stars. The night air was cool and sweet, and filled with the music of the fort's highly lauded military band. The prevailing mood about the place was one of excitement as men and women hurried along the walks toward the beacon of light in the midst of the darkened grounds.

Lorelei's heart pounded fiercely within her breast as she neared the site of the evening's festivities. She dreaded the task facing her. Although no stranger to the pleasures and triumphs of flirtation—she was, after all, every inch a Southern belle—she had never before played the game for such high stakes. And she had certainly never played it with a man like Reeve Cameron.

She frowned in displeasure and pulled her white lace shawl more closely about her. Glancing down toward the deep décolletage of her gown, she felt a knot of trepidation tighten in her stomach. The white gauze dress, silky in texture, clung to her every curve. A rich, green satin sash encircled her waist and was tied in the back above a stylishly full bustle. In front, the neckline of the fitted bodice was cut low and trimmed with delicate green lace. A cameo hung suspended from a narrow, black velvet ribbon around her neck, and her thick auburn tresses were arranged in a chignon from which loose locks of hair were arranged over one creamy shoulder. She had taken great care with her appearance; it had been a long time since she had sailed forth into the night with the single-minded purpose of enticement.

Dressed to kill, Hadley would no doubt have pronounced her. It was a favorite expression of his, one he had often used when teasing her about some latest conquest.

"Here we are!" said Abigail, beaming happily and looking quite elegant in a yellow silk polonaise gown. She drew Lorelei's arm through hers and led her inside, John following closely on their heels.

The hall was already becoming crowded. Dozens of lamps blazed above a lively, talkative collection of men in starched blue uniforms and their feminine counterparts in pretty, ruffled ballgowns. The tables and benches that normally filled the room had been cleared away, leaving plenty of space for the dancers. A makeshift platform had been set up at the far end of the polished wooden floor for the band, and a dazzling array of refreshments lay near the doorway. A single row of chairs lined the walls, providing a perch for those who either chose not to dance or were never fortunate enough to find partners. Whenever the music swelled to a crescendo, the murmur of voices increased to a parallel roar.

Lorelei's bright sapphire gaze instinctively searched the sea of faces for any sign of Reeve. She was torn between relief and disappointment when he did not materialize.

"Come along, Lorelei." Abigail was already propelling her toward a group of women to their left. "I want to introduce you to some of the other wives."

"Of course," she consented absently, then forced her attention to the ladies, who were eyeing her with a combination of curiosity, admiration, and outright envy. Recalling her earlier hopes to be able to rely upon them for any helpful bits of gossip, she smiled graciously and made a point of complimenting each woman on her impeccable choice of attire—no matter how much the opposite was true.

"I understand you are Private Montgomery's sister," remarked a woman Abigail had just identified as the wife of the post commander. Short and plump, and wearing a ridiculous feathered bonnet, she was, physically, the very antithesis of her husband. Her manner, however, was even more stiff and condescending than the colonel's.

"You understand correctly," Lorelei affirmed politely. She could feel the others staring at her in expectation, as if waiting to see how she would handle the formidable Harriet Jameson.

"What a pity!" the woman snapped. It was spoken with an unmistakable gesture of disdain.

"A pity?" echoed Lorelei, feigning ignorance. "Why is that, Mrs. Jameson?"

"Because, Miss Montgomery, you are destined for heartbreak." She frowned and fixed Lorelei with a stern, disapproving glare. "It would have been wiser to remain at home. There is nothing you can do for your brother here, and I suspect that he would not welcome your interference. It has always been the cavalry's way to take care of its own business. In any case," she concluded, drawing her purple-silk-clad bulk haughtily erect, "the colonel should not have to endure any further distraction from his duties."

"Lorelei's decision to come to Fort Concho was prompted by her love for her brother, not by a desire to interfere with Colonel Jameson's method of command," Abigail rushed to say in her new friend's defense.

"I would have done the same," one of the other women interjected bravely. A slender, petite blonde who had been married only a short time, she smiled at Lorelei and added, "Were it a member of my family imprisoned in the guardhouse, Miss Montgomery, I would not hesitate to interfere."

"I am quite sure you would not, Emily Rogers," Harriet remarked acidly. "But then, you have already had the misfortune to see one of your brothers imprisoned, have you not? For stealing a horse, I believe?" She smiled in malevolent satisfaction as Emily, looking mortified, colored and hastily excused herself from the group.

"Harriet Jameson, what a perfectly horrible thing to do!" Abigail exclaimed in reproach. "Why, poor Emily should not be continually reminded of her brother's transgression!"

"You, of all people, Abigail Merriwether, haven't the right to criticize *me*," said Harriet, her manner one of high indignation. "I may not have been here long, but I am already well aware of your less than stellar origins. Nothing but the daughter of an immigrant, a hardscrabble Virginia farmer, that's what you are! Everyone knows Captain Merriwether married beneath himself. He comes from a good family in Pennsylvania," she revealed smugly to the other women. "I would not be at all surprised if we were related in some way."

Lorelei's eyes blazed with anger. In spite of her resolve to make herself agreeable for Hadley's sake, she could no longer hold her tongue.

"It occurs to me, Mrs. Jameson, that you are no doubt quite an asset to your husband. I suspect that you have helped further his career at every turn," she remarked in a deceptively even tone. Aware of the bemused look Abigail cast her, she did not allow her own gaze to waver from Harriet's face.

"I have indeed, Miss Montgomery."

"Please tell me then," she challenged with a slow, calculated smile, "how it is that the colonel was given command of this primitive, godforsaken frontier outpost? Surely a man of his superior capabilities, and superior connections, deserves far better? Has he perhaps angered someone in Washington? Or, Heaven forbid, have you yourself been a trifle indiscreet in your conversation?"

Harriet's mouth fell open. She appeared extremely flustered for a moment, then struck a lofty pose once more and sliced Lorelei a venomous glare.

"Are you daring to imply—"

"I am implying nothing, Mrs. Jameson." She cut the other woman off deftly. "I am merely pointing out that a woman can do a great deal of harm—or good, if she so chooses—with her words." She exchanged a quick glance with Abigail before looking back to a visibly affronted Harriet and advising,

"You might do well to consider your own motives before you speak again this evening."

Telling herself that it would be impossible to carry on a significant conversation with anyone while the colonel's shrewish wife was around, she abandoned the idea and coolly announced that she had developed a sudden thirst. As she turned and made her way back through the crowd toward the refreshment table, Harriet's voice trailed relentlessly after her.

"Her ill-mannered behavior is nothing more than what we should expect from someone of her caliber! After all, she *is* the sister of a murderous traitor, and . . ."

Lorelei's temper flared, but she did not look back. She was soon out of earshot, and knew that Abigail would not be long in joining her. She had little doubt that she was to be presented to the many other officers' wives in attendance that evening, and the prospect was not an agreeable one. Absently scrutinizing the cookies and sandwiches spread out on the long, linen-covered table, and wondering when the devil Reeve Cameron would show up so she could finally get on with things, she had just reached for a cup of punch when a man's hand suddenly cupped her elbow.

"I was hoping the Merriwethers would convince you to come."

The voice, cultivated and smooth as silk, sounded close to her ear, causing her to give an involuntary start. She turned her head quickly and met Captain McNeil's gray, oddly unsettling gaze. He stood smiling down at her, looking very attractive in his dress uniform. She was reminded of the photographs that adorned the walls of the headquarters building, the ones where all the men appeared very much aware of their own importance. There was something about him, she thought, something she couldn't quite put a name to, that rang false.

"Good evening, Captain," she replied, cordially but with no true encouragement. She attempted to step away, only to find her path of escape blocked.

"May I have the honor of this dance, Miss Montgomery?" he requested. They both knew he would not accept a refusal. But nonetheless, Lorelei was tempted to tell him she was waiting for someone. Her eyes sought out Abigail, and then John, but they were concealed from view somewhere within the crowd. As if on cue, the band struck up a waltz.

"I give you my word, I am a capable dancer," Captain McNeil boasted with another polished smile. He was already slipping an arm about her waist. "Come along, Miss Montgomery. We don't want to disappoint everyone."

"Don't we?" she retorted, but did not protest as he took her hand and began whirling her about in the smooth, rhythmic movements of the dance. They were soon in the center of the floor, attracting quite a bit of attention and inspiring whispers of premature speculation among the more romantically minded ladies. It was generally agreed that they made a striking couple, and even Lorelei could not deny that her partner's boast had been well founded.

"I think we've created quite a stir, Miss Montgomery," he commented in satisfaction. He tried to pull her closer, but she would not allow it.

"Was that your intention, Captain McNeil?" she countered, performing the steps with a skill borne of experience as well as natural grace. She was surprised to hear him chuckle in response.

"My intention was to get to know you better." His eyes fell significantly to where the curve of her breasts swelled above the plunging neckline of her bodice. Looking up again, he was pleased to note the faint blush that warmed her cheeks. "It isn't often Fort Concho welcomes a visitor as beautiful as you, Miss Montgomery. We have our fair share of wives and daughters, but rarely any that provoke such a wealth of interest."

"*My* only interest is in seeing my brother cleared," she informed him with a frown.

"And understandably so," he concurred. "But he wouldn't want you to spend your days and nights pining away on his behalf. Apparently you agree, or else you wouldn't be here now."

"The only reason I am here tonight is because . . . because the Merriwethers refused to come without me," she lied, her eyes falling uncomfortably before his.

"Have you known them long?"

"The Merriwethers?" She shook her head. "No. They were kind enough to offer me a place to stay." An ironic smile touched her lips when she added, "It had been made quite clear to me that Santa Angela was an unsuitable alternative."

"Have you made any progress with your brother so far?" he inquired, changing the subject again.

"What do you mean?" Her eyes narrowed as she studied his face.

"I was hoping that he had decided to cooperate." His features grew very solemn. "Hadley is not a killer, Miss Montgomery. I don't care what the evidence shows, I will never believe him guilty."

"Nor will I, Captain McNeil."

His hand tightened about hers while the music rose toward its final crescendo. She sensed that he wanted to say more about Hadley, but he did not go on.

"I hope you'll allow me the pleasure of calling on you tomorrow."

"Thank you, Captain, but—"

"I have arranged for us to enjoy a ride together. It's perfectly safe, so long as we don't travel far from the post. I'm sure Mrs. Merriwether can spare you for a few hours."

"It isn't a question of being 'spared,' " said Lorelei, her temper kindling with annoyance at his latest presumption. She pulled free at the precise moment the music ended and told him, "While I am flattered by your attention, Captain McNeil, I regret that I cannot accept your offer. I scarcely know you, and even if that were not the case, I would not be inclined to encourage a friendship between us."

"Why not?" he demanded, his eyes glinting like cold steel.

He looked almost angry, not wounded, and Lorelei realized that he was probably unaccustomed to having his attentions spurned. She had little patience with men like him; she had encountered them often enough in the past.

"Because I will be returning to Georgia as soon as my brother's court-martial has taken place." She readjusted the lace shawl about her shoulders and turned to leave the dance floor.

"And what if something happens to change your mind?" Captain McNeil challenged, prompting her to face him briefly again.

"Nothing could ever induce me to spend one minute longer than necessary in Texas!" she asserted with considerable feeling.

She gathered up her skirts, headed back into the crowd, and found Abigail at last. After fortifying themselves with some punch, they completed their social rounds about the hall. Lorelei was relieved that, although some of the ladies were less than congenial, none were as outwardly belligerent as Harriet Jameson had been. The officers, on the other hand, were without exception charming and affable. Even Colonel Jameson, with his wife watching him like a hawk from across the room, put himself forth to smile and inquire if she was enjoying the evening.

The dance had been in progress for nearly an hour when Lorelei finally escaped outside for some fresh air. She had danced with more than half a dozen gallant partners, making endless small talk and wishing all the while that she could be putting her efforts to better use. Her disappointment had increased with each passing moment, for the one man she had come to see had never put in an appearance.

Releasing a long, angry sigh, she fingered the cameo at her throat distractedly and wandered around to the side of the building. There were no lamps to light her way in that direction, so she relied on the moon's soft glow. The lights of Santa Angela were visible across the river, and the plaintive ballad being played inside the mess hall mingled in the air with the more aggressive strains bursting from the saloons there.

135

Taking comfort in her momentary solitude, Lorelei breathed deeply and allowed her gaze to drift heavenward. She felt a sharp pang of homesickness. Aunt Matilda would be fast asleep by now, and the plantation—or what was left of it—would be still and quiet. She wondered idly if the moon was shining just as brightly over the green, rolling hills of Georgia. It all seemed so very far away . . .

"I didn't expect to find you waiting for me."

A sharp gasp of startlement broke from her lips. She spun about at the sound of that deep, splendidly masculine voice, her eyes growing wide before blazing with their magnificent blue fire.

"You are arrogant beyond belief, Major Cameron!" she charged indignantly. Torn between relief and dismay at the fact that he had come at last, she watched as he drew closer and gave her a smile that was both mocking and thoroughly disarming.

"So you keep telling me."

He came to a halt just inches away, towering over her in the moonlit darkness. She felt very small and vulnerable—and feminine. This man, damn him, always made her so completely aware of the fact that she was a woman. She remembered all too vividly what had transpired between them at their last meeting, and the memory threatened to send her running like a coward.

"Why aren't you inside?" asked Reeve, sparing a brief, uninterested glance toward the music-filled hall.

"I have *been* inside for quite some time."

"Do I detect a note of rebuke in your voice, Miss Montgomery?" he teased, the warmth in his tone throwing her completely off guard. Although he was wearing his dress uniform, there was nothing stiff or formal about him. No, indeed, she mused with a flash of resentment, he treated her with just the same bold familiarity as before.

But her breath caught in her throat as she stared up at him. He was without a doubt the most handsome man she had met since coming to Texas . . . or even before then, she amended honestly. *Dear Lord, how was she ever going to be able to go through with this?*

"I find it hard to believe you suffered from a lack of attention in my absence," he remarked, a light of roguish amusement in his green eyes as they flickered over her.

In truth, he experienced a powerful surge of jealousy at the thought of her dancing with anyone else. He cursed his own tardiness, even though an important development in the case had made it necessary, and vowed to spend the remainder of the evening making certain that no other man's arms held what was destined to be his alone.

"Believe what you will," she murmured noncommittally, too preoccupied for once to rise to the bait.

"I'm surprised to find you out here alone like this." He could see that she was troubled about something. And though his protective instincts compelled him to take her in his arms and kiss the frown from her beautiful brow, he knew that one simple gesture of comfort would lead to a lot more. Not that he didn't want a lot more—he did. Hell, he had never wanted anything more. But that would have to wait until later . . .

"I—I needed some air," Lorelei stammered finally in explanation.

137

Her gaze fell hastily before the piercing intensity of his. She battled the temptation to abandon her plan before she had even begun. Suddenly, her brother's face swam before her eyes, lending her courage.

She had to do it, of course. There was no other way. Only Heaven help her, she reflected with an inward groan, it was going to be even harder than she had feared.

"I hope you know how to dance, Major," she said, forcing a winsome smile to her lips. She moved to his side and slipped a hand lightly about his arm. "I believe you offered to escort me inside?"

"Not exactly," he was ungallant enough to point out. His mouth twitched. "Maybe we should stay out here." It was not meant to be taken seriously, though he wouldn't have minded being alone with her for the rest of the night.

"No!" She colored in embarrassment at the impulsive outburst, and took a deep breath before telling him calmly, "I am quite sure Abigail will begin to worry if I don't return soon."

"I don't think that's it at all." He was already leading her toward the front of the building. His hand came up to cover hers, and it seemed that a current of warmth shot through them both.

"You don't?" She stole a glance up at his face, and was nonplussed to see that his eyes were gleaming with wry amusement again.

"No."

"Then what *do* you think?"

"I think you're afraid to be alone with me, Lorelei Montgomery."

"I'm not afraid of you in the least, Major

138

Cameron!" she denied adamantly, lifting her chin proudly.

"Well you should be," he warned in a low, vibrant tone that made her pulse quicken alarmingly. A soft gasp escaped her lips as her eyes flew back up to his face.

They had reached the open doorway by now. Several people stood making conversation nearby, so Lorelei was forced to swallow the scathing retort that rose to her lips. It was just as well, she told herself with a sigh of reluctant acceptance, for her purpose that evening was to beguile, not berate.

"You'll want to pay your respects to John and Abigail first, of course," she assumed, pressing a bit closer so that she could be heard above the music. She did not fail to notice the way Reeve's eyes darkened with wholly masculine interest as they dropped toward her décolletage.

"John and Abigail can wait," he decreed, virtually sweeping her off her feet when, without warning, he caught her up against him.

She had little choice but to follow his lead as he spun her agilely onto the dance floor with him. It was evident after the first few steps that he was an even better dancer than Captain McNeil, a discovery that surprised her. She was unable to resist comparing them in other ways as well—though in truth there *was* no comparison, she admitted to herself. Reeve Cameron and Collin McNeil were as different as day and night, in spite of the fact that they wore the same uniform.

"You dance very well, Major," she remarked, her mouth curving into another smile. Her eyes sparkled appealingly up at him.

139

"So do you, Lorelei." His strong arm drew her closer, while his hand tightened about hers. He, too, wore a sardonic half-smile. "But I don't think the fact that we're well-matched as dancers will be what causes all the tongues to wag."

"What do you mean?" Being held so close to him was making her lightheaded.

"I mean, my dearest Miss Montgomery, that the entire post will be talking about us by tomorrow."

"But why?" she asked in puzzlement. Her gaze traveled swiftly about the room. "We're merely dancing together. What could possibly be—"

"We share an unusual connection." When she continued to stare blankly up at him, he explained, "Your brother."

"Hadley?" Her eyes lit with comprehension in the next instant. "Oh. Oh, I . . . of course."

She looked away hastily. Confound it, she thought in displeasure, she hadn't wanted them to talk about Hadley yet. She had intended to broach the subject only after she'd had time to make Reeve so infatuated with her that he couldn't possibly refuse her plea for special consideration. If she proved successful in flattering his ego to such an extent that he was convinced she was his for the taking, then surely he would do everything in his power to help. He was a man, after all, she told herself, and it had been her experience thus far that men were generally ruled by their basest instincts. He had shown himself vulnerable in that particular area on two separate occasions, she recalled, with a mixture of satisfaction and disquietude.

"I propose, Major, that we forget, at least for this one evening, about that connection," she suggested, tossing him a look designed to intrigue. It served its purpose quite well.

"All right," Reeve agreed without hesitation.

Although pleasantly surprised by the change in her behavior, he was also suspicious. He wondered if she had put aside her anger because she had finally decided to stop fighting the attraction between them, or because she had realized that he was the only man who stood a chance of clearing her brother. It occurred to him that Abigail might have influenced her in some way, but he told himself it didn't matter. Whatever had brought about this startling transformation, he was damned sure going to make the most of it.

The music ended soon thereafter. The band announced a short break in the dancing, so Reeve led Lorelei across the room to join the Merriwethers.

"You and our Miss Montgomery make a very striking couple!" Abigail told Reeve, smiling benevolently upon them. She did not fail to notice the way he maintained a light yet possessive grip on Lorelei's arm.

"I'm glad to see you here, Major," said John. "I was beginning to think you had decided to spend another night across the river." His careless remark earned him a sharp look of reprimand from his wife. Reeve's expression, however, remained impassive.

"You are staying in Santa Angela?" Lorelei asked, gazing up at him in surprise.

"No." He did not elaborate, but merely turned to Abigail and remarked, "I hope your cooking has improved, Mrs. Merriwether." His eyes delivered an affectionate challenge with which she was all too familiar.

"And I was hoping your manners had improved, Major Cameron!" she retorted in mock irritation. She smiled at Lorelei. "He has always been unforgivably rude, you know. I give you fair warning, my dear—don't encourage his impertinence in any way. He'll take full advantage of your weakness at every turn. Why, I myself have been a victim of his merciless teasing for more years than I care to remember. And John says he was an absolute terror when they were stationed together in Arizona!"

"Am I to be your victim now as well, Major?" Lorelei inquired saucily. She watched as a slow, devilishly appealing smile spread across the rugged perfection of his features. At times it was easy to see how he might be able to charm a woman into complete submission, she thought, as her heart skipped a beat. The thought of any other woman being the recipient of that smile provoked a sudden, inexplicable flash of anger.

"I'd say it's the other way around," countered Reeve. He shifted his unfathomable gaze back to John. "I'd like a word with you, Captain."

"Of course. Please excuse us for a moment, ladies."

Abigail grabbed Lorelei's hand as soon as the two men were safely on their way outside.

"Well?" the irrepressible brunette prompted. That one word was full of not-so-subtle meaning.

"Major Cameron and I have only shared one dance," Lorelei replied dampeningly. They had shared more than a dance, of course, but she certainly wasn't going to tell Abigail about *that*.

"Nevertheless, I'd say from the look of things that you have decided to take my advice," the other woman opined in satisfaction.

"A simple flirtation—nothing more," vowed Lorelei. She frowned as her eyes drifted with a will of their own toward the doorway. "I'm not at all certain it will do any good. Maybe I'm wasting my time, Abigail. He strikes me as the sort of man who likes to keep the line clearly drawn between duty and pleasure." Doubts had returned to plague her, in spite of her recent conclusions about his susceptibility to her charms.

"Normally, I would be inclined to agree with you, especially where Reeve is concerned. But I think you are going to prove an exception to the rule. And it's high time someone took him in hand and made him realize he is every bit as human as the rest of us!"

"I'm not going to 'take him in hand' at all! For Heaven's sake, I . . . well, I'm only going to dance with the man and make pleasant conversation," she insisted, feigning a great and sudden interest in making sure that her lace shawl was arranged correctly. "I might even allow him to walk me home. But under no circumstances will I—"

"Will you what, Miss Montgomery?"

She and Abigail turned in unison to find that Captain McNeil had approached them from behind. The woman who clung, so leech-like, to his arm was none other than Harriet Jameson. Lorelei exchanged a quick, chagrined glance with Abigail.

"I hope you'll pardon the intrusion," the colonel's wife spoke with no apparent trace of conviction, "but Captain McNeil has expressed a desire to dance with Miss Montgomery again."

"Then why didn't the captain simply ask her for a dance himself?" Abigail wondered aloud. She had never liked the man. John had declared him a capable soldier, but he was far too sure of himself for her taste.

"Because I was hoping Mrs. Jameson's verification of my good character would further my cause," he explained, smiling agreeably at Lorelei. "Well, Miss Montgomery? Has my little ploy worked?"

It was on the tip of her tongue to inform him that, even if she had approved of his choice of a sponsor, which she most assuredly did not, she'd have no use for a man who relied on others to fight his battles for him. Actions did indeed speak far louder than words; Reeve Cameron sprang to mind as a perfect example.

"I'm sorry, Captain," she turned him down with all politeness, "but I have promised the next dance to someone else."

"To Major Cameron, you mean." His features darkened, and she was surprised by the harsh glint of anger in his eyes.

"Not that it matters, but yes, to Major Cameron."

"It would appear that the major has decided to forfeit his claim upon you," remarked Harriet, her scornful gaze moving significantly past Lorelei. "He and Captain Merriwether have gone outside, have they not?"

"Never fear," Abigail exhorted with a hint of sarcasm, "they will return soon. The members of the band are only now taking their places again."

"Then I will act as Miss Montgomery's partner in the major's absence," announced Captain McNeil. His smug self-assurance was maddening in the extreme.

He nodded down at Harriet, who released his arm

and beamed with approval when he extended his hand toward Lorelei. She did not like the redheaded vixen in the least, but far be it for her to stand in the way of a young man's pursuit of romance. And having already made the acquaintance of Major Reeve Cameron—another one of those disgustingly bold, rough-and-ready Texans—she could not help but prefer Captain McNeil's more refined qualities. *He* was a true gentleman.

"But I have no wish to dance at the moment, Captain," Lorelei reiterated in a low tone brimming with ire. The blaze in her eyes warned of her rising temper, but the captain chose, unwisely, to disregard it.

"I won't be turned away this time, Miss Montgomery." His hand closed about her arm, while his gaze locked with hers in silent combat. "If you've the time to form a friendship with Major Cameron," he declared, "then I claim the right to an equal portion of your attention."

"Please take your hand off me, Captain McNeil," Lorelei demanded in a furious undertone. Two bright spots of color rode high on her cheeks and she was fairly quaking with the force of her anger. While she had no wish to cause a scene, she refused to let this man triumph.

"You are behaving very badly, Miss Montgomery!" Harriet rebuked sharply, glowering at her.

"I'm quite sure, Captain," Abigail hastened to intervene, "that you are far too much of a gentleman to—"

"Keep quiet, Abigail Merriwether!" snapped the colonel's wife.

If Lorelei hadn't been so angry, she would have

appreciated the utter absurdity of the situation. She couldn't recall ever having a man so intent upon dancing with her that he was willing to literally drag her onto the dance floor. Her eyes flew to the doorway once more, but there was still no sign of Reeve.

"I'm only asking for a dance," Captain McNeil remarked with a faint, humorless smile.

"You aren't *asking* at all!" she retorted hotly.

There was no help for it, she realized. Enraged by the defeat, however minor it was, she gave a curt nod of acquiescence and accompanied Captain McNeil to the center of the hall. Several other couples followed suit, and the band struck up a lively Virginia reel moments later.

Lorelei remained stiff and unyielding in her partner's arms, though she performed the steps with her usual proficiency. She refused to look up at him, even when he managed to draw her into conversation.

"Come now, Miss Montgomery, you didn't expect me to give up so easily, did you?"

"If you ever attempt such a despicable, cowardly maneuver again, Captain, I will not hesitate to slap your face!" she vowed.

"You're a regular firebrand, aren't you?" he said with a quiet, rather malicious chuckle. His eyes gleamed sensually at the thought of what he was going to do to her once her brother was out of the way. Love at first sight, that's what it had been, he mused sardonically. He would enjoy teaching her how to please him . . .

To Lorelei, it seemed the dance would never end. But it did — and quite unexpectedly.

"Captain?"

Her blue eyes grew wide at the sound of Reeve's voice. Relief washed over her as Captain McNeil stopped and turned to face the man who had just tapped him none too gently on the shoulder.

"Major," he ground out, his arm still clamped about Lorelei's waist.

"I believe Miss Montgomery promised this dance to me," drawled Reeve, a soft, inscrutable smile playing about his lips.

"The lady was abandoned," the captain parried in a tight voice.

He pulled Lorelei back to him with the obvious intention of resuming their dance. She looked instinctively to Reeve, an unconscious plea for rescue in her eyes. It was not necessary; his decision had been made the first moment he had seen her dancing with the captain.

"Let go of her," Reeve ordered in a low, deceptively calm tone. His gaze smoldered with fury, but he kept his emotions in check.

"Are you pulling rank, Major?" the other man challenged with a sneer.

"Please, Captain McNeil!" Lorelei tried appealing to him. While the other dancers continued whirling unaware about them, she hoped to prevent what threatened to be a particularly uncomfortable scene. Her luminous eyes traveled anxiously to Reeve, whose features remained dangerously grim. She turned back to the captain and continued, with a forced smile, "It is nothing more than tradition for you to allow Major Cameron the opportunity—"

"We are going to finish the dance," he insisted through clenched teeth. She gasped audibly when he tightened his arm abruptly about her. "That is, unless you *are* pulling rank?" he taunted Reeve, arching one eyebrow in a gesture of contempt.

It was his turn to gasp as Reeve's hand shot out with lightning speed and seized his wrist in a hard, punishing grip. Released at last, a startled Lorelei hastily regained her balance. Meanwhile, Captain McNeil had no time to react before he found his arm twisted behind his back, with the very real threat of serious physical injury. All this had been accomplished with such ease and lack of commotion that it was scarcely noticed by anyone else.

"You will apologize to Miss Montgomery, Captain McNeil," Reeve commanded with quiet yet deadly authority, "and then you'll confine yourself to your quarters for the rest of the evening. Is that understood?" The question was accompanied by a highly persuasive upward jerk on his arm.

"Yes, Major," the captain muttered furiously. He shot him a murderous glare, one that promised retribution, but Reeve was not impressed.

"Then do as I say, damn you, or I'll allow myself the pleasure of breaking your arm." His deep voice cut through the music like a knife.

Lorelei, watching in stunned silence, felt a tremor of very real fear when she viewed the savage gleam in Reeve's eyes. She had never seen a man so angry and so composed at the same time.

"My apologies, Miss Montgomery," Captain McNeil dutifully intoned once his arm had been released. She might have felt pity for him, if not for the glare of mingled vengeance and lust he turned upon her. "Until next time—goodnight."

"*Goodbye,* Captain," she replied pointedly.

A dull flush crept over his aristocratic features.

He shot Reeve one last murderous scowl, then strode away angrily through the crowd.

Lorelei released a long, pent-up sigh. She was smiling, ready to offer Reeve her gratitude as he stepped forward to claim her. Her smile quickly faded, however, when he seized her arm and, without so much as a word, began leading her from the dance floor.

Eight

"What in Heaven's name do you think you're doing?" she demanded breathlessly. He was making her feel as if she were a naughty child. Great balls of fire, she mused indignantly, she had done nothing wrong! "Major Cameron, where *are* we going?"

"I'm taking you home."

"Home?" She pulled to a halt and stared up at him in confusion. "But what about the dance? I thought we—"

"I'm taking you home," he repeated in a steely voice. He gave her no time to argue, propelling her masterfully along with him toward the mess hall's doorway.

Across the room, Abigail witnessed their sudden, unexpected departure and turned to her husband with a frown of mingled puzzlement and concern.

"John? John, shouldn't we—"

"We should do nothing, Abigail." He had seen them leaving as well, but appeared not the least bit worried.

"Where do you suppose they're going?"

"How should I know?" He smiled indulgently and tucked her hand beneath his arm. "Don't worry. She's perfectly safe with Reeve."

"Safe?" She looked far from convinced. "Why, John Merriwether, you know very well how . . . *influential* he can be with the ladies!"

"It's different this time," John declared confidently.

"What makes you so sure of that?"

"Because, my love," he revealed with a knowing look, "he told me so himself."

"He did?" she breathed in astonishment. "What exactly did he say?"

"Now, Abigail, you know I make it a point never to—"

"Either you tell me, or you can sleep in the parlor tonight!" she threatened, exasperated as always with his reticence.

"Blast it, Abigail Merriwether, that's blackmail!" He eyed her accusingly.

"Call it whatever you like," Abigail responded with an unrepentant smile of determination. "I'm sure you'll be very comfortable on the sofa."

"It won't work, Abigail," John insisted, shaking his head. "I'm going to sleep in my own bed—in *our* bed—and what's more, you're not going to interfere with Reeve and Miss Montgomery in any way."

"And what makes you so certain of that?" Her eyes flashed mutinously up at him. She gasped when his hand suddenly stole downward and landed a hard swat upon her bottom. Coloring in embarrassment, she looked about swiftly to make certain no one had witnessed her husband's unforgivable assertion of dominance. "How dare you, John Merriwether!" she whispered in shocked outrage.

"You'll obey me in this, Abigail," he told her, his expression quite solemn. "Reeve has his own reasons for spending time with Miss Montgomery."

"And she has hers!"

"What do you mean by that?"

"I make it a point never to betray a confidence, *Captain!*" she proclaimed, then sailed haughtily past him to seek refuge in the midst of a circle of women gathered some distance away. John was left to scowl darkly in her wake. He was tempted to go after her, but was prevented from doing so when one of his colleagues called upon him to settle an argument about the effectiveness of Colonel Mackenzie's latest campaign against the Indians.

At that same moment, outside, Lorelei was walking along with Reeve in thoughtful silence. His long, unaccountably angry strides had slowed to a more reasonable pace, so that she was no longer forced to hurry in order to keep up with him. She was more than a trifle annoyed herself, given the way he had hauled her out of the building with so little civility, but she was still determined to make the most of the evening.

Things might work out for the best after all, she told herself, her hopes rising again. She would simply focus all her efforts on conversation now, instead of dancing. The prospect of being alone with him, even within the relative security of the fort, made her feel several conflicting emotions.

They were passing the first of the six barracks when she cast a surreptitious glance up at his handsome, inscrutable countenance. Sensing that it was finally safe to question him, she inhaled deeply of the cool, rain-washed night air and tilted her head back to face him with a look of wide-eyed innocence. Moonlight combined with the soft golden

152

rays falling from a nearby lamppost to set her beautiful face aglow.

"Will you please tell me now, Major, what I have done to earn your displeasure?"

He did not answer immediately. His gaze burned down into hers, and she could have sworn she caught a glimpse of uncertainty within the magnificent, penetrating green depths of his eyes. A faint smile briefly touched his lips, then he sobered again.

"I want you to stay away from Captain McNeil."

"Stay away from him?" she echoed in bemusement. "Why, I don't know what you mean."

"You know exactly what I mean," he retorted curtly. His hand tightened about her arm. "Damn it, Lorelei, these men here are different from the kind you're used to."

That was exactly what Hadley had warned her about *him,* she recalled with an inward smile of irony.

"Are they indeed, Major?" She heaved a dramatic little sigh and brought her hand up to rest within the crook of his arm. "Well, then, I suppose I should count myself fortunate that I have you to protect me. However," she pointed out with a frown of mock reproach, "it wasn't at all necessary for you to treat Captain McNeil like that. The poor man had done nothing more than insist upon dancing with me." She did not add that she had never been so glad in her life to have a dance interrupted.

"And I suppose you offered him no encouragement," Reeve challenged wryly.

"None whatsoever!" She smiled and pressed a bit closer as they strolled leisurely along the walk. "Now that you're no longer angry, perhaps we

153

should return to the dance," she suggested on sudden impulse, then silently berated herself for being such a coward. "The Merriwethers will begin to wonder what has happened to me."

"I think they'll be able to figure it out." His eyes were brimming with an irresistible combination of amusement and desire as they roamed over her face, then dropped to where the exposed, provocative curve of her breasts seemed to be inviting his caress. *Damnation, every man who had seen her would be thinking the same thing,* he mused, another surge of jealousy running hotly through him.

"Besides," he observed when he met her sparkling gaze again, "this is the first chance we've had to get to know one another. I intend to take full advantage of it."

It wasn't so much what he said as the *way* he said it that struck fear in Lorelei's heart. She swallowed hard and tried to conceal her growing apprehension with an attempt to steer the conversation along a different route.

"According to Abigail, you might very well have been a general by now if you hadn't chosen to fight for the Confederacy."

"At least we have that in common." He smiled at her slight frown of puzzlement. "Our loyalties during the war, I mean."

"Yes, of course," she replied, her brow clearing. She released another sigh and directed a wistful glance overhead. "At times, it's difficult to believe such a terrible tragedy ever occurred." She looked back to Reeve. "But I suppose it's best forgotten, anyway." Such a thing was impossible, of course.

"What about your family?" Reeve asked suddenly,

his deep-timbred voice making her feel incredibly safe and warm in the moonlit darkness. "Did you lose anyone?"

"Yes. A number of cousins, and nearly all the young men from the neighboring plantations. And my parents." A shadow of painful remembrance crossed her face. "They died shortly after the war."

"I'm sorry," he said softly, his eyes holding genuine compassion. "What happened after that?"

"My aunt came to live with us. Hadley was still so very young," she recalled. "It was difficult for him to understand why his whole world suddenly fell apart."

"You couldn't have been much more than a child yourself."

"I was forced to grow up quickly," she admitted with a rueful smile. "You see there wasn't much left, and there was no one but me to make sure we survived. Aunt Matilda was a source of great comfort, but she was little help when it came to practicalities."

"So it fell to you to take care of everyone," said Reeve, anxious to hear more. His heart ached at the thought of her pain. "That couldn't have been easy."

"Oh, I was accustomed to taking charge. My father—completely against my mother's wishes, I might add—taught me all about running the plantation. It had been quite prosperous before the war, one of the finest in all of Georgia," she boasted proudly.

"And you're determined to make it so again." He could well imagine her as mistress of a great plantation. She was intelligent and headstrong, and certain to wreak havoc on the hearts of men who tried to

155

win her affection. His eyes warmed with admiration for the woman whose future, he had already decided, did not lie in the genteel countryside of Georgia.

"I have already enjoyed some measure of success in restoring my home to its former glory," replied Lorelei. That wasn't at all true, of course, she reflected with a sharp twinge of guilt. She would probably be forced to sell before the year was out. But she was reluctant to let Reeve know how difficult things had become. For some inexplicable reason, she wanted him to think her life was one of luxury and ease, the way it had been before the war. "Once Hadley . . . once I return home again, I hope to complete my plans for a more thorough renovation."

"What if things don't turn out the way you hope?" His steady, piercing gaze seemed to touch her very soul.

Catching her breath, she hastily looked away and tried to ignore the sudden racing of her heart.

"I prefer not to think about that at the moment. My brother . . . I suppose I've been more like a mother to him."

"Maybe that's why you're so obsessed with him," Reeve concluded aloud. His words startled her, and although his outward manner remained nonchalant, he studied her reaction closely. "I mean because you've been responsible for him all these years."

"I am not obsessed with Hadley!" she denied vehemently, her eyes flashing up at him as she pulled to a halt. "I've simply looked after him as best I could!"

"And who looked after you, Lorelei?" he asked,

his tone wonderfully low and vibrant.

"Why, I—I looked after myself." Why did her name always sound like an endearment on his lips?

"Did you?" There was only a ghost of a smile on his face. "Maybe it's time you turned the job over to someone else." With that enigmatic statement, he resumed their walk.

Lorelei's emotions were in utter turmoil by now. She didn't know what was happening to her. She had never felt so unsure of herself before, had never felt torn between the impulse to trust and confide in a man, and the urge to take flight before it was too late. *Too late for what?* she wondered dazedly.

Her confusion only increased when she glanced up to see that she and Reeve had reached the stretch of walk in front of the guardhouse. A single light burned in the center room, where she spied the night-duty guard leaning back restfully in his chair with his arms folded and his legs stretched out before him.

"It would make my job a hell of a lot easier if he decided to talk," pronounced Reeve, noting the direction of her troubled gaze. They both knew what he meant.

"He won't," she replied, shaking her head. "I tried to convince him, of course, but it was entirely useless. I'm afraid his silence will continue." She hesitated a moment before asking tentatively, "Have you . . . have you been able to find out anything yet?"

"I have." Without elaborating, he merely promised again, "I'll do my best, Lorelei."

"I'm sure you will, Major." She wanted desperately to press him for further details, but knew the time still wasn't right.

157

"It's 'Reeve.' "

"What?" Having become preoccupied with thoughts of Hadley for a moment, she smiled apologetically. "I'm terribly sorry, Major. What was that you said?"

"I said, Lorelei Montgomery, that if you call me 'Major' one more time, I'm going to drag you into the shadows and kiss you until you beg for mercy," he warned, in a tone that let her know it was no idle threat. She colored rosily and battled the wicked temptation to put him to the test.

"Tell me, Reeve Cameron, do you always go around bullying the women you're with?" she queried archly.

"That depends."

"On what?"

"On whether or not they're as obstinate as you."

"And how many have approached my level of obstinacy?" she asked, enjoying the raillery between them. Strangely enough, it was requiring no real effort on her part to flirt with him.

"None," he answered, with a smile of irony.

Lorelei gave a soft laugh and allowed her lace shawl to slip downward, exposing even more of her pale, creamy shoulders and bosom to his appreciative gaze. Reeve's green eyes darkened as they raked hungrily over her. Mentally he offered up a silent curse while he fought to control the fire raging in his blood.

"Are you a frequent visitor to Santa Angela, Ma—Reeve?" she inquired, prompted by a sudden thought.

"No." His gaze narrowed almost imperceptibly. "Why do you ask?"

158

"Oh, something Captain Merriwether said made me think you might be." Once again, the thought of him enjoying the company of the women at the saloons, or perhaps even at Miss Hattie's, made her eyes blaze with secret displeasure. "And I do recall having heard Charity Pardee extend a personal invitation to you yesterday," she added. The second it was out she could have bitten her tongue.

Reeve's mouth curved into a slow, challenging smile.

"Are you jealous, Lorelei?"

"Jealous?" She bristled visibly at the idea. "Certainly not!"

"Good. Because there's no reason to be," he declared, with maddening equanimity.

She was scarcely aware of the fact that they were approaching the officers' quarters now. Reeve, however, had noted their progress with increasing pleasure and anticipation. They lapsed into silence as he led her toward the small building behind the Merriwethers' house.

The darkness was much deeper now that they had moved away from the lampposts. Lorelei was dismayed to realize how nervous she felt. Her fingers trembled when she pulled the shawl about her once more, and she found herself wishing she had been more insistent upon remaining at the dance. She stopped in front of the door, turned to face Reeve, and gently disengaged her arm from his.

"Thank you for escorting me home," she told him, managing only a rather wan smile. She gave a quick worried glance toward the house. "I'm sure Abigail and John will be returning soon. The children—"

"Open the door, Lorelei," he broke in with quiet authority.

"Why?" She was almost afraid to ask. Peering up at him, she was acutely conscious of his nearness.

"Why do you think?" His deep voice held an undercurrent of tender amusement — and simmering passion.

His words threw her into a quandary. On one hand, she wanted to prolong the evening and thereby ensure an even better chance of success for her plan of enchantment; on the other, she was beginning to fear that she had already gone too far.

"I'm not at all certain I should answer that," she murmured finally.

"What are you afraid of?"

"Why, nothing!" she hastened to deny. Her smile this time was thoroughly captivating. "You know as well as I do that it would not be at all proper for a lady to entertain a gentleman in her private chambers at this hour of the night," she told him, her southern accent more pronounced than ever. "In any case, it *is* getting late, Major, and — "

She gasped in startlement when Reeve, completely ignoring her objections, reached behind her and turned the knob. The door swung open, sending a faint shaft of moonlight into the darkened confines of the room.

"What do you think you're doing?" she demanded breathlessly, her eyes flying wide.

"I want to have a word with you. Alone."

"But — we *are* alone!"

"Damn it, woman, are you going to get inside, or am I going to have to carry you?" he threatened with a strange half-smile that sent a

160

shiver coursing down her spine.

"This has gone quite far enough," she asserted sternly. "For Heaven's sake, what if someone should—"

"Please, Lorelei. Get inside."

For a moment it seemed she would refuse. But there was something so sweetly compelling about the way he spoke that she found it impossible to resist him. Maybe it was because he was asking, for a change, instead of demanding. She surprised herself—and made his eyes gleam with triumphant satisfaction—by capitulating.

"Very well. But you cannot stay long," she cautioned.

Pivoting about, she stepped inside and hurried across the room to light the lamp that rested on the table beside her bed. She bore it purposefully across the room and placed it on the washstand, a less intimate location. When she turned back to Reeve, she saw that he had closed the door and stood facing her solemnly.

"What is it you wished to speak to me about?" she prompted, with a composure that belied her inner turmoil. Moving to take a stance behind the rocking chair, she gripped the back of it for added support. She was relieved, and vaguely disappointed, when Reeve kept his distance. "Does it have anything to do with your investigation?"

"No." He frowned, his gaze burning across into hers. "I can't discuss that with you." He was every bit as aware as she, or perhaps even more so, that the two of them were completely alone together. It was all he could do to refrain from saying "To hell with patience" and sweeping her into his arms.

"Oh. Then what—"

"I think it's time we got something settled between us," he decreed.

"Settled?" she echoed, her throat constricting in alarm. She adopted an air of ignorance, insisting coquettishly, "Why, I haven't the faintest idea what you're talking about, Major Cameron."

"I think you do. But if you want to pretend otherwise, I'll be more than happy to enlighten you." The smile he gave her was both mocking and dangerously disarming.

Unable to think of a suitable response, Lorelei waited for him to speak again. Her eyes grew round in alarm when he began slowly advancing on her.

"I think you should leave now, Major!" she blurted out. Her eyes searched instinctively for a way to escape, but it was too late.

"I've already considered all the reasons why this shouldn't happen," he said, frowning at the memory. "It's been difficult to concentrate on anything else. I've tried telling myself that I'm a fool, that I'm courting certain disaster. Not only will it be looked upon as a serious conflict of interest in the investigation here, but I've little doubt it's going to interfere with my future assignments as well." A sardonic smile played about his lips when he remarked, "Hell, I'll probably find myself pulling duty at some rat-infested post out West that doesn't even have a name yet."

"What in Heaven's name are you talking about?" demanded Lorelei, staring at him as if he had suddenly taken complete leave of his senses.

She took an involuntary step backward when he finally drew to a halt before her. His tanned, rug-

162

gedly handsome features wore an expression of single-minded intent, and she could literally feel the heat and tension of his virile, hard-muscled body. Her trepidation increased tenfold as she lamented, quite belatedly, to herself that she should never have trusted him.

"I'm talking about *us,* Lorelei," he told her, his gaze smoldering with barely controlled passion. "About the fact that from the first moment I set eyes on you, I haven't been able to get you out of my mind. And damn it, I've certainly tried hard enough," he confided with another smile. "The last thing I wanted was to get mixed up with a woman — especially the sister of a man I've been sent to investigate."

"I beg to differ with you, Major Cameron," she retorted quickly, "but we are not 'mixed up' at all."

"We'll have to keep it quiet for a while," he continued, as if she hadn't spoken. "John and Abigail will have to be told, but no one else. I'll notify Washington of my plans just as soon as—"

"What plans?" Her breasts rose and fell rapidly beneath her tightly corseted bodice, while her eyes clouded with a mixture of confusion and alarm. "What is it that John and Abigail have to be told?"

"That we're going to be married."

"Married?" she gasped, not at all certain she had heard him correctly.

"Right away. Tomorrow, if I can arrange it."

Thunderstruck, Lorelei stared mutely up at him. He smiled tenderly at her astonishment and forced his arms to remain at his sides. One touch, he told himself, while the hypnotic glow in his eyes deepened; one touch was all it would take to make him

163

forget everything else but this beautiful, flame-haired wildcat who had stolen his heart and made his body burn to possess her. He wanted to make sure they reached an understanding before he allowed himself the pleasure of sealing their betrothal—a mercifully brief one, if he had his way—with a kiss.

"The idea took me by surprise at first, too," he confessed quietly. "I know it's sudden. I didn't plan on this happening any more than you did. But I want you more than I've ever wanted any woman, Lorelei Montgomery, and I mean to have you."

"This is absurd!" She recovered enough voice, finally, to respond. It was certainly the most shocking proposal she had received . . . but then, it wasn't a proposal at all. It was more like he was *requisitioning* her hand in marriage. "Surely you—you're not serious, Major Cameron!" she sputtered, while her head swam dizzily.

"Never more so." A light of unholy amusement danced in his green eyes. "I hope you don't intend to continue addressing me as 'Major' once we're married. I don't know if I much like the idea of being reminded of my duty to God and country every time we're in bed."

Lorelei crimsoned hotly and was dismayed to feel her knees weaken. She made a desperate attempt to restore sanity to the proceedings, which had gone unbelievably, ridiculously haywire.

"We scarcely know one another," she pointed out with admirable composure in the face of his warm, disturbing scrutiny. Gently clearing her throat, she retreated another step and lifted her chin to meet his gaze squarely. Her courage very nearly left her when he smiled at her again. "Why, until three short days ago—"

"We'll have a lifetime to get acquainted," asserted Reeve. "Besides, I have neither the time nor the inclination to court you in a 'proper' manner. I'll be leaving Fort Concho soon. And you'll be coming with me."

"But, I . . . you cannot do this!" Still reeling from the shock, she struggled to make sense of what was happening. Good Heavens, she mused numbly, she had certainly meant to captivate him, but she had never intended to be quite *this* successful! "Surely, as an officer in the United States Cavalry, you are answerable to a higher authority," she tried arguing. "Why, you said it yourself—I would not be at all suitable!"

"Suitable?" He gave a low chuckle and finally allowed himself the pleasure of reaching for her. "I think you'll suit me very well."

"But I . . . hellfire and damnation, Reeve Cameron, I don't love you!" she cried, her voice rising on a note of panic. A tremor shook her when his strong hands closed gently but firmly about her shoulders.

"Don't you?" he countered, his voice little more than a husky whisper. She struggled in his grasp, but he pulled her toward him. His smoldering, gold-flecked gaze seared relentlessly down into the stormy luminescence of hers. "You can fight against it all you like, Lorelei, but it won't do you any good. What's between us is—"

"There *is* nothing between us!" She raised her hands to push weakly against his chest.

"Then how do you explain what happens every

165

time I kiss you?"

"That is nothing more than . . . than mere physical attraction!" she insisted, her cheeks flaming. "And I am quite sure, *Major,* that you have experienced it with more than your fair share of willing partners!"

"Maybe," he responded with a crooked smile, then he grew serious again immediately. "But it's different with you. I've never asked a woman to marry me before."

"And I suppose I'm to count myself blessed among all women because you have decided to honor me as the first?" she parried caustically. Her sapphire eyes filled with an inordinate amount of fire. "Well, thank you very much, Major Cameron, but I did not ask for the honor!"

"Listen to me, you little wildcat!" Reeve commanded tersely, his expression growing thunderous as his fingers dug into her skin with almost bruising force. "If all I wanted was to make love to you, I'd have taken you that night at the Cantrells' and left us both the better for it! But I want more from you than that—much more! I want your heart and soul as well, Lorelei Montgomery, and I'll be damned if I'll settle for less!"

A soft, breathless cry broke from her lips when his arm caught her roughly about the waist and yanked her up hard against him. He entangled his other hand within the luxuriant thickness of her upswept curls, forcing her head back so that his fierce, possessive gaze could rake over her face.

"You're mine, Lorelei," he ground out. "You've been mine from the very first. If it pleases you to believe there's nothing but simple, unadulterated lust

166

between us, then so be it. You'll realize the truth soon enough. But either way, you're going to marry me."

"No!" she breathed, her heart pounding with fear at the look in his eyes. She made a last, desperate attempt to twist free, but his arm tightened about her like a band of steel. "Damn you, Reeve Cameron, let go of me!" she demanded frantically.

"No." He shook his head, and his voice was whipcord sharp in the lamplit silence of the room. "Not until I've heard you admit it."

"Admit what?" She stifled another cry as he crushed her to him with even more breathtaking urgency.

"That you want me as much as I want you. And that tomorrow, you're going to stand before the chaplain with me and promise to be mine forever."

"You've gone completely mad!" she pronounced, her voice quivering with emotions she did not wish to name.

"Maybe I have. But there's a method to my madness."

With that, he finally brought his lips down upon the parted softness of hers. She inhaled sharply and writhed in protest within his merciless grasp, her hands pushing at him in vain. He demanded a response they both knew to be inevitable. His hot, sensuous tongue ravished the sweetness of her mouth, and she moaned deeply before slowly melting against him in unspoken surrender.

Lorelei kissed him back with ever-increasing fervor, her hands stealing upward so that her arms could entwine about his neck. She knew she would hate herself again afterwards, knew she was behaving every bit as wickedly and wantonly—and *obedi-ently,* Heaven forbid—as he had wanted her to. But none of that seemed to matter whenever she was in his arms. A delicious warmth was spreading throughout her body, and she found herself wishing the sweet madness would go on forever . . .

Her eyes flew open in startlement when he suddenly lifted her off her feet. He gave her no time to protest. Within seconds, he had taken a seat in the rocking chair and settled her on his lap, one powerful arm remaining clamped about her waist while his other hand held her just below the roundness of her hips. His mouth continued its delectable assault upon hers, kissing her so deeply and so passionately that she grew lightheaded.

She was left gasping for breath when, quite abruptly, the kiss ended. Opening her eyes, she frowned in disappointment and confusion, but she was not left to wonder for long. Her eyes closed once more as his lips and tongue, after teasing provocatively at her ear, trailed a scorching path downward to where her breasts threatened to spill out of her low-cut bodice.

His hand came up to tug impatiently at the delicate white gauze. Before Lorelei could prevent it, his fingers had succeeded in easing the fabric far enough downward that her breasts were revealed in all their full, rose-tipped glory.

"Reeve!"

"I've been wanting to do that ever since I saw you standing there in this blasted dress," he murmured in a low, splendidly vibrant tone.

"Reeve—stop it!"

"At least you've learned how to say my name."

168

Coloring in shocked embarrassment, she made a hasty attempt to set her bodice to rights again, but he would not be denied. He captured both of her hands in one of his. His mouth roamed hotly across the tops of her naked breasts, branding her flesh and making her gasp repeatedly. Then, at last, his lips closed about one of the delicate peaks, his tongue flicking across the nipple with light, tantalizing strokes before he sucked gently.

"Sweet mercy!" she whispered huskily.

She gave a soft moan, her hips moving restlessly on his lean, hard-muscled thighs. Her head fell back, and her hair came tumbling riotously downward, shimmering like a magnificent, flame-colored banner. Reeve's hand gripped her about the hips and pulled her closer. He was soon inflicting the same exquisite torment on her other breast while she bit at her lower lip and felt her blood turn to liquid fire . . .

Certain she would be reduced to begging for mercy — just as he had earlier threatened she would — she didn't know whether to be glad or not when he raised his head. She found her hands released, and she gazed at him in stunned, breathless expectation as his arm tightened about her waist once more.

"Say it, Lorelei," he ordered, his face mere inches from her own. His unfathomable gaze burned into the passion-clouded sapphire depths of hers.

"Say . . . say what?" she panted.

"Say you'll marry me."

She stared at him in uncertainty, still struggling to regain some measure of control over her emotions as well as her breathing. Her hands had moved in-

169

stinctively to the neckline of her gown, pulling the fabric upward to cover her breasts while her face flamed anew. She would have slid from Reeve's lap if he had not continued to hold her captive.

"I'm afraid I—" she began, only to break off in confusion.

Reality was fast intruding, but Reeve Cameron was not a man to accept defeat so easily.

His green eyes darkened with a dangerous combination of anger and intent. Without another word, he reclaimed her lips in a kiss that was both punishing and rapturously intoxicating. She shivered as passion blazed to life within her once more. Her hands crept upward to clutch at his broad, powerfully muscled shoulders, and she strained against him while his mouth conquered hers with a vengeance.

He raked up her long skirts and petticoats, exposing a pair of white cotton drawers trimmed with lace and ruffles. His hand smoothed with bold appreciation across the alluring, thinly clad roundness of her bottom.

Lorelei moaned in halfhearted protest against his mouth. Once again, she tried to squirm free; once again, his determination to tame her became that much stronger. His fingers glided down the back of her thigh, then traveled around to insinuate themselves within the open seam of her drawers. She trembled at the touch of his warm fingers on the bare, satiny flesh of her inner thighs. But the tremble was nothing compared to the almost violent start she gave when he stroked upward to tease at the soft, delicate auburn curls between her legs.

"No!" she cried breathlessly, tearing her mouth

from his. She would have averted her shame-filled gaze, but he forced her to look at him.

"Say it, Lorelei," he insisted, in a low tone brimming with passion. He reinforced his command by capturing her lips in another hard, thoroughly inflaming kiss. Lorelei, in very real peril of losing all reason again, summoned enough strength of will to twist her head away.

"Reeve, *please!*" She pushed away from him while at the same time frantically trying to pull down her skirts.

"You're mine," he declared once more. His voice was one of deadly calm now. "And you will marry me. Even if I have to stay here all night in order to make you face the truth."

"You—you wouldn't dare!" she stammered, aghast at the threat. Her eyes quickly searched his face, and she shivered in fear at what she saw there.

"I would, Lorelei."

"Then you are no gentleman, Reeve Cameron!"

"I never claimed to be."

"Confound it, I . . ." she began, only to trail off as words failed her.

"Well?" Reeve demanded impatiently. His arm tightened again about her waist as his large hand closed over her buttocks with rough possessiveness. When she merely struggled in silence instead of offering him an answer, he muttered a curse and brought his lips down upon hers again.

A strangled cry rose in her throat when his fingers, strong and insistent, and sensuously persuasive, returned to the secret place at the juncture of her thighs. She blushed deeply at the wicked intimacy of his caress, but she felt a hot, unnamed

171

yearning building, to a fever pitch within her.

Her hips, wriggling with innocent seductiveness as she sought to escape the near-painful ecstasy he was subjecting her to, squirmed across his throbbing manhood. He gave a sharp intake of breath and felt his desire spiraling out of control . . .

A sudden knock at the door brought them both crashing back to earth.

"Lorelei?" Abigail called out softly. "Lorelei, are you in there?"

For a brief moment she froze at the sound of the other woman's voice, and then Lorelei came to life. She jerked her head about with a sharp gasp of alarm. Shooting Reeve a look of helpless desperation, she was surprised when he stood unhurriedly and set her on her feet beside him.

"Dear Lord, what—what do we do?" she whispered, smoothing her skirts quickly into place and raising unsteady hands to the thick mass of auburn tresses streaming down upon her face and shoulders in wild, telltale disarray. "What will Abigail think?" Without waiting for a response she rounded on him with eyes full of fire and cautioned sternly, "She mustn't know you're here!"

Reeve, looking damnably unruffled in his brass-buttoned uniform, stared down at her with a faint, ironic smile playing about his lips. His body still burned, and though his first reaction to Abigail's interruption had been one of almost murderous frustration, he was now determined to use it to his advantage.

"Why not?" he challenged softly.

"You know perfectly well why not!"

"Lorelei?" Abigail knocked again.

172

Reeve cast Lorelei a look that boded ill for her already strained nerves. Taking her by the shoulders, he moved her deliberately out of his path. Her eyes grew enormous within the flushed, delicate oval of her face, while her mouth fell open. She watched in stunned disbelief as he sauntered forward and opened the door.

"You've got the devil's own timing, Mrs. Merriwether," he quipped dryly, smiling down at the woman who had just raised her hand to knock once more.

Visibly startled, Abigail blinked up at him, then her eyes traveled across the room to where Lorelei stood blushing fierily and attempting, without any real degree of success, to set her hair to rights.

"Oh, I—please forgive me!" the brunette stammered in profound embarrassment, belatedly lamenting to herself that she hadn't listened to her husband. John had forbidden her to come, but she had not yet forgiven him for putting his foot down with such infuriating discourtesy, and so she had come anyway. She had little doubt that her defiance would be punished. Sighing inwardly, and musing that she would in all probability be the one to sleep in the parlor when John found out, she explained, "It's just that . . . well, I was certain I heard someone inside and I thought perhaps . . ." Her voice trailed away uncomfortably.

"It's all right, Abigail," Reeve assured her, his deep voice brimming with amusement. "You see, Miss Montgomery and I are going to be married."

"Married?" echoed Abigail, astounded at the news. She looked quickly to the younger woman for confirmation. "Good Heavens, my dear, I had no idea—"

"We are *not* going to be married!" Lorelei denied hotly. Her narrowed, blazing eyes looked daggers at Reeve's handsome head. "Major Cameron is deluding himself!"

"The post chaplain can perform the ceremony tomorrow," he told Abigail, calmly disregarding the protests of his future bride. "It will have to remain a secret for now. You can tell John, of course, but no one else."

"Tomorrow? But—do pardon me for saying so, Reeve, but isn't this all a bit sudden?"

"I'm not always the most patient of men," he conceded, with another brief smile.

"You shall receive no argument from me on that score! But what about the wedding? Surely you don't intend to deny Lorelei the pleasure of—"

"There isn't going to *be* a wedding!" cried Lorelei, furious at being ignored. She folded her arms indignantly across her breasts and declared with considerable feeling, "I am *not* going to marry you, Reeve Cameron, and I'll be hanged if—"

"Tomorrow," he cut her off masterfully. His smoldering gaze held the promise of passion as he subjected her to one last warm, intimate look, before nodding curtly at Abigail and striding away into the night.

"Lorelei Montgomery, what in Heaven's name is going on?" Abigail demanded breathlessly once he had gone. She closed the door and flew across the room to clasp one of Lorelei's hands within the comforting warmth of hers. "How did all this happen?"

"I don't know," she murmured, with a long, ragged sigh. She frowned and pulled away to sink dispiritedly into the rocking chair. "I certainly never intended for things to progress this far. It was supposed to be nothing more than a flirtation. I never, for one moment, expected . . . *this!*" Great balls of fire, how had the situation gotten so completely out of hand? she wondered, her senses still reeling.

"Well, are you going to marry him or not?"

"I most certainly am not!" Her eyes flashed as she gripped the arms of the chair. The sudden memory of what Reeve had done to her—and had attempted to do to her—in that same chair came back to taunt her with humiliating clarity. She gave an inward groan and felt her cheeks burn.

"It appears he is quite determined," Abigail pointed out unnecessarily.

"No more so than I!"

"I think you should at least give it some consideration," the other woman surprised her by advising.

"What?" She stared up at Abigail with an expression of incredulity. "How can you possibly—"

"Please, Lorelei, hear me out. It isn't every day that a man of Reeve Cameron's caliber comes along. And since he is so obviously in love with you, I think you should—"

"*Love* was never mentioned!" The thought provoked a sharp, inexplicable pain to slice through her heart.

"It wasn't?" Abigail appeared taken aback for a moment, but she quickly recovered and said with a bolstering smile, "Well, I'm sure that omission will be remedied without delay. In any case, it is clear to me that you haven't yet realized how advantageous a

175

marriage between the two of you would be."

"Advantageous?"

"Yes, and for the same reason you decided to charm him in the first place—your brother. Why, think of it, my dear! If you were married to Reeve, he would be all the more inclined to intervene on your brother's behalf."

"Abigail Merriwether, how can you suggest such a thing?" reproached Lorelei, completely appalled at the idea. "To flirt with a man on my brother's behalf is one thing, but to *marry* him?" She shook her head in a vigorous rejection, her tangled auburn curls sweeping about her shoulders. "No! No, by Heaven, I couldn't do it, not even for Hadley!"

Abigail opened her mouth to offer yet another recommendation, but was prevented from doing so by the sound of her husband's voice.

"Abigail?" He was calling angrily to her from the darkness outside.

"Good Heavens!" she gasped, flushing guiltily. She took Lorelei's hand again, her eyes full of compassion—and more than a twinge of dread. "I'm sorry, Lorelei, but I must go!" Whirling about, she hurried across to the door, then paused for a moment to opine in a breathless tumble of words, "I don't mean to be indelicate, but from what I observed when I intruded upon your 'discussion' with Reeve, there seems to be at least a small measure of affection upon which to build a marriage!"

"Abigail!"

"I'm coming, John!" she called back, grimacing nervously as she opened the door and finally slipped outside to face her husband.

Lorelei rose from the chair and crossed to the

doorway. She arrived just in time to witness Captain Merriwether take his wife's arm in a none-too-gentle grasp and propel her toward the house. They disappeared inside, the door slamming shut after them.

Offering up a silent prayer for Abigail's welfare and her own guidance, she sighed again and, leaning against the doorpost, allowed her troubled gaze to wander up toward the infinite, silver-dotted blackness of the night sky. Her mind drifted back over the events of the past three days, with particular attention given to those of the past half hour; and suddenly she realized that her life had been turned upside down from the first moment she had set eyes on Reeve Cameron.

Tomorrow, he had vowed. She shivered at the memory of his words, and the even more disturbing memory of his kisses and caresses. No matter what else she thought of him, he certainly had the ability to set her on fire. Heaven help her, she had never felt so aware of her womanhood before. Nor of its importance to men.

It was impossible, of course, she told herself, forcing her thoughts back to the issue at hand. Absolutely, unequivocally impossible. Even if she *could* consider marrying him for Hadley's sake, the solution to one problem would be the all too permanent cause of another. She would belong to Reeve, for better or for worse, until death. The prospect of spending the rest of her life with a man she scarcely knew — or loved — was frightening in the extreme.

Fears, however, have a way of being conquered.

She turned about and closed the door. Glancing down at the creased and hastily rearranged bodice of her gown, she rolled her eyes in an eloquent gesture of dismay, and hastened to get undressed. Her conscience was still waging a battle with her emotions when she climbed into bed a short time later. Sleep was remarkably fast in coming . . . but so was the dawn.

Nine

The morning flew by. And still there was no sign of Reeve.

Lorelei had already helped Abigail with breakfast, paid another visit to Hadley, made an unsuccessful attempt to speak with Colonel Jameson, and wandered about the post in the hope of finding someone who would talk to her about her brother—all before the hour of noon.

The women she had encountered were friendly enough in their way, but they had expressed complete ignorance about Private Montgomery and the charges against him. She had fared no better with the men; they had been reluctant to disclose even the smallest of details regarding the arrest of their comrade, although they had been more than willing to pay her effusive compliments, and press her for the favor of a walk, or a ride, or even, outrageously, the honor of her hand in marriage. The morning had proven to be an exercise in frustration, and it was with a heavy heart that she returned to her room and cooled her aching temples with a damp cloth.

At least she had followed Hadley's instructions about one thing—recalling his warning about the power of the conspiracy, and his fear of retaliation, she had made no mention of it to anyone. Reeve Cameron's caution against any interfering, however, was a different matter entirely. She suffered no pangs of remorse for having defied *him*.

Let the arrogant scoundrel toss her in the guardhouse if he would, she mused wrathfully, as she flung the cloth back down into the washbowl and faced her stormy-eyed reflection in the mirror above. Her efforts to help her brother were being thwarted at every turn. Indeed, the situation looked darker with each passing hour. And her sense of helpless desperation only increased whenever she thought about what had happened the night before.

If you were married to Reeve, he would be all the more inclined to intervene on your brother's behalf. Abigail's suggestion, which had at first seemed so distasteful, now began to appear more and more like the only viable solution.

Dear Lord, what else could she do? she thought, her gaze clouding with confusion and despair. There was always the hope that Reeve's investigation would result in Hadley's acquittal, of course, but the chances were just as good that the verdict would go against him. She knew she would never forgive herself if she had the means to help him all along, and chose to do nothing while he—

The possibility was unthinkable.

She turned away from the mirror and wandered distractedly to the bed, sinking down upon its quilt-covered softness. Her heart sank at the memory of her most recent visit with Hadley. His spirits had been lower than ever that morning, but still, he refused to cooperate.

Reeve Cameron wanted her. And she had little doubt that he would settle for nothing less than marriage at this point — he had made that abundantly clear.

Surely, if she *did* become his wife, it would be as Abigail had said: he would be bound to be influenced by the fact that Hadley was related to him through marriage. After all, he was a highly respected officer with strong connections to Washington; his pride and sense of duty alone would prompt him to seek mercy on behalf of a kinsman. There was also the likelihood, however slim, that he would make certain the outcome of the court-martial proved favorable.

"Lorelei Montgomery, how can you even consider doing such a despicable thing?" she challenged herself aloud. The thought of marrying a man she didn't love was contrary to everything she had always believed in. It would be so terribly unfair to both of them. She had intended to marry someday, of course, and to have a home and a family, but not like this. God help her, not like this!

She had been honest with him on that score, at least, she recalled with a heavy sigh. She had told him she didn't love him. But it hadn't seemed to make any difference. He had still been relentlessly determined to make her his bride.

Great balls of fire, what kind of man was he? she asked herself, rising abruptly to her feet and beginning to pace about the room. She had certainly never known anyone like him before. Proud, and stubborn, and infuriatingly mysterious . . . it was unbelievable that he was willing to sacrifice his future happiness in order to marry a woman he scarcely knew. The sacrifice on her part would be even greater, the motives entirely different; and yet the realization that he was willing to go to such drastic lengths to possess her made her deep blue eyes glow with wonderment and a certain perverse satisfaction.

There was still a great deal to think about, she mused with a frown of self-reproach. Even if she became so completely lost to reason as to go through with such a mercenary plan of action, what would happen afterwards?

She would be married to Reeve Cameron. He would be her husband, entitled to complete obedience and full marital rights.

"Marital rights," she whispered, and felt a tingling warmth spread throughout her entire body. She groaned in dismay and crossed back to the mirror to see that two bright spots of color stained her cheeks. One hand flew to her throat, before slipping downward to rest upon the full, rounded curve of her bosom, now modestly covered by a simple gown of sprigged cotton. The sudden, unbidden memory of Reeve's lips on her naked breasts made her knees weaken.

She couldn't allow herself to think about *that*. If she did, she knew she'd never have the courage to face the inevitable.

And inevitable it was.

Reeve finally came for her a short time after the bugler had sounded the last, mournful note of taps. The fort was calm and quiet beneath a sky rendered almost pitch-black by a heavy mantle of clouds. The scent of rain, usually a rarity during a broiling Texas summer, once again wafted softly along on the warm night wind.

Lorelei's nerves were strung so tightly that she found it impossible to sit still. She was furious with Reeve, and furious with herself as well. The past several hours had crawled by in an agonizing daze of expectation. Having begged off from supper with the Merriwethers, she had spent the entire evening wondering if Reeve had changed his mind, if she was really brave enough to make the sacrifice, and if there was some way she could persuade her new husband to postpone any "intimacies" between them, if she did indeed allow the wedding to take place.

"Tomorrow," she murmured, her gaze narrowing vengefully while she jabbed an errant hairpin back into place. Tomorrow, he had vowed. Well, the day was nearly gone. Where the devil was he?

Then as if on cue, she heard someone knock insistently on the door behind her.

She started in alarm and spun about. Her eyes flew wide. *Reeve!* It had to be him, she thought numbly. Who else would disturb her privacy at that time of night? She stood frozen to the spot, her heart pounding in her ears while frantic indecision gripped her once more.

Reeve did not wait. He swung open the door, his tall, muscular frame filling the doorway as his penetrating gaze met and locked with the luminous sapphire of hers.

"It's time, Lorelei," he decreed, his low, deep-timbred voice seeming to reverberate throughout the room. His handsome features were inscrutable, though she was certain she glimpsed the merest hint of a smile tugging at the corners of his mouth.

"Time?" she echoed weakly, then grew outraged at his smug confidence. "Do you have any idea, Major Cameron, how late it is?"

"Impatient to be wed, Miss Montgomery?" he countered, without explanation or repentance. His eyes flickered over her with a gleam of warm approval. "You'll make a beautiful bride." She detected a note of humor in his voice, which only added fuel to her anger.

"I am not going to be a bride at all!" In truth, now that the fateful moment had actually arrived, her courage had deserted her. But she would never let him know it. Lifting her head to a proudly defiant angle, she smoothed down the gathered folds of the embroidered, rose-colored sprigged gown she had donned after her bath that afternoon. "The very idea of a marriage between us is preposterous. And even if it were not, how dare you show up at this late hour and expect me to come along meekly—"

"The chaplain is waiting." Disregarding her indignation, he closed the distance between them in two long strides and took hold of her arm. "I'm sorry about the delay, but it was unavoidable."

"You—you really expect me to go through with this?" she stammered in disbelief. Sweet mercy, this couldn't be happening!

"I do." He smiled softly down at her. "Come on. John and Abigail are inside with the chaplain. I know you wish your brother could be in attendance as well, but under the circumstances . . ." He left the sentence unfinished, but Lorelei knew what he meant.

Hadley. Why, oh why did he have to go and mention Hadley? Her throat constricted. Memories, both good and bad, of their life together flooded her mind. He had been such an appealing, headstrong child; he had not really changed so much. Sudden tears sprang to her eyes at the thought, but resolutely she blinked them back.

She had vowed to do everything in her power to save him. He needed her help, needed it more than ever before. If she failed him, they would both suffer for it.

Once again, she knew she had little choice.

"Very well," she consented, in a voice that was scarcely more than a whisper. "But there's one thing I think you should know." She tilted her head back, her gaze searching his face. "One thing, Major Cameron, that must be understood between us before . . . before we are married."

"And what is that?"

All traces of amusement vanished when he saw the light of desperation in her eyes. He swore inwardly, his brow creasing into a frown. Were it not for the unwavering certainty that they were meant for one another, he might have been tempted to give her more time. But time was running out, and he'd be damned if he'd risk losing the only woman he had ever loved.

"If our situation as husband and wife should become intolerable, if we discover we are unable to find happiness together," she said, pausing to swallow a sudden lump in her throat before continuing, "then we must be free to seek an end to the union as quickly as possible."

"Are you asking me to grant you the option to divorce me?" His handsome face was dangerously grim.

"Yes."

"No."

"No? But surely—"

"No." He shook his head, and his fingers tightened their firm, unmistakably possessive grasp on her arm. "There will be no divorce, Lorelei. You're mine, now and forever."

His words threw her into a quandary. She had made the reluctant decision to marry him, and yet she didn't know how she could exchange wedding vows with a man who was obviously determined to hold her at all costs. No Montgomery had ever been divorced, and she would never have considered it under normal circumstances; but these circumstances were far from normal, and she was feeling more and more trapped . . .

Reeve, sensing her distress, lowered his head and pressed a tender, powerfully seductive kiss upon her lips. She swayed against him, closing her eyes as passion flared and the world receded.

But all too soon, the kiss ended.

"Let's go," Reeve commanded huskily, impatient to get the wedding over with.

Lorelei offered no resistance when he led her outside and across the darkened grounds to the Merriwethers' house. They entered through the back door, then headed immediately for the parlor, where John and Abigail stood talking with the post chaplain.

"Lorelei!" Abigail hurried forward to greet her with an affectionate hug. Her face was wreathed in smiles when she drew away again and pressed a bouquet of wildflowers into Lorelei's hands. "I do hope you won't mind not being married in a church, but there isn't one here at the post yet, and since this must remain a secret for now—"

"Abigail," John admonished gently. He smiled at Lorelei as well and turned to introduce the stout, somber-looking man in black beside him. "Miss Montgomery, allow me to present our post chaplain, Reverend Harmon. The bride, Reverend Harmon—Miss Lorelei Montgomery."

"I am honored to make your acquaintance, Miss Montgomery," said Reverend Harmon, his manner correctly paternal as he took her hand. He was all business when he turned to Reeve. "Well, Major?"

"We're ready," he confirmed. He clasped Lorelei's hand within the strong warmth of his and faced the chaplain. Abigail, with uncharacteristic solemnity, moved to stand beside Lorelei, and John assumed his position as best man.

It was over within a matter of minutes. Almost before Lorelei realized what was happening, Reeve was taking his new bride in his arms and claiming her lips in the traditional kiss. Except that it was a good deal longer and considerably more passionate than most wedding kisses, and it prompted the chaplain to clear his throat as a reminder that his services were required elsewhere.

"My felicitations to you both, Major," Reverend Harmon pronounced when the younger man finally allowed his new wife the much-needed opportunity to catch her breath.

"Thank you, Reverend."

"Oh, Lorelei, you are without a doubt the loveliest bride Fort Concho has ever seen!" exclaimed Abigail, bestowing another genuinely fond embrace upon her. "Don't worry, my dear!" she whispered in her ear. "Reeve has assured me that he will treat you with the utmost respect and gentleness!"

"Good Heavens, you discussed *that* with him?" she whispered back, crimsoning at the thought.

"Well no, not exactly." Abigail faced her again with a kindly, knowing look while the three men continued to talk amongst themselves. "But I'm quite sure he meant it to include every aspect of your marriage."

Respect and gentleness, Lorelei repeated silently. There had been nothing respectful about his treatment of her the night before. Gentleness, however . . . yes, there had been that, she recalled with another blush.

"I wish you all the best, Miss—Mrs. Cameron," Captain Merriwether offered, brushing her cheek with a congratulatory kiss.

"I must be going," Reverend Harmon announced on his way toward the doorway. Both Merriwethers went to see him off, leaving Lorelei momentarily alone with her new husband.

"We'll have to be careful," said Reeve. He smiled when she stared blankly up at him. "We don't want to arouse any suspicion. That's why I've decided to spend the night in town."

"You mean you're not going to—" she began, only to break off and look away as several conflicting emotions warred within her breast.

"I can't risk staying in that room of yours. Someone might see me leaving in the morning."

"No, of course you can't," she murmured. Telling herself she should feel overjoyed at the reprieve, she was dismayed to realize that it was disappointment, and not relief, washing over her. Why the devil did her heart ache so?

"I'll give you five minutes to pack your things."

"Pack my things?" Her gaze shot back up to his face. "But why?"

"Because, Mrs. Cameron," he explained in a rich, mellow tone, "I intend this night to be one we'll remember for the rest of our lives."

His words prompted a shiver to dance the length of her spine. Her eyes glowed with secret pleasure, then fell before the loving intensity of his.

"But I thought you said—" she protested.

"Surely you didn't think I'd let the simple matter of accommodations prevent me from doing my duty?" he teased. "I've arranged for us to occupy a room at the hotel. We'll have to travel there separately, of course. John has agreed to escort you. I'll join you shortly."

"The hotel?" she echoed in obvious bemusement. "But you once told me that it was entirely unsuitable!"

"Normally, it would be, but you won't be alone."

John and Abigail returned to the parlor a few moments later. As Lorelei soon learned, Reeve had taken care of everything, right down to how they would explain her relocation to Santa Angela for the night. Abigail had generously provided them with a wedding feast, packed in a basket, and John had insisted upon adding a bottle of wine—"borrowed" from the post hospital's collection of spirits kept for medicinal purposes only—to the basket's aromatic contents.

After giving his bride a quick, albeit thoroughly portentous kiss, Reeve took his leave. Lorelei, waving aside Abigail's offer of assistance, returned alone to the small building behind the house. She

189

felt strangely lightheaded, and found it difficult to concentrate while trying to decide what to pack. Finally, she tossed a few things into her carpetbag with a sigh of exasperation and hastily turned out the lamp. John came round to fetch her before she had reached the house again.

Abigail hugged her one last time, then watched as she set off on the short walk to Santa Angela with Captain Merriwether. She felt as though she had become lost in a dream, a dream from which she would surely awaken soon. But reality made itself known when she touched the gold band encircling the third finger of her left hand.

The lampposts illuminated their path until they reached the outskirts of the fort. They walked in silence across the bridge and into town, which was bustling with its usual horde of pleasure-seekers, sounds of raucous music and laughter, and a pervasive air of furious, near-desperate excitement. No one looked twice at them; it wasn't at all unusual to see a cavalryman wandering about the streets with a woman after dark. Unbeknownst to Lorelei, however, John was well prepared for any trouble that might arise. His Colt revolver was concealed beneath his dark blue coat, ready to be drawn and aimed with a deadly accuracy perfected during years of frontier duty.

Lorelei's trepidation grew as she accompanied him into the hotel. The interior was only slightly more promising than could be hoped. It was poorly lit, which might have been a blessing, and the furnishings had undoubtedly seen better days. There seemed to be a steady stream of people, mostly rough-looking men, passing through the crowded, dusty confines of the lobby, and the level of noise made it difficult for any one person to be heard.

"This way," John advised his beautiful charge. He took her arm in a purposefully solicitous grip and maneuvered her through the crowd of buffalo hunters, cowboys, and saloon girls to the narrow stairway in the far corner. Their progress was accompanied by a succession of lewd comments and open-mouthed stares, for Lorelei was noticeably out of place among the coarse revelers.

She went along with the captain in troubled silence. Her eyes filled with dismay at her surroundings; the hotel was even worse than she had been led to believe.

"It will be all right once we're upstairs," John reassured her, with a brief smile of compassion.

"Will it?" she murmured, obviously unconvinced.

They climbed a set of creaking wooden stairs and proceeded down the red-carpeted landing, pausing before a door at the very end. It was only a trifle quieter there than in the lobby; doors slammed, voices boomed, and, somewhere in the near distance, a gunshot rang out.

Apprehension was giving way to righteous fury as Lorelei swept inside the room.

Captain Merriwether hurried to light a lamp, then transferred the basket and carpetbag to the top of a small chest of drawers opposite the four-poster bed. Looking uncomfortable, he frowned and hesitated before saying, "I'm sorry, Miss Montgomery."

It was no mistake on his part that he used her maiden name, for he had left the door slightly ajar. "I know the accommodations are not what you would have wished." He cast a swift, critical glance

191

about the room, which was decorated in what had once been appealing shades of blue and gold.

"You've no need to apologize, Captain," replied Lorelei, managing a wan smile. "It certainly isn't your fault."

"I know, but I feel somewhat responsible. You see," he confessed, "it was at my suggestion that Ree—that these particular arrangements were made. I thought it would be best if, under the circumstances, you did not encounter any additional risks."

"I may not have been acquainted with him for long," she remarked in a voice edged with anger, and there was little doubt who she meant by *him,* "but I am absolutely certain that he cannot be persuaded to do anything unless it pleases him."

Feeling a sudden and desperate need to be alone, she crossed back to the door and opened it wide. A smile touched her lips when she viewed the baffled expression on Captain Merriwether's face.

"Thank you for your escort, Captain. You should be getting home now."

"But I am supposed to remain with you until—"

"I will be quite safe."

"He'll have my hide if I abandon you in this place," argued John, his eyes twinkling with both humor and perplexity. "And that is in addition to the scolding I will suffer at Abigail's hands."

"You can tell her that I was overcome with nerves," Lorelei asserted firmly. "It is not far from the truth. As for the other explanation required, I will handle it myself."

"Well, I suppose it would be ungentlemanly of me to stay where I am not wanted," he acquiesced reluctantly.

"It would." She watched as he strode past her and out into the hallway. He turned back to her with a worried frown.

"Are you sure—?"

"Quite sure."

"Very well. But I'll be downstairs in the lobby if you should need anything."

"Go home, Captain," she exhorted gently. She closed the door and leaned back against it for a moment, her gaze traveling about the room before she closed her eyes.

This was not at all how she had envisioned spending her wedding night.

Releasing a long, dispirited sigh, she wandered to the bed and sank down onto the clean but fraying and over-laundered quilt. The springs beneath the soft, lumpy mattress protested noisily under her weight. In spite of her anger and dismay, a smile of ironic amusement tugged at the corners of her mouth. She was torn between the desire to laugh at the utter absurdity of the situation, and the increasing urge to burst into tears.

It was perfectly understandable that she should be nervous; she was no different from other brides in that respect. But, Heaven help her, *other* brides weren't married secretly to men they had only known for a few days, they weren't faced with the heartbreaking prospect of pleading for their brothers' lives, and they certainly weren't sitting in the midst of some awful, broken-down hotel in the wilds of Texas, waiting for a husband who might or might not turn out to be a veritable monster.

Mercifully, the wait was a short one.

"Damn it, Lorelei, this door should have been locked."

Startled from her reverie, she leapt from the bed and whirled to face Reeve. He had slipped into the room without warning, closed the door behind him again, and now stood scowling darkly across at her.

"You might have at least had the decency to knock!" she reproached, her eyes shooting deep blue sparks. As usual, her indignation served to cast out her fear. "I suppose you have allowed Captain Merriwether to return home?"

"I have." Without further preamble, he sauntered forward and placed his own revolver on the table beside the bed. Lorelei's eyes grew round when he raised his hands and began unfastening the brass buttons of his coat.

"What—what do you think you're doing?" she stammered in a small voice, forgetting her anger with him.

"I am removing my coat," he explained, with a faint, sardonic smile. He drew it off and tossed it negligently across the foot of the bed. His loving gaze flickered over her as he unfastened the top three buttons of his long-sleeved, white cotton shirt. "You'll want a few minutes of privacy. I'll wait outside." He was already heading toward the doorway when she mentally shook herself and stepped out from her defensive position at the other side of the bed.

"No! I mean, please don't go yet." She forced a winning smile to her lips. "I thought we might talk before . . . before anything else. And I have suddenly realized that I am quite famished!" To add conviction to her words, she moved to the chest of drawers and began searching through the basket. "Abigail was remarkably generous. Why, she has provided us with chicken, and biscuits, and—"

She broke off with a soft gasp when he approached her from behind and slipped an arm about her waist. With his other hand, he reached up and slowly began pulling the pins from her hair.

"My hunger won't be satisfied with whatever you find in that basket," he murmured close to her ear.

Lorelei shivered and battled the temptation to struggle. A knot of panic tightened in her stomach, but she remained outwardly calm.

"There's something I'd like to talk to you about, Ma—Reeve," she announced, turning about to face him. Her thick, luxuriant auburn tresses tumbled down about her face and shoulders, and her eyes sparkled sweetly up at him. "Please?"

Reeve's own gaze, which had been smoldering with passion, now softened with tenderness. Though he wanted nothing more than to take his beautiful new wife to bed and love her with a vengeance, he cautioned himself to proceed slowly. If she wanted to talk first, then so be it.

"All right."

With admirable patience, he drew away from her and watched as she wandered across to the window. A pair of faded gingham curtains hung there crookedly, and the lights of the town's other establishments set the glass ablaze. Faint strains of music drifted up from below.

"Now that we are married, I would like to ask a favor of you," Lorelei began, choosing her words carefully. She clasped her hands together in front of her and tried, unsuccessfully, to keep her gaze from straying to the bed. A rosy blush stole over her face, but she lifted her head proudly and continued. "It concerns my brother."

"Your brother?" His green eyes narrowed as he folded his arms across his chest.

"Yes." She took a deep breath and charged ahead. "I am asking you to intervene on his behalf, to use your considerable influence to help him, in any way you can!"

"I'm sorry, Lorelei." There was genuine remorse in his gaze, and he frowned when he added, "I can't do that."

"Why not?" she demanded. Hastening back across the room to confront him directly, she looked up at him with eyes full of desperate, heartfelt entreaty. "I am your wife now! It would be perfectly natural for you to—"

"Natural or not, I can't do it."

"Can't? Or won't?" she challenged.

Reeve muttered an oath beneath his breath. His frown deepened as he reached out and took her arms in a firm but gentle grasp. His gaze burned down into hers.

"There's something you've got to understand, Lorelei. I can't allow anything—or anyone, for that matter—to color my judgment when it comes to my work. I was sent here to conduct an investigation, an *impartial* investigation, and that's what I'm going to do."

"Don't you care that your wife's brother might be found guilty of treason and murder? That he might hang for a crime he didn't commit?"

"Of course I care." His fingers tightened about her arms as he reminded her quietly, "I promised you I'd do my best, remember? If he's innocent, then I'll do everything I can to make sure he's cleared of all charges."

"And what if you reach the erroneous conclusion that he is guilty?" Her eyes glistened with hot, bitter tears.

"My job is to present the facts, not an opinion." He pulled her close, his arms surrounding her with their sinewy, hard-muscled warmth. "I know you love him, Lorelei. I know you can't bear the thought of losing him. But you can't ask me to forget everything I believe about duty and honor. You can't ask me to be less than what I am." He smoothed a hand across the unyielding stiffness of her back and urged, "You're going to have to trust me. And you're going to have to let justice run its course."

"I am sick of hearing about justice!" She surprised him with her vehemence when she suddenly tore herself from his grasp. Stumbling backward, she quickly regained her balance and stormed, "If there was any justice in this world, Hadley would never have been arrested in the first place!" Her voice was tremulous with disappointment as she fought back the tears. "I thought you would help me! I thought, once we were married—"

"Is that why you did it, Lorelei?" he asked in a low, deceptively even tone. "Did you marry me because of your brother?"

"What other reason could I have had?" she retorted, then grew defensive as she viewed the sudden, harsh glint in his gold-flecked eyes. "At least *my* motive was a noble one, Major Cameron! You married me only because of . . . because you wanted to *own* me!"

"You're wrong." He shook his head and moved closer again, his expression dangerously grim. "I married you because I love you."

Lorelei was stunned to hear him say it. She stared up at him in pain and confusion, hoping to read the truth in his face and yet afraid to. There was such incredible warmth in his eyes, such passion and affection, and, yes, anger. But she was too hurt to consider his declaration of love rationally. Once again, she sought refuge in fiery outrage.

"Do you really expect me to believe that? I have no doubt whatsoever that you would say anything to me to get what you wanted!"

"Damn it, you know—"

"Damn *you,* Reeve Cameron!" she cried hotly, feeling as though her whole world had come crashing down about her. "How could I have been so stupid? I wish I'd never set eyes on you! Dear God, I wish I had never gone through with this . . . this despicable charade!"

"It's no charade, Lorelei." His tone was one of deadly calm.

"Whatever it is, I certainly have no intention of allowing it to continue any longer!" she avowed.

Reeve's handsome features tightened, his gaze darkening with barely controlled fury as it raked over his bride's flushed and wrathful countenance. Her beauty was only heightened by her anger, and he found himself wanting her more than ever. But he was determined to be the master, if a benevolent one, in this marriage of theirs, and he really *would* be damned if he allowed her to continue denying what was between them.

He had expected a certain amount of conflict be-

198

cause of her brother. He had been prepared for the day when, depending on the outcome of the court-martial, she faced him with either reproach or gratitude. But he sure as hell hadn't come prepared to hear her claim that she had married him for the sole purpose of saving her brother's neck. Had it not been for the gravity of the situation, he would have been tempted to view her words with amusement.

Well, she might have been been able to convince herself that it was some grand and glorious sacrifice she had made, he concluded, his eyes darkening, but she'd never convince him. He knew the truth. He had known it that first night when he held her in his arms. And damn it, it was time she knew it, too . . .

Ten

"You're my wife now, Lorelei," Reeve pointed out, advancing on her with slow, purposeful steps.

The light of determination in his magnificent green eyes warned her of the inevitable, but she was not yet ready to surrender. Her heart still ached as a result of the disappointment she had already suffered at his hands; her wounded pride would not allow him yet another victory.

"No!" she countered defiantly, backing away from him. She gave a vigorous shake of her head, which sent her long, flame-colored locks swirling wildly about her. "I am every bit as much to blame as you, I suppose, but the fact remains that this was nothing more than a mistake, a terrible mistake, and I—I cannot be your wife!"

"You can and will."

"For Heaven's sake, don't you understand?" She paused in her desperate attempt to escape, and gazed across at him with eyes that were wide and full of an appeal for understanding—an understanding he would never give. "We were married for all the wrong reasons! It would only invite certain disaster if we were to continue with this . . . this travesty!"

"I'm willing to take my chances." A smile touched his lips as he drew relentlessly closer.

"Well *I'm* not!"

"You have no other choice." She attempted to dart past him to the other side of the bed, but he blocked her path. His hands closed about her shoulders, and a loud gasp broke from her lips when he forced her roughly about to face him. "You listen to me, you redheaded spitfire!" he commanded with affectionate gruffness. "I love you. I've never been so sure of anything in my life. You can rant and rave at me all you like, and you can try your absolute damnedest to deny it, but it won't do you any good."

"Let go of me!"

She struggled against him but he held fast, his superior size and strength making her feel terribly small and vulnerable. Her eyes were ablaze as she tilted her head back, and bright, angry color stained her cheeks. Faced with yet another humiliating defeat, she lashed out at him scornfully.

"I hate you, Reeve Cameron!"

"No you don't."

"Yes I do! And as God is my witness, if you dare to touch me again, I will never forgive you!" she threatened, her voice rising on a shrill note of panic.

"You'll never forgive me if I *don't*," he parried huskily, then crushed her to him at last. He kissed her with a fierce possessiveness that would normally have rendered her incapable of further resistance.

However, Lorelei was not so easily conquered

201

this time. Everything had changed, now that she had met with failure. She sensed that her entire future hinged on what occurred in that room. If she gave in to Reeve now, she would be lost forever. She would never be able to resume her life in Georgia again. And, perhaps worst of all, there was the fear that she would become like so many other women she had known, women who eventually served no other purpose in life than to decorate their husbands' arms.

Her own mother had been like that, but her father, bless his soul, had raised her to be independent; and how could she possibly hope to retain that independence if she submitted to someone as strong, as masterful and opinionated as Reeve Cameron?

With that highly alarming thought in mind, she brought her hands up and pushed at him with all her might, jerking her head aside at the same time.

"No! I will not let you do this!" she vowed, squirming furiously within his viselike grasp. She knew she was fighting herself as well as him, knew that if she was honest, she would admit Hadley wasn't the only reason she had allowed his whirlwind courtship to meet with such overwhelming success . . .

"*Lorelei*," he murmured by way of caution.

"Damn you! Let me go, you bastard!"

Reeve's mouth twitched with wry humor, but he sobered again quickly. He had meant to treat his bride with infinite patience, to tutor her gently in the pleasures of the marriage bed, but she was pushing his self-control beyond the limits of human endurance.

"I'm warning you, my love," he murmured in a low tone laced with desire as well as annoyance. Capturing one of her wrists, he yanked her up hard against him once more. "You'll either take advantage of the privacy I'm offering you, or I'll strip you myself."

"You wouldn't dare!" she breathed in horrified disbelief, recklessly putting him to the test.

"Wouldn't I?"

Their eyes locked in silent combat, his gleaming with a near-savage intensity, hers full of defiant, luminous, deep blue fire. If she had known him better, she would have realized that it was useless to engage him in a battle of wills and hope to win. But she had not yet truly discovered what sort of man she had married.

She gave a proud, willful toss of her auburn curls, thus sealing her own fate.

"I am going to leave now, Major Cameron," she announced with a good deal more bravado than she actually felt. "If you try to stop me, not only will I scream, but I will see to it that your superiors in Washington hear of your contemptible behavior!"

"Once again, you sweet vixen, you're forgetting a very important detail," he drawled, one eyebrow lifted mockingly. Although he had released her some moments earlier, she realized as he spoke that her skin still tingled from the warm pressure of his hands upon her.

"Oh?" she challenged, her heart pounding in

sudden dread. "And what is that?"

"You're my wife. You belong to me now, body and soul."

"I will never belong to you, Reeve Cameron, no matter what you do to me!"

"Well I intend to do plenty!"

His patience had run out. Lorelei gasped as he scooped her effortlessly up in his arms and lowered her to the quilt-covered mattress. Pushing at the broad, immovable hardness of his chest, she kicked and writhed in a frantic attempt to hurl herself from the bed. He imprisoned her body with his own, one arm holding her about the waist like a band of steel. His other hand wasted little time in reaching for the small pearl buttons running down the front of her fitted, primly high-necked dress. He flung one long booted leg across her skirts to hold both her flailing legs captive.

"Stop it!" she ordered wrathfully, desperate to thwart his threat to strip her naked. She managed to pull one of her arms free, and lifted her hand to bring it smashing forcefully against the side of his head. "Let go of me!"

Reeve swore, then seized her wrist and forced it behind her back. His handsome face was thunderous, and she felt a tremor of fear shake her when she viewed the hot, predatory look in his eyes. For a moment, she thought he meant to strike her.

"I have no desire to break your spirit, Lorelei," he proclaimed in a tense, even voice. "It's one of the many things about you I find endearing. But if you raise your hand to me one more time, you'll feel the flat of mine on your pretty bottom."

Her eyes shone with vengeful outrage. She had little doubt that his threat was a valid one.

"If you truly loved me, you would never say such a thing!" she retorted with great feeling.

"I do love you. With all my heart. But that doesn't mean I'm going to let you run roughshod over me."

"Well, I—I don't want your love, and I don't want to be married to you!"

"You were willing enough to go through with this when you thought it would help your brother," he noted ungallantly. "But we both know that wasn't the real reason you did it, don't we, Mrs. Cameron?"

"I don't know what you're talking about!"

"Yes you do. And before this night is through, you're going to face the truth."

His fingers returned to their skillful manipulation of her buttons, prompting her to renew her ineffectual struggles. It occurred to her to scream, of course, but she realized that it would serve little purpose since she was, indeed, legally wed to the man. And besides, there was serious reason to doubt anyone would either notice or care if a woman's scream was added to the pandemonium of the hotel. Cries for help were probably a commonplace occurrence in that rough, godforsaken place, she told herself resentfully.

In the end, she was powerless to stop him, though she protested loudly and very nearly without pause. It was only a matter of minutes before he had unfastened the last of the buttons and unceremoniously stripped the dress from her body.

205

Her checked muslin petticoats were the next to go, after which he turned his attention to her tightly laced, ribbon-trimmed corset.

Reeve pushed her back unceremoniously on the bed, loosening the strings with a swiftness and dexterity that made her suspect he had more than a passing knowledge of the intricate mysteries of feminine undergarments. The thought made her eyes spark with a fury that had nothing to do with the present situation.

She turned over and scrambled on to her knees, but he merely pushed her back down and tugged the corset free. Her bustle followed soon thereafter, joining the rest of the discarded clothing on the floor beside the bed. Realizing that she was clad in nothing but her chemise, drawers, and stockings, she fought him like a veritable tigress when he rolled her to her back once more.

"Stop it! This has gone *quite* far enough!" she seethed, twisting upward into a sitting position and glaring muderously at her husband through the tangled mass of curls that swept across her face. Her fiery sapphire eyes widened in startlement when he suddenly let go of her and stood upright beside the bed.

"What are—" she began, but there was no need to finish the question, for the answer became all too clear as he quickly unbuttoned his shirt and took it off. Her breasts rose and fell rapidly beneath the thin covering of her white cotton chemise as she stared up at him in dawning dismay.

Her eyes traveled with a will of their own over his magnificent, hard-muscled chest and powerful arms. His skin looked particularly smooth and bronzed in the soft lamplight. She held her breath and raised her eyes to his face again, then groaned inwardly when she saw the mocking expression on his face. She half expected him to say something, to offer some wicked, teasing remark about her fascination with his near nakedness, but he remained silent.

She watched while he tugged off his boots with an ease borne of much practice. His hands moved to the fastenings of his pants, at which time she came to life again. Rolling to the other side of the bed, she jumped up and would have fled the room if not for Reeve's timely intervention. He caught up with her before she had reached the door, slipping his arm about her waist from behind. She hurled another unladylike curse at his handsome head and tried, in vain, to pry herself loose.

"If you go out there dressed like that, Mrs. Cameron, I'll have to fight every blasted man in town to save your virtue."

"But *you're* the one who wants to . . . to steal it!"

"No, Lorelei," he insisted, forcing her around to face him again, "I don't want to steal anything from you. I want your love to be freely given."

"What?" she gasped in disbelief. Angrily she swept the curtain of wayward tresses from her face and opened her mouth to offer him another suitable defiant retort, but she never got the chance.

With an oath of impatience, Reeve lifted her in his arms and returned her to the bed. She had no chance to struggle. The lean, virile hardness of his body came down on top of her slender yet voluptuous curves, pressing her into the mattress with an accompanying creak of the springs. She raised her hands to push frantically at him, but he captured her wrists in one strong hand and held them captive above her head.

His other hand reached down to grasp the tapes of her frilly-legged drawers, which he loosened successfully while she squirmed and cried out in breathless protest. He yanked her drawers downward with merciless abruptness, leaving the gathered folds of white cotton bunched up about her knees. She crimsoned from head to toe at having her womanhood exposed to his burning gaze.

But he was not through yet. Her chemise was treated with an equal disregard for her maidenly modesty; he seized the hemline of the knee-length garment and jerked it upward. Her outrage and embarrassment increased tenfold as she felt a rush of cool air on her breasts. He pulled the chemise up over her head, off her arms, and flung it aside.

She was completely naked now, save for the drawers, a pair of black stockings, and her hightop boots. Reeve's gaze smoldered with white-hot desire as it traveled the length of her body in a bold, intimate appraisal.

"You're even more beautiful than I imagined," he murmured, his splendidly deep voice sending a delicious shiver up her spine.

She told herself that the tears stinging her eyelids were prompted by nothing more than bitter defeat. There was no denying the fact that she had lost the battle—but, as she would soon learn, losses can sometimes be turned into the sweetest of triumphs.

"I hate you for this!" she whispered brokenly.

"Then hate me. But by the devil, you *will* be mine!"

With that, he suddenly released her wrists and swept her up in his arms. The contact of bare flesh against bare flesh was both shocking and unbelievably pleasurable. Her eyes flew up to his. She felt her heart stir, felt it give a wild, inexplicabe leap, then his arms tightened about her and his warm lips claimed hers at last.

This time, there was more than enough fire to conquer whatever doubts remained in her mind. Lorelei trembled, moaning passionately as Reeve's mouth ravished the willing sweetness of hers. She entwined her arms about his neck and pressed closer, then shivered anew when she felt the undeniable evidence of his masculinity against her naked thighs. The kiss rapidly deepened and intensified, sending passion coursing like wildfire through them both.

Reeve's good intentions were shattered by a desire more intense than any he had ever known before. His plan of a slow, tender arousal became a reality of tempestuous haste as he fought to control the heat gathering in his loins.

Lorelei did not resist when his hand moved to the juncture of her slender thighs. She gasped when his fingers delved gently but urgently within the soft triangle of auburn curls, then began stroking the secret, silken flesh of her womanhood with such perfect sensitivity that she could not have put a stop to the madness even if she had wanted to. Her legs parted wider of their own accord, and her hips strained instinctively upward as her own desire blazed higher and higher.

Reeve's mouth left its delectable conquest of hers to roam ardently across her face, then trailed a tingling path downward to the beckoning curves of her naked breasts. His lips and tongue branded the satiny globes, caressing and exploring their rose-tipped fullness before his mouth closed about one of her breasts in hot, moist possession that made her moan and toss her beautiful head restlessly to and fro on the quilt.

Her breathing was a series of soft gasps as his velvety tongue darted and flicked and swirled about the nipple. He drew the delicate peak into his mouth so that his lips could suckle as greedily as a babe's while his tongue continued its tantalizing movements. Her head spun dizzily as near-painful ecstasy washed over her in great, forceful waves.

By the time Reeve began to inflict the same exquisite torture on her other breast, she was clutching almost convulsively at the bronzed muscles of his shoulders, her whole body suffused with the most captivating warmth and pleasure she had ever experienced. The sensations he was creating within her had successfully vanquished any thought of resistance or embarrassment, or even regret. She gave herself up to the wild, wicked mastery of his lovemaking, and in so doing found her innermost, carefully guarded emotions set free.

Desire flared hotter and hotter between them.

Carried away on a floodtide of passionate longing, Lorelei was certain she could bear no more. Reeve was apparently of a like mind, for he suddenly raised his head, stripped her bunched-up drawers down and off, and slipped a hand beneath his bride's alluringly rounded hips. He positioned himself above her while unfastening his pants.

"Reeve?"

Her eyes filled with a twinge of uncertainty when she felt him moving between her legs, but she didn't have long to wait or wonder. In the next instant, he began easing himself carefully into her. He summoned every ounce of self-control he possessed in an effort to spare her pain. She wriggled her hips beneath him and pushed at the waistband of his blue pants. While not intentionally seductive, the gesture prompted him nevertheless to groan and draw a shuddering breath.

"Damn it, woman, you'll drive me to madness yet!" he whispered hoarsely.

A sharp, breathless cry broke from her lips when his throbbing hardness suddenly plunged within the honeyed warmth of her feminine passage. She was surprised at the pain, but it was of mercifully short duration, giving way within seconds to a pleasure even more wondrous and irresistible than before. With consummate skill, his hips tutored hers in the age-old rhythm of love.

His thrusts grew deeper and swifter. She grasped at his powerful upper arms for support, riding the crest of passion along with him as she met his thrusts with a shameless abandon that would have shocked her, if she had been capable of rational thought.

The final blending of their bodies was achieved with the same blazing intensity with which it had begun. They soared Heavenward together, reaching the pinnacle of wild fulfillment in near-perfect unison.

Lorelei cried out, then collapsed back against the quilt while her beautiful, well-loved body trembled and her heart pounded erratically within her breast. Reeve tensed above her in the next instant. With a sharp intake of breath, he finally took his own pleasure and released his life-giving seed. She shivered as she felt it flooding her, filling her with its potent warmth. Somewhere in the recesses of her mind, she wondered how it was possible to feel conquered and triumphant at the same time.

Reluctantly, Reeve withdrew and rolled to his back on the creased, rumpled covers of the bed. Gathering his wife's pliant curves against him, he cradled her head upon his shoulder and released a long sigh of wholly masculine contentment. One arm remained wrapped about her with tender possessiveness, and his other hand rested warmly on the naked curve of her hip. Her long hair was spread across them both in glorious disarray.

In the soft afterglow of that first stormy union, Lorelei was thoroughly, breathtakingly stunned by what had just happened. The fact that she was naked seemed of no consequence at the moment; any attempt at modesty would seem irrelevent at that point.

Her sapphire gaze was clouded with a number of emotions, some of them conflicting ones. She had never been consumed with such fiery passion before, had never felt so . . . well, so *complete* in all her twenty-two years. It was little wonder that Reeve had been impatient to get her into bed, she reflected with a sigh, then blushed at the wickedness of her thoughts.

Neither of them spoke for several long moments. The music and laughter and other sounds of merrymaking continued to drift up from below, but they were each too engrossed in their own reverie to take any notice of the less than ideal surroundings. Finally, Lorelei heard her new husband give a soft chuckle.

"We're well-matched in every way, sweet vixen," he remarked, his green eyes brimming with love, amusement, and supreme satisfaction.

"I don't know what you're talking about!" She did, of course, but there was something about the way he'd said it that made her bristle.

She was rewarded for this display of defiance with a loud, familiar slap on her bare bottom, at which her eyes flew wide and a sharp gasp of indignation escaped her lips. She pushed herself up on one elbow to glare reproachfully at Reeve, but he pulled her back down and ran his hand in bold appreciation over the soft, provocatively rounded flesh that still bore a faint reminder of his playful chastisement.

"Taming you won't be easy," he murmured in a low, resonant tone that sent a delicious warmth stealing over her again. "Hell, I knew you'd be the worst kind of distraction. But I never counted on loving you this much, Lorelei."

Sudden tears sprang to her eyes. She offered him no response, but lapsed instead into pensive silence once more as his words burned in her mind. Plagued by confusion, she told herself she didn't know what to believe. There was no way to explain anything that had happened. She had professed to hate him one moment, but the next she had behaved like a virtual strumpet in his arms. The memory of his fierce yet loving mastery of her body, and her own shameless response, made her face flame anew. It also made her pulses give a wild leap.

Dear Lord, what am I going to do? she wondered. She was Reeve Cameron's wife now, in every sense of the word. There was certainly no getting around that. They were married, and he had a perfect right to command her obedience in all matters. The thought gave her little comfort.

She sighed again and closed her eyes. Reeve had said he loved her. Why did she want to believe him so badly? And why did her heart ache so at the possibililty that what he felt was really nothing more than simple, fleeting desire?

"I give you my word, Mrs. Cameron — as soon as my assignment here is completed, I'm taking you to New Orleans for a real honeymoon," he vowed, dropping a light kiss on the top of her head as he pulled her even closer.

His assignment, Lorelei repeated inwardly, her silken brow creasing into a disconsolate frown. His assignment was the reason they were together right now . . .

Her eyes glowed with renewed determination

when an idea suddenly occurred to her. Perhaps she hadn't failed Hadley after all.

"Reeve?"

"Yes?"

"You didn't really mean it when you said you wouldn't help my brother, did you?"

Her voice was soft and appealing, and she offered a subtle encouragement by trailing a hand across the bronzed, lightly matted expanse of his chest. Their lovemaking had bestowed her with a new sense of power, emboldening her to such an extent that she was willing to use her feminine wiles to her best advantage.

"If you love me as much as you say you do," she added, "then—"

"I do love you," he reiterated with quiet authority. "But I meant every word."

"You couldn't have!" she insisted. She raised herself up again so that her eyes could travel over the solemn, rugged perfection of his features. Her hair tumbled down about her face and shoulders, spilling across his naked chest. "Please, you've got to listen to me! Hadley is innocent—I know he is! And you're the only one who can help him!"

"Lorelei—" His eyes were glinting somberly and his lithely muscled frame had tensed beside her.

"Please, Reeve! I'm asking you to do it for *me*. I'm your wife now, and—"

"I thought we had settled this."

With startling abruptness, he set her away from him and rose from the bed. She scrambled up to her knees, watching with a mixture of bemusement

215

and angry frustration as he quickly fastened his pants and moved to the chest of drawers. He drew out the bottle of wine, opened it, and poured a small amount of the dark red liquid into one of the glasses Abigail had provided.

"It's getting late. I'll have to leave soon." He downed the wine and tried to ignore the pain in his heart. "I've arranged for someone I trust to keep an eye on you while I'm gone."

"But why are you leaving?" She tugged the quilt up over her nakedness now, clutching it to her breasts.

"Are you anxious for me to remain, Mrs. Cameron?" He turned back to face her with a faint, sardonic smile. His eyes darkened as they took in the sight of her beguiling dishevelment.

"Why should I be?" she retorted, lifting her head proudly. It seemed an incongruous gesture, given the fact that she was wearing nothing more than a frayed quilt. But, she reflected, she was supposed to be coaxing sweetly, not condemning shrewishly. Before he could answer, she sighed and added, with genuine regret, "It's just that I . . . we've had so little time to get to know one another."

"I'd say we know one another pretty well," he disputed, a gleam of roguish humor joining the glow of desire in his penetrating gaze. A faint, rosy blush tinged the smoothness of Lorelei's cheeks.

"You still haven't told me why it's necessary for you to leave."

"I've got work to do."

216

"At this hour of the night?" she asked in disbelief.

"I've found that men are willing to talk more readily after dark," he explained. "Especially when they've had a few drinks."

He set the glass down and crossed back to stand beside the bed. Lorelei stared up at him in breathless expectation, her fingers tightening their hold on the quilt.

"Are—are you leaving right this minute?" she stammered.

"Do you want me to stay?" Reeve responded softly.

He battled the impulse to reach out and yank the quilt free so that his eyes could drink their fill of her womanly charms. From what he had seen thus far, he knew she was beautiful enough to tempt a saint—and Heaven knew, he was no saint. He had every intention of making the most of the time left to them, but he longed to hear her say something, anything, that would indicate she was beginning to realize that her mercenary little heart had been captured right along with her sweet, damnably alluring body.

He knew she loved him. He also knew she was still reluctant to admit it. But now that she was his, he told himself, he could afford to be patient. At least for the next few days.

Lorelei, meanwhile, stared speechlessly up at him. She had meant to use physical temptation to bring him into accordance with her wishes, yet now that the opportunity presented itself, she was unable to proceed. The role of seductress was an

217

unfamiliar one, and she wasn't at all certain she had either the courage or the capability to play it.

"Well?" Reeve prompted.

"If you stay, I suppose you'll want to . . . to make love to me again?" She colored, her eyes falling beneath the loving amusement of his.

"You suppose correctly."

"Very well." She swallowed hard and arranged the quilt more securely about her, then said, with remarkable calm under the circumstances, "I have a proposal I want you to consider."

"A proposal?" The gleam in his eyes deepened.

"Yes." Her gaze traveled back up to meet his again, and she experienced a moment's hesitation before revealing, "I will agree to share your bed, without further resistance, if you will in turn agree to make a positive recommendation to the proper military authorities on my brother's behalf."

"No, Lorelei."

"No?" It wrenched her heart painfully, and did a great deal of damage to her pride as well, to think that her offer of willing participation in their lovemaking held so little attraction for him. As she would soon learn, however, that wasn't the case at all.

"No." Without another word, he began unfastening his pants again.

"Why not?" A knot of apprehension tightened in her stomach.

"Because, as I told you once before, you'll give me your love freely. There will be no bargains between us, Lorelei. Not now, not ever. I can't really blame you for what you're trying to do, but it's

218

time you accepted the situation for what it is."

"Perhaps, Major Cameron, you'll be gracious enough to tell me — exactly what *is* the situation?" she demanded with bitter sarcasm, stung by yet another failure.

"You're mine. And I hold what's mine."

He waited no longer before stripping off his pants. Lorelei gasped and hastily averted her gaze. Still clutching the quilt, she moved as far to the other side of the bed as possible. She toyed briefly with the idea of taking flight, but knew it was hopeless. Just as before, her husband would have his way with her. And, Heaven help her, she would be set afire by his touch.

Completely naked now, Reeve joined her on the bed. He wasted little time in carrying out his plan to make up for the tempestuous haste with which he had taken her earlier. The first thing he did was seize the quilt and send it flying to the foot of the bed.

Lorelei cried out in protest and made a furious attempt to preserve her reclaimed modesty. Folding her arms across her breasts, she clamped her knees together and rolled to one side. She stole a glance back over her shoulder at Reeve. Crimsoning, she looked away again when her eyes fell upon his manhood, which sprang from a cluster of tight brown curls between his lean, hard thighs.

"Look at me, Lorelei," he commanded, his deep voice laced with that devilish combination of passion and amusement that she had already come to know so well. When she refused to obey, he took her shoulders in a firm grasp and turned her to face him, where he knelt in the center of the bed.

"No!" She shook her head vehemently, then asked tremulously, "Are you really so lost to all sense of decency that you would take me by force again?"

In answer he grabbed her wrists and pulled her up to her knees before him. His searing gaze raked over her exposed loveliness, lingering with particular, disquieting significance on her breasts.

She grew warm all over and couldn't keep her eyes from straying to his naked, unmistakably virile body. The powerful muscles in his chest and arms suggested that he could have—and *had,* in fact, on more than one occasion—defended himself ably against any man foolish enough to cross him. Her fascinated gaze traveled downward, moving over a taut, flat belly, a pair of hard-muscled thighs, and legs that were long and athletic . . .

Her gaze was drawn back to the instrument of his passion, and she blushed anew. Although she didn't possess a great deal of knowledge upon which to base her comparison, she knew with a certainty that her husband's body was a magnificent specimen of hot-blooded masculinity.

Another loud gasp escaped her when he suddenly pulled her arms behind her back and brought her up hard against him. He smiled faintly.

"Force?" The word was a mocking challenge on his lips. His gold-flecked green eyes, at once piercing and unfathomable, seemed to bore into her very soul. "I won't have to force you, my love."

And he set about proving his point in a way

that would prove satisfactory, and highly pleasurable, to them both.

Lorelei had expected their second union to be as swift and stormy as the first, but she soon discovered that Reeve intended otherwise. He proceeded to make love to her with a slow, captivating thoroughness that resulted, as he desired, in making her beg for mercy.

She was startled to find herself being turned over and pressed face-down upon the bed. Startlement turned to shock and embarrassment when she felt Reeve's mouth trailing hotly over her saucy bottom. She wriggled in a halfhearted attempt to stop him, but he would not be denied. His hands gripped her about the hips, holding her captive while his eyes glowed with tenderly wolfish intent.

Her face flamed as his lips made a full, tantalizing exploration of her well-rounded buttocks. His teeth gently nipped while his tongue administered a series of light strokes across the satiny flesh. She moaned and squirmed restlessly on the bed, her arms tightening about the pillow beneath her head.

"You've got a beautiful backside, Mrs. Cameron," Reeve murmured huskily.

His mouth traveled upward, roaming over the slender, graceful curve of her back as his hand swept the luxuriant mass of auburn curls aside. He pressed one last kiss on her neck, then turned her over and finally captured her lips with his own. She inhaled sharply at the contact of his naked hardness, which fit atop her supple curves with such sensuous perfection that it seemed they had been destined for one another after all.

A marriage made in Heaven, an inner voice mused. It had to be true, at least in this one way, she conceded dazedly, since Heaven and earth joined together whenever Reeve took her in his arms . . .

She pulled him close, her body straining instinctively upward against his while she kissed him back with all the fire and passion he had awakened within her. Her tongue boldly parried the provocative thrusts of his, and the feverishness with which her arms tightened about him let him know that desire had blazed to life in her with a sweet vengeance once more.

But, still determined to make her burn to the extent that she would forget her stubborn pride and implore him to take her, Reeve ended the kiss and slid purposefully downward on her body. He brought his hands up to close about the satiny fullness of her breasts, and his warm, strong fingers kneaded her flesh gently before his mouth came down to pay moist, loving tribute. His lips closed about one of the quivering peaks, his tongue flicking back and forth across the nipple.

Lorelei gasped, her eyelids fluttering closed as she trembled and felt her senses reeling. Her blood turned to liquid fire within her veins as Reeve teased and caressed and suckled at her breasts with merciless resolve. She clutched at his broad shoulders, her fingers spreading across his heated, golden skin while she struggled for breath and arched her back.

Her eyes flew open when Reeve's lips seared even farther downward. He bestowed a series of soft, yet highly stimulating kisses as he went. His tongue dipped within the delicate hollow of her navel, prompting her to gasp again and squirm at the delectable sensation. His mouth glided across the silken planes of her abdomen, then moved lower still . . .

Her gaze filled with shocked dismay when she realized his intent.

Sweet mercy, she thought, surely he didn't mean to kiss her *there?* She had never imagined that a man would do such things to a lady, even if that lady was his wife.

She pounded insistently at his shoulders, but his hands were already parting her pale, slender thighs. Trying to roll to her side, she found her efforts thwarted when his hands seized her hips in an iron grip.

"Reeve, no!" she breathed, her blue eyes growing enormous in her flushed face.

"Oh yes," he decreed, an undercurrent of loving irony in his tone.

Lorelei caught her lower lip between her teeth, but was unable to stifle a moan of sheer, heart-stopping passion. She closed her eyes and threaded her fingers within the sun-streaked thickness of Reeve's hair. What he was doing was wicked, so utterly wicked and surely forbidden . . . and it was downright heavenly.

"Please!" she gasped out, her head tossing to and fro on the pillow as white-hot desire threatened to overwhelm her completely.

"Tell me what you want, Lorelei," her handsome tormentor commanded, his fingers taking over as he slid upward on her body once more.

"Reeve!"

"Say it!"

"Damn you, I—I want you to—to take me!"

"With pleasure, my love," he murmured in triumph.

He caught her up against him and suddenly rolled to his back. Lorelei frowned in confusion and pushed herself upward, wondering how they would possibly manage in that position, but she need not have worried. In the next instant, Reeve lifted her hips and brought her down upon his throbbing hardness, his manhood sheathing to the hilt within her velvety warmth.

There was no pain this time, only pleasure. She grasped at his arms for support, her long hair cascading down about them both. His hands and lips launched yet another rapturous assault upon her breasts while she rode atop him. The rotation of his hips beneath hers steadily increased, his slow, gentle thrusts growing swifter and more forceful. Their hearts and bodies, and perhaps even their souls, joined together in a wild, sweet vortex of fulfillment that easily surpassed what had come before.

Reeve was unable to tarry for long afterwards. Cursing the fact that it was necessary for him to leave his bride alone on their wedding night, he quickly washed up with the soap and water provided on the washstand, then dressed and pulled on his boots.

Lorelei had tugged the quilt up over her again. She felt both languid and inordinately happy.

MORE PASSION AND ADVENTURE AWAIT... YOUR TRIP TO A BIG ADVENTUROUS WORLD BEGINS WHEN YOU ACCEPT YOUR FIRST 4 NOVELS ABSOLUTELY *FREE* (AN $18.00 VALUE)

Accept your Free gift and start to experience more of the passion and adventure you like in a historical romance novel. Each Zebra novel is filled with proud men, spirited women and tempestuous love that you'll remember long after you turn the last page.

Zebra Historical Romances are the finest novels of their kind. They are written by authors who really know how to weave tales of romance and adventure in the historical settings you love. You'll feel like you've actually gone back in time with the thrilling stories that each Zebra novel offers.

GET YOUR FREE GIFT WITH THE START OF YOUR HOME SUBSCRIPTION

Our readers tell us that these books sell out very fast in book stores and often they miss the newest titles. So Zebra has made arrangements for you to receive the four newest novels published each month.

You'll be guaranteed that you'll never miss a title, and home delivery is so convenient. And to show you just how easy it is to get Zebra Historical Romances, we'll send you your first 4 books absolutely FREE! Our gift to you just for trying our home subscription service.

BIG SAVINGS AND FREE HOME DELIVERY

Each month, you'll receive the four newest titles as soon as they are published. You'll probably receive them even before the bookstores do. What's more, you may preview these exciting novels free for 10 days. If you like them as much as we think you will, just pay the low preferred subscriber's price of just $3.75 each. *You'll save $3.00 each month off the publisher's price.* AND, your savings are even greater because there are never any shipping, handling or other hidden charges—FREE Home Delivery. Of course you can return any shipment within 10 days for full credit, no questions asked. There is no minimum number of books you must buy.

Too tired to examine her emotions, she was content, for the moment at least, to lie abed and watch her husband.

"I probably won't be able to make it back before morning," he said, with obvious regret. "I'll come by after sunup to walk you back to the Merriwethers'."

"But won't that look suspicious?"

"Not if I've made a point of being seen at the post first." He finished buttoning his jacket, retrieved his Colt revolver, and told her firmly, "You're to stay in this room, understand?"

"What if I feel the need for a bath?" she asked, then realized that was exactly what she *did* feel.

"You'll have to make use of the facilities here in the room," he replied, nodding toward the washstand. His green eyes filled with a roguish light when he added, "I'd stay and do the job personally if duty wasn't calling me elsewhere."

"Haven't you done enough for one night?" she retorted, her eyes flashing up at him.

"Not by a damn sight."

He smiled, and leaned down to drop a quick kiss on her forehead, then left, making sure the door was locked behind him. Lorelei was tempted to call after him, but quelled the impulse and pulled herself up into a sitting position on the bed.

Wedded and bedded . . . and deserted, she mused with a long, disgruntled sigh. Why the blazes had Reeve insisted she spend the night at the hotel if he knew he was going to have to leave her alone within a few hours' time?

"You know very well why," she murmured aloud, frowning as another fiery blush stained her cheeks.

He had wanted to make love to her, of course. He had vowed to make their wedding night unforgettable, and he had certainly succeeded.

Angrily she flung back the covers, slid from the bed, and began gathering up the articles of her clothing that were strewn about the room. With disturbing clarity, she recalled how they had been stripped from her body. She muttered the same oath Reeve had used earlier and wandered distractedly to where her carpetbag rested beside the picnic basket. Following a brief search through its hastily packed contents, she pulled out a gingham wrapper and drew it on over her nakedness.

It was while she was tying the belt at her waist that a sudden impulse took her to the door. Having flown across the room and unlocked it, she eased it open, bent her head slightly and peered out into the hallway.

Her eyes widened in surprise when they fell upon a burly raven-haired man of indeterminate age sitting in a chair only a short distance away. He turned his head at the sound of the latch. He was dressed in civilian clothing, but she knew instinctively that he was the one Reeve had charged with the duty of keeping an eye on her.

"How do, ma'am," he drawled with a tip of his hat. A broad grin split his face beneath a thick black moustache.

Lorelei nodded mutely in response, then closed and locked the door again. It was obvious that she would indeed be remaining at the hotel. And there was always the chance that Reeve might come back . . .

Chiding herself for the traitorous direction of her thoughts, she poured fresh water from the pitcher into the bowl, reached for the sponge, and took up the cake of unscented lye soap. Then she virtually tore off the wrapper and set about scrubbing her body from head to toe.

Her skin was pink and glowing by the time she had finished bathing. She donned the wrapper again and wandered distractedly to the window. A flash of lightning suddenly streaked across the sky, followed seconds later by a resounding clap of thunder. She jumped at the sound and cast an anxious look toward the pitch-black sky. The storm blowing in would be a perfect match for her mood.

There was no sense in crying over spilled milk, as her grandmother would have put it. True, she was married to Reeve Cameron now. And she had reacted with shameful abandon to his lovemaking. But nothing that had happened would make any difference when it came to her brother.

Tomorrow, she vowed, her sapphire eyes filling with the light of determination once more. She was through with talking; the time had come for her to *do* something.

Eleven

Lorelei slept little, finally awakening for good shortly after dawn. She didn't know whether to be disappointed or relieved that her husband had not returned, but she told herself it didn't matter. She intended to be gone by the time he came for her that morning.

Quickly dressing, she took up her carpetbag and paused to cast one last bemused glance about the room. Several conflicting emotions played across her face as she looked at the bed.

"Mrs. Cameron," she whispered. The name still sounded foreign to her ears. No one but Reeve would call her that for now, and then only when they were alone.

Her eyes closed for a moment. If she removed the wedding band from her finger, it might just be possible to pretend the whole night had never happened. It was a silly thought, of course, she told herself with a small, humorless smile. Even if she could somehow manage to deceive her mind, it would be impossible to deny the evidence of her body. She was plagued by an embarrassing soreness; she ached in places she hadn't even known to exist before.

Groaning at the sudden, highly disconcerting reminiscence, she proceeded to the door of her room. The hotel was filled with an eerie silence at that early hour of the day. Most of its patrons were either sleeping off a night of drunken revelry or had taken themselves down the street to Miss Hattie's and never returned.

Lorelei carefully unlocked the door and eased it open, seeking and immediately finding the man who had maintained a vigilant watch over her all night long. Now, however, he had fallen asleep in the chair. A soft smile of irony touched her lips as her eyes traveled over his burly frame, which looked a good deal less threatening in repose. Offering up a silent prayer of thanksgiving for this unhoped-for piece of luck, she slipped from the room and closed the door behind her.

She crept as quietly as possible along the hallway, past her slumbering guard, and all the way down the upper landing to the staircase. There was no way to keep the steps from creaking beneath her feet, so she flew downstairs and across the lobby without looking back. The desk clerk came halfway out of his chair when he caught sight of her, but he shrugged to himself and sank back down again as she flung open the door and disappeared outside.

Lorelei stood on the boardwalk in front of the hotel, battling indecision. She knew only one person in town—Charity Pardee. Though she was loath to even think about setting foot in such a place as Miss Hattie's, she told herself there was no other way.

Desperate situations required desperate measures, and time was running out. Hadley refused to cooperate, Colonel Jameson refused to listen to reason, and Reeve had made it painfully clear that his feelings for her, whatever they were, would in no way influence his resolve to follow the military's usual course of justice. She had spent much of the night lost in contemplation of the matter—when she hadn't been thinking about her new husband—and had finally hit upon the idea that now prompted her to fix her bright, purposeful gaze on the sign hanging in front of the two-storied building a short distance away.

Gathering up her skirts with one hand and clutching her carpetbag with the other, she set off down the boardwalk. Last night's brief but impressively thunderous storm had settled the dust and left behind a somewhat cooler morning. Daylight revealed a main street that was practically deserted. A few horses remained tied in front of the saloons, and a wagon laden with buffalo hides sat waiting near the general store. Only a handful of men were up and about, and the majority of them appeared to be in dire need of a bath and a good night's sleep.

She saw no cavalrymen; she could only suppose that they were required to return to the post before reveille sounded. That thought was quickly followed by a sudden vision of Reeve's handsome face. Wondering if he had spent the entire night questioning men in the saloons, she frowned and tightened her grip on the carpetbag. The man she had married was still little more than a stranger . . .

A sharp gasp broke from her lips when a hand suddenly shot out to grasp at the hemline of her skirt. She looked down to see a young cowboy, apparently emerging from a drunken stupor, lying in the narrow space between two saloons. She jerked

230

her skirt free, then was startled to realize that her assailant was known to her.

"Virgil?" she uttered in disbelief. Her gaze immediately filled with concern. "For Heaven's sake, Mr. Baker, what are you doing here?"

"I don't know," he rasped truthfully. Staggering to his feet at last, he moaned and raised his hands to his aching head. His eyes, red-rimmed and bloodshot, focused on her face with some difficulty as he leaned heavily against one of the buildings. "Miss Montgomery?" It was his turn to look surprised. He turned beet-red with embarrassment, his eyes falling guiltily. "Aw hell — I mean, I didn't know it was you, Miss Montgomery."

"Are you all right?"

"Yes, ma'am." Grimacing as he leaned over, he snatched up his crumpled hat and used it to slap some of the dust from his clothes. "I must've fallen asleep."

"Shouldn't you be getting home now?" she suggested kindly, then cast a quick glance about. "Did you ride into town?" At his sheepish nod, she asked, "Well, then, do you remember where you left your horse?"

"I think I —" He broke off and swallowed hard before confessing, "I left it down at Miss Hattie's."

"What a fortunate coincidence," she remarked, a brief smile of wry humor touching her lips. "It so happens that I am on my way there at this very moment. Perhaps you would care to accompany me?"

"You're goin' to Miss Hattie's?" Visibly thunderstruck by her announcement, he ventured, "If you don't mind my askin', why in tarnation would a lady like you want to go in a place like *that?*"

"Because I need to speak to Miss Pardee." She hesitated a moment before explaining, "I am seeking information relating to a . . . a personal matter, and I believe she might be able to help me."

Virgil, still looking a good deal the worse for wear, nonetheless reached out and gallantly took her carpetbag. His legs were a trifle unsteady as he walked beside her, and he was grateful for the fact that they didn't have to travel far. Upon reaching Santa Angela's most infamous establishment, he opened the door and waited for Lorelei to precede him inside, then took himself off upstairs, saying he would find Charity for her.

Lorelei stood alone just inside the doorway, filled with curiosity as her gaze made a quick, encompassing sweep of the place. The downstairs portion of the building was obviously a saloon, and she was surprised to note the ornate furnishings. A huge gilded mirror hung on the panelled wall above a long, brass-trimmed bar. Half a dozen crystal chandeliers, unlit at the moment, were suspended from a pressed tin ceiling. A number of tables and chairs offered men the choice of poker, blackjack, or several other games of chance. Everything was neat and orderly; the only evidence of the previous night's wild celebration were the five new bulletholes in the floor near the roulette wheel.

"Charity said you could come on up," Virgil called down to her from the upper landing.

She raised her eyes and saw him leaning over the carved balustrade. He smiled and beckoned to her. Retrieving her carpetbag from beside the door, she approached the narrow, carpeted staircase and hesitated only briefly before climbing to the second floor. The smell of perfume, which had been pleasantly faint at the foot of the stairs, grew so strong as to make her wrinkle her nose in distaste by the time she reached the top step.

"I figure you'll probably want to talk to her alone," said Virgil, hastening forward to meet her. "But I'll stay if you—"

"No, thank you. I'll be perfectly safe."

She was, in truth, quite apprehensive about being there, but she consoled herself with the thought that it was now broad daylight and she had yet to encounter anyone at all. Everything was quiet, and the soft morning sunlight was streaming in through windows hung with lace curtains and red velvet drapes. There was certainly nothing to indicate danger of any sort. Her ears detected the sound of two women's voices at the far end of the landing, and she turned back to Virgil with a quizzical look.

"Which room is Miss Pardee's?"

"Third one on the left. Are you sure you don't want me to wait? Hell's bells, Miss Montgomery, I hate to go off and leave you here all alone!" Being young and in excellent health, he was already well on the road to recovery, and he liked the idea of staying there to protect her. But she wouldn't hear of it.

"I won't be staying long," she reassured him. "Besides, I'm quite sure your uncle will be expecting you back at the ranch."

"You've got the right of things there, ma'am. I was supposed to come on back last night," he confided, with a lopsided grin, then gave a sigh of resignation. "All right then, I'd better find my horse and get goin'. Maybe I'll run into you again some-time."

Lorelei thanked him once more and offered him her hand, which he proceeded to shake vigorously. Her mouth curved into a faint smile of indulgence as she watched him hurry down the staircase and out the door, but her eyes clouded with uneasiness when she started moving down the hallway toward the room he had pointed out to her.

"Miss Pardee?" she called out tentatively, her hand poised to knock as she stood before the door.

"Come in!" Charity called out from inside the room. "It ain't locked!"

Lorelei obediently opened the door. The first thing she noticed was that the entire room was an overwhelming blaze of crimson. Everything, from the curtains and wallpaper to the carpet and lamp-shades, was red. The only relief was provided by Charity herself, who lay stretched out on a velvet chaise in nothing but her white cotton undergar-ments.

"Hello, Miss Pardee," Lorelei said calmly.

"I never thought we'd be meetin' one another here, Miss Montgomery!" the buxom blonde re-sponded with a deep, throaty laugh.

She rose to her feet, wandered leisurely across the room to pause beside a canopied brass bed, and tossed a flimsy, pink gauze wrapper about her plump shoulders. Her eyes held an unmistakable spark of jealousy when they moved over Lorelei's trim figure, which was clad in a becoming gown of pale blue muslin.

"What is it you wanted to see me about?" Charity demanded sharply.

"I am looking for someone," proclaimed Lorelei, lowering her carpetbag to the floor. She was unable to keep her eyes from straying to the bed.

"What makes you think I know where they are?"

"To be perfectly honest with you, Miss Pardee, you are my last hope." She walked over to take a seat upon the chaise the other woman had just vacated. With an expression of heartfelt appeal, she looked at Charity and began, "You will no doubt recall that my reason for coming to Fort Concho was to visit my brother."

"Yes," Charity replied with a nod. She folded her arms across her ample bosom and prompted, with a touch of impatience, "Go on."

"My brother, Private Hadley Montgomery, was arrested for murder and treason a few weeks ago. I came as soon as I received word of it, of course, and . . . well, for reasons I cannot reveal, my brother has refused to cooperate with the investigation launched a few days ago."

"Why?" countered the blonde, eyeing her suspiciously. "Because he's got something to hide?"

"No! No, it isn't like that," Lorelei insisted. She frowned and rose to her feet. "You must believe me, Miss Pardee—my brother is innocent!"

"Why should I care one way or the other?"

"Because I need your help!" She released a heavy, ragged sigh and struggled to maintain her composure. It was impossible to deny the hostility in the other woman's attitude, but she was determined to win her over. "Please, Charity, you must hear me out!"

"All right," Charity agreed, with obvious reluctance. "But I'm bone-weary and dog-tired, so you'd

235

better do some fast talkin'." As if to emphasize the point, she took a seat on the edge of the bed and turned to rearrange the satin, lace-trimmed pillows atop the matching coverlet.

"I *am* sorry to intrude upon you this way, but I had no one else to turn to. And I thought, since you have no doubt become acquainted with a number of men here in—"

"Acquainted?" echoed the blonde, then smiled mockingly at Lorelei's faint flush. "I guess you could say that."

"I am looking for someone to help me arrange my brother's escape!" Lorelei blurted out finally.

She couldn't think of one good reason why she should trust the woman, or why she thought Charity would be able to provide her with a name. But she had exhausted all other options, and the idea had seemed worthy enough when she had hit upon it last night. What else was she to do? she thought in growing desperation. In less than a week's time, the court-martial would take place. The Montgomerys had always been honorable, law-abiding citizens, and yet she couldn't stand by the family's good name and do nothing, while her brother swung at the end of a rope.

You'll have to trust me, Reeve had said. Well, she couldn't do that. Not with something as important as Hadley's life. And not when her dear, damnably obstinate husband had made it known that his loyalties lay with the cavalry instead of with his own wife.

"Hell, honey, you ain't really serious?" Charity inquired, with a mixture of amusement and disbelief. She had shifted back around on the bed, and Lorelei's heart stirred with hope when she saw the glow of interest in the woman's eyes.

"I most certainly am!" she hastened to confirm. "I've tried pleading with — with the proper authorities, and there isn't much time! Do you know of anyone who might be able to help me?"

"Well, I don't know. Let me think on it a minute," murmured Charity. Lorelei waited in breathless anticipation while the other woman appeared to be giving the matter a great deal of consideration. Finally, her brow cleared. "How much are you willin' to pay?"

"Does that mean you've thought of someone?" asked Lorelei, her pulses leaping, while her eyes kindled with triumphant satisfaction.

"Maybe. But I don't know if he'll take on something like this. It's pretty risky. Matter of fact, I don't think you know what you're gettin' yourself into. Them soldier boys over there across the river won't take kindly to havin' anyone, 'specially a woman, make off with one of their prisoners. You might care to give it some thought — what would happen to you if you was unlucky enough to get caught, I mean."

"I am perfectly willing to take any risk involved! Now please, who — "

"You still haven't told me what you can pay," Charity reminded her.

"I haven't got much right now," admitted Lorelei. "But as soon as we reach our destination, I should be able to raise the remainder of the funds." She still had her mother's diamond and emerald brooch; it was easily worth a hundred dollars. "I can promise at least fifty dollars," she told Charity, hoping

237

the amount would be sufficient. She and Hadley would need money afterwards.

"Well, I don't know," the blonde responded, frowning thoughtfully again. "I'm probably doin' you more harm than good by this. The man's a rough sort, to be sure. You'll have to keep an eye on him. But so long as your brother's there . . ."

"What is his name? And where can I find him?"

"His name's Dugan. He'll still be sleepin' it off over at the hotel until noon or after."

The hotel, Lorelei repeated silently, then smiled at the irony of it.

"You can tell him I sent you," Charity added. Her own eyes shone with wry humor. "He ain't exactly what you'd call a friend, but we've done a bit of business together in the past."

"Thank you," said Lorelei. Her skirts rustled gently as she crossed the room and took the other woman's hand in an appreciative clasp with both of hers. "It is quite possible, Miss Pardee, that you have saved my brother's life!" she declared with a warm, grateful smile. "If you should ever need my help in any way—"

"Don't trouble yourself," the woman cut her off brusquely, as though embarrassed by her gratitude. "You said yourself I was your last hope. We both know you wouldn't have given me the time of day if it hadn't been for that."

"I'm not at all sure that's true, but I will never forget what you have done for me." She released her hand, moved back to pick up the carpetbag, and paused in the doorway. There was no need to caution Charity to secrecy, but she was curious about one thing. "I've no wish to pry, Miss Pardee, but would you mind telling me why you agreed to help?"

"I've got a brother myself," the weary-looking blonde answered, in a voice that was barely audible.

Lorelei started to say more, but decided against it. She left the room and turned back toward the staircase, anxious to return to the hotel and find the man called Dugan. If she could reach an agreement with him, and if things could be arranged on such short notice, there was a chance the escape could take place later that same day, sometime after nightfall.

Of course, she recalled with a troubled frown, pausing on the stairs, she had as yet to convince Hadley. He might voice stiff opposition to her admittedly desperate scheme, but she was convinced she could persuade him to go along with her. Her sapphire eyes glistened at a sudden memory. Hadley had told her that a crucial witness, perhaps the only man who could save him, had deserted and taken off for New Mexico Territory.

Very well, she decided then and there, they would head for New Mexico Territory and search for the man — Taggart was the name, wasn't it? — with the hope of bringing him back to Fort Concho to provide the testimony that would clear Hadley. Once they had proven the existence of the deadly conspiracy, surely the cavalry would understand why such drastic means had been necessary. There was always the possibility that, once he learned she had been right about her brother all along, Reeve would agree to help smooth things over with his superiors in Washington.

Strangely enough, she hadn't given serious

thought to what would happen between Reeve and herself once the source of their greatest conflict no longer existed. She would stay at the post long enough to see Hadley honorably discharged, or reassigned to another post if he insisted upon remaining in the cavalry, even after all he had suffered, and then —

Then what? she wondered. There was no doubt in her mind that Reeve would be absolutely furious with her for her part in the escape. Assuming he ever told anyone they were married, she would be a terrible blight upon his career. He might never be able to forgive her. He might even have her arrested. The prospect of facing his decidedly vengeful wrath was a dismal one. Fear gripped her heart at the mere thought of it.

And once he had done whatever he was going to do to her, would he insist that their marriage continue? Or would he seek to dissolve their ill-fated union? He would *have* to believe it ill-fated by then, she mused dispiritedly.

That particular issue still burning in her mind, she started downstairs again, reached the foot of the staircase, and swept across to the front door. Her hand had just closed about the doorknob when a dark figure suddenly loomed behind her. Before she could do anything more than give a faint cry of alarm, a pair of brawny arms had lifted her bodily and swung her high.

"Well, I'll be damned — a redhead!" exclaimed her captor. He was a veritable giant of a man, grinning down at her with undisguised pleasure while she struggled futilely in his grasp. "Hattie's got herself a real beauty this time!"

240

"Put me down!" Lorelei demanded indignantly, her cheeks flaming. "I am *not*—"

"Looks like I got one fresh off the stage!" he observed, his whiskey-reddened eyes falling on the carpetbag she had dropped in startlement. What little hair he possessed was greasy and slicked back, and he smelled worse than she had ever imagined a man could smell. "Hell, guess I get to be the first one to break you in!" he added, his gaze filling with the harsh, unmistakable glimmer of lust.

"No!" she shouted, her struggles intensifying. "Let go of me! Damn you, you blackhearted son of Satan, put me down!" Balling her free hand into a tight fist, she managed to land what she thought was a brain-rattling punch on the side of his head. But he merely chuckled gleefully and caught her wrist in such a brutal grip that she cried out in pain.

"You sure got a mouth on you, don't you, Red? Someone ought to teach you some manners. But that's all right—I like a whore who ain't afraid to speak her mind."

"I am not a . . . an *employee!*" Sweet mercy, this couldn't be happening! she thought in stunned dismay. She made a belated attempt to scream, but the foul-smelling giant clamped a dirty hand across her mouth and began carrying her up the stairs. Her eyes widened in growing horror, and her stomach churned as a wave of nausea threatened to overwhelm her.

Praying that someone, Charity or anyone else upstairs, would come along and confirm that she was not one of Hattie's girls, she kicked and squirmed frantically while she was borne to the top of the staircase. Her terror was made far worse by the fact that she now had more than a vague idea about what happened behind those closed doors at Miss Hattie's. The thought of sharing with this man, or any other man for that matter, what she had shared with Reeve made her shudder with revulsion.

"Put her down."

Lorelei's heart gave a wild leap of joy and relief at the sound of that familiar voice. Her struggles ceased abruptly as her captor, poised on the top step, spun about with her in his arms. Her eyes flew to Reeve, who stood at the foot of the staircase. His handsome face was inscrutable, but she did not miss the savage gleam in his penetrating gaze.

"Who the hell are you?" the man growled, his coarse features suffused with a dull, angry color. Quickly he took note of Reeve's uniform. "You got no right to come in here and tell me what to do, you blue-coated son of a bitch!"

"Put her down," Reeve ordered once more, his tone one of deadly calm.

Although he had yet to move, his body was tensed for action. A near-murderous fury had gripped him at the first sight of Lorelei in the man's arms; he knew that he could easily pound the bastard's ugly face to a pulp and feel not one damned ounce of remorse for it. The fear he saw in his wife's wide, luminous eyes only added fuel to the fire raging in his blood.

Lorelei gasped as she was suddenly lowered to her feet and thrust roughly aside. She stumbled, and would have fallen if she hadn't managed to catch hold of the balustrade. Hastily sweeping several wayward curls from her face, she watched in breathless apprehension as the man started moving down the stairs toward Reeve.

"I've had a bellyful of you fancy horse-handlers across the river actin' like you own the place!" he snarled menacingly. "The redhead's mine, damn your hide, and I ain't—"

"The *lady* is unwilling," Reeve cut him off, still not retreating. A single muscle twitched in the clean-shaven ruggedness of his cheek, while his green eyes narrowed. He was looking forward to the fight.

"Lady?" The man stopped his advance and gave a loud snort of derisive laughter. "You must've been out chasin' after them Comanches too long, Soldier Boy!"

"He's right!" Lorelei intervened indignantly.

"Stay out of this," her husband commanded tersely.

But she was not inclined to obey. Anxious to prevent what she believed would be certain disaster for Reeve, she hurried forward to confront her assailant, who had turned at her words. She came to a halt two steps above him, which allowed her to meet his befuddled gaze squarely.

"My name is Miss Lorelei Montgomery, and I am most assuredly *not* among the women employed at this establishment!" she reiterated, drawing herself proudly erect. She planted her hands on her hips and fixed the open-mouthed giant with a look of stern admonishment. "How dare you behave as though you have a perfect right to accost any woman unfortunate enough to cross your path! If it were not for Major Cameron's timely intervention, you might very well have found yourself facing imprisonment, for I would not have hesitated to see you arrested! In fact, I've a good mind to contact

243

the proper authorities and—"

"No harm was done," he muttered sullenly. It was clear that he had finally accepted her protests as being well-founded. The hot, feral gleam in his eyes had been replaced by a dull glint of begrudging resignation. "Hell, what was I supposed to think? It ain't every day a lady comes into Hattie's."

"Lady or not, there is no conceivable excuse for your behavior!" She swept haughtily past him and down the stairs to Reeve's side. "Shall we go, Major?"

"Wait outside," he told her.

"What?" She blinked up at him in puzzlement.

"Wait outside."

The tone in his voice warned her to obey. She did so, but with an ill grace. Narrowing her eyes resentfully at him, she crossed to the front door again, picked up her carpetbag, and escaped into the welcoming brightness outside.

He joined her a scant two minutes later.

"What happened?" she asked in a small voice, her gaze shifting back to the doorway as he took the carpetbag from her and seized her arm.

"Nothing." He began leading her down the boardwalk. His handsome face wore a tight-lipped expression, and his green eyes were unfathomable.

"Nothing?" She could literally feel his anger, and she felt a moment's trepidation before retorting, "I find that difficult to believe! Why, you must have done *something*, or else you wouldn't have—"

"Damn it, Lorelei!" he growled. He stopped abruptly and pulled her around to face him. His low, deep-timbred voice was whipcord sharp as he

244

demanded, "What the *hell* were you doing in that place?"

"I . . . I ran into Mr. Baker!" she was lucky enough to recall in time. She blanched at the way his fierce, steady gaze burned down into hers, but somehow she was able to maintain her composure. "You remember—Virgil Baker, from the stagecoach? He wasn't feeling well, and I offered to help him find his horse. As it turned out, he had left it in front of Miss Hattie's."

It wasn't a complete lie, she rationalized to herself. But even if it had been, she refused to let him intimidate her. Her eyes flashed up at him as she jerked her arm free.

"I owe you no explanation, Reeve Cameron! Indeed, I should be interrogating you! How did *you* happen to be in that . . . that house of ill repute? Is that where you spent the night? Did your 'work' include personal interviews with the women there?" she demanded, with biting sarcasm.

"As a matter of fact, it did." His expression softened and the merest hint of a smile touched his lips. "But your jealousy is unfounded, my love."

"I am not jealous!" she denied, bristling visibly at the suggestion.

"Why did you leave the hotel?"

"Because I wanted to!"

"I seem to recall, sweet wife, that you were told to stay there until I came for you this morning," he reminded her, in a voice meant for her ears alone.

"And I seem to recall, *Major,* that I never agreed to do anything of the sort!" she countered defiantly, then added with perverse satisfaction, "It was no great difficulty to leave, in spite of your efforts to

245

have my every move watched!" She regretted the remark immediately when she observed the way his countenance tightened with anger once more.

"I've already had a word with him," he assured her grimly.

Feeling a sharp pang of guilt at the realization that she had been the cause of the man's undoubtedly severe reproval, Lorelei looked up at her husband with a plea for mercy in her glowing sapphire gaze.

"It was my fault, really!" she insisted. "I shouldn't have—"

"You're right. You shouldn't have."

He took her arm in a firm grip again and propelled her wordlessly across the street with him, toward the bridge that separated a life of strict duty and discipline from the unbridled pursuit of pleasure. Lorelei made no attempt to renew their conversation until they were nearing the row of officers' quarters at the post. The grounds were already bustling with activity, and she was aware of the curious looks directed their way by the soldiers.

She glanced toward the building where Hadley sat under lock and key. Her mind was racing to think of a way to contact the man named Dugan without Reeve's knowledge; she knew she would have to be especially cautious from now on.

"I suppose, since you have apparently been up all night, you intend to get some sleep?" she ventured, her manner deceptively nonchalant. She still wanted to know more about his fortuitous presence at Miss Hattie's, and it suddenly occurred to her to wonder if Charity Pardee had been among those he had questioned; but she told herself there were more important matters requiring her attention at the present time. There was so much to be done . . .

"Unless you'd like to persuade me to stay awake," Reeve drawled in response. He turned his head and cast her a look that could best be described as tenderly wolfish. "I could spare an hour or two."

"But for Heaven's sake, it's broad daylight!" she protested. Shocked at the utter boldness of the idea, she colored and looked away. "And besides, I—I don't think we should be seen spending too much time together. As you yourself have said, we certainly don't want to arouse suspicion." She cleared her throat gently and hurried to change the subject. "Where will you be for the remainder of the day? I mean, if my appeal to Hadley to talk this morning should prove successful, how will I get word to you?" It sounded unconvincing, even to her own ears, but fortunately Reeve was too preoccupied with other thoughts to notice.

"Colonel Jameson was kind enough to allow me to bunk in with the other unmarried officers, at the end of the row." His lips curved into a faint, sardonic smile. "Of course, after next week, you and I will both be looking for new quarters."

Lorelei swallowed a sudden lump in her throat, and was glad when they reached her temporary home. Her heart pounded with a strange mixture of apprehension and excitement as she wondered if he would insist upon coming inside, but her fears were ungrounded.

"There's something I think you should know," he announced, once he had opened the door and set her carpetbag inside.

"Something about Hadley?" she asked, her brows

247

knitting together into a frown of concern. Reeve nodded and lifted his hands to her shoulders.

"I know I said I couldn't reveal any details of the investigation, but I wanted to warn you." His fingers glided down her arms before he forced himself to release her. His heart ached at the anxiety reflected in her gaze. "He's going to *have* to talk, Lorelei. There are a number of men willing to testify against him."

He wanted to reveal more, but did not. If she had any notion of how bad things looked for her brother—no, confound it, he couldn't tell her. It was already difficult enough to prevent his personal feelings from interfering with his work. Just as he had told her last night, he hadn't counted on loving her so much.

"Who are these men?" demanded Lorelei, her voice quavering with emotion while she stared up at him.

"I can't tell you that." He frowned and surrendered to the urge to touch her again. Raising a hand to her face, he smoothed his warm fingers across her cheek. His eyes were full of such incredible warmth and compassion that she felt her own heart stirring. "I don't want to see you hurt. God knows, that's the last thing I want. But no matter how things turn out, you've got to believe that I love you. I'll always love you."

Sudden tears gathered in her eyes. She caught her breath when he bent his head and pressed a tender, intoxicating kiss upon her lips. Then, without another word, he turned and left.

She opened her eyes and stared after him, cursing the fact that her emotions were in utter turmoil and

248

every square inch of her body had come alive. Why did this man possess the ability to set her afire with a single kiss?

Damn him, she thought without any conviction whatsoever. Damn him for being so irresistible and obstinate — and for caring. It would make what was to come that much harder.

She pivoted about and went inside. Her husband's warning had strengthened her determination to act without delay. It was now or never . . .

Twelve

Lorelei paced restlessly about the lamplit room, her bright, troubled gaze shifting with a will of its own toward the doorway again.

"Ten o'clock," she murmured aloud. It was already a few minutes past that now.

Reeve was late.

Releasing a long, pent-up sigh, she wandered back to the rocking chair and sat down. She clasped her hands tightly together in her lap and closed her eyes for a moment. A silent prayer for strength, and a second one for success, rose in her mind as she listened to her heartbeat pounding in her ears.

Everything was arranged. Mr. Dugan stood ready nearby, and the necessary supplies and horses were waiting for them just outside the boundaries of the fort. God help her, she had never felt so nervous in her whole life. Getting through the next few hours would require every ounce of courage and determination she possessed.

Her thoughts drifted back over all that had happened since Reeve had escorted her home that morning, starting with the unpleasant yet ultimately productive meeting with Abner Dugan. She had managed to slip away to town again on the pretense of having forgotten something at the hotel. Abigail had even volunteered to accompany her, and it would have looked suspicious if she had refused. Fortunately, however, the other woman had remained in the lobby downstairs while she had searched out the man Charity had recommended.

He had been willing enough to help her, and had agreed to accept the fifty dollars she had offered him, but he had treated her with such familiarity and outright insolence that she had breathed a sigh of relief upon leaving his room. She wasn't at all sure she could trust him, and yet she had little choice.

She had warned him about Reeve—but only to a certain extent. Without revealing the truth of their relationship, she had said that Major Cameron was a special investigator assigned to the case and would no doubt pose a very real threat to their plans. It was Dugan himself who had come up with a scheme to get Reeve safely out of the way . . .

Great balls of fire, she wished she had never agreed to go along with *this* part of the plan! she thought, standing abruptly to her feet once more. She folded her arms across her breasts and resumed her pacing. Her eyes flew back to the clock ticking softly on the wall.

"Where the devil is he?" she lamented, her voice edged with impatience.

It hadn't been difficult to arrange a meeting with her husband, especially since she had given him the distinct impression that her reasons for wanting to see him alone were of a highly intimate nature. What else was he to think, when her note had invited him to pay her a call in the privacy of her room after everyone else had retired for the night?

In truth, she hadn't been sure he would agree; it would involve taking a risk he had already declared himself anxious to avoid. But he had delivered the reply in person, stopping by the Merriwethers' earlier that afternoon. Thank Heavens Abigail had been in the very next room, she mused with another sigh. God only knew how she would have managed to carry out the deception if he had stayed any longer. She had never been particularly good at lying, and it had proven even more difficult than usual with Reeve.

With Hadley, of course, there had been no need for lies. At first, he had been every bit as reluctant as she had thought he would be. He had been absolutely furious at the mere suggestion of an escape. But after she had outlined her intention of finding Taggart and bringing him back to Fort Concho, he had begun to think that her plan was not so rattle-brained after all. Like her, he had finally realized that it was better to take action—even as desperate and fraught with danger as this—to prove himself innocent rather than simply sit in the guardhouse and wait for the worst to happen.

Still, he hadn't wanted to place her in jeopardy. She had faced the greatest resistance in convincing him that her participation was necessary. And in the end, he had faced the fact that it was entirely useless to argue with her. She would have her way, as usual.

You're as jumpy as a cat with a knot in its tail, she told herself, recalling another of her grandmother's delightfully southern adages. Wandering to

252

the bed, she bent and cast a quick glance underneath it. Her carpetbag, fully packed, lay waiting on the bare wooden floor.

She started in guilty alarm when a knock sounded at the door. Inhaling sharply, she raised a hand to her throat and whirled about.

"Who—who is it?" she called out. Dismayed to feel a telltale blush rising to her cheeks, she hastily composed herself. She smoothed down her full skirts and checked to make sure her rebellious auburn curls were still secured in the single long braid that reached all the way down her back to her hips.

The door swung open. Reeve's tall, muscular frame filled the doorway.

"If I thought for one minute you were expecting someone else, my love, I'd wring your beautiful little neck," he teased, with mock severity. He stepped inside and closed the door behind him. His warm gaze raked hungrily over her. "I shouldn't have come, you know."

"Then why did you?" she retorted saucily. Her eyes widened as he advanced on her.

"Why do you think?"

"I'm sure I can't possibly imagine, Major Cameron." She forced a smile to her lips. "I suppose you're planning to return to Miss Hattie's tonight?" she demanded, only half in jest. Her gaze shifted anxiously to the doorway before moving to his face again. She hated playing him for the fool, hated the prospect of what was to come, but she told herself it was too late to back out now. Mr. Dugan would arrive on the scene any moment now, and Hadley was waiting.

253

"Feeling jealous again, Mrs. Cameron?" he challenged, with a low, affectionate chuckle. He pulled her into his arms and gazed lovingly down into her upturned countenance. If he noticed that she was behaving a little strangely, he made no mention of it. "As I told you before, there's no reason. Besides, you're all I can handle."

"Am I indeed? Well then, I . . . I think you should prove it," she parried, with convincing seductiveness. Surprised at how much her heart was aching, she felt a sudden and powerful urge to call the whole thing off. *Where was Mr. Dugan?* she thought in rising panic.

"As always, sweet vixen," Reeve murmured, while his arms tightened about her and his head lowered toward hers, "with pleasure."

From the first touch of his mouth upon hers, he demanded a response she could not help but give. She moaned in surrender and swayed against him; her arms lifting to the corded muscles of his neck while her lips parted to allow the hot, rapturous invasion of his tongue. For a moment, she completely forgot about plans and deceptions and the guilt of betrayal. She forgot about everything save Reeve, and this wild, sweet madness that only he could create within her.

She was brought crashing back to reality when Abner Dugan made his appearance at last.

Even though she had been expecting him, she did not hear the door easing open, but a soft creak of the floorboards warned of his arrival. Her eyelids fluttered open just in time to observe him slipping into the room. A gasp of startlement rose in her throat when she saw that the man he had brought along as an accomplice—the "friend who owes me a favor"—was the same man who had accosted her at Miss Hattie's that morning.

The sudden tensing of Reeve's body against hers let her know he had become aware of their presence as well. In one swift motion, he spun about and thrust her protectively behind him. His hand moved to the revolver holstered on his belt, but he never got the chance to withdraw it.

"Hold it right there, Soldier Boy!" the loathsome giant ordered. His right eye was swollen and discolored, his ugly face battered, and Lorelei knew without asking that the damage had been inflicted by Reeve. "I got a score to settle with you, remember?" He was unarmed, but his huge fists were clenched in readiness at his sides. In one hand was a coiled length of rope.

Abner Dugan stood holding a gun aimed directly at Reeve. He was a slender but wiry man of average height, with lank black hair hanging to his collar, and eyes that were so pale a blue as to seem almost colorless. Though not yet thirty, he looked much older. The scars on his body certainly testified to years of hard living. His mouth curved into a broad, contemptuous smile as he motioned to Lorelei.

"Come on, Miss Montgomery. Let's get goin'."

"Stay right where you are," Reeve instructed her. His eyes darkened with a savage gleam and he warned Dugan, "I don't know what you want, but if you make one move toward her, you're a dead man." If not for his fear that Lorelei would be caught in the crossfire, he wouldn't have hesitated to draw then and there.

"Time's wastin', ma'am," Dugan advised, responding to Reeve's threat with another scornful smile. He glanced toward his scowling, brawny friend and said, "All right, Clayton. Tie him up."

"Miss Montgomery goes free," Reeve insisted, in a voice of deadly calm. His gaze smoldered with barely suppressed violence, while a murderous, vengeful fury turned his blood to fire. Without any concern for his own safety, he vowed to do whatever it took to make sure Lorelei escaped their clutches.

"I—I have to go with them," she stammered behind him. She tried to move forward, but his hand seized her arm.

"Stay put!" he ground out, his handsome face thunderous.

"No!" She jerked free and felt hot, bitter tears stinging her eyes when she rounded on him. Her heart felt as though it was breaking in two. "Damn it, Reeve Cameron, don't you understand? I didn't have any other choice! I had to do something, and you wouldn't help me!"

"What are you talking about?" His eyes filled with dawning suspicion as they searched her face for the truth.

"I couldn't let my brother hang! I don't have time to explain, but . . . I'm sorry! Dear God, *I'm sorry!*" she cried brokenly.

Blinded by her tears, she whirled and fled to the doorway, where she stood with her back turned resolutely toward him. Abner Dugan watched as the man he'd called Clayton stalked forward with the rope in his hands.

"You ain't so all-fired superior now are you, Soldier Boy?" the giant sneered menacingly.

"Lorelei, don't do this," Reeve cautioned her, his eyes glinting with pain and rage. "You can't trust these men. God only knows what will happen—"

"Shut up!" growled Clayton.

"Lorelei," Reeve's deep voice reached out to her.

"I have no choice!" she reiterated, still refusing to face him again.

His features became a hard, inscrutable mask. He forced himself to wait until Clayton drew closer, then suddenly he sprang into action.

His fist smashed forcefully upward against Clayton's unprotected chin. While the larger man staggered backward, Reeve drew his gun. But it was too late. Dugan had been prepared for just such an attack and had already moved into position behind the pair. Lorelei spun back around to watch in horror as he raised his arm and brought the handle of his gun crashing down on the back of Reeve's head.

"No!" came her hoarse cry as he crumpled, unconscious, to the floor.

She flew across the room and dropped to her knees beside him. The tears were streaming freely down her face now, and she was choking back sobs as she cradled Reeve's head in her lap.

"He wasn't supposed to be hurt!" she accused Dugan, her voice rising shrilly.

"The son of a bitch ain't dead," muttered Clayton. He pushed her out of the way and began tying Reeve up. "Guess this means we'll have to hightail it out of Santa Angela for a while, don't it, Dugan?"

"Where are your things?" Abner Dugan asked

257

Lorelei curtly. When she did not answer, he grabbed her and yanked her to her feet. "We're leavin' now, Miss Montgomery. Either you get your things or we'll go without them!" Prompted by nothing more than greed, he was anxious to get his hands on the fifty dollars she had promised him.

Lorelei glared venomously at him before retrieving her carpetbag from beneath the bed. She would have returned to Reeve's side once more, but Dugan prevented her by reaching out and catching hold of her arm.

"Let's go!" he snapped. He half dragged her back across the room with him.

Clayton had just finished tightening the bonds about Reeve's hands and feet. He stood and surveyed his handiwork with malicious satisfaction.

"That ought to hold him for a while." He turned and prepared to join the others near the doorway. But he stopped dead in his tracks when he saw that Dugan was aiming the gun at him. "Dugan? What the hell—"

"Do as I say and I won't have to shoot you, you stupid bastard," cautioned Dugan. "Put your hands up and turn around."

"What?" Clayton stared at him in disbelief, then grew visibly enraged. "Why, you—"

"*Now!*"

The other man reluctantly did as he was told.

"Good Heavens, what are you doing?" Lorelei demanded.

She tried to pull free, but Dugan's fingers bit into her arm. Before she could guess his intent, he took one step forward and struck Clayton on the head, the same way he had struck Reeve minutes earlier. She watched as the large man fell heavily to the floor.

"Why did you do that?" she breathed, aghast at the thought of Clayton's huge body lying a short distance away from Reeve's.

"He would've slowed us down too much," Dugan explained indifferently.

He holstered his gun and pulled her swiftly outside with him. She hung back for a brief moment as they headed away from the Merriwethers' house. Although tempted to call out, she told herself that Reeve would be all right, that Abigail would discover him in the morning if he didn't manage to summon help before then.

She dashed impatiently at her tears and felt her throat constrict as the vision of Dugan knocking Reeve unconscious flashed across her mind once more. But that wasn't the memory that would haunt her. She knew she would never forget the look of pain in Reeve Cameron's eyes when he had realized the truth of her betrayal. *Never.*

Muttering an oath of impatience, Dugan urged her along with him through the concealing darkness behind the buildings and on toward the guardhouse. Lorelei was forced to run to keep pace with him. She was nearly out of breath when they reached the building, where Hadley was pacing anxiously back and forth in his cell.

"Go on!" Dugan whispered, nodding toward the front of the guardhouse.

He stood waiting in the shadows around at the side, watching as she followed the plan they had agreed upon that afternoon. Unable to stop thinking about Reeve, she moved along the lamplit walk in a haze of guilt and apprehension—and misery. Dear Lord, she had never felt so wretchedly unhappy before.

Somehow managing a coquettish smile, she gathered up her skirts and swept inside. The guard leapt to his feet, his eyes widening with surprise.

"Miss Montgomery?" he said in disbelief. He frowned and cleared his throat before asking, "What are you doing here? Colonel Jameson didn't leave orders—"

"I am so terribly sorry to bother you, Private," she told him, in her most engaging manner, "but I was unable to sleep, and I thought it might be possible to have a word with my brother."

Her color was high and her eyes bright as the result of her recent, desperate flight around the perimeter of the fort. The young man before her, no older than Hadley if she had to venture a guess, was not immune to her charms, but it soon became clear that he took his duty seriously.

"I'm sorry, ma'am," he answered with sincere regret written on his face, "but no visitors are allowed after final retreat's been sounded."

"Come now, Private, surely that doesn't have to include me, does it?" She edged closer to him and gazed imploringly up into his eyes. "Please, just this once, couldn't we bend the rules a little?"

"No, ma'am, I—I'm afraid we can't do that," he stammered, looking decidedly uncomfortable at her proximity.

"Why not? Who's to know if I speak to him for a

few minutes?" she appealed sweetly. She allowed her hand to rest upon his arm. "Please?"

Dugan made his move then. He slipped inside with his gun already drawn, his eyes making a quick, encompassing sweep of the room.

"Give her the keys!" he ordered the guard.

The young cavalryman hesitated, his eyes flying to where his rifle sat propped up in the corner a few feet away. Lorelei, noting the direction of his gaze, shook her head as she retreated a step.

"Please, don't," she cautioned. The contrition in her own gaze was genuine. "I'm sorry. But you'll have to give me the keys."

"You don't want to do this, Miss Montgomery," he insisted somberly. "It'll only make things worse for your brother, and you're letting yourself in for a lot of trouble if—"

"Shut up, damn it, and give her the keys!" growled Dugan, emphasizing the command with a curt, threatening motion of his gun.

Lorelei breathed an inward sigh of relief when the guard finally complied. She took the ring of keys from him and hurried to the first door. After trying three of the keys without success, she found the one that worked. The door swung open, and she raced down the narrow corridor to Hadley's cell.

He was standing at the door, his fingers grasping the bars, when she appeared before him with the keys.

"I was beginning to think something had gone wrong!" he whispered. Watching nervously while she searched for the right key, he raised his eyes to her face and frowned. He knew her better than anyone, and he could see that something was troubling her greatly. "What is it, Lori? What's happened?"

"Nothing!" she denied in a tremulous undertone. "I—I'll explain later!" Her hands were shaking so much it was difficult to turn the key in the lock. But she managed it at last and quickly stepped out of the way while Hadley flung the cell door open.

"Come on!" he said. He seized her hand and urged her back down the corridor to the central room, where Dugan had kept watch with his gun leveled at the guard.

Hadley nodded wordlessly at the man who had agreed to help them. Dugan scowled in response.

"Don't just stand there, boy!" he snapped in a low, malevolent voice. "Gag him and lock him in one of the cells! Hell, you want him to bring the whole damned post runnin' before we can clear out?"

Hadley flushed with anger, but nevertheless did as he was told. Murmuring an apology to the young guard, who had been a friend, he tied his yellow kerchief about the man's mouth, bound his hands behind his back with a length of rope Dugan tossed to him, and marched him swiftly down the corridor to the same cell where he himself had been imprisoned for more days than he cared to remember.

When he returned to join Dugan and Lorelei, he snatched up the guard's rifle and cartridge belt, took his sister's hand once more, and faced the older man with an expression of simmering fury.

"Don't ever call me 'boy' again," he warned, his blue eyes narrowing.

"You got me quakin' in my boots," Dugan

262

sneered, then jerked his head toward the doorway. "Let's go!"

Hadley pulled Lorelei outside and made for the darkness behind the stables. Dugan followed closely on their heels. In a matter of seconds, the three of them had reached the waiting horses. Dugan flipped a silver dollar to the boy he had paid to watch the animals. The twelve-year-old pocketed his reward and took off, anxious to boast to his friends, with no small amount of embellishment, about how he had helped a prisoner escape from Fort Concho.

Dugan mounted up while Hadley waited to assist Lorelei. She paused briefly to unhook her skirt, which fastened separately from her white cotton shirtwaist, and draw it off. She was wearing a pair of men's dark blue pants underneath. They were too loose in the waist and too tight across the hips, but they were all she had been able to find at the general store in town. It would require several long days on horseback to reach New Mexico Territory; she prayed that she had the strength to endure the difficult journey.

She turned back to her horse and lifted her carpetbag so that the handle caught on the saddlehorn. Hadley seized her about the waist and helped her mount, then hurried to swing up into his own saddle. Dugan swore at the delay.

"Damn it, we're all gonna hang if we don't get goin'!" he whispered stridently.

"I'm ready!" Lorelei assured him.

Dugan reined about, his heels digging into the horse's flanks. He rode swiftly away into the dark-

263

ness, with the two Montgomerys following after him.

Lorelei cast a heavyhearted glanced over her shoulder. She knew with certainty that Reeve Cameron would come after them. God help her if he caught up with them before they had found Taggart . . . God help them all.

Thirteen

Lorelei slid wearily from the saddle. She was grateful for the support of Hadley's arms about her; she was afraid her legs would give way beneath her if she attempted to move them just yet.

"It will get easier, Lori," her brother reassured her. He helped her over to where Dugan was already making preparations for a fire. She sank down onto a large rock beside the stream, only to wince in pain as her saddlesore bottom made contact with the hard surface.

"Remember when we used to spend all day riding like wild savages across the county?" she asked Hadley with a rueful smile. "I'm afraid I have spent far too little time in the saddle since you went away."

"Lori—"

"No, don't say it!" she commanded. "I had to come. And I *will* get better at this." She was aching all over, her skin felt raw from the combined effects of the wind and the sun, and her nerves were strung as tight as a bowstring after a day spent worrying about Reeve.

Everyone would know about the escape by now, she mused with a ragged sigh. According to Hadley, Colonel Jameson wouldn't have sent a patrol after

265

them until daybreak. But that was nearly twelve hours ago. She wondered if Reeve would be leading the soldiers in pursuit, or if he would come after them alone. The mere thought of facing him again sent a tremor of fear coursing through her body.

"We shouldn't be risking a fire," said Hadley, frowning as he turned to Dugan.

He didn't want to frighten Lorelei, but he had been in the Cavalry long enough to know that a fire would signal Indians of their presence. They had been lucky so far. The threat of an attack was constant out there on the *Llano Estacado* — the "Staked Plains," as that part of Texas had been known for centuries, since the first white men came. There were few trees to offer shelter, only a vast, limitless expanse of prairie, where water was scarce and where they could travel for days on end without encountering another human being. It was Indian country; and the farther away they got from Fort Concho, the more dangerous their situation would become.

"Boy, you're a damn fool if you think they don't already know we're here," replied Dugan. His use of the insulting *boy* earned him a furious glare from Hadley.

With a gesture of contempt for the younger man's ignorance, Dugan struck a match and set the collection of sticks ablaze. The site he had chosen as their camp for the night was well known to him. It featured the rare, encircling protection of trees, the convenience of a stream right at hand, and the added bonus of a drop-off in the land. They'd be able to see anyone who tried to sneak up on them.

266

He was glad they hadn't been forced to share the campsite with any of the buffalo hunters he'd run into before, particularly since he had decided his services as guide and nursemaid were worth a hell of a lot more than fifty dollars. His eyes gleamed with malicious intent as he threw a quick, furtive look toward Lorelei.

"What are you talking about?" she asked in puzzlement, having waited in vain for the two of them to finish their conversation. She rose to her feet, her gaze shifting anxiously from one man to the other. "Who knows we're here?"

"Now, Lori, there's no sense in worrying about—" Hadley started to reassure her once more.

"Comanches," Dugan answered. He plunged the coffeepot into the stream to fill it, then set it on the fire to heat.

"Comanches?" gasped Lorelei. Her eyes flew to her brother. He hastened back to her side and slipped a comforting arm about her shoulders.

"That's why I told you it was too dangerous for you to come." He scowled and exclaimed angrily, "Blast it, Lori, I deserve to hang for getting you into this mess! I must have been clean out of my mind to let you talk me into—"

"Mr. Dugan warned me about the Indians, Hadley," she interrupted in calm, measured tones, "and about the other hardships we would be facing. I . . . well, it's just that I hadn't really given serious thought to the possibility until now."

That was true enough. She had been too engrossed with thoughts of Reeve, and too concerned about keeping up with the more experienced riders, to be able to concentrate on much else. Perhaps that was a blessing in disguise, she reflected with an inward sigh. Now, of course, she would have to add the very real threat of Indians to the growing list of dangers in her mind.

It struck her—not for the first time since leaving Fort Concho—that she hadn't thought things through very well. In fact, she was beginning to realize that she was quite ill-prepared for what lay ahead. She had acted impulsively, had allowed her emotions to rule her head, and yet, sweet mercy, what else could she have done?

"The time to worry's when it gets good and dark," said Dugan. He tossed a perfunctory glance overhead. The sun had nearly disappeared below the western horizon, turning the sky into a blaze of color as twilight approached. "There'll be a full moon tonight. A Comanche moon. Them murderin' bastards like to raid in the summer when the moon's all big and shinin'. Yessir, some poor son-of-a-bitch rancher might find his stock gone come mornin', or maybe even his—"

"I told you to watch your language around my sister, Dugan!" snapped Hadley. He stalked over to the water's edge and took up the reins of the three horses, which he had already unsaddled. He led the animals beneath the trees, looping the reins over a low branch to secure them for the night.

"Why haven't we seen any buffalo yet, Mr. Dugan?" Lorelei queried, in an attempt to change the subject. She knelt beside the fire and began stirring the potful of beans he had just placed there.

"We might run across a herd or two up north," he

answered casually, though he was fairly burning with the desire to reach out and lay hands on her.

His eyes glinted hotly as they traveled over her bent head, down to where the curve of her full breasts was evident beneath the thin white cotton of her blouse. He had watched the sway of her hips when she walked, noting with lustful pleasure the way those men's pants she was wearing stretched tightly across her well-rounded backside. She was a cut above the whores back at Miss Hattie's, no doubt about that, but she was all woman just the same.

That brother of hers would be a problem, he mused in annoyance. But he'd find a way to take care of him. Hell, the boy was still green. He'd probably run scared at the first sign of trouble . . .

"Coffee's ready," he announced. Anxious for the night to come, he sat back on his heels and watched as brother and sister sat beside one another to enjoy a meal of beans and salt pork that Lorelei had served.

After supper, Lorelei rinsed the tin plates and forks in the stream and stacked them near the fire. She had placed her bedroll next to Hadley's, and she fell to her knees on her blanket while working to unbraid her hair.

"How I long for a hot bath," she sighed. She had washed up in the stream, but she knew she would never feel clean until she could scrub from head to toe. If it had not been for Abner Dugan's presence, she would have stripped down to her chemise and done just that. "Hadley?"

"What?" He had already stretched out, his hands

pillowing the back of his head while he lay staring up at the moonlit sky. Dugan had volunteered to take the first watch; he sat a short distance away, on the other side of the fire.

"Now that we're no longer at Fort Concho, why don't you tell me why you refused to cooperate with Ree—with Major Cameron?" She was dismayed to feel another sharp twinge of pain. Why did her heart ache so at the mere sound of his name on her lips?

"I guess it's time you knew the truth," he conceded. He turned on his side, propping up on one elbow while his eyes met hers. When he spoke again, he lowered his voice to little more than a whisper so that Dugan wouldn't hear. "I told you the conspiracy was a powerful one. I might have gone up against them anyway if . . . if you hadn't come. I shouldn't have sent you that telegram, Lori. It was selfish of me, and I'll regret it to my dying day," he declared earnestly.

"Oh Hadley, don't say that!" She reached out and touched his arm in a gesture that was both affectionate and reproachful. "Don't ever say that again! I told you before—I would never have forgiven you if you hadn't sent word to me!"

"Maybe so, but it only made things worse." A shadow crossed his face before he revealed, "You see, once they found out you had arrived at the post, they let me know in no uncertain terms that your life rested in my hands." He pulled himself into a sitting position and frowned in remembrance. "They used you against me, Lori. They threatened to kill you, and then me, too, of

270

course, if I opened my mouth to anyone."

"But why didn't you tell Major Cameron about this? And for Heaven's sake, *who* threatened—"

"I couldn't tell the major because I wasn't sure I could trust him! For all I know, he might have friends among them, friends he doesn't want to see accused of murder and treason. What chance would a lowly private have against veteran officers? As for names, I'd rather not tell you just yet. There's still a good chance I'll be caught. We both know it, even if we don't want to admit it. And if that should happen, you'll be able to claim in all honesty that I wouldn't identify anyone."

"You could have trusted him," Lorelei insisted, as Reeve's face swam before her eyes. She drew in a long, shuddering breath and felt the sudden urge to disclose the whole unbelievable story to her brother.

"How do you know that?"

"Because I—I became well acquainted with Major Cameron these past few days," she stammered evasively.

She had finished separating the long auburn tresses and turned away slightly in order to take up her hairbrush. Acutely conscious of Hadley's eyes on her, she began dragging the brush through her hair with movements that seemed almost mechanical.

"Just how well *did* you and the major get to know one another?" her brother demanded, his gaze narrowing in suspicion. When she did not answer immediately, he grabbed her wrist and forced her to look at him. "Lori? Answer me! What happened between you and the major?"

"Dear God, Hadley, I've made such a terrible mess of things!" she whispered brokenly. She cursed the tears gathering in her eyes once more, and did not resist when he pulled her into his arms.

"Tell me," he prompted, with loving gentleness.

"I wanted to tell you before now, but I wasn't sure how to do it!" She took another deep breath, and composed herself a bit before confessing, "At first, I played up to him in the hope that he would agree to help you in some way. Abigail Merriwether had told me he was highly regarded up in Washington, and I thought he might use his influence, at least to make certain you did not receive a sentence of — of death. But then the plan backfired on me, and I found myself deeper and deeper in trouble!"

"What do you mean, it 'backfired' on you?"

"Well, instead of merely flirting with the man to get what I wanted, I married him."

"You *what?*" Wearing an expression of stunned disbelief, he seized her arms and urgently pulled her up to face him again. "Lorelei Montgomery, what the—"

"Cameron," she corrected him, with a faint smile of irony. "My name is Lorelei Cameron now. Mrs. Reeve Cameron, to be precise."

"You can't be serious!"

"I'm afraid I can." She swept the wildly tumbling locks from her face, and related in a breathless rush. "It all happened so quickly! One night, I was attending a dance with the sole purpose of captivating the man, and the next, I was standing beside him in Captain Merriwether's parlor while the chaplain pronounced us man and wife! I suppose you could say my efforts succeeded all too well, and now I . . . I'm married to him," she concluded, her voice trailing away at the end.

"Blast it all, Lori, this is without a doubt the most pointless, dim-witted thing you have ever done!" he blurted out irefully. He let her go and released another heavy sigh. "I can't believe you sacrificed yourself like that. And for no reason. *For no reason!*" His gaze bored across into the glistening depths of hers. "Don't you understand? You can't bribe a man like Major Cameron!"

"I didn't bribe him!" she protested indignantly.

"That's exactly what you did! Only you used something far more valuable than money!"

She paled and looked away before blushing hotly. Hadley groaned at the guilty embarrassment written on her face.

"You mean you—"

"Yes, damn it!" she admitted in a furious undertone. "I was no kissless bride! And if you dare to say one more word on the subject, Hadley Montgomery, I'll—"

"Why?" he cut her off to demand, his own voice tinged with anguish now, as the full impact of her confession finally sank in. Heartsick at the realization that he was to blame for ruining her life, he asked with brotherly compassion, "Why did you do it, Lori?"

"I already told you why! I was afraid you would be found guilty and sentenced to hang, and I thought he—oh, what difference does it make now?"

"Married," he repeated, slowly shaking his head

273

in wonderment. An uncomfortable silence fell between them until he asked at a sudden thought, "And what about the major? How did you manage to get him to go along with your little plan?"

"He said he loved me," she revealed, with a catch in her voice. Her blue eyes clouded at the memory.

"Then I guess he must. A man like him wouldn't marry a woman simply because he wanted to . . ." He left the sentence unfinished, adding after a moment a less direct, "Well, you know what I mean."

"Yes. I know what you mean." A brief, humorless smile touched her lips as she dashed impatiently at tears that would not be denied.

"What about you?" He gently took her arms again, subjecting her to a close scrutiny. "Did you really marry him just because of me, Lori?"

"I tried to make myself believe you were the only reason. But, great balls of fire, I don't know anymore!" she burst out. "Everything is so dreadfully mixed up now, Hadley, and it isn't going to make any difference how Reeve feels or how I feel, because after this he's *never* going to forgive me!"

"If he loves you, he will," Hadley said soothingly. "A man can forgive anything if—"

"You're so very young!" sighed Lorelei. "What could you possibly know about such things?"

"A lot more than you think!" He turned away and stretched back out on his bedroll. "I'm not a child anymore, Lori," he declared in a low, faintly resentful tone. "I've had to grow up fast since I came to Texas."

"I know, and I'm sorry," she hastened to apologize. "I shouldn't have said that. It's just that I—I'm terribly confused right now." She lifted the hair-brush again, but merely fingered the bristles while her eyes drifted toward the dwindling blaze nearby. "And in truth, I'm worried about what's going to happen."

"You mean when we reach New Mexico Territory?"

"Yes. And when we return to Fort Concho."

"No matter what happens, I want you to promise me you'll ask Major Cameron to help you. Tell him I made you come with me. Tell him I was the one who planned the whole thing, and that you—"

"No!" She shook her head in adamant disagreement. "No, Hadley, I won't do that!"

"You've got to!" he insisted. "It's bad enough, your being involved in my escape and all, but they'll got a lot easier on you if they believe you were a reluctant accomplice."

"No."

"Why the blue blazes *not?*" he demanded angrily.

"Because I'm so very tired of lies and secrets and deceptions!" She frowned and glanced uneasily toward their guide, who sat cradling his rifle just within the grove of trees. "And while we're on the subject of deceptions—I don't know what to think of Mr. Dugan," she divulged in a particularly cautious whisper. "He's been behaving quite strangely all this evening." She shuddered when she recalled the way she had caught him looking at her during supper. It was as if he had been undressing her with his eyes. "I don't think he's very trustworthy, do you?"

"I don't think a man of high moral character

275

would have agreed to help us," her brother noted sardonically; then he sobered and told her, "Don't worry. I have no intention of allowing him to come near you." He touched the rifle at his side and allowed his gaze to follow the direction of hers. "I don't think he'll try anything so long as I keep an eye on him."

"Do you really think he's going to lead us into New Mexico Territory?"

"Yes, if for no other reason than it being every bit as dangerous for him to remain in Texas right now as it is for us. Las Vegas, New Mexico is a haven for outlaws and desperadoes, and anyone else on the run from the law. Which only adds to the fact that I must have been insane to let you come along!"

"How can you be so sure Private Taggart has gone to Las Vegas?" she asked, pointedly ignoring his last remark. He had told her that the town, only a day's ride from the northwest border, was considerably larger and wilder than Santa Angela; she wondered how they could possibly hope to find someone there, especially someone who in all likelihood didn't *want* to be found.

"Taggart once mentioned that was where he was going to head if things started looking bad. He said he had a friend at one of the saloons there." He rolled over onto his side again, apparently having decided that they had talked enough for one night. "Try to get some sleep. We'll be riding out at first light."

"What about you?"

"I'll catch a few winks," he promised. His mouth curved into a broad, mischievous grin that belied the gravity of their circumstances. "Besides, I'm young, remember? I don't need as much sleep as you old-timers."

In spite of the fact that she was still greatly troubled, Lorelei smiled. She lay down and settled her curves on the hard ground, wishing for all the world that she was back home in Georgia—or back at the hotel room in Santa Angela with Reeve.

Good heavens, where had that thought come from? Her mind branded her a traitor for it, and yet her heart stirred wistfully. It was difficult to believe that at this time last night, she had been lying in her husband's arms . . .

A coyote's mournful wail rose somewhere in the darkness nearby. The fire hissed and crackled, sending a shower of sparks flying heavenward. Lorelei stared up at the deep, starlit panorama of the Texas sky, musing that she would never get used to the limitless beauty of it.

"Hadley?"

"Hmmm?"

"You wouldn't really have let them hang you, would you?"

"I don't know that I would have had much say in the matter." His eyes twinkled at her in the firelight before he grew serious again. "You've been taking care of me my whole life. It's time I learned to stand on my own two feet. I did what I had to do back at the post. To be perfectly honest, I'm not sure if I would have been brave enough to keep silent until the very end. I've never been through a court-martial before." For a moment, he looked even younger than his nineteen years. "But what

277

kind of man would I be if I had risked my sister's life to save my own? No," he concluded, shaking his head once more, "I didn't have any other choice."

"Yes, you did," she maintained with sudden, heartfelt conviction. "You could have told Reeve about the conspiracy. You could have told him about how they threatened to—"

"You barely know the man, Lori! What makes you so all-fired certain he would have been able to do anything?"

"I . . . I just know, that's all."

They lapsed into another long silence, each lost in their own chaotic reverie. Nearby, Abner Dugan shifted on the ground and leaned negligently back against a tree. Hadley watched him for a moment, then turned to Lorelei again.

"What are you planning to do when we get back to Fort Concho?" he surprised her by asking. "Will you be going with Major Cameron?" Before she could answer, he told her with a frown, "You don't have to, you know. You could return home and forget you ever had a husband."

"No, Hadley, I couldn't." No matter how hard she tried, she could never forget Reeve Cameron.

"Then get a divorce!" Warming to his own suggestion, he added eagerly, "We can head down to San Antone when this is all over with. I'll help you find a good, reputable lawyer, and—"

"Major Cameron has already made it quite clear that he will never entertain the thought of divorce," she informed him in a low, measured tone.

"Maybe you don't want to be rid of him at all, Lori." He settled himself on his back again and tugged his broad-brimmed hat farther down on his forehead. "Now shut up and let me get some sleep. It will be my turn to stand watch in another couple of hours. But don't worry about Dugan," he reiterated. "I'm a light sleeper."

Lorelei's brow creased into a frown. Following his none too chivalrous request, she closed her eyes and drew a light woolen blanket up over her fully clothed body. It was a bit too warm for cover, but she felt that she needed extra protection from Dugan's lustful gaze. She was glad her brother lay close by; she prayed that there would be no need for the rifle he was clasping in defensive readiness. Soon, and with remarkable ease, she drifted off to sleep.

She awakened with a start only a short time later. Her eyes flew wide, instinctively searching for the dark form of Hadley's body beside her. He was gone.

"Hadley?" she called out softly. There was no answer.

Her heart drummed in her ears as she sat up and shifted her apprehensive gaze toward the fire. It had burned down to nothing more than a glowing mass of embers, but the full moon cast enough light on the rugged, nighttime prairie landscape so that she could easily make out the outline of a man coming toward her.

"Hadley?"

Too late, she realized it was Abner Dugan. A warning bell sounded deep in her brain. Without being told, she knew something was terribly wrong.

"Where is my brother, Mr. Dugan?" she demanded, scrambling hastily to her feet.

The thick, luxuriant mass of flame-colored tresses swirled about her face and shoulders, making her even more desirable in the eyes of the man who had decided the first time he saw her that he would take her. Hell, he told himself, she'd probably never even had a man inside her before. He'd change that soon enough. Yessir, he thought, his eyes shining hotly at the prospect, he'd take her hard and fast the first time, and then he'd strip off her clothes and spend some time getting to know that sweet body of hers.

"Me and the boy had ourselves a little disagreement," he drawled mockingly.

It hadn't been at all difficult to lure the young bastard over to the other side of the trees and then knock him out with a well-placed blow to the chin. The struggle had been a brief one, he recalled with malevolent satisfaction. The boy had proven himself to be a sorry fighter, just as he'd thought. If not for the fact that he was reluctant to add murder to his already impressive list of crimes, he'd have finished him off. As it was, he had settled for leaving him hog-tied at the bottom of the hill. And now it was time to do what he'd been itching to do all day long.

He drew closer and gave Lorelei a slow, rapacious smile that caused a shiver of fear to run the length of her spine.

"A—a disagreement?" she stammered weakly.

"Yeah. He lost."

"Dear God, what did you do to him?" she breathed. "Where is he?"

She backed away in rising panic, her gaze wide and horror-struck as she looked about frantically for a means of defense. Her brother's rifle was missing, and there was nothing else around—save one of the jagged-edged rocks that peppered the ground about her bedroll. Hope sprang to life in her breast when her eyes fell on them.

"There's no need to worry yourself about him," Dugan sneered contemptuously. "Nothin's hurt but his pride."

"Stay away from me!" she cried, edging nearer to her intended weapon. She made a quick, mental note of the fact that he had set aside his own rifle, and had removed his holster as well.

"I could tell right away that what you needed was someone to show you that you ain't no better than the rest of us." He unbuckled his belt and tugged it off. "Miss High and Mighty Montgomery. Hell, you're nothin' but a redhaired little bitch!"

"As God is my witness, Mr. Dugan, if you come any closer, I will do whatever it takes to protect myself!" The threat earned her a derisive snort of laughter.

"Go ahead." Wearying of talk, he lunged for her. His hand closed with bruising force about her arm.

"No!"

She bent swiftly and grasped the rock. Dugan yanked her up hard against him in the very next instant, twisting her arm cruelly behind her back so that she cried out. She raised her other arm and brought the rock crashing down against the side of his head.

He cursed and released his brutal grip on her, staggering backward. Blood gushed from the jagged wound just above his temple. Momentarily forget-

281

ting about the woman responsible for his pain, he ripped off his kerchief and raised it to his head in a futile attempt to staunch the flow of blood.

Lorelei was already halfway through the cover of trees by the time he thought about seeking revenge. She paused to catch up the rifle Hadley had dropped, then looked about instinctively for her brother. Her eyes widened in further dismay when they fell on his bound, unconscious form lying at the foot of the hill.

"Hadley!" she screamed. Flinging a terrified glance back over her shoulder, she raced down the moonlit slope. She dropped to her knees beside her brother and worked desperately to untie the rope about his hands and feet, all the while fearing that Abner Dugan would materialize at the top of the hill.

Miraculously, however, there was still no sign of her attacker. Both puzzled and relieved by the fact that he had not come after her yet, she succeeded in loosening Hadley's bonds and began slapping lightly at his face.

"Hadley!" she repeated in a hoarse, urgent whisper. Her fingers clenched about the rifle and she cast yet another apprehensive glance up toward the grove of trees where she knew Dugan lay in wait. "Hadley, wake up! Dear God, you've got to wake up!"

He moaned at last, his eyelids fluttering open as he struggled to return to consciousness. Grimacing at the pain in his jaw, he pulled himself unsteadily into a sitting position and frowned in groggy confusion at his sister.

"Lori? Wha—what happened?"

"It's Mr. Dugan!" she disclosed in a breathless tumble of words. "He tried to force himself on me! I managed to fight him off, but—"

"I'll kill that double-crossing son of a bitch!" he growled in vengeful fury. He snatched the rifle from her grasp and climbed slowly to his feet. She clutched at his arm, her eyes full of desperate entreaty.

"No! Please, Hadley, you can't go up there!"

"Damn it, Lori, we can't just stay here and let him finish us off! We're like sitting ducks!" He jerked away from her and started up the hill. Lorelei was close behind him, still intent on stopping him before it was too late.

But there was no need. They had traveled only a few steps when they heard the unmistakable sound of hoofbeats breaking the silence of the night.

"He's getting away!" exclaimed Hadley. Darting up the hill as swiftly as he could, he arrived just in time to see Dugan riding away into the moonlit darkness.

Lorelei drew to a halt beside her brother. She was glad the man had gone, even though she understood all too well the significance of his departure.

"What are we going to do now?" she asked Hadley. She swept her long, wildly streaming hair from her face and tried to catch her breath. "At least he left us our horses," she noted, momentarily directing her bright gaze toward the two animals still secured beneath the trees. She looked back to her brother, her brows drawing together into a frown of worriment on his behalf, as she raised a gentle hand to

283

his bruised, scowling face. "Are you all right?"

"I'm fine," he assured her, his voice edged with bitter anger. "Just fine. Only now, blast it all, we're left in the middle of nowhere, without a guide and with only one rifle between us!"

"We can still make it, Hadley," she insisted. "We can leave right now and —"

"We're not going anywhere until morning!"

"Why not?"

"Because it's too dangerous for us to travel any farther tonight," he replied with a heavy sigh. "The horses aren't rested enough. We couldn't ride for more than a couple of hours at most, and then we really *would* be stranded. If we stay put for now, we've got at least a chance of making it." He lowered the rifle and walked over to drop down on one knee beside the dwindling fire. Piling the last of the wood on top of the embers, he said despondently, "There's nothing more either of us can do tonight. Try to get some sleep, Lori. I'll keep watch."

"Are you sure you're all right?"

"Yes." Carefully he touched his chin, which was already turning an ugly shade of purple. Then suddenly his eyes lit with guilty realization. He rose to his feet again and lifted his hand to Lorelei's shoulder. "What about you?" he demanded, his gaze anxiously searching her upturned countenance. "Dugan didn't hurt you, did he?"

"No." She shook her head and started to say more, but sudden tears of release, both physical and emotional, choked the words back. Her eyes closed as her brother drew her against him.

"I'm sorry, Lori. I'm sorry I let you down like

284

that. And I'm sorry I ever got you into this mess!" he lamented once more. His youthful features tightened with self-reproach and misery, and with no small amount of trepidation.

Lorelei buried her face in his shirt and allowed the tears to flow unchecked. She remembered how Reeve had tried to warn her about Dugan. She remembered everything . . . everything he had ever said or done to her since the first moment she had set eyes on him back at the stage office in Fort Worth. And she yearned for his strong, comforting arms about her right now instead of Hadley's.

When the storm of weeping had finally subsided, she drew away from her brother and sank down onto her bedroll. The two of them sat together in silence for a long time, staring at the dancing flames of the fire while the night deepened about them.

"Hadley?" Lorelei murmured, as she stretched out again after a while and stared up at the full moon.

"Go to sleep, Lori," he chided gently. Although his own body ached with the need for sleep, he would remain awake. "We can talk tomorrow."

"I just wanted you to know that I don't think I'll be going back to Georgia, after all."

Too tired to examine what had prompted that statement, which had startled her every bit as much as it had her brother, she closed her eyes obediently and fell into a deep, dreamless sleep.

Fourteen

"Wake up, Lori. It's time to go."

Lorelei reluctantly opened her eyes to see her brother's face smiling down at her.

"Good Heavens, is it morning already?" she asked, stifling a groan as she pushed herself up from the bedroll. She focused with an effort and made a quick, encompassing sweep of her surroundings. The sky, brilliantly blue and cloudless, was already lit with the pink-hued rays of the dawn.

"The sun will be up in a few minutes," said Hadley. He offered her a strip of beef jerky and a small square of hardtack. "Here. Eat this. Maybe we can get a hot meal later."

"Thank you," she murmured, eyeing the food dubiously. She took a bite of the crunchy, unappetizing biscuit and climbed to her feet. Noting that the horses were already saddled, she frowned and cast an anxious look at her brother. "Did you get any sleep at all?"

"No. But we'll take time for a decent rest once we reach a town."

"And when will that be?"

"I don't know," he admitted honestly. He squinted

toward the horizon and said, with more conviction than he actually felt, "As long as we continue heading northwest, we should reach New Mexico in another day or two."

Lorelei nodded wordlessly and hurried to get ready. She washed her face and hands in the stream, braided her hair, and sought the concealing privacy of the trees for a moment while Hadley led the horses a short distance away.

"Do you think we'll ever meet up with Mr. Dugan again?" she wondered aloud when she emerged again. She swung up into the saddle without assistance, secretly dreading the prospect of another long day spent on horseback.

"I hope so," answered Hadley. His eyes gleamed at the possibility of a chance for revenge. Although he still lacked the maturity and experience to make him the leader he aspired to be, he was determined to right whatever wrongs he could. And Abner Dugan, damn his soul to hell, had committed an unforgivable sin.

"Come on!" He urged his mount forward, turning his head to make certain his sister followed.

They had ridden scarcely a mile from the campsite when Lorelei was suddenly seized with the impulse to cast a look back over her shoulder. She did so — and felt her whole body flooding with a contradictory mixture of heart-stopping alarm and the most profound joy she had ever known

Reeve!

"Hadley!" she called out to her brother, who was several yards ahead of her by this time. Raising her voice to be heard above the wind and the thunder of

287

the horses' hooves, she tried again frantically. "Hadley!"

"What is it?" he flung back at her.

"It's Reeve! He—he's here!"

Hadley reined his horse to a sudden halt and jerked his head about. His face paled at the sight of the lone rider bearing down on them.

"Are you sure it's Major Cameron?" he asked Lorelei, though he already knew the answer.

"I'm sure!" she affirmed, drawing up beside him. Even at this distance, she could make out his rugged, sun-bronzed features. There was no mistaking the familiar broad shoulders, nor the grim set of his jaw. He rode a horse as if he had been born to it, and he was swiftly closing the gap between them.

"You've got to go on without me!" she told Hadley, her mind racing to think of a way to help him escape once more.

"I'm not going to leave you behind!" he protested, shaking his head in a stubborn, vehement denial.

"You've got to! Don't you see?" she pleaded desperately, conscious of the fact that, in a matter of seconds, it would be too late to do anything. "Our only chance is for you to continue on to Las Vegas, find Private Taggart, and bring him back to Fort Concho!"

"But what about you? Hell's bells, Lori, I can't go off and leave you with—"

"I'll be perfectly safe!" she assured him, with a confidence she was far from feeling. "Reeve is my husband, remember? He'll follow me, not you! I love you, Hadley—*now go!*"

With that, she reined about and headed due west.

Her brother hesitated, his conscience waging a fierce battle with his begrudging realization that her suggestion made sense. Finally, he did as she bid. He bit out a curse and rode away to the north.

Lorelei's blue eyes sparkled with triumphant satisfaction when she glanced back and saw that Reeve was giving chase. She hadn't been at all sure he would choose to pursue her instead of Hadley; she had simply listened to her instincts. They had told her that, just this once, he would follow his heart instead of his head. And he had. Thank God, *he had!*

She held on for dear life as her horse galloped wildly across the vast prairie landscape. The longer it took for Reeve to catch her, she told herself, the more time Hadley would have to get away. It was with that sole purpose in mind that she bent low in the saddle and allowed the animal beneath her to obey his own instincts.

Moments later, she turned her head and noted with dismay that her husband was so close that she could literally see the white-hot fury smoldering in his magnificent green eyes. Trembling with very real fear, she snapped the reins together and pressed herself even lower.

Suddenly, disaster struck.

A sharp, breathless cry escaped her lips as her horse stumbled and fell. Without warning, she was thrown free. The cinch snapped in two, sending the saddle tumbling downward in her wake. She was almost certain she heard Reeve call her name, but there was not time to think about that or anything else. While the panic-stricken animal quickly regained his balance and took off like a shot again, she found herself hitting the ground with such force that the breath was knocked from her body.

She landed on her side, her hip and shoulder absorbing the impact of the fall before she rolled over and came to rest on her back. Dazed and bruised, but otherwise miraculously unhurt, she lay there staring up at the sky while her heart pounded heavily in her chest and a merciful numbness filled her entire body. The next thing she knew, Reeve was bending over her.

"Lorelei?" His splendid, deep-timbred voice was raw with emotion as he dropped to his knees beside her. He ran his hands swiftly over her arms and legs, then across her hips and shoulders. Satisfied that she had suffered no broken bones, he breathed a long, ragged sigh of relief and muttered hoarsely, "Dear God, I thought you were dead!"

She offered no resistance when he swept her up against him. Her head spun dizzily, and her muscles had begun to scream in protest at what they had just endured, but she closed her eyes and felt her heart give a leap of pure happiness.

"Are you all right?" he asked quietly.

"Yes. I . . . I'm all right," she assured him.

"Good. Because I want some answers!" he ground out.

She gasped when he stood abruptly and hauled her up before him. His handsome face was thunderous, his gaze was filled with a dangerous, near-savage light, and she was painfully aware of the hot, barely controlled rage that simmered just below the surface. She had never seen him so angry before—

and she prayed that she never would again.

"What the devil did you think you were doing?" he demanded tersely. "Damn it, woman, you might have broken your neck!"

"I was trying to help my brother get away," she answered in a small voice. Her gaze fell beneath the burning intensity of his, and she swallowed hard before adding, "I thought if I could lead you—"

"What you've *done*, you little fool, is lead yourself into a hell of a lot more trouble than you bargained for." He swore under his breath and forced his hands away from her, though the look in his eyes left little doubt that he was battling the urge to exact a sweet revenge for her betrayal. There would be time for that later, he promised himself. He frowned down at her and gave a passing glance back toward the campsite. "What happened to Dugan?"

She was reluctant to tell him. Knowing full well what his reaction would be, she did her best to conceal her lingering distress over the matter.

"Mr. Dugan rode away last night," she replied evasively, averting her gaze once more.

"Why?" Reeve demanded, in a voice that let her know he wouldn't settle for anything less than the truth. His eyes darkened when he glimpsed a telltale shadow cross her beautiful features.

Lorelei inhaled sharply when his hands shot out to grasp her arms. She looked up at him, only to shiver when she saw the fierce, tight-lipped expression on his face.

"What did that bastard do to you?"

"He . . . nothing! I was able to get away in time, and then he left!"

She blanched at the murderous look in his eyes, mistakenly believing that it was directed at her. Actually, he was contemplating the pleasure he would get out of killing Abner Dugan with his bare hands.

"Come on," he ordered, virtually dragging her over to where his horse stood pawing impatiently at the ground. He snatched up her carpetbag, which had fallen with her saddle, on the way.

"Are we going back to Fort Concho?" She was almost afraid to ask.

"No." With curt, angry movements, he tied her bag securely on one side of his saddle.

He seized her about the waist and tossed her effortlessly up onto the horse's back, then swung up behind her. She trembled when he pulled her back against him, her softly rounded hips making intimate contact with the lean hardness of his thighs.

"Then where—" she started to ask.

"Las Vegas, New Mexico." His arms came about her as he reached for the reins.

Her eyes widened with incredulity. She turned her head to look at him again. Suddenly it dawned on her that he was wearing civilian clothing, but she was too preoccupied with other thoughts to ask him why he was out of uniform.

"How did you know that's where we were headed?"

"I know all about Private Taggart. And about the conspiracy," he startled her by revealing.

"You *do?* But—why didn't you tell me? For Heaven's sake, Reeve Cameron, if you knew about it all along, why couldn't you have told Hadley? And *me?*" she demanded accusingly. "He was afraid to

292

cooperate with you, and I—"

"Should have trusted me," he finished for her. He clamped an arm about her waist and gripped the reins expertly with one hand. "None of that matters now. We've got a hard day's ride ahead of us, so keep quiet and hold on."

"Reeve—"

"Later," he cut her off brusquely, already reining about. "You'd better pray that we catch up with that brother of yours before the Comanches do."

Lorelei's throat constricted in alarm. She hadn't paused to consider the dangers Hadley might face traveling alone. Once again, she thought with an inward sigh, she had acted with an impulsiveness she would no doubt live to regret. More and more, she was beginning to realize that, as Reeve had said, she should have trusted him . . .

Feeling sick at heart, and yet still inexplicably contented, she clung to the saddlehorn as her husband touched his booted heels to the horse's flanks. They set off after Hadley at a gallop, the morning sun blazing to life behind them and setting the plains afire with a sudden burst of gold.

True to Reeve's words, the day's journey gave every indication of being long and hard. They stopped to rest twice that morning, when it was necessary to feed and water the horse. Lorelei was grateful for these respites, however brief they were, and would spend the precious minutes quenching her own considerable thirst, stretching her saddle-weary legs, and cooling her skin with a wet handkerchief. With surprising thoughtfulness, Reeve allowed her a few moments of privacy each time.

Then, with scarcely a dozen words having passed between them, he would lift her back up to the saddle and mount behind her.

She soon realized that her husband was familiar with this countryside; he never once seemed to doubt what lay ahead. There was no opportunity for conversation between them as they rode like the very devil across the boundless, uncivilized prairie, but she remained painfully aware of his anger with her. His arm was like a band of steel about her waist, and his face was disturbingly inscrutable whenever she stole a look at him.

The sun was almost directly overhead when she caught a glimpse of what she thought was a herd of cattle in the distance. As she and Reeve drew nearer, however, she was pleased to discover that the animals weren't the expected longhorn cows at all — they were buffalo. She had seen a number of jackrabbits and prairie dogs, and even antelope, thus far, but nothing could compare with the impressive sight before her now.

The buffalo were magnificent-looking beasts, huge and shaggy, and moving across the grassy earth with methodical slowness. They were scattered into small groups and spread out over a large area, perhaps some sixty or seventy in all, and Lorelei mused that they appeared far less than threatening at the moment. Recalling the wagons she had seen loaded with bloody hides back in Santa Angela, she felt a renewed twinge of horror at the thought they were being slaughtered so mercilessly.

"Can't we get any closer?" she asked Reeve, daring for the first time to break the silence while they rode. He shook his head, and his eyes glinted beneath the brim of his hat.

"No. We don't want to risk a stampede."

She frowned and shifted back around. Unaware of the way her husband's features tensed as the roundness of her hips nestled against his manhood, she heaved a sigh of disappointment. Her gaze remained fastened on the buffalo until they were out of sight. A short time later, Reeve guided the horse toward a stand of mesquite and cottonwood trees, which, at least in the barren wilds of far-west Texas, signaled a welcome oasis.

"We'll stop and eat here," he announced, slowing the weary, sweat-coated animal beneath them to a walk.

"I suppose I'm to receive nothing but bread and water so long as I'm your prisoner," remarked Lorelei, her tone laced with bitter sarcasm. She was hot and tired, and anxious to have it out with him once and for all. Heaven help her, she couldn't bear any more of this dreadful anticipation. "Or perhaps you've another punishment in mind, Major Cameron?" she challenged tauntingly. "I do recall you once threatened to have me imprisoned!"

"It would be no more than you deserve," he retorted gruffly.

He reined to a halt beside the trees, dismounted, and hauled her unceremoniously down from the saddle. His hands remained at her waist, and his gaze burned down into hers. He was torn between the vengeful urge to tan her beautiful, traitorous little hide and the infinitely more appealing temptation to throw her on the ground and take her with

295

such furious, unbridled passion that she would never again be able to deny that she was his.

At the moment, however, he was still too angry with her to trust his emotions. He had never loved anyone as much as he loved her; her betrayal had hurt him more than he'd ever been hurt before.

"You'll find food in one of the saddlebags," he instructed in a low, distant voice, forcing himself to release her. "We'll get a hot meal tonight."

That was the same promise Hadley had made her, she recalled with a disconsolate sigh. She turned and watched in silence while Reeve, after tossing the saddlebags to the ground, led the horse over to the thin trickle of water that passed for a stream in that part of the country. Suddenly realizing that she had very little appetite, she decided to forego the meal, and settled instead for dropping to her knees beside the stream. Her troubled gaze swept across the surrounding plains, absently scrutinizing the endless clusters of sagebrush, cactus, and yucca plants.

She closed her eyes and splashed generous handfuls of the cooling liquid on her face, then sat back on her heels and allowed the water to course freely down her throat. Where her full breasts thrust upward against her white cotton blouse and chemise, the thin, wet fabric became virtually transparent, offering Reeve a tantalizing glimpse of the rose-tipped peaks, which seemed to be inviting his touch.

He cursed inwardly and felt his loins filling with a heat that had nothing to do with the sun blazing relentlessly overhead.

"I don't think we have a chance of catching up with Hadley," opined Lorelei, smoothing the damp, wayward tendrils from her forehead. She opened her eyes and climbed to her feet, but did not look at Reeve. "He should easily outdistance us, given the fact that we are forced to share your horse." Turning about, she strolled back to where the saddlebags lay.

Reeve's deep green gaze darkened as it fastened on the seductive sway of her backside, displayed to full advantage in the tight-fitting pants she wore. Vowing to make sure she never dressed like that in any other man's presence, he left the horse grazing beside the stream and joined her. He set his rifle beside the saddlebags.

"What you said before, about . . . about the Comanches," Lorelei stammered with a frown, as she glanced anxiously at the gun. "Mr. Dugan warned us about them, but we saw nothing—"

"You wouldn't see anything until it was too late." He bent his tall frame downward, coming to rest on one knee as he pulled a packet of food from the saddlebag.

"Then Hadley really is in danger," she murmured. She sank down onto the ground and nibbled distractedly at the hard biscuit Reeve offered her. Moments later, she stole a look at him from beneath her eyelashes, and colored warmly when she saw that he was staring at her. "Will you tell me now why you didn't mention anything about the conspiracy to either me or Hadley?" she ventured, still amazed that he had known all along.

"I never reveal anything before I've completed an investigation," he explained, his tone very low and level. "In your brother's case, his cooperation had to be based on nothing more than a desire to see himself cleared. That was the only way I could be sure he was telling the truth. I was told about the conspiracy before I ever left Washington," he surprised her by adding. His penetrating gaze met and locked with the liquid blue fire of hers. "For some time now, Colonel Mackenzie has suspected that some of his own men were involved in the raids taking place near the post. He believed that a number of enlisted men, as well as officers, were responsible for inciting the Indians to violence against the settlers, then sharing in the plunder."

"But how could my brother have gotten involved?" she asked in confusion. "Hadley would never—"

"The extent of his involvement, or lack of it, hasn't been decided yet," Reeve pointed out. "But he was standing as sentry the night Lieutenant Fitzhugh was killed. Private Taggart was there, too."

"But why was Hadley arrested for the murder? And why didn't you see fit to question Private Taggart before he so conveniently deserted?" she demanded, outraged that the only man who could clear her brother had managed to slip through the military's fingers with such ease.

"I don't have an answer yet to your first question. But as for Taggart—let's just say he had ample help and persuasion." A faint, sardonic smile touched his lips before his expression became one of grim determination once more. "I've already dispatched someone to Las Vegas to find him."

"You have?" she breathed in astonishment. "Why didn't you tell me?"

"Because you were supposed to trust me to do my

298

job, remember?" His eyes darkened again, with reproachful fury this time. He rose to his feet and scowled down at her. "Damn it, Lorelei, do you have any idea how much trouble you've caused?" he exploded finally. "Your brother's in worse danger than before, I'm going to have to fight like hell to keep you from being arrested, and it will be a miracle if I manage to keep my hands off you long enough to let my temper cool!"

"You are every bit as much to blame as I am, Reeve Cameron!" she retorted, standing now as well. She flung the piece of hardtack aside and tilted her head back to confront him squarely. Her eyes flashed resentfully up into his. "If you had only bothered to let me know what was going on, I might have been able to give you the trust you seem to think you deserve! How was I to know that there was any hope of Hadley being cleared? You said yourself that things looked bad for him, and that if he didn't talk it was almost certain the court-martial would go against him! What was I supposed to do—sit back and watch him hang? I told you once before that I couldn't do that!"

"So you chose to hire a sorry, no-account bastard like Abner Dugan and break your brother out of the guardhouse!" he countered harshly, finding it more and more difficult to keep his hands at his sides. "I wouldn't have believed even *you* could be that naïve!"

He would have given his very life for her, and yet no one, *no one,* had ever infuriated him as much as she had with her reckless interference. His pride stung at the memory of how she had lured him to her room and then betrayed him. He wanted to make her pay, to make her beg for forgiveness . . . damn it all, he wanted to make her love him as much as he loved her.

"I don't care what you think of me!" she declared, her beautiful face flushed and defiant. Her breasts rose and fell angrily beneath the wet, revealing cotton. "I did what I had to do! I would have done anything to save Hadley!"

"As I recall, that was the same reason you gave for marrying me, wasn't it?" He tried, unsuccessfully, to prevent his gaze from straying downward from her face. Desire had already turned his blood to fire, and his self-control was taking a beating. "Damnation, you little hellcat," he ground out, "you can give whatever reason you want for arranging that stupid, misguided attempt at justice, but don't ever try telling me again that becoming my wife was a sacrifice on your part! You married me of your own free will, because you wanted me every bit as much as I wanted you!"

"That's not true!" she denied hotly.

"Yes it is! And what's more, your body isn't the only thing that belongs to me now. Your heart is mine as well, Lorelei Montgomery Cameron, and I'm tired of waiting to hear you admit it. I've run out of patience!"

She gave a loud gasp of startlement, her eyes growing wide as he reached for her at last. She turned to run, but it was too late. He seized her wrist in an iron grip and yanked her up roughly against him.

"When this is all over with, no matter how things

turn out for your brother, you're coming with me!" he decreed, his arms enveloping her with their sinewy hardness. His gaze smoldered down into the stormy depths of hers. "I love you. And you love me. But don't *ever* make the mistake of playing me for a fool again!"

"Let me go!" she cried, battling her own desires as well as his. She struggled wildly within his grasp, but he held her captive.

She didn't want to love him. She didn't want to acknowledge that what she felt was anything more than a wicked, highly pleasurable attraction, even though her heart held the truth. It couldn't be possible that she had fallen in love with the man who might very well end up being responsible for her brother's death—it couldn't be! But, sweet mercy, she came alive whenever he took her in his arms, she had suffered terrible remorse for having caused him pain, and, perhaps most damning of all, she couldn't bear the thought of being apart from him any more.

She opened her mouth to speak, but Reeve's lips silenced her. His mouth branded hers in a hard, fiercely demanding kiss that took her breath away and sent passion blazing through her body like wildfire. She moaned in surrender and pressed her soft, trembling curves against him, offering no resistance whatsoever when he swept her up in his arms and carried her to the shelter of the trees. He lowered her to the ground and lay down beside her, his fingers already tugging the shirtwaist free of her pants.

She ran her hands feverishly across the broad, rock-hard planes of his back and down his arms.

Her own fingers moved to the front of her blouse, but Reeve tore impatiently at the damp garment. The buttons went flying as the fabric gave way. His mouth temporarily relinquished hers as he yanked the straps of her chemise downward, baring her breasts.

"Oh, Reeve!" she breathed, her skin feeling scorched by his hot, appreciative gaze. She made no move to cover her nakedness as his eyes raked hungrily over her, but instead tugged with growing impatience at his blue cotton shirt.

Rising to his knees beside her, he swiftly peeled off his shirt and flung it aside. Lorelei's arms tightened about him in a rapturous welcome when he lowered himself on top of her and claimed her lips in another sweetly savage onslaught. A delicious shiver ran down her spine when her naked breasts made contact with his bronzed, lightly matted chest, and she arched her back instinctively beneath him as his tongue plunged within her mouth and his hand came up to caress the full, satiny roundness of her breasts.

She moaned again, clinging to him as the familiar yearning turned her blood to liquid fire. His mouth ravished hers completely and without mercy, then trailed hotly downward to close about one of her breasts. His warm, wet tongue swirled about the nipple, his lips suckling greedily, while her eyes closed in ecstasy and her hips moved restlessly on the ground.

His fingers, moving to unfasten his pants, accomplished their task with amazing speed and dexterity. He did the same to Lorelei's and, having tugged them down and eased them off, he was suddenly seized with an idea. Deftly, he turned her over. He longed to bury himself deep inside her and knew that her fire matched his own. Urging her up to her knees, he pulled her back against him. His hand moved around to delve within the inviting triangle of auburn curls between her thighs. She cried out softly, her thighs parting as she strained upward against his wildly erotic caress.

The next thing she knew, he was pushing her forward so that she came to rest on her hands and knees. Her eyelids fluttered open, and she turned her head to glance at him in confusion, wondering how he would take her when he had yet to turn her around. Her unspoken question was answered an instant later when he plunged into her from the rear, his hardness sheathing expertly within her feminine passage.

Another breathless cry escaped her lips as she accepted the full, throbbing length of him. He pulled her back against him once more, one hand continuing its exquisite torment between her thighs while the other came up to caress her breasts. Her hips followed the sensuous, fiercely loving motion of his, and their perfectly blended flesh and hearts became as one. The tempestuous union ended in a blaze of mutual fulfillment, leaving them both fully sated, gasping for breath, and more than a little stunned by what had happened.

After a few moments, Reeve stretched out on his back beneath the trees, and pulled his beloved bride close. She rested contentedly in his arms for a while, until finally awakening to the fact that she was lying there almost naked in broad daylight. An inner voice pointed out that it certainly hadn't seemed to matter a short time ago; but now that reality was fast intruding, so was modesty.

She sat up and pulled her chemise upward to cover her breasts. Reeve's hand closed gently about her arm, but she refused to look at him as she tugged and squirmed to pull her pants back on once more.

"Need some help?" he drawled, his eyes brimming with amusement and a roguish smile playing about his lips.

"No!" She blushed and finally succeeded in pulling the pants up, then climbed to her knees while she fastened them. A frown creased her brow when she took in the sight of her torn, buttonless shirtwaist. "I hope you don't intend to make a habit of tearing off my clothes," she murmured. But her sigh of exasperation was woefully unconvincing, even to her own ears.

"Not unless you intend to make a habit of parading around in those damned pants." Though he wanted nothing more than to pull her back down, he forced himself to let her go and reluctantly got to his feet beside her. He set his own pants to rights again and donned his shirt, watching her closely while she marched over to her carpetbag and searched in vain for another shirtwaist. "You'll put on a dress before we get to Tascosa," he commanded masterfully.

"Tascosa?" She straightened and turned to face him with a puzzled expression. "Is that a town?"

" 'Town' is too generous a description, but it's the

best we can do. It's still half a day's ride from here." He went back to the stream, cupped his hands and took a drink, then told her, "You'll find a shirt in that other saddlebag."

"Thank you," she replied, with only a hint of sarcasm. She followed his instructions, withdrawing a white cotton shirt that fairly swallowed her when she put it on. She rolled up the sleeves and tucked the knee-length shirttail into her pants. Acutely conscious of her husband's watchful gaze, she returned to the stream and treated herself to one last drink of water.

"Lorelei."

Her head came up at the sound of her name on his lips. Hastily she scrambled to her feet when she saw that he was advancing on her with an all-too-familiar light in his piercing green eyes.

"Stay away from me, Reeve Cameron!" she insisted, her pulses racing alarmingly. Good Heavens, she thought with an inward groan, she really had become shameless. "I—I don't want to talk about what happened! As a matter of fact, I don't want to talk at all!"

"All right," he agreed, much to her surprise. "Have it your way then—for now."

She took a deep breath as his easy, masculine strides led him past her to retrieve the saddlebags. She dreaded the moment when he would lift her up into the saddle; the prospect of having him touch her again was a disquieting one, especially after their wildly rapturous lovemaking.

Just as she had feared, she grew warm and breathless when it came time for them to leave and his hands closed about her waist. He did not lift her immediately, but stood gazing down at her purposely bent head.

"For whatever it's worth," he proclaimed in a low, warm tone, "I'm sorry I didn't tell you what I knew."

She tilted her head back, and her eyes met the steady, fathomless intensity of his.

"You are?" she whispered in disbelief. Her heart stirred with emotion. She felt sudden tears starting to her eyes, and found herself battling the impulse to fling herself on his broad, capable chest and let him hold her for as long as he liked. "Well, I . . . I am sorry for not trusting you," she replied sincerely. "And for deceiving you." She drew in a long, shuddering breath before explaining in a rush, "Mr. Dugan promised me you wouldn't be hurt! I didn't know he was going to bring that man Clayton with him, and—"

"That's not important now," he assured her, his fingers tightening about her waist while his eyes glowed softly. "We're going to put the past behind us, Lorelei. Someday, we'll tell our children about our less-than-auspicious beginnings. But for now," he concluded, finally hoisting her up to her place in the saddle, "we've got to find that brother of yours. And Taggart, too, if we're lucky."

"Reeve?"

"Yes?" He mounted behind her, his arm slipping possessively about her waist as he reined the horse away from the stream.

"Why do you know your way around this part of the country so well?" she asked, the thought

306

prompting her brows to knit together into a slight frown. She glanced back at him and saw a smile touch his lips.

"I thought we were going to forget about the past."

"Not entirely," she corrected. She sighed, and faced forward again. "I don't know very much about you at all. And in truth, there are a good many things about me you would be surprised to learn."

"Nothing about you would ever surprise me, sweet vixen," he said wryly. "But if it pleases you to confess all your past sins, you can do so tonight when we reach Tascosa."

"It isn't *my* sins I'm worried about!" she retorted.

He gave a low chuckle and pulled her closer against him, then urged the horse into a gallop. The sun beat down on them with merciless zeal as they rode, and the hot wind flung dust in their faces, but Lorelei's spirits were lighter than they had been in days. For the first time since leaving Fort Concho, she felt truly hopeful.

Fifteen

They reached Tascosa shortly before nightfall. Just as Reeve had warned her, the settlement, which had sprung up in the very midst of the *Llano Estacado,* was little more than a collection of small Mexican adobes, tin-roofed shacks, and tents. It was a rough place, a stopping point for buffalo hunters, cattle drovers, and even renegades. But it offered an abundance of water, due to its enviable location on the wooded banks of the Canadian River, and the luxury of a "real" hotel.

Lorelei did not feel even the slightest twinge of disappointment when Reeve pulled the horse to a halt in front of a single-story building that looked as if it had been erected overnight. The Longhorn Hotel would have been called a shack back home in Georgia, yet it was one of Tascosa's finest establishments.

The waning sunlight revealed a wide, dusty street flanked on either side by structures which proclaimed themselves, by virtue of faded, handpainted signs, to be places where one could get a variety of things such as a bath and a shave, a hot meal, general merchandise, and, surprisingly, the services of a dentist. And then, of course, there were the hell-town essentials of saloons and gaming halls.

Horses and wagons, many loaded with buffalo hides, choked the main avenue as darkness approached and the need for shelter grew more pressing. The few women about were either the wives and daughters of the original Mexican settlers, or the "soiled doves," who wore tight satin dresses and forced smiles. An overwhelming abundance of men crowded the planks that had been laid end to end along the street—young, fresh-faced cowboys who participated in the many drives that followed the nearby Goodnight-Loving Trail, sheep ranchers who had come to the river valley years ago, and others who obviously earned a living killing and skinning the great beasts of the plains.

Lorelei shuddered involuntarily as she recalled the horrible sight she and Reeve had witnessed earlier. Vultures had swarmed and circled above dozens of rotting buffalo carcasses in the near distance. A few miles farther on, they had come upon a veritable sea of bones, bleached white by the sun. Reeve had told her that summer always brought with it hordes of men anxious to make an entire year's wages for three months of hard, dangerous work.

"Hell, it's not much to look at, but at least we'll have a roof over our heads," he pronounced as he swung her down.

"Do you think I'll be able to get a bath?" she asked hopefully. Her long braid was twisted up beneath the hat he had given her, and he had flung a canvas duster over her shoulders before they had ridden into town.

"Of course." He gave a faint smile of irony before

turning away to loop the reins over the hitching post. "I'll have to keep my gun handy."

"Why?"

"Because, Mrs. Cameron, you're a beautiful woman in a town full of men who probably wouldn't think twice about slitting my throat just to have a good look at you." He took her arm in a firm, possessive grasp and began leading her toward her hotel. "And since I have no intention of allowing that to happen, you'll stay safely out of sight until morning."

"Do you think there's a chance Hadley came through here?"

"A chance, yes," he answered, then cautioned, "But don't get your hopes up yet. Even if he did manage to find his way this far, there's still more than a hundred miles of open country between here and Las Vegas."

She grew silent then, and as he had instructed earlier remained quiet while he obtained them a room. It required a bit of persuasion on his part, since the stout, gray-haired older man at the front desk insisted quite adamantly that the hotel was full to overflowing. Reeve was successful in the end, however, having learned a long time before that accommodations could always be found for the right price. Lorelei accompanied him down a narrow, dimly lit hallway to a room at the very back. He turned the key in the lock and swung the door open.

Too tired to be distressed by the fact that the room was little more than a low-ceilinged cubicle boasting no other furniture than an iron bedstead and a splintered washstand, Lorelei hurried to throw wide the single window. A blast of warm, smoke-scented air filled the room.

"Stay here," Reeve told her, dumping the saddle-bags, bedrolls, and carpetbag on the bare wooden floor. "I'll be back just as soon as I've seen to the horse."

"All right. But don't be long!" she called after him as he closed the door on his way out.

She felt a sharp twinge of uneasiness once he had gone, and hurried to slip the interior bolt into place. That done, she shrugged thankfully out of the duster and tugged the hat from her head. She had just started unbraiding her hair when a knock, loud and insistent, sounded at the door.

"Reeve?" Surprised that he had returned so soon, she unlocked the door and opened it with a smile of welcome already on her lips. The smile faded quickly when she saw that it wasn't Reeve who stood glowering at her, but a hawk-featured stranger with furiously narrowed brown eyes and dirty, rumpled clothing that looked as if it had been worn continuously for the better part of a week.

"Where's Cameron?" the man snarled at her without any attempt at civility.

"Cameron?" she asked, pretending ignorance. She had no idea why this man was looking for Reeve, but her instincts warned her against making his search an easy one. "I'm afraid I don't know—"

"He's your man, ain't he?"

"My man?"

"Damn your hide, girl, I saw him come in here with you! Now where the hell is the son of a bitch?" he demanded in a voice that was more like a growl.

311

"I don't know what you're talking about!" she lied, haughtily drawing herself erect. "And if you do not leave at once, I will scream and bring the entire town running!" To lend credence to her words she snatched up the rifle Reeve had left beside the bed and aimed the barrel at the man's chest. "Now go!"

The threat was no idle one and fortunately the coarse stranger realized that. He capitulated with an ill grace, treating her to one last venomous glare before ramming his hat back down upon his dark, greasy head.

"Tell him I came lookin' for him!" he bit out. "The name's Stanton!"

She remained on her guard until he had disappeared back down the hallway. Then, releasing a long, pent-up sigh of relief, she closed and locked the door again. Her heart was pounding as she lowered the rifle, and her eyes clouded with apprehension at the thought of what would happen when Stanton found Reeve. The man was evidently bent on revenge for something; she was anxious for her husband to return so she could ask him why.

The next time she heard a knock at the door, she made Reeve identify himself before she slid the bolt free. He stepped inside, only to frown at the troubled expression on her face.

"What's wrong?" he asked quietly, reaching for her shoulders.

"A man named Stanton was here! He said—" she started to explain, only to be cut off by his muttered curse. She gazed up at him in surprise as his handsome features grew taut with anger.

"He didn't threaten you, did he?" he demanded,

312

his eyes searing down into hers. "Damn him, if he dared to touch you—"

"No!" she hastened to assure him. "He didn't do anything at all, other than to tell me to say he is looking for you! For Heaven's sake, Reeve, who *is* he?"

"An old acquaintance," he answered evasively. He released her and tossed his hat onto the bed. Unwilling to accept his less-than-illuminating explanation, she grasped his arm and gave him a narrow, blazing look that would have made a lesser man tremble.

"I have a right to know what this is all about!" she declared with true wifely insistence. In spite of the gravity of the situation, Reeve's gaze filled with amusement.

"I suppose you do," he conceded softly.

"Well?" she prompted, folding her arms across her chest in an eloquent gesture of impatience. "Who is he? And why is he so angry with you?"

"His name is Buford Stanton, he's a two-bit outlaw who's been on the run for the majority of his sorry life, and I was his commanding officer back during the war."

"But why—"

"I had him brought up on charges of desertion. He was guilty as hell." His eyes darkened at the memory of how Stanton and thirteen others had run like cowards under fire. Their actions had cost the lives of nearly an entire company. "He spent the last eighteen months of the war in prison," added Reeve, turning away to lift the saddlebags up to the bed.

"You mean he's still seeking revenge for something that happened all those years ago?" she queried in wide-eyed disbelief. "Why should he blame you for his own crime?"

"Men like Stanton don't possess a conscience, Lorelei. They have no sense of right and wrong." He drew out a bundle of clothing, then went on, "And since I've told you this much, you might as well know that there's every likelihood Stanton has more than a passing knowledge of what's been going on back at Fort Concho."

"What?" she gasped. "Are you saying that he—"

"What I'm saying," Reeve clarified grimly, "is that he was among the civilians Colonel Mackenzie believed to be connected in some way to the conspiracy."

"Do you think he knows Hadley?" she queried, her gaze wide and anxious. "Do you think that's why he's here in Tascosa?"

"It's probably nothing more than a coincidence. There isn't much in the way of civilization this far west. It isn't unusual for me to run into an old 'friend' or two wherever I go. But I intend to question him, all the same."

"You can't do that!" she protested, her throat constricting in sudden alarm. She flew to his side and raised her hand to his arm again, scarcely aware of the fact that he had just opened her carpetbag and pulled a dress and clean undergarments from it. "If he truly is bent on revenge, then you'd be in certain danger if you tried to question him! Why, he might even attempt to kill you!"

"That's the general idea."

"Blast you, Reeve Cameron, don't you dare laugh at me!" she warned, her eyes flashing indignantly up

314

at him. "I'm perfectly serious!"

"So am I." His gaze softened as it roamed over her stormy, upturned face. He wrapped his arms about her and drew her forward until her soft curves were fitted with intimate, breathtaking perfection against his lithely muscled hardness. "Don't worry, my love," he said in a rich, mellow tone that made her pulses race. "You won't get rid of me that easily. No, you're not going to play the role of merry widow for at least another fifty or sixty years, if I have anything to say about it."

"Reeve—"

"Come on." He set her firmly away from him, but seized her hand in the strong warmth of his. "It's getting late."

"Where are you taking me?"

"To get you that bath you've been mooning about all day," he replied with maddening equanimity. He thrust her clothes at her and took up his own, then retrieved her borrowed hat and duster and stood watching her while she put them on.

"I have not been 'mooning'!" she retorted, bristling visibly again. "And besides, won't it be too dangerous for us to go anywhere? After all, Mr. Stanton—"

"Has been threatening to get even with me for as long as I can remember."

"Then he is bound to succeed sooner or later!" Although it was uttered as a riposte, she felt anything but lighthearted about the man's threats. Still, she told herself with an inward sigh, Reeve seemed to know what he was doing.

He pulled her from the room with him, catching

up his rifle on the way out and locking the door behind them. They left the hotel and traveled along the planked walk to the bathhouse, which was in actuality a series of tents featuring big wooden tubs and makeshift canvas curtains to separate one "room" from another. Huge bucketfuls of hot water were carried by male attendants, who discreetly averted their gaze so as not to offend the modesty of their customers, which was largely unnecessary since most of them were male. Towels and soap were provided at an extra fee, even though a bath would hardly be worthwhile without them.

Lorelei followed her husband as the proprietor showed them to a tent set apart from the others. It was at the very back, and a sign above the doorway read LADIES ONLY.

"You'll have to keep yourself outside," the man informed Reeve with a cautionary frown. "We run a decent place. But your woman can take all the time she wants. 'Course, it'll be dark soon, and then you got to watch out for snakes. We ain't had any use for this here tent for nigh on to a week. It was the missus' idea," he rattled on. "She said the womenfolk for miles around would come stampedin' just to take turns soakin' in the newfangled tub we got from back East." He shook his head. "It ain't happened. Guess everyone's still doin' their washin' up in the river."

Handing the towel and bar of lye soap to Lorelei, and the lamp to Reeve, he took himself off to deal with the steady stream of cowboys and buffalo hunters who were more than willing to pay a hard-earned dollar for a real, all-over bath. For many, it

316

would be the first washing they'd done in weeks.

"If this wasn't such a 'decent place,' I'd join you," Reeve drawled, as he ducked inside and set the lamp on a table beside the bright red metal bathtub.

"You most certainly would not!" She opened her mouth to say more, but a young man suddenly appeared with the hot water. Once he had filled the tub and gone, she reminded her husband sternly, "You heard what the man said—you are to wait outside!"

"Are you sure you don't need any help?" He towered above her, his eyes raking over her with bold significance.

"Quite sure!" She colored rosily and looked away before stammering. "I—I suppose you'll be bathing as well?"

"Not until you've finished." He turned and sauntered outside, taking up a protective stance just beyond the doorway.

She pulled the edges of the canvas together before moving back to the tub and quickly stripping off her clothes. Acutely conscious of the fact that Reeve was only a few feet away, she lowered her naked body into the hot, steaming water and closed her eyes as she lay back to enjoy its soothing warmth for a while—until she remembered the warning about snakes. She wasted no more time, but took up the cake of soap and scrubbed herself vigorously from head to toe.

Reeve was in easy earshot of the sounds of her bathing, and he could envision all too well what was taking place on the other side of the canvas. He gave an inward groan and tried not to think about his wife's beautiful body as it would look now — naked and wet, and damnably alluring. It required a supreme effort of will for him to refrain from joining her, as he had teasingly threatened to do.

Lorelei bent forward and washed her dust-coated auburn tresses, then got out of the tub and hastily wrapped a towel around herself. She gave a worried glance to the dirt floor, then twisted her long, dripping hair into a thick single coil in order to wring some of the water from it. Her eyes strayed in the direction of the doorway again as she removed the towel and drew on her chemise and drawers, followed by a simple, rose-colored dress, white cotton stockings, and her high-top leather boots. A frown of annoyance creased her brow when she mused again that Reeve Cameron seemed to possess far too much knowledge about feminine attire, for he had omitted nothing that she might need.

She had just begun rubbing at her hair with the towel when her husband suddenly materialized behind her. Sensing his presence even before he spoke, she whirled to face him.

"What are you doing in here?" she demanded breathlessly. "You cannot—"

"I can, and I will." He unbuckled his holster and placed it beside the bathtub, then set his rifle down as well. Lorelei's eyes grew round as saucers.

"What are you doing?" she reiterated, a blush stealing over her. She clutched the towel to her chest and watched while he began unbuttoning his shirt.

"Exactly what it looks like," he answered, his deep voice brimming with humor. He gave a nod toward the bathtub. "There's no sense in letting all

318

that water go to waste." He removed the shirt, then his boots and socks.

"This tent is for ladies only!" she protested, casting an anxious look toward the doorway.

"Yes, but there's no stampede, remember?" His eyes glowed warmly as he unfastened his pants and drew them off. He stood before her in all his masculine glory, an indulgent smile playing about his lips when he observed the way her face flamed.

"Reeve!" she gasped, spinning about again. "What if someone should come in?"

"They'll get more of an eyeful than they bargained for."

She heard the splash as he lowered himself into the water. It was ridiculous for her to be shocked— after all, she told herself, she had certainly seen him in the "altogether" before—and yet she could not help feeling uncomfortable. Resolutely keeping her back turned toward him, she braided her hair again, caught up the discarded clothing, and headed for the doorway.

"Where do you think you're going?" Reeve demanded nonchalantly.

"To wait outside!"

"No, you're not. You'll stay right here, where I can keep an eye on you."

"But—"

"Damn it, woman, don't you ever do anything without an argument first?" he cried in mock reproach.

"I might, if you didn't persist in giving me orders at every turn!" she retorted, folding her arms across her breasts. "For your information, Major Cameron, I am not under your command!"

"Come here."

"What?" She uncrossed her arms, her eyes widening again.

"Come here," he repeated, his voice, low and resonant, sending a delicious shiver up her spine.

"I—I most certainly will not!" she sputtered, shaking her head in stubborn, unwifely defiance. "Since I am quite sure you have nothing but mischief on your mind, I will remain exactly where I am!"

"I only want you to scrub my back, you little wildcat," he declared, with a quiet chuckle.

"If we were in more private surroundings, I might be inclined to obey," she parried loftily.

"I'll hold you to that."

He rinsed quickly, washed his thick, sun-streaked hair, and drew himself out of the tub, all the while keeping one eye on his gun and the doorway. Lorelei waited until he had dressed, then pivoted finally to face him.

"Feel better?" Reeve asked her, buckling on his holster again.

"Immensely," she confirmed.

"Good." He gave her a disarming half-smile that made her knees weaken. "Because I've still got that mischief on my mind."

"It will have to wait!" She swallowed hard as he slowly closed the distance between them, his bold, penetrating gaze flickering over her in a swift but thorough appraisal. He made no move to touch her, yet she felt branded all the same.

"That's another promise I'll hold you to," he

murmured softly.

She caught her breath, but he sauntered past her and ducked outside. He called for her to follow a moment later. She did so, only to find that twilight had crept over the rough, bustling riverside settlement.

"Are we going back to the hotel now?" she asked, tossing a glance overhead at the darkening sky.

"Yes. And then we're going to see what kind of meal we can find. From what I remember, Tascosa isn't known for its culinary excellence," he remarked dryly. He took her arm and led her away from the tent.

They stopped at the hotel room only briefly, relieving themselves of the dirty clothing before setting off for a building, a little farther down the street, which proudly advertised itself as a restaurant. Lorelei was conscious of the many appreciative looks, stares, and muttered oaths of surprise she elicited as she walked alongside Reeve—it would have been impossible *not* to be aware of them—but determinedly she kept her gaze straight and steady, and tried not to let her nervousness show. She was becomingly flushed by the time they reached the restaurant, and every head in the place turned when she appeared in the doorway.

The strong, mingling smells of food, smoke, and unwashed bodies met her as she stepped inside with Reeve, and she groaned inwardly upon discovering that, other than the two harried waitresses, she was the only woman in the place.

"Don't worry," her husband exhorted quietly, bending his head a little so that his lips were close to her ear, "they just want to get a good look at you."

He maintained a possessive grip on her arm as they made their way to an empty table near the front. There were at least two dozen men seated at benches and tables crowded indiscriminately within the lamplit room, and a quick glance at the handwritten menu revealed that there was only one choice for supper—beef stew.

A short time later, they were enjoying their first decent meal in two days when suddenly Buford Stanton came barreling into the restaurant. Lorelei tensed in alarm, her eyes flying to Reeve. He gave her a faint but reassuring smile before lifting another forkful of stew to his mouth. His manner was deceptively indifferent as the other man caught sight of him. Beneath the table, his left hand moved in defensive readiness toward his gun.

"Cameron!" roared Stanton.

A sudden hush fell over the room. Lorelei's heart twisted with dread.

"Reeve?" she whispered, desperately wondering why he didn't do something, anything, in response to the man's threatening presence. Her wide, anxious gaze shifted back to Buford Stanton's hawkish features, which were contorted in rage.

"Damn your soul to hell, Cameron, it's time you and me settled things once and for all!" he snarled vengefully. Most of the other diners got up at that and beat a hasty retreat, leaving only a handful of interested observers.

"I've told you before, Stanton," drawled Reeve, "I'm ready whenever you are."

322

"Well I'm ready now!"

"Reeve?" Lorelei stared at him in horrified disbelief, her voice rising shrilly. "Dear God, surely you're not going to—"

"Stay there," he commanded, standing up finally.

"But you—you can't do this!" she stammered breathlessly.

"It won't take long." He tossed his napkin to the table and put on his hat, his movements purposeful and unhurried. His mouth twitched when he added, "It never does."

"You mean you've done this before?" gasped Lorelei, rising abruptly to her feet as well.

"You plannin' to stand there and jaw all day, Cameron?" Stanton complained with a growl of impatience.

"I hope you've been practicing since last time, Stanton," Reeve said mockingly. He pushed Lorelei back down into her chair, then headed outside. Buford Stanton was right behind him.

"Reeve, no!" Lorelei pleaded. *Sweet mercy, this can't be happening,* she told herself numbly. She wasn't about to sit back and allow her husband to be shot down without doing anything to prevent it!

Disregarding his orders once again, she leapt to her feet and raced outside after them. Her wide, luminous gaze moved instinctively to Reeve when she drew to a halt on the planked walk in front of the restaurant. He was taking up a position in the center of the street, with his furious adversary doing the same a few yards away. A crowd was already gathering to watch; gunfights were frequent events in Tas-

323

cosa, and always popular.

"No!" cried Lorelei. She had to stop them!

Without pausing to consider the wisdom of her actions, she darted out into the moonlit street, making straight for Buford Stanton.

"What the—?" he muttered in startlement.

"Lorelei!" Reeve ground out. "Go back!"

"Please, Mr. Stanton!" she exclaimed, her skirts flying about her ankles as she ran toward him. She stopped and looked up at him with an imploring expression. "I am Lorelei Montgomery—perhaps you know my brother, Hadley Montgomery?"

"Yeah, I know him!" he snarled. She gasped when his hand suddenly shot out and closed about her wrist in a brutal grip. He yanked her in front of him, his arm coming around her waist like a vise, and at the same time he drew his gun. His eyes gleamed with malicious triumph when he yelled at Reeve, "Hell, Cameron, maybe I ought to just take your woman and ride on out of here!"

"Let her go!" Reeve ordered curtly, his features a grim mask of fury. His gold-flecked eyes filled with a savage gleam as he observed the shadow of fear crossing Lorelei's face, and his hand ached to draw his own gun and shoot her captor right between the eyes. "Damn you, Stanton, she isn't part of this. Now let her go," he called, in a voice of deadly calm.

"Yessir, I think I've finally found a way to make you pay, you self-righteous bastard!" the other man taunted recklessly.

His arm tightened about Lorelei's waist until tears of pain started to her eyes. Her mind raced to think of a way to break free. It was all too obvious that none of the men who were watching would dare to interfere. Fearing that any sudden move on her part would make Buford Stanton shoot Reeve, she fought back the tears and prayed for guidance. *Please God, tell me what to do,* she beseeched silently.

Her prayer was answered—and none too soon.

"You'd like to come with me, wouldn't you, honey?" Stanton sneered at Lorelei, jabbing the gun into her side. "Hell, yes, you pretty little whore, you're gonna like what I put between your legs so much you'll beg for more!"

"Let her go," Reeve warned one last time, his fingers inching down toward his gun.

Lorelei finally took action. Throwing her husband a conspiratorial look, she doubled over suddenly and went completely limp against Stanton's arm. He swore and stumbled, and she broke from his grasp to fall to the ground.

That one moment of distraction was enough for Reeve. He drew his gun from the holster with lightning speed, firing a bullet into the other man's shoulder. A sharp howl of pain broke from Stanton's lips as he collapsed in the dusty street. He clapped a hand to his bleeding wound and rolled heavily onto his back, crying out for help.

Lorelei climbed to her knees nearby. Reeve was there in the next instant, pulling her upright before him and wrapping his strong arms about her trembling body. He held her as though he would never let her go.

"Oh, Reeve!" she whispered brokenly, her face buried against his broad chest. "I thought he was

325

going to kill you!"

"It wasn't me I was worried about," he murmured, his arms tightening about her with fierce, loving possessiveness. "Are you all right?"

"Yes." Content to remain forever within his warm and comforting embrace, she was disappointed a few moments later when he pulled away and frowned down at her.

"Why did you do it?" he demanded, his eyes glinting angrily at the heart-stopping memory of how she had placed herself in danger. "Why didn't you do as I said and stay put inside the restaurant?"

"Because I didn't want to be a widow yet!"

"I'm pleased to know you hold such confidence in my abilities, my love," he countered sardonically.

"How was I to know what would happen?" she pointed out. Her sapphire eyes kindled with resentment. "For Heaven's sake, Reeve Cameron, did you really expect me to stand and watch while my husband was gunned down in the street by that madman?" She glanced toward Buford Stanton, who was moaning loudly as he was helped to his feet and led away by two of the onlookers.

"What I *expected* was for you to trust your husband enough to obey him. Damn it, you little fool," he said, wavering between fury at her disobedience and a deep, intense pleasure at the realization that she cared so much, "aren't you ever going to learn to do as you're told?"

"No!" She shook her head and raised a hand to dash impatiently at her tears, which had overflowed to course down the flushed smoothness of her cheeks. "And if that's the kind of wife you . . . you expect me to be, then you are going to be sorely disappointed!"

"I'll never be disappointed," he replied, sweeping her close again. The crowd had already dispersed, and the saloons and gaming halls were filling up, as the night brought with it the usual frenzied search for entertainment. Reeve kept an arm about Lorelei's waist as he led her back toward the hotel.

"You don't think Mr. Stanton will die, do you?" she asked in a small voice, her eyes full of concern for the man in spite of what he had done.

"He's too mean to die yet," Reeve said wryly. He smiled down at her, and revealed, "This is the third time he's called me out—and the third time he's lost."

"You mean you've shot him twice before?" The thought was an unsettling one, to say the least.

"No. Until now, it's never been necessary to do anything more than beat him to the draw. It doesn't take much to send a coward running for cover." He frowned and added grimly, "I'll probably have to kill him someday. I would have gladly done so tonight, but he might be able to give me some answers about Fort Concho." His blood boiled with vengeful rage at the thought of her in Stanton's grasp.

"Then you're still planning to question him?" She was beginning to realize just how foolish she had been to go flying out into the street like that. But she couldn't regret her motives; she'd have done anything to save Reeve's life. She shuddered anew as a vision of Buford Stanton's coarse, acrimonious face swam before her eyes.

"As soon as I get you locked away at the hotel,"

confirmed Reeve. "He won't be in much of a mood for conversation, but I don't intend to come away empty-handed."

Lorelei waited alone in the room for what seemed like an eternity. She had stripped down to her chemise and belted on her gingham wrapper immediately after Reeve had taken his leave. He had promised to return within an hour's time, but she was certain it had already been much longer than that. Her eyes strayed continuously toward the door as she unbraided her hair and pulled the hairbrush through the luxuriant, flame-colored tresses what she thought was one hundred times. In truth, she was much too distracted to keep an accurate count.

Perching on the edge of the bed, she stared toward the open window and allowed her mind to drift back over the startling, life-altering events of the past few days. Reeve dominated her reverie, just as he dominated her every waking thought, and even her dreams.

"Oh, Reeve," she sighed. Her deep blue gaze softened as she conjured up an image of his devilishly handsome face. He could be so authoritative and infuriating—yet so tender and comforting. And passionate, an inner voice added. So skillfully, hot-bloodedly passionate.

She had never known anyone like him before. He was a man of honor, integrity, and complete self-assurance, a man who knew exactly what he wanted and wouldn't let anything stand in the way of his getting it. He had certainly proven that with her, she mused, smiling to herself while a delicious warmth stole over her.

Her eyes clouded with sudden pain as she recalled what had happened that night. An awful feeling of dread had shot through her when Reeve had gone outside to face Buford Stanton. In that moment, she had been able to think of only one thing — saving the man she loved.

"Love?" she said aloud.

The truth hit her like a bolt of lightning. Finally her head acknowledged what her heart had known all along.

She loved him.

Her eyes widened while her pulses leapt wildly. She rose to her feet and flew to the cracked mirror hanging above the washstand. Her reflection stared back at her, fixing her with a knowing look that could not be denied in the lamp's soft golden glow.

She loved him! Dear God, it was true, she thought, filled with both incredulity and exultation at the discovery. She was in love with Reeve Cameron . . . in love with her own husband! That was how it should have been from the beginning, of course, and yet she had only just realized why she had been unable to prevent the successful outcome of his bold, whirlwind courtship. Great balls of fire, she had never had a chance! He had been right about that, and about a good many other things as well.

Finally it all made sense — the way his touch never failed to set her aflame, her inability to resist his kisses, and even the wildly immodest way she responded to his lovemaking. She wasn't a shameless hussy after all; she was simply a woman in love. Then again, there was nothing simple about their relationship, she thought with another sigh. Everything was stormy, and complicated, and likely to remain that way until God only knew when. She couldn't imagine the two of them ever settling into a peaceful, commonplace existence. Nor did she really want them to . . .

How had it happened? she wondered dazedly, returning to the bed and sinking down upon its lumpy, creaking mattress once more. And when? A chaotic jumble of questions and answers flooded her mind.

She must have loved him from the very first. If there was such a thing as fate, it had most assuredly arranged for them to travel along paths that had finally intersected at Fort Worth. Hadley's arrest, the stagecoach journey, Reeve's assignment as special investigator—everything had worked together to bring about the inevitable. And Heaven be praised, she told herself with another soft smile, the inevitable had been worth the wait. Well worth it.

Her heart swelled with emotion as her body stirred with longing. She yearned to be with Reeve, to express her newfound love with all the fire and passion he had awakened within her. For the first time, she intended to be the one to take the initiative. Her eyes lit with warm pleasure, and a touch of apprehension, at the prospect. She wasn't entirely certain how to go about seducing her husband, but she had learned enough about sensuous persuasion to be able to improvise. Yes, indeed, she had been blessed with a willing and thoroughly capable teacher.

By the time Reeve knocked at the door some

thirty minutes later, she was fairly burning with impatience to put her plan into action. She hurried to unfasten the bolt.

"I thought you'd never get back!" she breathed, flinging her arms about his neck as he stepped inside and closed the door behind him.

Delighted by her enthusiastic greeting, Reeve swept her up against him and gave her a smile that would have conquered her heart if it had not already been his.

"I'm glad to know you missed me, Mrs. Cameron," he murmured huskily. He gathered her closer, the glow in his magnificent green eyes deepening. "And I'm pleased to see that you were wise enough to remove most of your clothing. I seem to recall a complaint earlier today about the methods I used in asserting my husbandly rights."

"Reeve, I . . . there's something I want to tell you," she began tentatively, at the same time musing that now she would have no complaints whatsoever if he chose to repeat the earlier episode. Husbandly rights, her mind repeated. She loved the sound of that, especially when it pertained to the physical aspect of their marriage. Blushing at the wickedness of her own thoughts, she cleared her throat gently and said, "I think it's very important that we are honest with one another in all matters."

"All right," he agreed. "We'll get business out of the way first."

"It has nothing to do with business!"

"Doesn't it? I thought you'd want to know how my discussion with Stanton went," he remarked dryly.

"Of course I do, but—"

"Before you say anything more, I want you to promise me you won't get your hopes up too high."

"Why not?" she asked, eyeing him suspiciously.

"Because Buford Stanton isn't what you'd call a reliable witness." He drew away from her and unbuckled his holster. "But his testimony might just shed some new light on your brother's case."

"Oh Reeve, what did he say?" she demanded anxiously, watching as he took a seat on the edge of the bed and tugged off his boots.

"He said that Hadley was never part of the conspiracy, and that Private Taggart was only marginally involved. He claims to have been nothing but a go-between, arranging for the sale of the livestock taken in the raids. But he wouldn't give me any names." He stood again, unbuttoned his shirt, and peeled it off. His brows drew together in a sharp frown of displeasure when he recalled how Stanton had declared himself too damned scared to point a finger at any of the ringleaders. "Of course," he cautioned Lorelei, "getting him to tell the truth at the court-martial won't be easy."

"I told you Hadley was innocent!" she exclaimed triumphantly, her eyes shining. She gave silent thanks for the first hopeful news she'd heard thus far. "I told you, he could never have murdered anyone or done anything even remotely treasonous!"

"I know you did. And I wanted to believe you. But Stanton's testimony won't have any bearing on the murder charge. We still need Taggart for that."

"Then we'll find him!" she vowed with renewed determination. "But—what about Mr. Stanton?

332

How can you be certain he'll stay put once we leave town?"

Reeve's mouth curved into a brief, crooked smile. Clad in nothing but his pants now, he went to blow out the lamp. It was too hot to lower the window, and there were no curtains to block the view of any prying eyes that might feel inclined to stray in their direction. But at least they'd have a bed instead of the hard ground. And they'd have the rest of the night to make good use of it.

"Mr. Stanton is enjoying the hospitality of a mutual friend," he told her, his voice sounding wonderfully deep-timbred in the room's darkness.

"Male or female?" she demanded archly.

"What difference does it make?" He wasted no time in stripping off his pants and reaching for her. She surprised him by slipping out of his grasp and retreating to the other side of the bed. "Damn it, Lorelei, what—"

"If you'll stop hurling curses at my head long enough to listen to me, Reeve Cameron, I promise you won't be disappointed! Now please," she requested, in a more conciliatory manner, "sit down and don't say a word."

She was satisfied when he bent his tall, muscular frame downward to the bed and slipped between the sheets. Stuffing a pillow behind him, he leaned back against the wrought-iron headboard and folded his strong arms across his naked chest.

"Well?" he prompted with gruff, loving impatience.

"You're to keep quiet, remember?" she parried.

While he subjected her to a narrow look, she took

a deep, steadying breath, and brought her hands up to the belt of her wrapper.

"I scarcely know where to begin." She experienced a moment's hesitation, then proclaimed, in a voice that was little more than a whisper, "I . . . well, I want you to know that I realize now you were right all along. It *wasn't* a sacrifice when I married you, Reeve."

Feeling both nervous and wonderfully excited, she untied the belt and slowly eased the wrapper off her shoulders, leaving only the thin white chemise to shield her lush curves from his burning gaze. He remained obediently silent, but she was aware of the way his body tensed in the bed.

"I think I must have known the truth on our wedding night, but I wasn't ready to admit it. And then there was my brother, and your stubborn refusal to help him. I didn't see how I could possibly feel anything but anger and resentment toward you. But I did," she confessed with a soft, tremulous smile. "I felt a great deal more."

Trembling slightly, she grasped the hemline of her chemise and eased it upward . . .

Pale, silvery moonlight streamed in the window to fill the room, providing her thoroughly captivated audience with a clear sight of her naked, voluptuous body as she pulled the chemise all the way off and sent it floating downward to join her wrapper on the floor.

"I finally realized why I was powerless to resist you," she sighed. It was a sigh of total surrender, and a complete acceptance of her destiny. "And I understand now why, in spite of our differences, I couldn't let Buford Stanton shoot you." She didn't notice the way his mouth twitched briefly at this last confession.

Shocked at her own boldness, she knelt on the side of the bed and tugged the sheet free of her husband's naked form, a few provocative inches at a time. He had still not moved a muscle; he continued watching her with an inscrutable look on his handsome face and a smoldering light in his eyes.

"I love you, Reeve Cameron," she declared at last. She pulled the sheet all the way off, and she caught her breath as her sapphire gaze met and locked with the fathomless green depths of his. "I didn't want to love you, I fought against it, but there was nothing I could do. God help me, I've fallen in love with you! I've fallen in love, for the first time in my life."

"And the last," he decreed in a low, vibrant tone, brimming with both triumph and passion that coursed through his veins like liquid fire. He had longed to hear her say it; his heart swelled with love, and with pride at her courage. He reached for her again, but her hands came up to press him insistently back down.

"And the last," she affirmed softly. Warm color rose to her cheeks as she straddled the lean hardness of his hips and knelt above him. She gave him a slow, mischievous smile, which made him groan inwardly. "I think, my dearest Major, that it's time you learned you are not the only one in this family who can play the conquering soldier." It was a daring boast, one which made her blush all the more.

"You have my permission to demonstrate, Mrs. Cameron," drawled Reeve, willing to let her continue with her little game, if only for a short time longer.

His manhood was already rigid and throbbing with desire, the condition increased when his eyes roamed hungrily over her full breasts, which were mere inches away from his face. It was all he could do to prevent his hands and mouth from claiming them. His gaze darkened even more when it flickered downward to her parted thighs and the delicate auburn curls between them, her womanly flesh so close to its virile, masculine counterpart that he could have moved things along quite well with a simple thrust of his hips. If not for his curiosity to see just how far his beloved spitfire would go, he would have rolled her over then and there and shown her just how "conquering" he could be.

Lorelei wasted no more time, but bent downward and dropped a light, tantalizing kiss upon her husband's naked chest. She took care not to touch him with anything except her lips, which pressed a whole series of feathery kisses across the hard-muscled expanse of his chest. Her long hair streamed about her, sweeping down across Reeve as well. His body grew taut with the effort it was costing him to lie still.

Her blue eyes glowed with wholly feminine triumph as she moved toward the foot of the bed. Her mouth trailed a fiery path downward along the center of his chest to the flat planes of his belly. Her tongue dipped playfully within his navel, eliciting a response from him that provoked her to even greater audacity.

She straddled his hips again and smoothed her hands up along his sinewy arms. She gave him another slow, thoroughly bewitching smile while her fingers curled about the bronzed muscles of his shoulders.

"You have a magnificent body, Major Cameron," she pronounced, her voice hushed and seductive. She bent forward until her breasts just touched his chest.

"And how the devil would you know that?" Reeve countered with something akin to a growl. Although thrilled by her boldness, he wanted to be done with this exquisite torture and quench the raging fire in his blood. He vowed to make her pay for tormenting him. The revenge would be a sweet one for them both, and his eyes gleamed hotly at the prospect.

"I told you there were things about me you would be surprised to learn," she teased saucily. She bent even lower, her breasts making intimate contact with his chest while she kissed the spot where his pulse beat so rapidly, at the base of his throat.

"So help me, woman, if I ever catch you looking at another man—" he threatened, his hands clenching into fists at his sides as she stretched out full-length atop him. They both shivered as naked flesh met naked flesh.

"You won't," she murmured, sliding downward on his body until her head was nearly on a level with his hips. Her hands immediately followed, her fingers tracing along his sides. "You are more than enough for me, Reeve Cameron." As if to emphasize the point, her hands glided around to where the undeniable evidence of his arousal sprang from a

337

cluster of tight curls.

"Lorelei," groaned Reeve. He'd had just about all of this he could stand.

She gazed in fascination at the remarkable instrument of his passion for a moment, then allowed one of her hands to close about it. Her eyes lit with another glow of satisfaction when he inhaled sharply. Acting on a sudden wicked impulse, she lowered her head and dropped a soft kiss upon his burning masculine flesh.

"Damn it, you little vixen, *no more!*" he ground out.

She gasped as he sat up, seized her roughly about the waist and tumbled her to her back on the bed. Before she could do anything more than whisper his name, he began a fierce, delectable assault, which prompted her to moan again and again with pleasure.

His hands, lips and tongue played together over her sweet body, caressing, tasting, stroking until she thought she would faint. She was virtually crying for release when he plunged into her honeyed warmth, and her hands ran feverishly across his broad back while her legs came up about his hips. His swift, wildly rapturous thrusts did not cease until he and his passionate Southern belle had become lost in a whirlwind of ecstasy that took them to dizzying new heights of fulfillment.

In the sweet aftermath of their passion, they lay entwined together in the bed. A slight breeze danced across their naked bodies as the moonlit summer night deepened. Somewhere in the distance, a piano played. Reeve's hand rested possessively on the curve of Lorelei's hip, while her fingers traced light, repetitive patterns on the hard muscles of his chest.

"I never thought it was possible to love someone as much as I love you," she sighed contentedly.

"And I was beginning to think I'd never hear you admit it," he parried, with a sigh of his own. He smiled crookedly down at her before adding, "You are a headstrong woman, my love, but I wouldn't have you any other way."

"Reeve?" Her eyes were shining softly as she looked up at him.

"Yes?"

"Will it . . . will it always be like this between us?" she asked, a faint blush staining her cheeks when she recalled their tumultuous union.

There was something rather indecent about it, she mused guiltily, the way she always took part in their lovemaking with such lusty abandon. She had certainly never been taught to behave like that. Properly bred young ladies from old, well-connected families in Georgia did not go about marrying men they scarcely knew and then becoming absolute wantons in their husbands' arms. And yet, she concluded with a secret smile of delight, she couldn't be sorry. Not one bit.

"I mean," she went on to clarify, while Reeve's hand began roaming across her bare bottom in a warm, highly distracting caress, "do you think what happens whenever we are in bed will always be like it was tonight?"

"No."

"No?" She raised herself up on one elbow and faced him with a crestfallen look. He pulled her back down.

"I give you my word, it will only get better," he whispered, in a tone laced with an intoxicating mixture of affection and amusement.

Lorelei was completely satisfied with his answer—and with the way his fingers were trailing upward to pay loving tribute to her naked breasts. She caught her lower lip between her teeth to stifle a moan as his thumb flicked gently back and forth across one of the delicate, rosy nipples.

"Reeve?" His name was little more than a gasp on her lips. She squirmed restlessly against him.

"What is it now?" he asked with an indulgent smile, his green eyes already smoldering with renewed desire.

"I—I don't know anything about being a—a cavalry wife!" She did not protest when he pulled her on top of him. Sweeping the silken tresses from her face, she felt his hands closing about her hips.

"Don't worry." His mouth curved into a thoroughly devastating smile. "You're a quick learner."

"But Reeve—"

"Shut up, woman."

She frowned, but did as he ordered, then was rewarded for her compliance in a manner that proved more than adequate to make her forget about anything else.

Sixteen

There were dark circles beneath her eyes and a slight, telltale soreness in certain parts of her body, but Lorelei was not at all inclined to complain about the lack of sleep. Her sapphire gaze still glowed with warm pleasure at the memory of the night's enchantment when she and her husband rode away from Tascosa the next morning.

Reeve had purchased another horse for her, a spirited but sturdy-looking animal for which he had paid roughly half what the owner of the stables had demanded. She had been impressed with his bargaining skills, and also with the fact that he had managed to appear well-rested, in spite of having had only a few hours of sleep.

It crossed her mind that his many years on the frontier must have conditioned him to endure all sorts of deprivation. Of course, she thought with an inward sigh, she knew almost nothing about those years. His past life was a mystery to her. But he had another life now, with her at his side, a life in which, God willing, they would be able to know one another as completely as two people can.

By noon, they had reached the border between Texas and New Mexico Territory. Lorelei could see no evidence of it; the rugged, sun-baked prairie landscape looked the same. She reined her mount to a halt beside Reeve's after he had called back that they were stopping.

"How much farther is it to Las Vegas?" she asked, pushing the front brim of the hat upward on her forehead. She had lost a brief but heated argument with him over her desire to wear pants again, so she had settled for hiking her skirts and petticoats above her knees while she rode. It pleased her in more ways than one when she caught his eyes straying to her exposed, white-stockinged legs.

"Another full day's ride still," he answered. His gaze narrowed a bit as it made a swift, encompassing sweep of the countryside. He settled his own hat farther back on his head and shifted in the saddle.

"I can see why this is referred to as a no-man's-land," remarked Lorelei. There were no signs of civilization—no cattle or buildings, or even more than a scattering of wildlife. They had seen a couple of ranches earlier that day, close to Tascosa, but now there was nothing save the endless blue sky above the treeless plains all about them. She tugged the kerchief from about her neck and rubbed some of the dust from her face. "Are we going to rest the horses now?"

"No." He shook his head, muttered a savage curse under his breath, and said in a low and level tone, "There's a watering hole a few miles farther on."

"Then why did we stop here?" A frown of puzzlement creased her brow.

"Because we're being followed."

"Followed?" she echoed, her frown deepening.

342

She twisted about in the saddle and looked hastily about, but saw nothing. "How do you know? And who—"

"Indians. Comanches, most likely."

"Comanches?" she gasped in disbelief.

"Stay calm, Lorelei," he ordered, with quiet authority. His steady, penetrating gaze sought the alarmed roundness of her blue eyes. "There can't be more than half a dozen of them. They've been following us for the past quarter of an hour."

"Dear God, Reeve, what are we going to do?" she blurted out, her terror-stricken gaze flying about until it finally came to rest upon the undeniable evidence in the far distance. Several dark specks had appeared on the horizon, and she did not need to ask Reeve how he could be so certain they were Indians.

"Nothing. At least, not yet." He smiled faintly and continued, "We haven't got a chance in hell of outrunning them. We're going to just keep riding, and hope they either give up the chase or let us know what it is they want."

"What they want?" She shook her head in fear and confusion. "I don't understand! I thought the Indians always—"

"If they'd wanted to kill us, we'd be dead by now," he insisted firmly. "No, they're after something else." He didn't say what that something else might be. But as long as he drew breath, they'd not take her. And, damn it to hell, he had every intention of staying alive. "Come on," he said, tugging his hat low upon his head again. "Let's see how serious they are about this game they're playing."

343

Lorelei wanted to say more, to tell him how much she loved him and how desperately sorry she was for getting them into this predicament, but there was no time. She nodded mutely and followed as he urged his mount into a gallop.

They rode at a hard, breakneck pace, keeping a tight grip on the reins as the animals beneath them raced across the plains. But when they had reached the spot where Reeve intended for them to rest and water the horses, they saw that the pursuing riders were still bearing down on them.

"Whatever happens, I want you to keep quiet and do as I say," Reeve cautioned, dismounting and then swiftly pulling her down beside him.

"I know how to use a gun!" she informed him in a breathless rush.

"Good." He withdrew the revolver from his holster and handed it to her. "Because it might just come to that. Keep this hidden in your skirts until I tell you to use it."

He took her arm and led her over to a nearby rock, instructing her to sit down and not move a muscle. She was gripped by an awful, heart-rending apprehension as she watched him lead the horses to drink at the small spring that bubbled out of the parched earth there. He took the precaution of tying the reins to a stake before drawing the rifle from the holster on his saddle and moving back to take a protective stance beside her.

"Don't worry," he reassured her, with a smile and a quick, hard kiss. "I've been in worse situations than this and haven't lost my scalp yet."

"You'd have been able to escape this time if it

wasn't for me," she observed remorsefully. "Oh Reeve, I slowed you down and—"

"Damn it, Lorelei, don't ever let me hear you talk like that again," he snapped. "Now keep quiet!" He stood tall and impassive as the Indians approached, his rifle cradled with deceptive nonchalance in his arms.

Just as he had thought, they were Comanches—six young braves, riding half-wild horses and armed with military rifles. They were quite handsome, with strong features and bronzed, gleaming bodies displayed to full advantage, for they were almost entirely naked. Small, apron-like cloth garments were tied around their waists, and their coarse black hair was fastened in long braids on either side of their heads. Each wore a lone feather in the traditional headband. Their chiseled, stoic faces were unpainted, which signaled to Reeve that their purpose was hunting, not war.

They drew to a halt a few yards away. Lorelei tensed, her fingers clenching about the gun concealed within the folds of her skirt. She cast a hasty, questioning glance up at Reeve, only to see that his expression was still dangerously inscrutable. Her fearful gaze shifted back to the Comanches. All six of them were staring at her intently.

The oldest of the group nodded curtly in her direction and said something to his companions. There ensued a brief and enthusiastic discussion, after which the leader separated from the others. He guided his mount closer and addressed Reeve with a few terse, guttural words of the Comanche language.

Lorelei swallowed hard and looked to her husband again, her eyes widening in amazement when he answered the young warrior. They continued to speak for a moment, leaving her to fight back rising panic as the other members of the hunting party subjected her to a close, highly alarming scrutiny. Finally, Reeve translated for her what had been said, though his wary gaze never left the Comanches.

"They want you to take off your hat," he told her quietly.

"Take off my hat?" she echoed in confusion. "But — why?"

"It's your hair," he explained. "They think redheads have special powers."

"Special powers?" Sweet mercy, this couldn't be happening, she thought, in dismay and astonishment. "What should I do?"

"Go ahead. Take it off," commanded Reeve. "Maybe if they get a good look at you, they'll be satisfied." If not, he was ready. His eyes narrowed almost imperceptibly as he calculated which of them to shoot after he'd taken out the leader.

She nodded dazedly and did as he said, her hand shaking as she reached up to pull the hat from her head. Six pairs of keen black eyes widened at the sight of her flame-colored locks. The braves murmured amongst themselves once more, and then the group's spokesman looked at Reeve again. They exchanged words that grew angry. By the time the Comanche fell silent, Reeve was smoldering with barely controlled fury.

"Well. What did he say?" Lorelei demanded anxiously, having long ago forgotten that she had been warned to keep quiet.

"It doesn't matter," he ground out.

"I have a right to know!" Her heart leapt in alarm at the look on his face. "What is it? What do they want?"

"You."

"Me?" She inhaled sharply and she looked back to the Comanches. They sat proud and erect astride their horses, their eyes boring into hers. Her fingers trembled as they moved upon the hidden revolver. "Why do they want me?" she whispered hoarsely.

Her bright, horrified gaze traveled swiftly to her husband's face once more. The merest ghost of a smile played about his lips.

"They think you'll bring them good luck." But all traces of amusement vanished in the next instant, and she shuddered at the fierce, bloodthirsty gleam in his eyes. "Stand up, Lorelei. And get ready to use that gun."

Her knees felt perilously weak as she drew herself upright. Reeve moved slowly in front of her and tightened his grip on the rifle. The young warrior scowled darkly and bit out a few more angry words. He jabbed a finger toward the two horses. Reeve answered him tersely, shaking his head in a firm denial.

"What did he say this time?" Lorelei asked in a tremulous undertone. Dear God, she prayed silently, please don't let it end this way!

"He offered to let me keep the horses if I'd turn you over to them."

"What did you tell him?"

"I told him that if they didn't leave now, you'd

347

put a curse on them," he replied, with another small smile of irony.

"A curse?" she repeated in stunned disbelief. "For Heaven's sake, Reeve, how do you expect —"

"Quiet!" he ordered, in a voice that was whipcord sharp.

Feeling as though she had become trapped in a nightmare, she fell silent and listened to what she could only surmise was another brief, volatile argument over the less-than-generous terms the Indians had offered. Her mind raced to think of a way to convince her would-be captors that she did indeed possess the ability to work some magic on them.

It was to this end that she suddenly reached around to the single long braid of hair down her back, and tugged the ribbon at the end free. She raked her fingers through the plaited thickness, then shook her head so that the luxuriant, flame-colored tresses cascaded about her face and shoulders in beautiful disarray. Satisfied that she had captured the Indians' attention, she forced a smile to her lips and stepped out from behind Reeve.

"What the hell do you think you're doing? Get back!" he hissed in a low, furious tone.

"I've got to do *something!*" she countered.

Disregarding his glare of warning, she moved forward to the spring and knelt to scoop up a handful of the water. She acted solely on instinct, pretending complete disinterest in her audience as she lifted her hand to her mouth and drank. She could feel Reeve's eyes burning into her back.

"Tell them . . . tell them I'm preparing to curse them," she advised softly.

"Lorelei, come here," he enjoined in a voice of deadly calm.

"No! At least this way, if they decide to shoot they'll have to aim at two separate targets," she reasoned stubbornly. "Now tell them!" She dipped her hand into the spring once more and tried to mask her trepidation by rising to her feet and allowing the water to escape through her fingers. Her eyes lit with a faint glow of satisfaction when she glimpsed the sudden, bemused frown on the leader's face.

Reeve's green eyes darkened with rage, but he knew he couldn't risk forcing his recalcitrant wife back to his side. He nodded curtly toward her and told the other man what she had said about the curse. It would have sounded foolish to anyone else, but he knew how much the Comanches were ruled by their superstitions and their strong beliefs in the supernatural.

Lifting her head to a haughty angle, Lorelei transferred her gaze to the group's spokesman. His eyes narrowed and glittered hotly as they searched her face. Her mouth curved into a slow, purposefully enigmatic smile. It seemed that she stood there for hours, forcing herself to remain silent and motionless while the Indians took their measure of her.

Behind her, Reeve's hard-muscled body tensed for action. He knew that he could manage to shoot two or even three of the young warriors before any of them had fired a single shot; he prayed that Lorelei would not hesitate when he ordered her to get down. His savage, piercing gaze flickered over the group of riders as the seconds crept by.

But miraculously, Lorelei's ploy worked — or the

Indians decided she wasn't worth dying for. It wasn't often they encountered a white man who could speak their language, and it wasn't often they came up against an adversary as formidable-looking as Reeve. For whatever reason, they abandoned their efforts to obtain "the woman with hair the color of fire."

The leader muttered what might have been an oath, then let out a bloodcurdling yell. He lifted his rifle high above his head in a final gesture of defiance, before digging his heels into his horse's flanks and riding away. The five other braves followed, thundering back across the plains. Lorelei stared after them in breathless astonishment.

"Thank God," she sighed raggedly once they had gone. She flew into Reeve's welcoming arms, pale, shaken, and lightheaded with relief. He held her for only a few moments before seizing her by the shoulders and roughly setting her away from him.

"You were supposed to keep quiet and do as I said!" he exclaimed, his gaze furious and reproachful as his fingers clenched about her upper arms. "Damn it, you little fool, you might have gotten both of us killed!"

"But I didn't!" she pointed out. Her beautiful, fiery blue eyes locked in silent combat with the gleaming viridescence of his. "It seems to me, Reeve Cameron, that you should be offering me gratitude instead of raking me over the coals! After all, if I hadn't done something they might very well have shot *you* and carried *me* off to be some sort of good luck charm!"

"Why doesn't it ever occur to you that I might

just be able to handle a situation without your interference?" he challenged harshly.

Once again, in spite of the fact that he was so angry he wanted to shake her, or beat her, or both, he felt a certain begrudging admiration for what she had done. She always faced danger head-on, without complaint, and with more courage than he had seen most men display. Confound it, he mused to himself, she was unlike any woman he had ever known. And she was his! The thought prompted his heart to swell with love and pride. His temper cooling, he drew her back against him and wrapped his arms about her tense but soft body.

"I think you were born to scare the hell out of me," he remarked in a wry, mellow voice.

"I . . . I suppose I should have listened to you," she conceded, with an audible sigh of surrender. She raised her arms to his neck and pressed herself even closer to his warm and virile hardness. "I told you I wasn't very good at taking orders."

"You were right." He tightened his arms about her before murmuring, with a low chuckle, "I'll bet you were a holy terror when you were a child."

"Absolutely." She tilted her head back and smiled lovingly up into his rugged countenance. "But perhaps, with time and patience and a great deal of affection, Major Cameron," she teased, "I might learn how to be a good cavalry wife."

"You'll never be that," he retorted ungallantly. His eyes filled with roguish humor. "But it will be a pleasure to try and tame you."

She merely smiled again and settled her head back upon his chest. Finally, he announced that it was time for them to be on their way. They quickly ate and drank, and Lorelei braided her hair again. She pulled her hat back on as Reeve led the horses forward.

"Do you think Hadley came this way?" she asked, at a sudden thought. An involuntary shiver ran down her spine when she imagined her brother meeting up with the same band of Comanches she and Reeve had just faced.

"I've seen no evidence of it," he answered. He lifted her up into the saddle before mounting his own horse. "He could easily have come across farther south. Either way, I hope to find him when we get to Las Vegas."

"And what . . . what if we can't?" she asked reluctantly, her eyes clouding at the thought. "What will you do if he isn't there?"

"I've got a friend who owns a ranch just east of Santa Fe. If need be, I'll leave you in his care while I find your brother," he declared grimly. "But I don't expect it to come to that." He was already reining about when she detained him with one last question.

"Reeve?" She met his gaze when he turned wordlessly back to her. "Why did you come after us alone?"

"Because I love you." He gave her a smile. "And because I always work best on my own."

"Not any longer," she asserted, with a determined toss of her head. "You have taken on a partner, Major, and you might as well get used to the idea!"

She snapped the reins, causing her horse to take off like a shot. Reeve smiled to himself, then rode after her. They galloped farther into New Mexico Territory, while a thick ominous line of clouds advanced on the western horizon.

By the time they made camp for the night, Lorelei was weary of battling the wind and rain that stung against her face. The storm, violent and thunderous, had broken late that afternoon. Although she'd had the protection of her husband's yellow canvas slicker, she was still drenched to the skin and longed for the opportunity to rest.

She was profoundly grateful when Reeve found them an old, abandoned cabin in which to take shelter, and she wasted little time in sliding from the saddle in order to make her way inside. Reeve was close on her heels.

"I'll see to the horses," he told her, dumping the wet saddlebags on the floor. "There's a barn out back. You try and get a fire started."

Nodding, she lowered her carpetbag to rest beside the saddlebags and turned to inspect the cabin. It took a moment for her eyes to adjust to the darkness, but she was able to make out the stone fireplace on the opposite wall. Other than a lopsided table near the doorway, the cabin was empty—and none too clean, judging from the smell. But at least the roof was sound, she told herself, noting with relief that there were only a few minor leaks.

She hurried across the room and was pleasantly surprised to discover a pile of broken furniture, which had apparently been used as firewood by some former occupant. Water dripped off her clothes and hair and puddled on the rough wooden floor around her when she knelt and began stacking the splintered chair legs in the fireplace.

She was still trying to set the wood alight when Reeve returned. Muttering in frustration, she stood and angrily peeled off the slicker.

"I suppose we'll have to eat hardtack and jerky again!" she pronounced, with a heavy sigh of displeasure.

"Here," he said, sauntering forward to take the matches from her. He suppressed a smile and told her, "Find the blankets. You'll feel better once you get out of those wet clothes."

Watching in amusement as she took herself off to follow his advice, he turned and went down on one knee before the fireplace. It was only a matter of seconds before his practiced efforts yielded success. The tiny flame took life and soon grew to a healthy blaze, filling the room with a soft, flickering glow.

Lorelei stripped off everything but her chemise, then wrapped one of the blankets about her and crossed back to stand before the fire. Reeve had already found their food in one of the saddlebags and set the beans and bacon to cooking. The mouth-watering aroma drifted upward, reminding them of how hungry they were after the hard day's ride.

"Aren't you going to get undressed?" Lorelei asked her husband, whose clothing was even more thoroughly soaked than hers had been.

"If you think you can make a decent pot of coffee," he drawled. He smiled when she lifted her head proudly.

"Of course I can." Tucking the corner of the blanket into the folds wrapped above her breasts, she knelt and began scooping the richly scented grounds

354

into the coffeepot. "It so happens that I am an excellent cook," she informed him, with perhaps a trace of boastfulness.

"My mother will be relieved to hear it." He removed every stitch of clothing he had on before wrapping the other blanket about his waist. His damp hair waved rakishly across his forehead, while his naked chest and arms glowed, bronzed and powerful, in the firelight. Lorelei smiled up at him when he moved back to her side.

"Reeve, why don't you tell me about your family?" she urged. She put the coffee on to heat and sat back, tucking her legs beneath her. Her hands moved up to unbraid her hair as she stared toward the dancing flames. "I know your father owns the stage line, but that's *all* I know," she added, with another sigh.

"There's not much to tell," he replied, bending his tall frame down to sit close beside her. He lifted one knee and rested an arm negligently across it, his other hand bracing on the floor. His steady gaze followed the direction of hers. "We lived near San Antonio until I was twelve. My father started the ranch at Fort Worth just after my youngest sister was born."

"You have a sister?" Somehow, she had never envisioned him with any siblings at all.

"Why should that surprise you?" he parried with a half-smile. "I have two, actually. And three brothers. All younger—and mean as hell." His deep voice was laced with an undeniable pride and affection that belied his teasing assessment.

"I had no idea you came from such a large family," she remarked in wonderment. She ran her fingers through the liberated auburn curls and shook her head to send them tumbling down about her shoulders. A sudden shadow crossed her face when she confided, "My parents always wanted more children."

"And what about you?" he asked softly.

She turned her head to look at him, her heart stirring at the love she saw in his splendid green eyes. A faint blush rose to her cheeks before she turned her luminous gaze to the fire once more.

"I — I haven't given it a great deal of thought," she murmured, in a small voice. *Children,* her mind repeated. Yes, she thought, her pulse racing wildly, she wanted to have his children. And soon . . . very soon, if she had her way!

"I have."

"Indeed?" Secretly thrilling to the undercurrent of passion in his resonant voice, she readjusted the blanket about her. "And what path have your thoughts taken?"

"I think we should have an even dozen."

"A dozen?" Her eyes flew back to his face, only to find that he was scrutinizing her with an unholy light of amusement in his gaze. She frowned in mock reproach. "You have a wicked sense of humor, Reeve Cameron."

"I have a wicked desire for you," he corrected, smoothing a hand up her bare arm.

"You still haven't told me anything about your family," she complained halfheartedly. She did not protest when he slipped an arm about her waist and settled her back against him. "For instance, where

356

are your brothers and sisters now? And your parents? I suppose you intend to let me meet them eventually?"

"Eventually." His fingers swept her long hair aside so that he could press a warm, highly intoxicating kiss upon the graceful curve of her neck.

"I — I think the coffee is ready." A delicious shiver coursed along her spine when his lips glided upward. He tugged the edge of the blanket free and the woolen folds fell to the floor. "Aren't you hungry?" she asked breathlessly, then stifled a moan when his tongue plunged within her ear.

"Yes." His strong hands clasped her about the waist and turned her slowly toward him. He settled her across his lap, pulling the blanket away from her scantily clad body. "I have a hunger that only you can satisfy, sweet vixen," he declared, in a husky, mischievous tone. His arms lifted her higher, his head lowering toward her breasts.

"Reeve!"

She gasped as his mouth closed wetly about one of her breasts. The thin fabric of her chemise was little protection against his searing caress. Another moan rose in her throat when he sucked hard on her breast, his tongue snaking out to tease boldly at the pert nipple. The sensation was one of near painful ecstasy, and her fingers curled almost convulsively upon his broad shoulder while he did the same to her other breast.

The next thing she knew, he was tugging the chemise from her body with wholly masculine impatience. He yanked his own blanket free, then positioned her so that she was facing him. She crimsoned to find herself straddling him as he sat on the floor, her naked bottom resting on his hard-muscled thighs and her legs parted wide across his hips.

"Reeve, please!" she whispered, squirming in his grasp. Her color deepened when she glanced down and saw just how shockingly intimate her position was.

"Please what?" he retorted, with a soft laugh. He was already drawing her closer so that his mouth could return to its delectable torment of her breasts. One of his hands smoothed up her back while the other roamed downward to take gentle, loving possession of the womanly treasure between her thighs. His fingers delved within the soft triangle of hair, parting the silken folds of flesh, which were so conveniently placed for his masterful touch.

"Reeve!" Her hands grasped at his shoulders for support as she closed her eyes and felt the familiar wildfire blazing through her.

"I love the way you say my name, Mrs. Cameron," he murmured against her breast. His warm mouth and insistent tongue worked their hot, sensuous magic, ravishing both of her breasts so thoroughly that she thought she would faint with the sheer pleasure of it all.

Almost panting, she instinctively arched her back, her long hair shimmering down across her buttocks. Reeve waited until he could bear no more. His lips finally claimed hers in a deep, wondrously compelling kiss, and his hands gripped her hips and brought her down upon his burning hardness.

Her soft cry was lost against his mouth. Her fingers clenched about his shoulders as he slid all the way inside her moist, well-prepared warmth. She shuddered with passion and obediently followed the rhythm of his hips, meeting his slow, provocative thrusts with a bold enthusiasm that quickly drove him to move faster and harder, in spite of his efforts to prolong the exquisite torture.

The storm of passion raging inside the cabin was a fitting match for the one that continued to lash out at the plains with flashing, loudly thunderous intensity. By the time their sweet madness reached its final and infinitely satisfying conclusion, the coffee was starting to boil and the food had overcooked. But neither of them cared.

It was several minutes before Reeve allowed his beautiful, becomingly flushed bride to rise and draw the blanket about her once more. A disarming smile played about his lips as he watched her glance down at him with a noticeable touch of shyness.

"I . . . I suppose you know a good many ways to make love," she murmured, her voice still breathless and uneven. The firelight set her gloriously tousled hair aglow and shed riotous light and shadow over her face.

"I know enough to get by," Reeve answered softly, his voice brimming with ironic humor. He secured the blanket about his own nakedness and rose to his feet beside her. His arms enveloped her with their strong, muscular warmth as he pulled her back against him. "But I'm sure I could still learn a thing or two."

"So could I," she said with a contented sigh. Reeve's arms tightened about her.

"Have I ever told you that I think you are aptly

named?"

"No. What do you mean?"

"I can well imagine you luring poor, besotted sailors to their deaths," he replied with a wry smile. "Lorelei, the siren of the seas. Yes, one look at you would do it."

"I'm not quite certain that's what my mother had in mind," she countered, then added saucily, "But if there's been any luring done, Reeve Cameron, you had best look at yourself! I seem to recall a certain Charity Pardee wanting to know you better! And there have probably been countless other women eager to get better acquainted with you!"

"Countless." His low, vibrant chuckle made her knees weaken. "Don't tell me there weren't any men back in Georgia with enough sense to try and get you to the altar." The thought never failed to provoke a surge of jealousy within him.

"I suppose I received my fair share of proposals," she conceded. Her brow creased into a sudden frown of remembrance as she stared into the fire. "But the only man I might have considered marrying didn't really want anything more than a pretty wife to grace his home and entertain his guests while he lived his own life. I didn't love him," she hastened to add. "And I couldn't ever have settled for someone like him. I realize that even more now."

"Your life with me won't be an easy one," Reeve cautioned her. "Hell, I never know from one year to the next where I'll be posted. And there are always short-term assignments like the one at Fort Concho." He turned her about to face him, his eyes staring deeply into hers. "But I give you my word,

360

I'll do my damnedest to make you happy."

"You're doing quite well already, Major," she assured him with a provocative little smile. Swaying against him, she tilted her head back and gave him a look that lent credence to her words.

His gaze warmed with loving triumph before his lips descended upon the parted, inviting softness of hers. The kiss was both tender and demanding, and might have led to yet another passionate interlude if not for the fact that the coffee boiled over just then, and sizzled loudly upon the stone hearth.

Reluctantly letting his wife go, Reeve spun her about and landed a hard, playful swat upon her backside.

"Stop tempting me, woman, or I'll never get anything to eat."

"Why, you . . . *you're* the one who—" she sputtered indignantly, only to be cut off when he grabbed her hand and pulled her down beside him.

They ate their supper at last, then stretched out between the two blankets on the floor. Lorelei drifted off to sleep in Reeve's arms, listening to the rain drumming on the roof and the soft, steady sound of her husband's breathing.

Seventeen

The storm had ended sometime in the night. Lorelei gave silent thanks for that fact as she and Reeve saddled up and rode away from the cabin after a hearty breakfast. The morning air was filled with the fresh, lingering scent of rain, and the unmistakable smell of sagebrush—mile after mile of sagebrush, she reflected with an inward sigh. She inhaled deeply and glanced up toward the cloudless summer sky.

"Do you think we'll be able to reach Las Vegas before nightfall?" she asked as they slowed their horses to a walk across the sunlight prairie. Reeve had told her they would be following the Santa Fe Trail, once the route of wagon trains heading West.

"Yes," answered Reeve, "and I've got a friend who runs a hotel on the plaza there. We should be able to get a room for the night."

"You seem to have friends everywhere," Lorelei observed, with a thoughtful frown.

"A few." His green eyes twinkled when he added dryly, "And some of them are men."

"Don't you dare start *that* again!"

"I'm thirty years old, Lorelei," he told her, a brief smile touching his lips. "I haven't lived like a monk, but I haven't left a trail of broken hearts, either. You're the only woman I've ever loved, and it's time you stopped worrying."

"Who said I was worrying?" she retorted loftily. She ignored his soft laugh and shifted in the saddle. Her gaze drifted out across the rugged landscape once more, and another frown creased her brow. "Reeve?"

"You're thinking about your brother again, aren't you?" His perceptive remark earned him a look of wide-eyed surprise.

"How did you know what—"

"Because I know you." His features became grim, and his eyes glinted. "Even if we don't find Taggart, Hadley still has a chance if he cooperates. He'll have to give me names. And he'll have to be able to offer a convincing argument about why he found it necessary to escape. The United States Cavalry doesn't take lightly to losing its prisoners. And innocent men don't usually run."

"I know," Lorelei sighed disconsolately. She blamed herself, of course. If she hadn't interfered, Hadley wouldn't be facing even more charges now, and neither would he be facing the many dangers of the *Llano Estacado* alone. But rather than waste time in self-recrimination, she could try and think of a way to help once they caught up with him. Dear God, she entreated silently, let him be in Las Vegas.

The long day wore on. They stopped several times, once at a collection of adobe houses where the inhabitants—Mexican sheepherders and their families—welcomed them with a hot meal of *tama-*

363

les and *frijoles,* and plenty of feed for their horses. Lorelei received yet another surprise concerning her husband's abilities when he began conversing with their hosts in fluent Spanish; she wondered if he would ever cease to amaze her. By the time they resumed their journey, the sun was hanging low in the western sky and the heat was rising off the land in visible, undulating waves.

Finally, Las Vegas materialized in the distance.

Lorelei's heart pounded with anticipation as her gaze narrowed to take in the sight of the beckoning oasis, which had sprung up some twenty-five years before on the banks of the Gallinas River. There were mountains to the north and west of the town, their awesome, green-mantled heights providing a striking contrast to the barren plains.

"It looks a good deal larger than Tascosa," she observed, nodding toward the town as she and Reeve slowed their weary horses to a walk once more.

"It is," he confirmed.

"How many people live there?" She hoped it wasn't too heavily populated, since that would make their search for Hadley all the more difficult.

"A couple of thousand, I'd say. Most of the men passing through are prospectors or cattlemen, a few soldiers." He smiled briefly. "Come on. Let's see about that hotel room."

Not in the least bit inclined to argue, she shifted in the saddle again, and following his lead set a course down the hill. Evening was already upon them, and she was anxious to get a better look before total darkness fell.

Not only was Las Vegas larger than Tascosa, it

was also more permanent-looking. The town had taken shape around a rectangular plaza, flanked on all four sides by the typical Spanish-style, flat-roofed structures made of adobe. More buildings had been erected along the roads leading out from the central square. There were several saloons and gambling halls, but also an impressive array of mercantile stores, hotels, and even a sawmill and flour mill. A beautiful church stood on the west side of the plaza.

The population was indeed varied, mused Lorelei as she and Reeve urged their horses along the dry, dusty street through the center of town. The plaza was crowded, not only with men, but with women and a surprising number of children. Although the original settlers had been of Mexican descent, the inhabitants were now from an intriguing mixture of cultures. She found it difficult to believe that the town was a haven for outlaws and renegades, as Reeve had said it was. If first impressions counted for anything, she would pronounce it to be remarkably civilized.

They reined to a halt in front of a two-story building on the southeast corner of the plaza. A sign out front read "The Imperial." Like everything else in Las Vegas, it had been constructed of thick adobe bricks, but it was unique in that it featured white columns on both levels, and a wide front porch.

Lorelei was pleased to see that the hotel was a vast improvement over the one back in Tascosa. She smiled at Reeve when he lifted her down.

"You never did tell me if your friend was a man

365

or a woman," she reminded him archly.

"Her name is Annie Leary," he replied, his eyes brimming with amusement. "And I expect you to behave yourself."

"Annie Leary," she echoed. "I suppose she's a beautiful Irish girl you knew many years ago." She heaved a dramatic sigh and turned to pull her carpetbag down.

"She's pretty enough. And it hasn't been all that long since I knew her."

Tossing the saddlebags over one shoulder, he handed the reins to a young man who rushed forward to see to their horses and lead them to the stables and corrals out back. Reeve took the carpetbag from Lorelei, ushering her up the front steps and into the hotel. He left her alone near the doorway, with a promise to return soon.

The lobby was immaculate and brightly lit, and crowded at the moment with travelers anxious to find accommodations in a town that was always full. The furnishings, Lorelei noted with surprise, were of exceptionally high quality. Blue velvet draperies hung at the windows, the wooden floor had been polished until it shone, a sofa and chairs upholstered in heavy brocade offered seating in the middle of the spacious room, and the front desk was topped with marble. Such elegance was not at all what she had expected to find this far west; Reeve's friend—if indeed that's all she was—had either married well, inherited a great deal of money, or, Heaven forbid, earned a fortune by other, less reputable means.

"Lorelei, this is Mrs. Leary," she heard Reeve announcing behind her. She turned, her eyes widening with dismay when she found herself facing a woman who was far beyond *pretty enough*.

Annie Leary couldn't have been more than thirty, and she was only a few inches shorter than Reeve. Incredibly lovely, she possessed a splendid, well-rounded figure, eyes that were more green than blue, and dark golden hair pinned low on the nape of her neck. Her red silk gown hugged her lush curves to perfection, and, perhaps most disturbing of all, she flashed Reeve a smile that was more than friendly before looking back to Lorelei.

"Welcome, Lorelei," she offered, taking her hand in a cool grasp. "You can imagine my surprise when Reeve told me he had brought along his bride this time. I had no idea he was contemplating marriage. This all happened rather suddenly, didn't it?" Her words were laced with a subtle rebuke that was not lost on Lorelei.

"How do you do, Mrs. Leary," she responded in measured tones, wondering where Mister Leary was. Her gaze traveled back to Reeve. His features were inscrutable, but she glimpsed a devilish light in his eyes.

"Annie has managed to find us a room," he told her casually.

"Would you expect anything less from such an old friend?" the woman retorted. She smiled coquettishly at him again and confided to Lorelei, "He knows he's welcome here any time. Why, he's certainly relied upon my hospitality often enough in the past! But I shouldn't be going on like this. We need to get you settled for the night. And from the look of it, my dear," she concluded as her eyes flickered over Lorelei, "you could do with a bath."

"Thank you," Lorelei told her with forced politeness. She cast Reeve a narrow, speaking look. "My husband and I have traveled a long way."

"So I understand."

Lorelei's eyes flashed with irritation as Reeve took her arm and led her across the lobby in the hotel owner's wake. They climbed the wide, carpeted staircase and Annie showed them to a room at the far end of the landing. Fitting a key into the lock, she opened the door and swept gracefully inside to light the lamp.

"It isn't our largest room, I'm afraid, but I think you'll be more than comfortable." She pivoted about to face them, and her mouth curved into a slow, meaningful smile as she said to Reeve, "Do you remember that time back in San Antone when we had to share a room above the jail?" Conscious of the way Lorelei stiffened, she clarified smoothly, "Oh, we weren't alone, of course, my dear. Jacob was with us."

"Jacob?"

"My late husband. He and Reeve were—"

"I believe you said something about a bath?" Reeve cut her off with a frown. He tossed his hat onto the four-poster bed. "And how about a change of clothes while you're at it?"

"I'll send someone up with the water right away," the comely widow assured him. "The bathroom is at the other end of the hall. But then, you already know that, don't you?" She walked back over to the door, then paused to tell Lorelei, "Jacob and Reeve were enough alike to be brothers, you know. I always keep some of his things handy in case Reeve happens to be passing through. He never fails to stop by."

"Really? Well, how very fortunate he is to have a friend like you, Mrs. Leary." It was all she could do to refrain from demanding to know just how deep their friendship truly was. She already disliked the woman, and she had little doubt that the feeling was mutual.

"Yes. I've missed him terribly." Annie sighed feelingly, then with one last knowing smile, she took herself off to see to the bath.

" 'He never fails to stop by,' " Lorelei muttered with biting sarcasm as she closed the door with a good deal more force than was necessary. She rounded on her husband with fire in her eyes. "And just how often is *that,* Reeve Cameron?"

"I thought you were going to behave." His mouth twitched as he lowered the bags to the floor. "Annie's a friend—nothing more."

"Indeed?" She tore off her hat and lifted angry hands to her long braid. "Perhaps you should try telling *her* that!" Tugging the ribbon free, she loosened her hair and sank down upon a chair to unlace her boots. Reeve watched her with a mixture of exasperation and humor.

"I knew the two of you would hit it off," he said sardonically.

"What a coincidence that you should mention hitting. It would give me the greatest of pleasure to slap her smirking face!"

"Stop being childish."

"I'm not being childish!" she denied hotly. She pulled off the boots and folded her arms across her heaving breasts. "I simply find it offensive when a woman from my husband's past behaves as though she would like to renew the acquaintance!"

"Damn it, Lorelei, I don't have time for this." Frowning, he closed the distance between them in two long strides. He seized her arms and hauled her up before him. "Annie Leary was married to a man who served with me during the war. We've known each other a long time."

" 'So I understand,' " she countered, mimicking the other woman again. She knew she was behaving irrationally, but she couldn't help it. Her stormy gaze locked with the annoyed glint of his.

"Take your bath," he directed, in a low and level tone. "I'm going downstairs."

"What for?" She eyed him suspiciously.

"To ask a few questions."

"Of Mrs. Leary, I suppose?" she challenged, her temper flaring at the thought.

"I'll be back soon," was all he would say. His lips were compressed into a tight, thin line of displeasure as he released her and left the room.

She battled the impulse to call after him. A long, ragged sigh escaped her lips before she dropped back down into the chair. Her heart ached, and even though she told herself there was no reason to be so jealous, she could not forget the way the statuesque blonde had looked at Reeve.

A young Mexican woman knocked at the door a short time later to announce that the bath was ready. Lorelei had already undressed and donned

370

her wrapper, so she thanked her and hurried down the hall to the bathroom. When she opened the door she found an immense, porcelain bathtub with clawfoot legs. It dominated the small, brightly decorated room. Steam curled up from the surface of the water, and someone had placed a large white towel on the table beside the tub. Lorelei smiled; this bath would be very welcome.

She closed the door and turned the key in the lock, then unbelted her wrapper. Drawing it off, she hung it on a peg beside the door and turned to step into the tub. Her eyes closed as she lowered herself into the tub and leaned back. The liquid warmth eased her tired muscles, and soothed her troubled mind as well.

Making a silent vow to try and put aside her jealousy, she sighed and wondered if Reeve was having any success in his efforts to gather information about Hadley. It was possible that her brother was in that same hotel, but unlikely. He had no money. And she couldn't envision him wasting time in the pursuit of comfort when he was so anxious to find Private Taggart.

Of course, *she* was doing that. She experienced a sharp twinge of guilt upon realizing that she was enjoying a nice, leisurely bath while her brother was . . . well, wherever he was, she was quite certain it wasn't anything like this. It struck her that she had experienced far too much pleasure these past two days, while he had probably known nothing but hardship and worriment.

But although she felt more than a little contrite, there was none of the desperate responsibility that

371

had always burned within her. Hadley had been right when he'd said it was time he lived his own life. She suddenly realized that he wasn't foremost in her thoughts anymore — Reeve was. After all these years, her life had taken on a new focus. Love had changed everything.

She sighed again and sank lower in the tub. Her thick auburn tresses fanned about her, soaking up the water to turn an even darker shade of red. Her body began to relax, and she could easily have drifted off to sleep . . .

A blast of cool air startled her from her languor. She gasped, her eyes flying wide in alarm as she came bolt upright in the tub and hastily tried to cover her breasts with her arms. Water splashed everywhere. Opening her mouth to scream, she was shocked instead into silence by the dawning realization that it was her own husband who had intruded upon her privacy.

Reeve closed the door behind him. His eyes glowed warmly when they lit upon his wife's naked, glistening body.

"Great balls of fire, Reeve Cameron, what do you think you're doing?" she demanded in breathless indignation. "How did you get in here? Why, I — I distinctly remember locking that door!"

"You did. But I've had a little practice when it comes to locks." A purposeful, utterly wicked smile spread across his handsome face as he sauntered forward to take a seat on the chair beside the bath.

"I thought you were going downstairs."

"I'm back."

"Did you find out anything?" Her eyes widened

once more when he tugged off his boots. "And what *are* you doing?" she demanded again.

"Taggart's here in Las Vegas all right," he told her, ignoring the last question altogether. "But no one's heard of your brother." He stood, his hands lifting to the buttons of his shirt.

"Private Taggart is here?" Relief washed over her. "Oh Reeve, then that means Hadley will be cleared!" She swallowed hard and slid lower in the water as she watched him remove the shirt and toss it aside. A sudden frown of puzzlement creased her brow. "But how did you find him so quickly? And why aren't you out arresting him?"

"I told you I had already sent someone to Las Vegas, remember? Taggart's got friends here. He's a frequent visitor to the saloon downstairs, but he won't show up before nightfall. Which means I've got a little time to kill," he concluded, unfastening his pants now. "It won't do me any good to check the other saloons until later, either. If that brother of yours is in town, then I stand a better chance of finding him after dark."

"Dear Lord, I hope he's here," she murmured, then charged with a renewed burst of annoyance, "I suppose you made a point of interrogating the enchanting Mrs. Leary?"

"A very wise and capable woman."

None too pleased with his rejoinder, she fought the temptation to hurl the sponge at his head. But her thoughts were drawn back to the situation at hand when he stripped off his pants.

"For Heaven's sake, I haven't finished my bath yet!" Her whole body became suffused with rosy color as he stood naked and unashamed before her. Thinking he meant to use the water as he'd done in Tascosa, she frowned again and said, "If you will please allow me to finish first, I will be more than happy to let you—"

"There's plenty of room for both of us," he cut in complacently.

"Reeve!" she breathed in shocked protest.

It did no good. He stepped into the tub behind where she sat and bent his tall, muscular frame downward, sending more water cascading over the edges to puddle on the floor. Lorelei gasped when he sat behind her and drew her against him.

"You're making a terrible mess! What will your dearest Annie say?" she taunted, shivering as her soft, supple curves fitted with absolute perfection against his virile hardness.

"You talk too much, you redheaded wildcat," he murmured huskily. He smiled when she reached her arms back to entwine about the corded muscles of his neck and pressed herself even closer.

"Then I suppose you'll have to silence me." She was rewarded for her impertinence when he leaned back against the tub and pulled her full-length on top of him in the water.

"With pleasure," he consented, with a soft chuckle.

Lorelei had never imagined it could be so pleasurable to make love in a bathtub, but it was—sweet mercy, *it was*. Reeve took her right there in the water, first turning her over and setting her passions aflame with the skillful, highly stimulating endeavors of his mouth and hands, and then sliding into her wet, silken passage while she cried out and clung to his hard-muscled shoulders. Afterwards, they took turns soaping one another's bodies, which led to another brief but tempestuous encounter on the floor beside the tub.

By the time they emerged from the bathroom, darkness had fallen and they were both of a mind to get something to eat. Reeve escorted his wife back to their room. While she dressed in a clean gown and pinned up her hair, he exchanged his own damp and dusty clothing for the shirt and trousers Annie had left on the bed.

The restaurant downstairs provided them with a delicious meal of roast beef and potatoes, hot biscuits, and the added delicacy of fresh peaches. After she had emptied her plate, Lorelei downed the last of her wine and frowned thoughtfully across at her husband.

"I think I should come with you tonight. If Hadley sees you without me, he won't stay around long enough to hear that you believe he is innocent."

"No, Lorelei." He shook his head, returning her frown with one of his own. "I'm sorry, but I can't take you with me."

"Why not?"

"Because women, at least women like you, don't belong in saloons," he explained patiently.

"But—"

"No."

She fell silent and cast him a mutinous look. A ghost of a smile played about his lips when he drew himself up from the table.

"Come on."

"Where are we going?" she asked, rising to her feet as well.

"Upstairs. I'm taking you to our room, and that's where you're going to stay until I get back." His warm hand closed about her arm, but she proved obstinate.

"So I'm supposed to sit and wait while you spend half the night searching all over Las Vegas for my brother?" she challenged, her blue eyes flashing spiritedly up at him. "I thought I had made it clear to you, Major Cameron, that you have a partner now!"

"What I have," he corrected, "is a *wife*. And I expect her to do as she's told."

"Does your good friend Annie do as she's told?" she retorted. The thought of him spending even one minute more in that woman's company provoked her to anger. "Oh, but I forgot—she's a very wise and capable woman, isn't she? How the devil did she acquire such wisdom and capability?"

"Blast it, you little spitfire, don't start that again," he warned quietly. His fingers tightened about her arm, and he propelled her none too gently along with him as he strode from the restaurant. They had the misfortune to cross paths with the troublesome Mrs. Leary herself just before they reached the staircase.

"I was hoping to run into you again," the widow said, though she spared only a passing glance for Lorelei. As usual, her smile was for Reeve. "I need to talk to you. Why don't we go into the saloon?"

"The saloon?" echoed Lorelei. She looked pointedly up at Reeve before turning to Annie. Deter-

376

mined not to be ignored, she lifted her head to a proud angle and inquired, "Tell me, Mrs. Leary—do you make it a habit of inviting other women's husbands to join you for a drink so late in the evening?" The words fairly dripped from her tongue in an exaggerated Southern drawl.

"Only when the husbands are as handsome and charming as yours," Annie countered, with a soft, unrepentant laugh. She told Reeve, "You'd better watch out, my dearest Major, or else you'll find yourself well and truly henpecked by your little bride. And there's nothing worse than a man who allows a woman to run his life." She made a quick, calculated adjustment to the low-cut bodice of her gown before adding, "I'll be waiting for you in the saloon." With that, she sailed blithely away, her hips swaying beneath her red silk skirts.

"We have a name for women like that back in Georgia," Lorelei pronounced in a low, seething tone, "but I am far too much of a lady to repeat it!" Her sapphire gaze blazed at the woman's retreating back. "So help me, Reeve Cameron, if you have any intention of meeting her—"

"She knows more about what's going on in this town than anyone else," he insisted, with maddening equanimity. Turning to lead her up the stairs, he was unable to prevent a smile of irony from touching his lips. "Jacob Leary had the patience of a saint. God knows, Annie can be a real hellion at times."

"What happened to her husband?" she asked, then opined before he could answer, "It wouldn't surprise me to learn that he had simply run out of patience and taken flight." She regretted the careless remark immediately.

"He was killed a couple of years ago," answered Reeve. A shadow crossed his face at the memory, but he did not elaborate. He unlocked the door to their room and slipped his arms about her. "I don't know when I'll be back, but it will be late. Don't wait up."

"I certainly will not," she parried with a frown, still simmering over his refusal to let her come along. "Reeve, if you should find Hadley—"

"I'll bring him back here," he promised. He bent his head and gave her a quick, hard kiss. "Go to sleep, Lorelei."

She watched as he turned and strode back down the hall. Feeling restless, irritated, and apprehensive all at once, she stepped inside the room, closed the door, and leaned back against it, her mind a chaotic jumble of thoughts.

Reeve had told her to stay put, and yet how could she? It simply wasn't in her nature to sit and wait like some meek, mousy little female, while he plunged himself into adventure—and perhaps even danger. She had always taken life by the horns, as her father used to say. Such impetuosity had gotten her into trouble on more than one occasion, it was true, but it had also meant that she found solutions to her problems more readily than most of the other women she had known.

Without further hesitation, she unfastened her dress and pulled it off. She searched in her carpetbag for the pair of pants she had been wearing when she left Fort Concho. They were neatly folded at the bottom, where she had hidden them in defiance of Reeve's orders to throw them out.

Lacking a shirtwaist to wear with the pants, she was forced to settle for her chemise. She dressed quickly, laced up her boots again, and found the canvas slicker. Thankfully, it covered her from her neck to her ankles when she buttoned it on. She donned the hat and tucked her hair securely beneath it.

She hurried across the room to face herself in the large, gilded mirror. Her eyes sparkled with mingled defiance and satisfaction at what she saw.

"Women don't belong in saloons," she murmured, repeating the statement Reeve had made a short time earlier. "Very well: have it your way, Major Cameron." She tugged the front brim of the hat lower and prayed that no one would look too closely.

Slipping from the room, she headed downstairs. She forced herself to maintain a natural, unhurried pace, since she certainly had no wish to call attention to herself. A smile of triumph tugged at the corners of her mouth when she managed to stroll all the way across the crowded lobby without attracting so much as a sideways glance.

It was much too risky to pay a visit to Annie's saloon, she decided reluctantly as she stood outside on the front porch. Reeve would recognize her in an instant. She could well imagine how surprised he would be when he learned of her little deception; surprised and furious, she amended with a frown. A knot of trepidation tightened in her stomach at the thought of his wrath, but she was determined to charge ahead. If she could find Hadley, then any chastisement she suffered afterwards would be worth it.

Keeping her head down, she directed her steps toward the nearest saloon. The plaza was ablaze with lights, the cool night air filled with the strains of music and the smell of food, horses, and woodsmoke. Men crowded along the boardwalks and called out to one another in the darkness, while the sound of women's laughter rose above the whole boisterous roar. Just as in Tascosa, gunshots rang out at regular intervals, though no one seemed to take much notice.

Lorelei took a deep, steadying breath and followed a group of young cowboys into the saloon. She moved unobtrusively toward one corner, her gaze scanning the noisy, smoke-filled room for any sign of her brother. There was none. Disappointed, she slipped back outside.

There were at least half a dozen places on the plaza to try, and she was determined not to return to the hotel until she had visited each and every one of them. She realized that it might still be too early, or that Hadley might decide not to risk coming into town at all, but her hope was that he had indeed reached Las Vegas by now and would waste little time in searching for his former comrade.

She walked along the boardwalk to the saloon next door and waited so that she could enter in the immediate wake of five rough-looking men who were much too preoccupied with their own conversation to notice her. Unfortunately, the room in which she found herself was even larger and more crowded than the last. The smoke stung her eyes, and she resisted the impulse to cough as she peered surreptitiously about. The din of human voices and piano music was almost deafening, while the smell of unwashed bodies blended with the aroma of strong spirits to choke the air. It all prompted her to wonder why any man in his right mind would choose to spend his evenings in such a place.

She did not see Hadley anywhere. Heaving another sigh of disappointment, she turned and headed back toward the swinging double half-doors. She kept her eyes downcast as she went, and in so doing accidentally passed too close to one of the poker tables. Her foot landed a glancing blow to the table leg. The four men participating in the game of five-card stud raised a loud, angry protest at her clumsiness, as several cards and coins went flying.

"Damn your hide, you stupid son of a bitch!" one of them snarled, jumping to his feet to confront her.

"I—I'm sorry," she murmured, keeping her voice as low as possible. She ducked her head again and tried to continue on her way, but the man was not appeased.

"Sorry ain't good enough!"

His hand shot out to close about her arm in a hard, punishing grip. She gasped in alarm and raised her eyes to his face. He glowered menacingly down at her, his own eyes narrowing when he took in the sight of her pale, heart-shaped face.

"What the hell we got here?" he cried, in a voice full of scorn. "Why, you ain't nothin' but a pretty little boy!" He looked to his friends and jeered, "Must be one of them greenhorns from over at that

381

Englishman's spread!"

"Take your hands off me!" Lorelei rasped out. She tried to pull free, but her vengeful, half-drunk captor wasn't about to release her yet.

"Somebody ought to teach you 'bout buttin' in where you ain't wanted!" he threatened. Warming to the thought, he smiled malevolently and reached down with his other hand to unbuckle his belt. He yanked it off and caught the other end, up against the buckle, apparently meaning to use it on her. "I'll give you a hidin' you won't forget, boy!"

"No!" She struggled in his grasp, frantically wondering if she should appeal to the other men for help. If she revealed her identity, there was a chance the situation would become even more dangerous — and in an entirely different way. "I said I was sorry, now let me go!" she demanded hoarsely.

"Not 'til you've learned some manners!" He spun her about and pushed her hard against the table. She gave a breathless cry as her midsection connected forcefully with the edge. He clamped a hand on the back of her neck and bent her forward.

"Damn you, let go of me!" She managed to twist about and deliver a loud, stinging slap to his face. A number of the onlookers laughed and shouted encouragement, watching as she struck out at him again.

"Aw come on, Judd, let the boy go," one of his friends drawled, frowning in mild displeasure. "He didn't mean no harm."

"Mind your own business!" He grabbed her arm once more and twisted it cruelly behind her back.

"Let him go!" someone else dared to intervene.

382

Lorelei's heart leapt at the sound of that voice. *Hadley!* She jerked her head around to see her brother standing a few feet away, his hand clenched in readiness about his gun.

"What the—" the man called Judd ground out, only to break off when his eyes fell on the revolver, which was aimed directly at his heart. He swallowed the lump of fear in his throat and relaxed his grip on Lorelei. "You the boy's nursemaid?" he challenged, with a gesture of contempt.

"You might say that," Hadley replied evenly. He nodded at Lorelei. "Now let him go."

Judd hesitated visibly, torn between the wisdom of obedience and the folly of drawing his own gun. Wisdom won out. Muttering an oath, he let go of Lorelei. Laughter erupted about him, and there was more than one uncomplimentary remark made about his brief tangle with a greenhorn.

"Oh, Hadley, thank God you're here!" breathed Lorelei, flying across to his side.

"Get behind me," he instructed in a low, cautious tone. When she had done as he'd said, he motioned at the other man with his gun. "Sit down and get on with your game."

"Yeah, I'm tired of holdin' this hand," one of the other three participants complained gruffly.

Relief washed over Lorelei when the hot-tempered Judd sank heavily down into his chair once more. A million questions were whirling about in her mind as she and her brother made their way safely outside.

"When did you get into town?" she asked, rounding on him once they paused on the boardwalk a

383

short distance away from the saloon. Her hand closed anxiously about his arm. "Are you all right? How did you—"

"I'll explain everything later." He cut her off with a faint smile. He looked tired, but otherwise in good health. He frowned at her, his eyes searching her face in the semidarkness. "What about you? Where's Major Cameron?"

"I'm fine!" she assured him hastily. "And Reeve is at the hotel, waiting—good Heavens, Hadley, he's waiting to arrest Private Taggart!"

"And me," he added, his frown deepening.

"No! I mean, yes, he wants to take you back to Fort Concho, but he believes you now!" Her eyes glowed warmly up into his. "He knows you're innocent. He knows it, and he's determined to help you prove it!"

"The only proof I need is Taggart."

"But I just told you, Reeve is—"

"No, he isn't." He shook his head and drew her a bit farther into the shadows. Lowering his voice to an undertone, he confided, "I'm meeting Taggart tonight. I managed to get a message to him through a friend of his, the one at the saloon he told me about, and he's agreed to meet me outside town. As a matter of fact, he's probably waiting for me there right now."

"Why couldn't you talk to him here in Las Vegas?" she asked in puzzlement.

"Because this is the way he wanted it." He took her arm and started leading her toward the hotel. "I was trying to find out if you and the major had arrived in town yet when I saw you in that saloon." A

384

brief smile of irony touched his lips. "It's a good thing I recognized you back there. You could have ended up with far worse than a hiding from that new admirer of yours. Hellfire and damnation, Lori, I can't believe the major was fool enough to let you—"

"He didn't let me," she interrupted. "He told me to stay at the hotel, but I wanted to find you before he did!"

"And as usual, you did as you pleased," he observed wryly.

"It worked, didn't it?" She lifted her head and fixed him with a steady look of determination. "I'm coming with you to meet Taggart."

"You are not!"

"Yes, I am! What if he's planning to double-cross you? I don't think he will try anything if I'm there, especially after I tell him I'm married to the man who intends to take him back to Fort Concho."

"No," Hadley insisted, shaking his head in a firm denial. "I'm meeting him alone. It's too dangerous for you to come. I have very little doubt that Major Cameron would have my head if I let anything happen to you!"

"You can joke all you want to, Hadley Montgomery," she countered, "but I *am* coming with you! If you try and go without me, I'll simply follow. And then you really will have cause to worry, won't you?"

"Lori—"

"It's useless to argue with me, and you know it." She flashed him a conciliatory smile and added, "Besides, you could probably use a fresh horse. I'll

385

tell the man at the stables what we need, and I'll have him apply the charges to our hotel bill. You don't have any money, do you?"

"No," he conceded reluctantly.

"I didn't think so." She looked him up and down, noting for the first time that he was wearing a shirt and pants that were decidedly ill-fitting. "Where on earth did you get those clothes?"

"You might say I borrowed them." In spite of the gravity of the situation, his eyes twinkled at her. "I certainly didn't want to advertise myself as a desperado on the run."

"You look much worse than that," she opined with sisterly honesty, then concluded as they reached the hotel, "Well, then, it's settled."

"All right, damn it." His brows drew together into a dark scowl of warning. "But you're to keep quiet and let me do the talking, understand? Taggart's not the most congenial of men. He's something of a hothead, and I wouldn't put it past him to call the whole thing off if he so much as suspects that we want to take him back to Fort Concho."

"Reeve said you could still be cleared if you cooperated with him," she said earnestly. Her gaze softened as it met the similar, deep blue depths of his. "He's a fair man, Hadley. And he's been on your side all along. We should have trusted him."

"Thank you for your completely unbiased assessment of the man," her brother retorted. Then his features grew solemn. "Maybe when this is all over, I can get to know the man you married, Lori. I'd like that. But for now, he's still a special investigator with the United States Cavalry—and I'm an escaped

386

prisoner."

She offered no reply, but instead led him around to the stables in back of the hotel. They were soon on their way, riding away from the plaza and along one of the dusty roads that led up into the hills outside the town.

Eighteen

Lorelei felt a sharp pang of guilt as her thoughts drifted back to Reeve. She wondered how long he would wait at the hotel before setting out to search the other saloons. Praying that Hadley's meeting with Private Taggart would prove successful, she shifted in the saddle and cast a glance up toward the night sky. The lights of Las Vegas shone in the near distance, but all about them was a cloaking darkness relieved only by an occasional glimmer of lamplight from one of the outlying ranches.

"How much farther?" she asked her brother. She was getting hot in the slicker, but dared not remove it yet.

"We're almost there," he answered. Slowing his horse to a walk, he pointed toward a bend in the road just ahead. "There's the place. But I don't see Taggart."

He frowned and reined to a halt. Lorelei drew up beside him, her eyes searching along with his. The road was completely deserted.

"He should have been here by now," murmured Hadley. His voice was edged with worry.

"Maybe Reeve has already found him," Lorelei suggested reluctantly. "If he did, then the only thing to do is ride back to town and —"

"Not yet. We'll wait a while first."

"All right. But I . . . I don't have a good feeling about this, Hadley," she confessed, glancing uneasily about her.

"I told you not to come!" he reminded her. He dismounted and looped the reins about a tree beside the road. Grabbing the hat from his head, he breathed a curse and realized that he felt just as uneasy as his sister. He blamed the feeling on the desperate hope that tonight would finally bring an end to his ordeal. For Lorelei's sake as well as his own, he wanted to put it all behind him and get on with his life. "It's only a little past nine," he said, trying to sound nonchalant.

"Yes, and it's possible that he simply lost track of time." Following his example she dismounted and wrapped her reins over the tree's low branch. "You know, you never have told me what really happened the night Lieutenant Fitzhugh was killed," she remarked, at a sudden thought. "Why were you accused of his murder?"

"Taggart and I were standing guard that night," he related grimly. "The lieutenant was returning from Santa Angela. I called out to him as he approached, but he didn't answer. And that's when it happened."

"When *what* happened?"

"Someone jumped me from behind. I remember struggling, then I felt a pain in the back of my head and blacked out. The next thing I knew, Taggart was bending over me, claiming that I had shot Lieutenant Fitzhugh. I couldn't believe it. He was right there and saw everything."

389

"But he lied and said that you were the one," Lorelei murmured, her eyes blazing at the man's treachery.

"He didn't have much choice. They would have killed him," he said. "That's why he took off when he did. He was afraid I might talk."

"But how could you be charged on such flimsy evidence? And what about the injury you suffered? Shouldn't that have lent proof to your story?"

"The murderer killed the lieutenant with my gun," he told her. "I never got a look at him. Taggart did, of course, but he never told me who it was. As for my injury—it was claimed to be self-inflicted as an attempt on my part to cover up what I had done."

"Do you have any idea *why* Lieutenant Fitzhugh was murdered?" she queried next, her mind still spinning as she tried to take in what she had just heard.

"There was talk that he wanted out, that he was threatening to expose all those involved. It was incredibly foolish of him to think he could just walk away. Those men are ruthless. They won't hesitate to do whatever it takes to get what they want," he declared, angry resignation in his voice.

"Oh, Hadley, I don't understand any of this! Why didn't you go to the colonel and tell him what was happening? And if so many officers and enlisted men are involved, why couldn't you have sent word to Washington?"

"You can't understand," he insisted. "You don't know what it's like to be looking over your shoulder all the time, wondering who's standing ready to put a knife in your back. There was nowhere to run, nowhere to hide." He paused for a moment, his gaze darkening at the bitter reminiscence. "When I first discovered what was going on, I tried to talk to Colonel Mackenzie about it. He listened politely, even asked a question or two, then told me he'd look into the matter. He did nothing."

"That's not true!" exclaimed Lorelei. "It's because of a report Colonel Mackenzie made that Reeve was sent to Fort Concho!"

"I'd like to believe that," he responded with a faint smile, then sighed raggedly. "But I don't know what to believe anymore. These past few weeks have been a nightmare, Lori. First, there were the raids. There had been plenty in the past, but they suddenly increased to an alarming frequency. The Indians seemed to know exactly where and when to attack. Innocent men and women, and dear God, even children were killed." He shuddered at the awful memory. "It sickened me when I found out that some of my own friends were involved. They didn't care about anything but their share in the plunder."

"They've got to be brought to justice, Hadley," she declared quietly, her gaze full of horror. "You can't let them go unpunished. You can't!"

"I don't intend to. I never did." He sighed again, and met her gaze. "But I can't take them on alone, Lori."

"You won't have to. Reeve will help you. He has a great deal of influence in Washington. You can rest assured that he will see justice done," she concluded, with heartfelt sincerity. "If Taggart doesn't come tonight, you've got to promise me that you'll

391

tell Reeve everything you know. Even the names. He's got to know everything!"

"You meant it when you said you wouldn't be going home to Georgia, didn't you?" he challenged unexpectedly, a light of amusement in his eyes.

"Yes, I meant it," she confirmed in all seriousness. "I love him, Hadley. and I'm going to follow him wherever he goes."

"Are you sure, Lori? You may not be happy sharing his kind of life. It won't be anything like what you've known back home."

"I'm sure." There was no denying the certainty in her beautiful sapphire eyes.

They lapsed into silence for a few moments. All about them, the sounds of the night rose in the cool, pine-scented air. Finally, Lorelei decided to venture another question.

"Hadley, why do you think Taggart agreed to meet with you tonight?"

"I think he wants to get things settled, too. He won't be willing to return to Fort Concho, but I don't plan to give him a choice."

"I know, but—"

"Quiet!" he hissed sharply. "Someone's coming!"

Lorelei heard the distant sound of hoofbeats. Instinctively she moved closer to her brother and waited as the sound grew louder.

"That can't be Taggart!" Hadley whispered.

"Then who . . .'" Her words trailed away as her heart filled with sudden dread. It was increasingly apparent that a good many riders were approaching.

"Let's get out of here!" directed Hadley, his voice holding more than a touch of apprehension.

Lorelei hastened to do as he said, but it was too late. They had done nothing more than unloop the reins when the horsemen rounded the bend in the road and cut off their escape.

Catching sight of them, the lead rider raised his arm in a silent command and all the men, more than a dozen, reined to a halt directly in front of them.

Even in the darkness, Lorelei could make out their faces. A few were white, others were Mexican, while still others were of mixed blood. With coarse, unshaven features, sinister eyes, and clothing that was dusty and rumpled, they seemed to be the epitome of the type of lawless, unscrupulous men Reeve had warned her about. Hadley's next words reinforced that opinion.

"Comancheros," he whispered. "Keep quiet!"

She wasn't sure exactly what the term signified, but she knew these men were outlaws. Nodding wordlessly, she pressed closer to Hadley. Her frightened gaze traveled to the leader of the desperadoes, who was staring down at her with unnerving intensity. He spoke a few words of Spanish to the man beside him, then gave her a broad, calculating smile.

"You are very young still," he observed, his English heavily accented. His dark gaze lit with pleasure. "I could get a very good price for you." He looked to Hadley and frowned. "You, *señor,* are too old to fetch much. But I will try."

A good price, Lorelei's mind echoed. What did he mean by that? She ducked her head lower and battled the panic welling up deep within her.

"My brother and I were headed for Las Vegas,

393

when my horse threw a shoe," Hadley announced with deceptive calm. His hand was already inching down toward his holster. "We'd like to be on our way."

The other man laughed. His companions did the same.

"No, *señor,* you will not be on your way. You and your little brother there are coming with us."

"I'm afraid we can't do that," insisted Hadley. He pulled Lorelei behind him and drew his gun. "We want no trouble with you, but we're heading to Las Vegas."

The leader of the group spoke to the man beside him again. When he turned back to Hadley this time, there was no trace of amusement in his hotly glittering eyes.

"Put down your gun and live," he suggested.

"I'll go with you, if you let my brother ride on," countered Hadley.

"No!" Lorelei burst out, her terror-stricken gaze shooting back to the desperado.

The leader eyed her suspiciously and ground out a command to one of the other riders. The man dismounted and advanced on her. Hadley took a defensive step forward.

"Stay back!" he cautioned, leveling the gun.

Everything happened with lightning swiftness after that. A shot rang out, splitting the silence of the night. Lorelei screamed as Hadley clutched at his chest and collapsed on the ground.

"Hadley! Dear God, no!"

She fell to her knees beside him, tears of rage and pain stinging against her eyelids as she saw blood staining his shirt. He was alive, but just barely. Her gaze widened with horrified disbelief, and then she snatched the gun from his hand and scrambled to her feet.

"Damn your soul to hell!" she cried brokenly, pointing the barrel of the revolver toward the leader. She never got the chance to fire. Seized roughly by the man who had been moving toward her when Hadley was shot, she screamed again as the gun was wrenched from her grasp. Her hat was knocked off in the ensuing struggle, allowing her thick, luxuriant auburn curls to tumble freely about her face and shoulders.

The sight of her beautiful countenance and flame-colored locks prompted the *comancheros* to gasp with admiration—and avarice. They knew this woman would command a top price from the Comanches.

"So, you are no little brother at all," the leader said, with a low chuckle. "Come, *señorita*. It is growing late and my men are tired."

"I'm not going anywhere with you!" she proclaimed in vengeful defiance, twisting furiously within the grasp of her captor. "My brother needs medical attention at once! He will die if—"

"He will die more quickly if you do not do as I say."

"You can't leave him here like this!" she protested, the tears coursing hotly down her cheeks now. She choked back a sob and pleaded with him in growing desperation. "Please, I . . . I will do as you say, if you will only send someone into town to deliver a message!"

"No message," he decreed, unmoved by her tears.

At another wordless signal, she was suddenly caught up in her captor's arms and carried, still struggling with all her might, to the leader himself. She found herself seated before him on horseback, his arm like a band of iron about her waist and his voice low and full of menace next to her ear.

"Obey, *señorita,* and you will not be harmed."

"Why are you doing this?" she demanded raggedly, her stricken gaze moving back to Hadley's unconscious form.

"For the money—what else?" He gave a soft, triumphant laugh. "A woman with red hair will be much valued by the Comanches."

"Comanches?" she gasped, terror gripping her at the word.

"They will pay more for you than all the other captives put together, *señorita,*" he boasted. He raised his voice in a brusque directive to his men, then reined about and rode away. The others followed close behind, one of them leading the two horses Lorelei had rented from the hotel's stables.

She managed to catch one last glimpse of her brother before she was spirited away into the darkness. Her heart ached terribly, and she feared she would never see him alive again. She closed her eyes and prayed that he would be discovered before it was too late. Private Taggart might still show up for the meeting—if indeed the *comancheros* weren't part of a double cross he had arranged.

Only then did she offer up a prayer on her own behalf. *Please, God, please let Reeve find me in time!*

She felt as though they rode for hours. At first holding herself stiff and unyielding against her captor's arm, she began to slump wearily as the long night wore on. She wept in silence, haunted by the burning memory of her brother's shooting. It seemed impossible that he would die like this. After al they had been through together . . . surely fate couldn't be so cruel.

Reeve's face swam before her eyes. Her heart cried out for him. If only she had listened to him, Hadley might not be lying in the road with a bullet in his chest, and she wouldn't be facing the ghastly prospect of being sold to the Comanches. Dear God, would she ever see him again?

Just when she feared she would faint from the combined effects of physical and emotional exhaustion, the wild ride across the rugged New Mexico countryside came to an end. The *comancheros* headed through a narrow canyon to a surprisingly large, protected settlement in the foothills of the mountains. A number of women and children raised a warm greeting for the returning men, in spite of the fact that it was nearly midnight. Dogs barked and scampered excitedly about as the riders drew their mounts to a halt and swung down. The aroma of food and woodsmoke provided a comforting reminder of yet another triumphant homecoming.

Lorelei's desolate gaze traveled wearily over the many adobe houses, corrals, and outbuildings. It looked like a small, rough-hewn kingdom, and she had little doubt that the man who dismounted and pulled her down beside him presided over it with an iron hand.

"You will eat and rest tonight, *señorita,*" he told her. "Tomorrow, we will have a visitor. He will want to see for himself what valuable *contrabando* I have taken."

"I suppose he is a Comanche!" she hissed, jerking her arm from his grasp. "Well, I won't be sold to him, do you hear? You have no right to keep me prisoner, and as God is my witness, I'll see you hanged for what you've done!"

"He is no Comanche," the desperado replied, with a chuckle. "He was our *patrón,* our leader. And maybe he will buy you for himself." His dark, sinister eyes flickered over her, and he gave her another malevolent smile. "He will have to pay a very good price."

Lorelei cried out and struck him as hard as she could across the face. He merely seized her wrist in a brutal grip and called to two of his men to take her away. She fought them like a wildcat, kicking and flailing and even biting one of them on the hand, but to no avail. They carried her inside a nearby building and thrust her roughly into a back room. She scrambled to her feet and flew to the door, only to cry tears of furious, helpless defeat as the key was turned in the lock.

Dashing impatiently at her eyes, she spun about and searched for any possible means of escape. It was very dark inside the small, airless room. The only source of light was a high window, covered by bars and too narrow to be of any use. A cot rested in one corner, a table beside it, but there was nothing else.

She cautioned herself not to give in to despair,

and yet there appeared to be little hope of escape. Reeve would come for her—of that, she was certain. But when? And, Heaven help her, what was she going to do in the meantime?

Her spirits wretchedly low, she sank down onto the cot and buried her face in her hands. A moment later, she heard the key turning in the lock again. She sprang to her feet, her pulses racing as she looked about for something she could use as a weapon.

Three women appeared in the doorway. Two were young and comely, but the third was much older, very tall, and wore an expression of unmistakable antagonism. It was she who stepped forward to eye Lorelei narrowly.

"Here's food and drink," she announced, then motioned to the other women. They hurried into the room and set a try laden with bowls of *frijoles* and *tortillas* and a jug of water on the table. After stealing a hasty, curious glance at her, they returned to the doorway.

"Please, you've got to help me!" Lorelei entreated the gray-haired woman. "I must get away! My brother has been shot, and—"

"You can have a bath in the morning." She frowned as her rancorous gaze moved over the canvas slicker. "Take that off," she ordered tersely.

"Please, you have to listen to me!" Lorelei tried again. Her eyes held a desperate appeal as she approached the woman and offered tremulously, "I—I will see that you are well rewarded if you help me! My husband is waiting for me in Las Vegas, and he—"

"Shut up!" Without warning, she raised her hand and gave the smoothness of Lorelei's cheek a stinging slap. "Now take it off!"

Lorelei's eyes blazed with vengeful fire, but she drew herself up proudly and shook her head.

"No," she uttered in defiance.

The woman signaled for the other two to come forward again. Before Lorelei could move to prevent it, they had each seized one of her arms. She struggled against them, but the older woman managed to unbutton the slicker and yank it off.

"Take off them pants, too!" she demanded, in a harsh, angry tone of voice.

"Go to the devil!" Lorelei shot back.

She knew it was hopeless, but still she fought them. They stripped off the pants in a matter of minutes, leaving her clad in nothing but her chemise. It reached only to her knees, and the thin white fabric revealed far too much of her womanly charms. Feeling virtually naked, she crossed her arms against her breasts and faced her principal tormentor with the light of battle in her eyes.

"Damn you!" she cried hotly. "The least you could do is leave me something to wear!"

"You'll get something tomorrow," the woman told her, then smiled for the first time. It was a chilling smile, full of malice. "We want you to look all clean and pretty for *El Lobo,* don't we now?"

"And who is *El Lobo?*"

"You'll find out soon enough."

The two young women gathered up the slicker and pants, then preceded the hostile, gray-haired giantess from the room. Lorelei thought briefly about trying to dart past them, but decided against it. Reluctantly telling herself that it would be wiser to wait for a more advantageous opportunity, she listened to the sound of the door being locked and released a heavy, despondent sigh.

There was nothing more to be done that night. Still feeling terribly sick at heart, she lay down upon the cot and closed her eyes. Sleep eluded her for most of the night; when it did come, her dreams were filled with horrible visions of Hadley's death and her own fate among the Comanches. Her last waking thought, however, was of her beloved husband.

"Reeve," she whispered into the surrounding darkness. Her heart twisted anew, but she could weep no more . . .

Nineteen

The promised bath arrived soon after breakfast. But the promised clothing did not.

"You said I was to be given something to wear!" Lorelei reminded the woman who had treated her with such contempt the previous night.

"You'll fetch a higher price if he can get a good look at you."

"And who the devil decided *that?*" she demanded, stepping out of the old, metal hip tub and wrapping a towel about herself. Her eyes strayed nervously toward the doorway, where a man stood guard on the other side of the door instead of the two young women who had come the night before.

"You cause me any more trouble, you red-haired bitch, and I'll fix it so no one'll want to look at you ever again," the woman threatened ruthlessly. She flung Lorelei's chemise at her. "Put it back on and shut your trap!"

Lorelei was given no time to argue, for her reluctant caretaker stalked from the room and slammed the door behind her. She heard the woman say something to the guard, but she was unable to decipher the words.

Faced with no other choice, she slipped on the chemise once more. She sat down, took up the comb she had been given, and dragged it through her wet hair.

Her sapphire gaze kindled with another burst of proud defiance. She had no intention of being displayed before the mysterious *El Lobo,* or any other man. If it came down to it, she would risk her life before she'd allow herself to be taken. The thought of anyone else claiming what belonged to Reeve alone was unbearable. She would never submit. *Never.*

The sound of children's laughter, women's chatter, and other evidence of life outside drifted into the room through the barred window above. As the sun rose higher in the sky, the air became hot and stifling, and she felt increasingly drained of energy. The only time the door opened was at mealtimes. She received no other visitors. The hours crawled by in a never-ending haze of painful remembrance and apprehension at what lay ahead. Thoughts of Hadley, Reeve, and escape tumbled about in her mind, giving her hope whenever her spirits sank.

It wasn't until nightfall that the awful waiting came to an end.

She had just finished bathing again, using the pitcher of water and the large wooden bowl that had been delivered along with her meal. It had been decreed that her hair should be left unbound, but she had rebelliously caught it up into a knot, which rested on the nape of her neck. The air was mercifully cooler now that darkness had crept over the settlement, and the bustling activity outside had died down to nothing more than an occasional murmur of voices.

Having wondered if she would ever be given the

403

chance to try and escape, Lorelei was vastly relieved when the door opened to admit the gray-haired woman once more.

"Come on."

"Where are we going?"

"El Lobo is here." She took Lorelei's arm in a none-too-gentle grip and pulled her toward the door. "Don't try anything, you hear?"

"Will you at least allow me to cover myself while I am being taken to him?" she requested, with deceptive civility. "It occurs to me that this *El Lobo* would not approve of what is intended for his eyes alone being ogled by every man here." Her gaze sparked with triumphant satisfaction when she observed the look of begrudging acquiescence on her wardress's ugly, sharp-featured face.

"All right. Here," said the woman, snatching up the towel. "Wrap it around your shoulders. But let down your hair!"

Lorelei obeyed without argument. She did not protest when the woman took her arm again and led her swiftly from the room. They walked outside and headed across the darkened compound to a large, two-story adobe building a short distance away. A man followed close behind, his arms cradling a gun in the event that the beautiful prisoner tried to escape— or in case the *comancheros* watching them decided to make off with such a prize.

Her gaze made a broad, encompassing sweep of the grounds, her mind racing to formulate a plan. She toyed with the idea of taking flight then and there, but realized that she had no chance of success. No, she couldn't act solely on impulse. She had to wait for the right moment. And she prayed that it would come soon.

The blood pounded in her ears as she was led into the building and up a flight of stairs. A single lamp was burning in the center of the room in which she found herself. It was spacious, and decorated in an unexpectedly grand style, with heavy velvet draperies and massive carved furniture. The floors were covered by expensive carpets, and along one wall sat a huge, four-poster bed with a lacy canopy.

Her eyes blazed at the sight of that bed. It renewed her courage, and lent fuel to the fire of determination already burning within her.

"Stay here," the woman instructed gruffly. She turned and started to leave, but paused for a moment to offer a bit of advice. "You'd better hope *El Lobo* likes you, girl. Better him than the Comanches, wouldn't you say?"

Lorelei did not answer. She waited until she was left alone in the room, then dropped the towel and flew about in a frantic effort to find something, anything at all, she could use to defend herself against the man who would soon be there to "inspect" her. If she could manage to incapacitate him, she could climb out the window and drop to the ground below. The darkness would aid her in making her way across to the corrals. She could take one of the horses and ride away, back to Las Vegas . . . back to Reeve.

There was always the danger that she would be caught, of course. She surmised correctly that there were men assigned to keep watch over the settlement at every hour of the day and night. But she was willing to do whatever it took to obtain her freedom. God help her, she would even kill if she had to.

Her eyes lit upon a crystal decanter. Musing that her captors had foolishly underestimated her, she hurried across to the table beside the bed and grasped the decanter. It was quite heavy, and contained a small amount of brandy. After emptying the liquid into a glass, she tried the feel of the intended weapon in her hands, then moved back across to the doorway.

Raising the decanter high, she waited for the door to open. Her hands shook, but her resolve never wavered. She would be ready when *El Lobo* arrived.

The wait was not a long one.

Her arms were just beginning to get tired when she heard someone coming up the stairs. She tensed, her hands clenching about the heavy crystal. Saying a quick prayer that her desperate plan would work, she watched in breathless anticipation as the doorknob turned.

The door swung open. A dark head appeared—and Lorelei made her move.

A breathless cry broke from her lips when her intended victim suddenly caught her about the waist and toppled her to the floor. The decanter fell harmlessly onto the carpet. Lorelei found both her wrists seized in a strong, relentless grip. The man rolled so that he was atop her, his weight crushing her half-naked softness while she struggled wildly beneath him.

"No! Let me go!" she cried, twisting her head from side to side.

"Damn it, Lorelei, it's me!"

Her eyes flew wide and her struggles ceased abruptly. She stared up at him in shocked disbelief.

"Reeve?" In the next instant, her whole body

406

flooded with the most profound joy and relief she had ever known. "Dear God, it—it's really you!"

"Quiet!" he cautioned sharply. He climbed to his feet and pulled her up as well, his strong arms wrapping about her as her legs threatened to give way beneath her. "Are you all right?"

"Yes!" she fought back a fresh wave of tears. "But how did you get here? And what about the *comancheros?* Oh Reeve, Hadley was—"

"He's going to be fine," he hastened to assure her. Casting a quick glance over his shoulder, he put a finger to her lips and left her for a moment to close the door. He returned to take her in his warm embrace once more, and explained, "Taggart found him and brought him back to town."

"So, he . . . he didn't double-cross Hadley after all," she murmured tremulously.

"No. Your brother lost a lot of blood, but the doctor said he'll recover. He's young and healthy, Lorelei." He tightened his arms about her and pressed a kiss to the silken smoothness of her forehead. "I nearly went wild when Hadley regained consciousness this afternoon and told me what happened!" he confided, his deep-timbred voice raw with emotion. "His description of your abductors was right on target."

"Oh, Reeve, there's a man coming here, a man they call *El Lobo!* He could be here any minute! We've got to get away while there's still time!" she insisted, drawing away and trying to pull him toward the window.

"It's all right, my love."

"What do you mean, 'it's all right'?" she demanded in bafflement. She raised her hands to his arms and pleaded anxiously, "Don't you understand. If you're

407

found here, they'll kill you!"

"They won't kill *El Lobo.*"

"What in Heaven's name are you talking about?" Her frown of confusion deepened when she observed the slow, crooked smile spreading across his handsome face.

"I'm *El Lobo,* Lorelei."

"But how could that be?" she gasped, incredulous at the declaration. "They told me he was some kind of former leader of theirs, and they . . . they knew he was coming today!"

"I rode with them several months ago," he revealed. "It was part of another assignment. My orders were to infiltrate the *comancheros* and find out how many guns they were selling to the Indians. The reason they expected me today was because I had already sent word of my return. I was planning to question them about Fort Concho."

"Why? What makes you think they could have been involved?"

"Because they're what's known as the middlemen. They trade guns and ammunition for the livestock and other contraband taken by the Indians in the raids. Comanches, Kiowas, Cheyennes — they've dealt with them all. I don't know if these particular men are involved with what happened back at Fort Concho, but they probably know who is." His expression became dangerously grim, and he added, "Whenever they can, they take white captives and sell them to the Indians. Which is why you're here."

"I was supposed to hope that you would pay a high price for me, so I wouldn't be sold to the Comanches," she recalled with a shudder. Her eyes met his again. "They don't know who you really are, do they?"

"No," he confirmed, with a faint smile of irony. "They think I'm on the run from the law."

"We've got to get out of here!" she reiterated.

"We can't leave yet."

"Why not?"

"Because it would look suspicious if I didn't stay at least a day or two. We're perfectly safe," he maintained, pulling her close again. "I've given orders that we're not to be disturbed for the rest of the night."

"Oh, Reeve, I still can't believe you're really here! she sighed. She entwined her arms about his neck and gazed lovingly up at him. "Thank God you came when you did. And thank God I didn't kill you!"

"You never had a chance of that, sweet vixen," he remarked, with another soft smile. "I've had too many years of practice dodging bullets, and a host of other objects, to be taken down by a redheaded wildcat." His brows drew together in a frown when his eyes dropped to her scantily clad body. "Where the devil are your clothes?'

"They thought *El Lobo* would be more inclined to buy me if I looked like this," she disclosed, warm color staining her cheeks.

"They were right." He scooped her up in his arms and carried her to the bed.

"Reeve!" she protested weakly. "Surely you're not planning to — "

"Nothing would give me greater pleasure," he admitted, his gaze brimming with love and passion, "but you've been through hell these past twenty-four hours. And I think it's a good idea if I keep an eye out for any trouble."

"I thought you said we were perfectly safe."

"We are. But I've never found it a waste of time to be cautious."

"Couldn't you . . . hold me for a while?" she entreated in a small voice, wanting desperately to lie in his arms and feel his heart beating against hers.

"All right," he agreed readily. He lowered her to the bed and stretched out beside her, then placed his gun on the table at arm's reach. Drawing her sweet, thinly covered curves against his fully clothed hardness, he cradled her head upon his chest and tenderly smoothed the hair away from her face. "I love you, Lorelei. Hell, if those bastards had harmed you in any way, I'd have killed every last one of them," he vowed, his low voice simmering with rage. "Maybe now my superiors will listen to me and clean them out for good."

"It's finally coming to an end, isn't it, Reeve? Now that you have Taggart, and Hadley is going to be all right, we can go back to Fort Concho," she remarked, with another sigh. She pressed even closer and, for the first time since the terrible ordeal had begun, smiled. "What does *El Lobo* mean?"

"The Wolf."

"The Wolf," she echoed softly. "Yes, I can see why they would call you that. You're canny, and arrogant, and only half tamed, but I love you with all my heart."

"Go to sleep, my love," he whispered. He placed a finger beneath her chin and gently tilted her head back so that he could bestow a brief yet thoroughly affectionate kiss upon her lips. "Go to sleep."

She complied with remarkable ease, drifting off into a deep and dreamless sleep within minutes. Reeve continued to hold her for quite some time, then left the bed and covered her with the quilt. He returned his gun to the holster buckled low on his hips, and moved to blow out the lamp. Bending his tall, muscular frame down into a chair, he settled down for the night.

Lorelei awoke the next morning to the feel of her husband's lips upon hers. She moaned softly and raised her arms to his neck, kissing him back with such sweet ardor that he was sorely tempted to throw all caution to the winds. But reason prevailed.

"It's time to get up, Mrs. Cameron," he told her, reluctantly turning away. "Our hosts will be arriving with breakfast any moment now."

"Our hosts?" She sat up and stretched contentedly, only to pale when the belated memory of their surroundings hit her. "Good Heavens, I forgot!" Hurriedly slipping from the bed, she looked about for something with which to cover herself. Reeve, as if possessing the ability to read her mind, handed her a blue silk gown.

"Here, put this on. I found it in one of Joaquín's trunks. He probably intended to give it to one of his mistresses." The merest ghost of a smile touched his lips when she took it from him.

"Who is Joaquín?" she asked, drawing the gown over her head. It was a far from perfect fit, but she was grateful for it nonetheless. She swept her tangled mass of curls aside so that Reeve could fasten the row of tiny pearl buttons up the back for her.

"Joaquín is the man who brought you here. He's the leader of this particular band."

"You mean there are others?"

"Yes. They are all over Texas and New Mexico, even down across the border." He frowned and turned her to face him again. "I've never found my good friend Joaquín to be entirely trustworthy, but at least he didn't question my authority. Strange as it may seem, these people do have a code they live by—'honor among thieves,' I guess you'd call it."

"What honor can there be in shooting innocent men and selling women and children to the Comanches?" she wondered aloud. She smoothed down the full skirts of the gown and took the hairbrush Reeve offered her. "And why haven't they been arrested?"

"Because the government, in its innate and highly peculiar wisdom, would rather focus on the Indians. The irony of it all is that, if the *comancheros* were forced out of business, the raids would eventually stop."

"Reeve?" Momentarily she ceased her efforts to bring order to her wayward auburn locks and gazed up at him with a troubled expression.

"Yes?"

"Did you have a mistress here, too?"

Her eyes glared with annoyance when he gave a soft laugh of pure amusement.

"Hell, I had my own harem," he teased.

"I'm serious, blast it!" she stormed in exasperation. "If you were with the *comancheros* for any length of time—"

"Don't you ever give up?" He moved forward, towering above her while her eyes shot sapphire sparks up

412

at him. His hands closed gently about her upper arms. The smile he flashed her was disarming in the extreme. "Am I going to have to spend the rest of my life facing a barrage of questions about my colorful past?"

"You had better make certain, Major Cameron, that neither your present nor your future have any color whatsoever!" she retorted saucily.

"Consider it done." He swept her into his arms at last, his lips branding hers in a kiss that left them both wanting a good deal more.

A knock sounded at the door. Lorelei started in alarm, but Reeve assured her quietly that there was no reason to be afraid. He left her standing beside the bed and crossed the room to open the door.

"Good morning, *El Lobo*," said a woman who was balancing a heavy tray on her hip. She was young and quite pretty, with long raven hair and eyes that sparkled invitingly up at him. "I have brought you and the *señorita* your breakfast."

"Thank you."

He smiled at her and stood aside so that she could carry the tray to the table near the window. Her gaze shifted to Lorelei, but she said nothing else. After she had gone, Reeve closed the door and turned back to find his wife confronting him with an arch look.

"You appear to be quite popular," she noted.

"I'm like a brother to them all," he quipped in response. He smiled again and said, "Let's eat. I'm expected to meet with Joaquín and give him my answer this morning."

"What answer?"

"About you. He'll want to know if I'm willing to

413

pay his price—which, I might add, is a substantial one. You should feel honored."

"Oh, Reeve, are there any other captives here?" she asked seriously, her eyes clouding at the thought.

"None that I know of. But I'll make certain before we leave."

They ate quickly, then washed up and traveled downstairs for the meeting with the man known as Joaquín. Lorelei, following Reeve's instructions to behave like a woman being held against her will, held herself stiffly erect as she walked beside him in the morning sunlight. She was conscious of the many pairs of eyes upon her, and she looked about surreptitiously, still finding it difficult to believe that Reeve had lived with these people. He led her back across the grounds to yet another building. Upon entering, they found Joaquín seated at a table with a pretty young woman on his lap. He did not bother to get up, but merely smoothed one hand caressingly along the woman's hip and toyed with his cup of coffee with the other.

"Ah, so you have left your bed at last, my friend," he remarked, smiling broadly at Reeve. His dark eyes moved with bold significance to Lorelei. "I would not have been so hasty."

"I didn't want to be greedy," drawled Reeve. "Especially since you've not yet been paid."

"So, you have decided you want to buy the woman?"

"I have." His hand closed possessively about Lorelei's arm. "She is worth the price."

"Then maybe I should keep her for myself," suggested Joaquín, with a low chuckle. Finally he pushed

414

he woman away and rose to his feet. His smile this ime was for Lorelei alone. "You are a lucky woman, *eñorita*. When *El Lobo* was our *patrón,* the women vere fighting to see who would share his bed."

"Indeed?" she responded icily. Her beautiful blue yes, however, were full of fire as they shot to Reeve.

"But the Comanches might pay me even more," aid Joaquín, apparently still undecided. He stepped orward and lifted a hand to her hair. "You would be nuch honored among them, *señorita.*"

"Don't you ever touch me again!" she snarled. It reuired no playacting on her part to slap his hand away uriously. She cried out when he retaliated by tangling is hand in her hair and giving a cruel yank.

"You had better learn some manners, *señorita!*"

"Let her go," Reeve commanded, his tone one of leadly calm as his hands clenched into fists at his ides.

It required every ounce of self-control he possessed o refrain from knocking his former *compadre* across he room. But he knew it would appear suspicious if le reacted so violently over the welfare of a mere capive. Still, the savage gleam in his green eyes was :nough to warn the other man that defiance would be anwise. Joaquín was unaware that he had just sealed lis own fate.

"I think I will have to double my price," he obverved, giving another soft, malicious laugh. He urned away and took up his hat. "Come, my friend. Ve will talk of this while we are riding."

"Riding?" Lorelei repeated, looking anxiously to Reeve.

"All right," he agreed. "But I must have your prom-

415

ise that the woman will be left alone."

"She can stay here with Angelita," he said, nodding toward the young woman who was clearing away the dishes. "No one will come near her." He met Reeve's gaze squarely for a moment. "You have my word."

Lorelei tensed, her pulses racing in alarm at the prospect of being in the compound without Reeve. But she knew she had little choice in the matter.

"How long will you be gone?" she asked him, forgetting for a moment that she was supposed to behave like a prisoner.

"You have tamed her already, *El Lobo*," Joaquín remarked with a grin. He pulled his hat on and sauntered leisurely outside.

"Don't worry," Reeve assured her. He resisted the impulse to touch her. Flashing her a brief smile, he joined Joaquín.

Lorelei heaved a sigh once they had gone. She pivoted slowly about, only to find herself facing a visibly angry Angelita.

"You stupid little *puta!*" the woman hissed venomously. Her eyes glittered with a lethal combination of hatred and jealousy as they flickered over Lorelei. "Because of you, my Joaquín will be the *patrón* no more!"

"I—I don't know what you're talking about!" stammered Lorelei.

"*El Lobo* has come back! And with you as his woman, the Comanches will deal only with him!" She muttered a curse and whirled away, snatching up the dishes and disappearing into a back room.

Lorelei stared after her in bewilderment. She was not given much time to ponder Angelita's words.

416

however, for the other woman returned with the news that there was work to be done outside—by both of them.

"But I thought I was to remain here," protested Lorelei. In truth, she welcomed the opportunity to get some fresh air, and keeping busy would certainly help pass the time, but she felt uneasy about being seen by the many *comancheros* who had remained in the settlement to enjoy a day of rest.

"What is the matter, *señorita?*" Angelita challenged, with biting sarcasm. "Are your fine hands not used to getting dirty?" Not waiting for a reply, she marched forward and flung open the door. "You will work, or you will not eat!" she threatened.

"I am not opposed to working," Lorelei insisted, with remarkable calm. She swept proudly past the woman, having decided that it was worth any risk to be able to escape the stifling heat that would soon fill the building.

She followed Angelita's example and tucked her long skirts up almost to her knees, before starting to work in the garden that had been planted near the corrals. There were dozens of horses secured within the split-rail fences, and her brow creased into a frown when she mused that every one of them had probably been stolen. Other women drifted outside to work alongside her as the morning wore on, but they kept their distance. They gossiped and laughed with one another, while their children scampered about like happy little savages. It was difficult to believe that the domestic scene about her concealed a very real proclivity toward murder and thievery, and the selling of captives.

A number of men had gathered at the corrals by the time the sun hung directly overhead. Lorelei did her best to ignore them, but she was painfully conscious of their eyes upon her as she bent to her task. She was relieved when Angelita finally announced a break for the noon meal. There was grudging respect in the other woman's gaze when the two of them hurried away to wash up and prepare the food.

She was beginning to worry when the afternoon lengthened and Reeve had still not returned. His continuing absence wreaked havoc on her emotions. Plagued by visions of him lying injured or even—*God forbid*—dead somewhere, she mentally shook herself and attempted to concentrate on what they would do once his assignment at Fort Concho had been completed.

She didn't care where they were sent, just as long as they were together. She had meant what she'd told Hadley—she belonged at her husband's side and would remain there for the rest of her life. But, sweet mercy, she reflected with an inward sigh, they had to get away from the *comancheros* first. And the waiting was becoming unbearable.

Afternoon gave way to twilight. She was helping Angelita gather up the wash when a man rode into the compound. She looked with only mild interest in his direction as she lifted the basketful of clothes and started back toward the building, but something about him, she suddenly realized, seemed familiar. He rode closer.

Lorelei's throat constricted in dread, her face paling at the sight of his coarse, unshaven features.

Abner Dugan! Dear God, it couldn't be!

She spun about, her heart pounding fiercely within her breast as her mind raced. He mustn't see her, she thought in rising panic. And even more importantly, he mustn't see Reeve. She had little doubt that he would reveal their true identities to the *comancheros*.

Grateful for the hat Angelita had given her earlier, she bent her head and hastened inside the building. She flew to the window and stood watching cautiously as Abner Dugan rode past. He reined to a halt a short distance away, swung down from the saddle, and was greeted with welcoming smiles by two men who were obviously well acquainted with him.

Still reeling from the shock of seeing him there, Lorelei prayed that he would not witness Reeve's return. She would have to warn her husband, and she would have to do so without arousing the suspicions of Joaquín or anyone else.

She waited until Dugan had accompanied the two men into the small adobe structure that served as the *cantina,* then slipped outside once more. Angelita frowned as she came forward with her own basket.

"What is wrong?" she demanded, her brown eyes narrowing.

"Nothing!" Lorelei hastened to deny. She forced a smile to her lips and affected an air of nonchalance. "I am simply feeling the need for some fresh air."

"If you go too far, the guards will shoot you." It was more of a warning than a threat.

"I won't go far."

She smiled again and set off with purposeful, unhurried steps toward the other end of the compound. Surely Reeve and Joaquín would return soon, she told herself, glancing up toward the darkening sky. Night

419

was fast approaching, and she knew Reeve would be anxious on her behalf. His worry could be nothing compared to hers, though, she thought, her nerves strung so tightly that it was difficult to breathe.

One of the guards shouted at her to turn back when she reached the outermost boundary. She raised a hand to indicate that she had heard, but did not immediately follow his command. He called out to her again, this time in a voice edged with anger. But the thunder of hoofbeats echoed from the canyon before she could reply. Reeve, Joaquín, and a number of other *comancheros* came riding home at last.

Lorelei ran forward. One look at her face was enough for her husband to know that something was wrong. He swung down and turned to grasp her arm, aware of the fact that Joaquín was watching them closely.

"Don't tell me you missed me," Reeve asked her with a sardonic half-smile. His gaze was steady and penetrating.

"I . . . of course not!" she denied hotly. To lend credence to her role as defiant captive, she jerked her arm free and rounded on him with eyes ablaze. "I demand that you give me my freedom at once! I have a husband in Las Vegas, and he will kill you when he finds out what you've done! As a matter of fact, I saw a man who knows my husband — *he is here!*"

She was satisfied when she observed the way Reeve's handsome features tightened. Joaquín prevented any further conversation between them by slipping an arm about her shoulders.

"Come, *señorita,* it is time we settle your fate." He laughed when she tried to escape his grasp, and held her tighter, so she pretended weariness and went along with him meekly. Glancing back over her shoulder, she saw that Reeve followed them as they moved inside the building where Angelita waited.

"Get out," Joaquín ordered the young woman curtly. She flung him a mutinous glare, but did as she was told. Reeve came inside and closed the door, while Joaquín pressed Lorelei down into a chair. He remained beside her, his hand lightly caressing her shoulder. "I meant it, my friend, when I said I might keep her. I think she would warm my bed even better than Angelita."

"We made a deal," Reeve reminded him. His eyes filled with a dangerous light at the sight of the other man touching his wife.

"Yes, but you have not yet paid me."

"Damn it, you know I can't do that until I can get word to my partner to bring the horses up from Texas."

"Then maybe I will 'guard' her for you until then," Joaquín suggested meaningfully. He moved away from her and poured himself some whiskey from the bottle Angelita had left on the table. "We'll have a drink first. Then we'll decide."

"It's been decided," said Reeve, his low tone steely. He took the drink Joaquín offered him, and met Lorelei's wide, fearful gaze. "I'm riding out tonight. With the woman."

"I can't let you do that," the other man disagreed smoothly. "Not even *El Lobo* can take what is not yet his. It would not be a good example for the *patrón* to set. My men might think they can do the same."

"Why should I care what your men think?" He

421

downed the whiskey and set the glass forcefully down upon the table's rough surface. "The woman is mine. You'll have your horses in a few days. And if you've got it in mind to double-cross me, you four-flushing bastard, I'll see you in hell."

Lorelei was surprised when Joaquín, instead of being angered by the insult, merely smiled and poured himself another drink.

"I thought you knew me better than that, my friend."

"I know you better than you think."

"All right. I will let you take the woman. But only on one condition." His hand lowered to rest upon Lorelei's shoulder once more. She stiffened, holding her breath while waiting for him to finish.

"Well?" Reeve prompted impatiently.

"You must give me your word that you will not return."

"Agreed."

Lorelei could scarcely believe it was over. Weak with relief, she was afraid she would not be able to stand. Reeve took hold of her hands and pulled her up before him, his strong arm going about her waist to lend support as he propelled her toward the doorway.

"I am a generous man," Joaquín added behind them. "I will even give you the woman's horse."

"Thanks." His mouth curved into a faint smile. *"Adiós."* Opening the door, he led his wife outside. They were already on their way toward the corrals, where Reeve had left his horse tied, when disaster struck.

Abner Dugan sauntered out of the *cantina* a short distance away. He stopped dead in his tracks when he caught sight of Lorelei. His gaze widened, then narrowed as it shot to Reeve. He muttered a blistering curse and went for his gun.

"Cavalry!" he yelled in warning to the *comancheros*.

Reeve thrust Lorelei aside. She fell to her knees on the ground, a loud gasp breaking from her lips when a gunshot rang out. She jerked her head about, her terror-stricken gaze flying back to Reeve. He was still standing, his revolver in his hand. Abner Dugan's lifeless body lay sprawled in the dirt.

"Come on!" Reeve rapped out. He grabbed her arm and pulled her to her feet. "We've got to make a run for it — *now!*"

She needed no further encouragement. Gathering up her skirts, she raced along with him toward his horse. The whole camp erupted into pandemonium in the next few seconds, as Dugan's body was discovered and someone raised a cry of alarm. Men came running outside, women followed closely behind, and the armed guards standing watch made ready to fire at anything suspicious.

Reeve tossed Lorelei up into the saddle and mounted swiftly behind her. He clamped an arm about her waist, his booted heels digging into the horse's flanks as he caught up the reins and guided the animal toward the only avenue of escape.

"Stay low!" he ordered Lorelei. She bent forward until her cheek rested on the horse's mane. They rode hell-bent for leather out of the compound and into the canyon just ahead, knowing full well that the *comancheros* would be in hot pursuit.

Bullets flew all about them in the darkness, but

Reeve never allowed the animal galloping wildly beneath them to slow its pace. On and on they rode, their only thought one of freedom. Lorelei's fingers clenched within the horse's mane, and she stifled a cry of pain when a bullet grazed the back of her neck. She could feel the warm blood trickling downward into her gown, but she dared not raise a hand to her burning flesh.

Behind them, Joaquín had already mounted up and was leading more than a dozen men in furious, vengeful pursuit. That one word Dugan had shouted before being killed was enough to let him know why his old friend had taken flight. He'd had an uneasy feeling ever since *El Lobo* had come back, but he had never suspected that their former *patrón* was connected to the military. The realization made his blood boil, and he swore to give himself the pleasure of killing Reeve.

Lorelei was feeling perilously lightheaded by the time they emerged from the canyon and set a course across the rolling, night-mantled countryside. She fought back a wave of nausea and clung to the horse, all the while praying in silent desperation that she and Reeve could somehow manage to outrun the *comancheros*. It required very little imagination to envision what would happen to them if they were caught. The memory of Joaquín's eyes, glittering with sinister intent, made her shudder.

She lost all track of time as they rode, but she knew the horse could not continue its frenzied pace forever. Las Vegas had to be hours away yet. Dear God, how could they possibly hope to make it?

But Reeve was the one who had been underestimated this time.

He did not head toward Las Vegas at all. She sensed that he knew exactly where they were going.

Her instincts proved correct a mercifully short time later, when they topped a rise in the land. At first certain that she was hallucinating, she narrowed her pain-clouded eyes and took in the sight of a soft, flickering glow on the horizon. They made straightaway for that light.

"Reeve?" she shouted, above the noise of the wind and the horse's hooves beating against the hard ground.

"It's a patrol from Fort Union!" he told her.

Her heart leapt at his words. She straightened her back and cast a quick glance behind them. The *comancheros* were nowhere to be seen.

They rode closer to the light, and soon Lorelei could see campfires blazing in the middle of a surrounding circle of cavalry tents. She watched as the soldiers leapt into defensive readiness at the sound of their approach.

"How did you know?" she asked Reeve, leaning back into his strong, comforting embrace as he finally slowed the horse to a walk.

"We saw them when we were out riding today." The merest hint of a smile touched his lips when he added, "Joaquín boasted of being able to outrun them every time they got too close."

He called out to identify himself to the soldiers as he reined the exhausted animal to a halt and dismounted. He pulled Lorelei down into his arms, carrying her into the camp while the patrol's commanding officer hastened forward to offer assistance.

Lorelei knew she would never forget the kindness of

the soldiers, nor the loving ministrations of her husband. In the privacy of their own borrowed tent, he gently cleansed her wound and bandaged it, then peeled off her bloodstained gown and placed a jacket about her shoulders. He raised a cup of hot coffee to her lips while cradling her on his lap.

"Damn it, woman, I told you to stay put at the hotel," he finally saw fit to remind her. His voice was low, and brimming with a mixture of reproach for her disobedience and heartfelt gratitude for her safety.

"I know. I'm sorry," she sighed, genuinely contrite. "I always seem to be making a mess of things, don't I?" She raised her arms to his neck and tilted her head back to face him in the lamplight. Her blue eyes were glowing softly. "Will you ever be able to forgive me? I—I nearly got you killed, and Hadley."

"I know, my love," he assured her with a tender smile. "But it's over now."

"What will happen to Joaquín and the others?"

"I'm going to make sure they pay for their crimes," he promised grimly. He set the cup of coffee aside and drew her closer. "We'll head back to Fort Concho as soon as your brother is well enough to travel. Hopefully, we'll arrive before the court-martial is scheduled to take place."

"Oh, Reeve, is Hadley really going to be cleared at last?" She was almost afraid to believe it, for fear that something else would happen.

"He is," confirmed Reeve.

"But what about the escape? And what's going to happen to Private Taggart?"

"I'm going to recommend leniency for both of them. I expect your brother to draw an extra term of duty, but Taggart won't get off so lightly. Strange as it may seem, desertion is a more serious offense than escape. Still," he concluded, drawing her head down to rest upon his broad and wonderfully capable shoulder, "I'm going to ask the tribunal to take into account the fact that he saved your brother's life and gave himself up in the process."

She sighed again, her eyes closing. Reeve pressed a kiss upon her forehead, then carried her to where the bedrolls were spread out upon the ground. She did not protest when he lowered her to one of them and covered her with a blanket. He blew out the lamp before settling down for the night close beside her, his heart beating with hers. Outside, the soft hiss and crackle of the campfires provided a comforting reminder of deliverance . . . and the dream of a bright future.

Twenty

The days they spent in Las Vegas were among the happiest Lorelei had ever known. She didn't even mind Annie Leary any longer — which turned out to be a good thing, since the widow seemed determined to make a complete nuisance of herself. Annie was forever bustling about, taking charge of Hadley's convalescence, offering Lorelei unsolicited advice about marriage in general and Reeve in particular, even going so far as to tell her "good friend" Reeve that the fastest way to settle his bride was to do his duty and get her with child.

But Lorelei realized that there was nothing truly threatening about the woman. And when the time came for them to head back to Fort Concho, she said goodbye to the indomitable Mrs. Leary with genuine warmth and affection. Las Vegas, New Mexico Territory, she realized, would always hold a special place in her heart.

The return journey was a good deal less dangerous than the trip there had been. Reeve arranged for an escort from Fort Union; twenty cavalrymen were sent to ensure them safe passage across the *Llano Estacado* and down into Texas.

Hadley had recovered enough from his wound to

be able to travel without too much discomfort. He continued to blame himself for his sister's ordeal, until finally she made him agree that the blame was both mutual and completely pointless. She was glad that he and Reeve were getting to know one another at last. God willing, the three of them would be able to maintain a close relationship for the rest of their lives.

Private Taggart, she discovered, was every bit the hot-tempered man Hadley had said he was. She could not like him, even though he had saved her brother's life, and yet neither could she wish him ill. He was a very troubled and confused young man, a boy really, and she hoped that the tribunal would indeed show him mercy.

They rode into Fort Concho in the late afternoon, only a short time after drill had ended. Hadley and Private Taggart were immediately taken to the guardhouse. Reeve left his wife in the care of a beaming Abigail Merriwether, then went to make his report to the colonel.

"I couldn't believe it when I heard you had helped your brother escape!" remarked Abigail, leading her inside and away from the many prying eyes. Her tone held no rebuke, only excitement. "John was absolutely livid when he came running in to tell me he'd found Reeve tied up in your room, and I don't think I've ever seen Reeve Cameron look so *dangerous* as he did then!"

"It wasn't meant to happen like that," Lorelei murmured, with a frown of remorse.

"Well, I can see that all is well between you now!" She placed an arm about her shoulders and smiled

429

again. "You must tell me everything, for I am simply dying with curiosity! I must say, no one expected to see you here at the post again, and there's been talk of little else since the night you disappeared!"

"I'll be happy to satisfy your curiosity," agreed Lorelei, "but not until I've had a long, hot bath. Great balls of fire, I don't care if I never see a horse again!"

Abigail laughed and promised to grant her request without delay. She showed her to the small building she had occupied before, then left her alone with the promise of sending Caroline out with the soap and towel.

Lorelei did not see Reeve again until nearly two hours later, when she was dressing for supper. He had already bathed and changed into a clean uniform. Her heart swelled with love and pride at the sight of him. She had forgotten how handsome he looked in his uniform. *He looks even more handsome out of it,* an inner voice declared, with wicked audacity. She blushed and wondered if she would ever stop feeling this way about him.

He drew her into his arms, kissed her soundly, and released her again before telling her that the court-martial would take place the very next day. She felt a sharp twinge of apprehension at the thought.

"Oh, Reeve, are you sure nothing else can go wrong?" she asked, securing her flame-colored tresses with one last hairpin.

"I can't promise you that," he conceded, with a slight frown. "But I've posted extra guards to keep watch over the prisoners, and Colonel Jameson has assured me that every precaution will be taken tomorrow. I spoke to him about you as well. It was necessary to reveal the fact of our marriage. Needless to say, he was quite surprised."

"And is he . . . is he going to have me arrested?" she stammered, her voice quavering.

"No. Thank God, the man's not as big a fool as I thought. I don't think he much liked the idea of having to fight me to see you prosecuted. He may outrank me, but I have a few friends up in Washington he isn't particularly eager to irritate."

"Have you told anyone else yet—about our marriage, that is?"

"No." A faint smile of irony played about his lips. "But I think our connection was noticed on the trip homeward. And it won't be a secret here at Fort Concho after tonight."

"What do you mean?" She turned and faced him with an expression of bemusement he found absolutely delightful.

"I mean, my dearest Mrs. Cameron," he replied, reaching for her again, "that I am going to spend the night here, with you."

"But what will everyone think?" she protested without any real conviction, as his arms gathered her close. "Wouldn't it be better to wait until after—"

"I've already sent word back to headquarters of my altered status," he informed her. His green eyes twinkled roguishly down into the luminous blue depths of hers. "Are you sure you'll still be willing to follow me wherever I go? There's every possibility that I'll receive my new orders by the week's end. I could end up pulling duty at one of those rat-infested hellholes, after all."

"You can't scare me off so easily, Major!" She threaded her fingers through the dark, sun-streaked thickness of his hair and smiled seductively. "You know you'd absolutely wither up and die without me," she opined in her best southern belle voice.

"I'm certainly not withering now," he murmured in a low, intimate voice. His hands swept down her back to close about her hips, pressing her lower body hard against his and thereby offering her undeniable proof of his arousal.

"The Merriwethers expect us to arrive promptly at seven o'clock," she reminded him, with another playfully taunting little smile.

"They'll wait."

Lorelei gave a breathless cry as he suddenly toppled her to the bed and did what he'd been burning to do ever since they had left the hotel in Las Vegas. Her dress was sadly creased afterward, and her hair required a complete rearrangement, but she was not in the least bit inclined to complain.

She slept little that night—and not only because Reeve took it in mind to "elaborate" upon the rapturous episode they had enjoyed before supper. Her mind was troubled by thoughts of the next day's proceedings. No matter how hard she tried, she could not shake the feeling of uneasiness that had plagued her ever since they had returned to Fort Concho that afternoon.

The next morning dawned bright and clear. Lorelei awoke to find her husband gone. Reveille had already sounded, but miraculously she had slept through it. She smoothed a hand across the empty space in the bed beside her. The mattress still bore a slight indentation where the weight of Reeve's virile, hard-muscled body had been only a short time ago. Heaving a sigh of half contentment, half disappointment, she tossed back the covers and reluctantly climbed from the bed.

Anxious to visit Hadley before the court-martial began, she dressed quickly and hurried in to breakfast. Abigail sensed her friend's uneasiness and did her best to keep the children quiet, but Lorelei insisted that she was glad for their company, for it was a pleasant distraction and would help to lift her spirits. Caroline shot what seemed like a million and one questions at her, while the two little boys were content to provide a background of happy noise throughout the meal.

"John says the court-martial will of a certainty result in your brother's acquittal, but I am praying for him nonetheless," Abigail confided, as she walked Lorelei to the front door. She embraced her with true affection, then added, "I hope that we will see one another often in the future, my dear. Now that you're a cavalry wife as well, there is always the possibility that our husbands will be serving at the same post."

"I would like that very much," declared Lorelei, her eyes sparkling warmly. She set off across the sunlit parade ground, dressed in a very becoming gown of pale blue muslin and wishing for all the world that the next few hours had already passed. Life at the frontier fort was going on about her as

433

usual, with the soldiers performing their everyday duties and offering up their everyday complaints about them.

Reeve had promised to meet her outside the head-quarters building shortly before eight o'clock, which was when the court-martial was scheduled to begin. She glanced apprehensively toward the building on her way to the guardhouse, knowing that Reeve was probably inside at that very moment. He would be serving as Hadley's defense officer—a highly irregular arrangement, but one he had insisted upon. As he had told her, the only other people allowed in the room would be six court officers, the military tribunal, and a junior officer who would record the proceedings. There would be no observers present, and no way to know how the trial was going until after the verdict had been reached.

She released a long, pent-up sigh, and approached the guardhouse. Two armed guards stood at attention on either side of the doorway. They moved to block her way when she attempted to go inside.

"Sorry, ma'am, no visitors allowed," one of them informed her, his voice polite but firm.

"But I am Private Montgomery's sister!" she protested in disbelief. "Colonel Jameson gave—"

"The colonel has rescinded all visiting privileges until further notice."

"You don't understand. I have to speak with my brother before . . . before the trial begins!"

"No visitors," the young cavalryman reiterated. Viewing her obvious distress, he lowered his voice to an undertone and suggested, "Maybe you can catch a word with him when they bring him out."

"Thank you." Her brief smile was full of gratitude.

Sorely disappointed, she moved farther along the walk. Her gaze remained fastened upon the door to the guardhouse. She stood and waited for several long minutes, until finally Hadley appeared. Her heart twisted at the sight of him—his face was very pale, and he wore shackles on his wrists and ankles. He was flanked on either side by a guard, with two others in front and two following behind as he was led outside.

"Hadley!" she called out to him. She hurried forward, but was prevented from getting too close. Tears started to her eyes when he turned and gave her a smile.

"It's all right, Lori," he assured her, with brotherly compassion. "It will all be over soon."

"I know," she replied tremulously. She could think of nothing else to say; but words were not necessary between them.

Her eyes were clouded with worry as she watched him being taken away. Only when he had disappeared inside the headquarters building did she start forward herself. Reeve came outside to speak with her shortly thereafter. She was grateful when he wrapped his arms about her and pulled her close.

"Oh, Reeve, I'd give anything if it were tomorrow already," she murmured unevenly.

"I want you to go back to the Merriwethers' house, and stay there until I come for you," he commanded with quiet authority.

"Why?" She tilted her head back to meet his gaze.

"An added precaution," he explained, with a faint

435

smile. His features grew solemn again in the next instant, and his eyes bored down into hers. "Do as I say, Lorelei. I don't think you're in any real danger, but there's always the chance I might be wrong." He did not reveal that he'd had a man watching over her ever since they had returned to Fort Concho; the last thing he wanted to do was alarm her unduly.

"Surely no one will try anything now," she insisted. "Why, the court-martial is about to begin, and everyone knows that Private Taggart—"

"You'll obey me in this," he decreed firmly. "I can't be worrying about you and do my best as your brother's defense officer."

"All right," she acquiesced with obvious reluctance, swayed by this last argument. She frowned up at him. "But come as soon as you can!"

"As soon as I can." He kissed her quickly, then set her away from him. "Now go on."

Slowly she turned and directed her steps back toward the row of officers' quarters. Glancing over her shoulder at Reeve, she watched his long, purposeful strides carry him inside the building. Guards were posted at all the doors, and there was little doubt that Hadley was safe from the threat of reprisal, at least for now.

Although she dismissed Reeve's concern for her as nothing more than that of a loving and overly protective husband, she decided to follow his instructions. She was nearing the Merriwethers' house when Captain Collin McNeil suddenly materialized in her path.

"Miss Montgomery," he said, smiling down at her.

"Captain McNeil!" she exclaimed in surprise. Recalling their last, highly unpleasant encounter, she colored faintly and managed only a cool smile in return. "If you'll please excuse me, I was on my way—"

"I'd like a word with you, if you don't mind."

"A word with me?" She frowned up at him in puzzlement.

"It concerns your brother, Miss Montgomery."

With a sharp intake of breath, she searched the man's aristocratic features for any sign of malevolence. His expression was guarded and impassive, but his gray, hawkish gaze burned with a strange light.

"What is it?" she demanded.

"If you will consent to walk with me, I will be more than happy to tell you." He smiled again and gallantly offered her the support of his arm. She hesitated, torn between the desire to hear what he had to say about Hadley and the impulse to flee from his annoying presence with all haste. Curiosity won out.

"Very well, Captain," she replied, slipping her hand about his arm. She held herself stiffly as they began strolling along the walk. "But I promised my . . . I promised Mrs. Merriwether that I would return shortly."

"This won't take long," he assured her. He did not speak again for several moments, until after they had passed Abigail's house. "I trust you are well, after your long journey?"

"Yes, thank you." Impatient to hear what he had to say about Hadley, she muttered an inward curse, and quickened her steps in the hope that she could bring about a swifter end to their meeting. "Please, Captain McNeil, you know I am anxious about my brother!"

"Understandably so. I have heard that court-martial proceedings can be very difficult." He flung a quick, sideways glance in her direction. "But since Private Taggart has been brought back to testify, there can be no question of the outcome."

"I certainly hope not." They were approaching the outer boundary of the fort now. The bridge across the river was just ahead, and it occurred to her that he meant for them to cross into Santa Angela. "I think we should head back to the Merriwethers' now," she insisted, pulling to a stop. "As a matter of fact, Captain, this has gone on *quite* long enough. I would appreciate it if you would reveal whatever information you have about my brother!"

"Keep walking," he startled her by growling.

"What?" she gasped. Her eyes flew wide when he suddenly drew a knife and pressed the tip of it up against her side.

"Try and call for help, Miss Montgomery, and I'll kill you," he threatened, his tone low and edged with barely controlled violence. He slipped his other arm about her waist and forced her to accompany him toward the bridge, which saw little use at that early hour of the morning.

"Why are you doing this?" whispered Lorelei, her terrified gaze sweeping about her as her mind raced frantically to think of a way to escape. "For Heaven's sake, what do you —"

"I'm clearing out. And you're coming with me." He gave a chuckle of malicious amusement. "I'd like

438

to see Major Cameron's face when he finds out I've made off with his whore."

"I'm not his whore!" she snapped angrily. "I'm his wife!"

"Oh, even better." His arm tightened like a vise about her, and she stifled a cry as the point of the knife jabbed against her flesh. "It really makes no difference, Mrs. Cameron, since I have no intention of making our relationship legal."

"I won't go with you, Captain!" she defied hotly, her whole body trembling with a mixture of rage and fear.

"You'll go—unless you'd prefer to have your pretty throat slit." He gave another soft laugh. "We'll be miles away before they learn the truth. Taggart will probably be too scared to tell them about me. He'll always wonder if I might take it into my head to come back and kill him."

"You . . . you're part of the conspiracy!" breathed Lorelei, as realization dawned on her.

"Not 'part,'" he corrected smoothly, his eyes gleaming with triumph. "I was in command."

"You were the one who killed Lieutenant Fitzhugh!" she accused. She knew with a certainty that it was true, even before he answered.

"And your brother, dim-witted son of a bitch that he is, was the perfect one to frame for it."

They had reached the outskirts of town. The main street was practically deserted, and the few people about took no notice of the cavalry officer walking along with a woman at his side. Captain McNeil propelled Lorelei toward the livery stables, where he had already made arrangements for the long journey ahead.

"I can understand, Captain, why you are so anxious to leave Fort Concho," she told him, her calm, measured words belying the panic deep within her. Reeve's face swam before her eyes, and it was all she could do to choke back the scream rising in her throat. "But why am I to be part of your escape? I will only slow you down, and—"

"I made a vow to have you the first time I saw you," he interrupted, his eyes glittering with lust now, while a sinister smile played about his lips. "I watched you standing there outside the guardhouse in the rain, your clothes all wet and clinging to your body, your face so incredibly beautiful. You looked like an angel . . . an angel in the midst of this godforsaken excuse for a post. My resolve was made all the stronger when I held you in my arms at the dance." He scowled darkly at the memory of Reeve's interference. "If it hadn't been for that Johnny Reb bastard, I'd have taken you that night!"

A shudder of revulsion shook her as he pulled her to the rear of the livery stable. Once there, he released her, but drew his gun and leveled it menacingly at her.

"Mount up," he directed, motioning toward one of the two horses already saddled and waiting outside the corral.

"Please, Captain, don't do this!" she entreated. "If you have any hope of getting away, then—"

"Mount up, damn it!" he growled, his eyes narrowing to slits of fury.

Still determined to escape somehow, Lorelei lifted her head proudly and did as he said. She swung up into the saddle and thought of trying to make a run for it, but Captain McNeil guessed her intent and moved forward to take the reins. He clutched them in the same hand as the revolver while he mounted the other horse.

"Now ride out to the street. Slowly." He flung the reins at her.

She gathered them up and urged the animal toward the front of the building. *Reeve!* her heart cried out to him. Dear God, how would he find her this time?

Lorelei told herself she couldn't allow this to happen, no matter what danger she might face as a result of her resistance. Although she knew Captain McNeil was right behind her, she decided to take the risk and try to break away. *If she could only make it to the post.*

She gripped the reins more tightly, her mind offering up a silent prayer as she prepared to kick the horse into a gallop. She bent lower in the saddle, but waited until she reached the street before cautiously lifting her heels . . .

A sharp gasp broke from her lips when suddenly she caught a glimpse of movement out of the corner of her eye. Before she knew what was happening, she was snatched from the saddle. Two strong arms came about her, breaking her fall as she tumbled downward.

In the very next instant, a shot rang out. She gave a cry of alarm and pushed at the man who held her, her head jerking about to see that Reeve had yanked Captain McNeil from his mount and sent him crashing to the ground.

"Reeve!" she cried breathlessly. Her terror-stricken gaze moved to Captain MeNeil's gun, which now lay harmlessly in the street. Her eyes flew back to her husband as she scrambled to her feet. A shiver ran the length of her spine when she observed the look on his face.

Reeve's handsome features were a mask of savage, vengeful fury as he hauled the captain upright. He smashed his fist into the other man's face with such force that blood poured from Captain McNeil's shattered nose. With merciless intent, Reeve hit him again and again.

Lorelei was certain he meant to kill her abductor. She was about to intervene, but the man beside her did so instead.

"Enough, Major," he cautioned.

Turning her head toward him at last, she was surprised to see that he was the same good-natured, brawny fellow Reeve had assigned to keep watch over her on their wedding night. Unbeknownst to her, he was the "guardian angel" who had seen Captain McNeil abduct her and had gone to warn Reeve. She looked back to her husband, her eyes wide and anxious.

Reeve muttered an oath and finally allowed the man in his grasp to crumple to the ground. Captain McNeil gave a low moan, his face a bloody mass of cuts and bruises.

Lorelei raced forward and threw her arms about her husband's neck. Her eyes closed in relief as he pulled her against his hard warmth.

"Oh, Reeve, he—he's the one who framed Hadley!" she murmured brokenly. "And he told me he was in command of the conspiracy!"

"I know." His arms tightened about her as though he would never let her go. "I didn't have enough proof to arrest him until this morning. And by then, it was too late." He was still enraged at the memory of how, only a short time ago, Colonel Jameson had refused to have Captain McNeil confined to his quarters.

"He was going to take me away." She shuddered anew at the thought.

"I'm sorry, my love," Reeve told her quietly, his voice full of self-reproach as well as anger. "Sorry I didn't suspect that he'd do something like this."

"How could you know?" She drew away a little and gave him a tremulous smile. "In spite of what you may think, my dearest Major, you are only human."

He smiled down at her, his eyes glowing with such love that she felt herself shiver deliciously.

"Thank God for that." His arm remained possessively about her shoulders when he began leading her way. "Keep an eye on the captain," he instructed his friend. The man nodded curtly and flashed Lorelei a broad grin.

"Glad you're all right, ma'am."

"Thank you," she answered sincerely. "What will happen to Captain McNeil now?" she asked Reeve as they headed back toward the fort.

"I'm sending him back to Fort Union to await trial. And unless I miss my guess," Reeve added grimly, "he'll be sentenced to hang."

"What about Hadley? Now that someone else has been exposed as the true murderer—"

"The court-martial will be nothing more than a formality," he assured her, with another brief smile.

"I should have listened to you," she sighed, her thoughts turning to other matters now that the nightmare had ended. "Great balls of fire, will I ever learn?"

"I doubt it." His green eyes twinkled down at her. "But keep working on it."

"Yes, Major." Her own eyes shone with all the love in her heart as she walked with him across the bridge.

Twenty-one

The stagecoach waited in front of the hotel in Santa Angela, the horses pawing impatiently at the dry, dusty ground while Ollie Newcomb tossed the baggage up into place and bellowed at the top of his lungs for the passengers to climb aboard. This was rather unnecessary, since there was only one, and *she* was the boss's new wife.

Lorelei turned to say a last goodbye to her brother as they stood together on the boardwalk.

"You'll write as soon as you can?" she asked, wanting confirmation of a promise he had already made.

"Yes." He embraced her warmly, his arms hugging her close. "Don't worry, Lori. Everything's going to be fine."

"I know. But Reeve said it may be quite some time before we can see you again, and—"

"I'm a grown man now, remember?" He drew away and gazed down at her with an indulgent smile tugging at his lips. "You've done a good job taking care of me all these years. It's the cavalry's job now."

"Fort Laramie is so far away!" she sighed. "Still, I suppose it *is* for the best that you won't be at Fort Concho any longer."

"You might say that," he drawled wryly. "With more than thirty men on their way to Fort Union to face court-martial, I don't think Colonel Jameson wants me around as a reminder of what happened."

"Why, you should be treated as a hero—not an outcast!" Lorelei protested with great feeling. "Because of you, the conspiracy was finally destroyed, and Captain McNeil won't be able to hurt anyone else!"

"I had a little help," Hadley reminded her, his eyes lighting with amusement once more. He grew serious before asking, "Do you have any idea where you'll be heading, once the major reports back to Washington?"

"No. But we're going to stop in Fort Worth for a day or two first. Reeve wants me to meet his family." She viewed the prospect with no small amount of trepidation. She desperately wanted his parents, brothers, and sisters to like her.

"They can't help but love you," said her brother, as if reading her thoughts. He opened the door of the stagecoach and took hold of her arm to help her up. Once she was settled inside he closed the door again, and smiled across into features that were so similar to his own, and yet so utterly feminine. "I'll miss you, Lori."

"I'll miss you too, Hadley." Silently she cursed the tears that sprang to her eyes. Having vowed not to cry, she returned his smile and proclaimed, "I'm sure I will make a terrible cavalry wife, but I'll do my best anyway."

"An accurate prediction if ever I heard one." Reeve sauntered forward to join Hadley beside the

446

coach. He offered the younger man his hand. "Take care of yourself, Private Montgomery."

"Take care of my sister, Major Cameron," Hadley retorted with a grin. He shook Reeve's hand and stepped away.

"Ready?" Reeve asked Lorelei. At her nod, he gave her a long, lingering kiss and promised huskily, "Tonight, Mrs. Cameron, I'm going to take you behind Cantrell's Station and finish what I started the last time we were there."

"Nothing would give me greater pleasure," she replied, her beautiful face becomingly flushed.

She leaned out of the window and watched him climb agilely up to take his place beside Ollie, who had already gathered up his reins. The two men exchanged a quick look of understanding.

"Home?" asked Ollie, grinning broadly.

"Home," confirmed Reeve. His own mouth twitched as he settled back.

Ollie snapped the reins above the horses' heads. The stagecoach lurched forward. Inside, Lorelei grasped at the leather strap for support and waved at her brother until he was out of sight.

She leaned back against the cushioned leather seat and smiled to herself, as the coach rolled back down Santa Angela's main street and toward the beckoning plains. Her heart's journey had come to an end, but her life's was just beginning. And with Reeve Cameron at her side, she knew the trip would be full of excitement and adventure . . . and love.

DISCOVER DEANA JAMES!